Praise for the novels of Al

CHURCHILL'S SECRET MES

"Hlad does a nice job of intertwining the romance and action stories, treating both realistically and largely without melodrama. The early parts of the novel, detailing Rose's work in the below-ground War Rooms and her encounters with Churchill, prove every bit as compelling as the behind-the-lines drama. Good reading for both WWII and romance fans." —*Booklist*

THE LONG FLIGHT HOME

"Hlad's debut snares readers with its fresh angle on the blitz of WWII, focusing on the homing pigeons used by the British, and the people who trained and cared for them. . . . Descriptions of the horrors of war and the excitement of battle are engaging, and the unusual element of the carrier pigeons lends an intriguing twist. This story will speak not only to romance readers and WWII buffs but also to animal advocates and anyone who enjoys discovering quirky details that are hidden in history." —*Publishers Weekly*

"I've always been fascinated by homing pigeons, and Alan Hlad makes these amazing birds and their trainers shine in *The Long Flight Home*—a sweeping tale full of romance and espionage, poignant sacrifice and missed chances, uncommon courage and the ongoing costs of war. A compelling debut told with conviction and great heart." —Paula McLain, *New York Times* bestselling author of *The Paris Wife* and *Love and Ruin*

"Hlad's debut delves into an obscure piece of World War II history: the covert mission of the National Pigeon Service, which deployed an army of homing pigeons to send messages to Britain from Nazi-occupied France. . . . Ollie's attempts to escape from France are gripping, and Hlad adeptly drives home the devastating civilian cost of the war." —*Booklist*

"Alan Hlad tells a dramatic, fictionalized story about the real use of pigeons during World War II. . . . Compelling. . . . The engaging plot and fascinating details of the National Pigeon Service make it a rewarding read. Many civilian pigeon-keepers volunteered to try to turn the tide of the war, not knowing if it would work or be worth the loss of their birds in the dangerous process. *The Long Flight Home* captures the contributions of the average citizens who, in a time of peril, rose to meet the challenge in heroic ways." —*BookPage*

THE BOOK SPY

Books by Alan Hlad

THE LONG FLIGHT HOME

CHURCHILL'S SECRET MESSENGER

A LIGHT BEYOND THE TRENCHES

THE BOOK SPY

Published by Kensington Publishing Corp.

THE BOOK SPY

ALAN HLAD

JOHN SCOGNAMIGLIO BOOKS
Kensington Publishing Corp.
www.kensingtonbooks.com

JOHN SCOGNAMIGLIO BOOKS are published by

Kensington Publishing Corp.
119 West 40th Street
New York, NY 10018

This book is a work of fiction. Names, characters, businesses, organizations, places, events, and incidents either are the product of the author's imagination or are used fictitiously. Any resemblance to actual persons, living or dead, events, or locales is entirely coincidental.

To the extent that the image or images on the cover of this book depict a person or persons, such person or persons are merely models, and are not intended to portray any character or characters featured in the book.

All Kensington titles, imprints, and distributed lines are available at special quantity discounts for bulk purchases for sales promotion, premiums, fund-raising, educational, or institutional use.

Special book excerpts or customized printings can also be created to fit specific needs. For details, write or phone the office of the Kensington Sales Manager: Kensington Publishing Corp., 119 West 40th Street, New York, NY 10018. Attn. Sales Department. Phone: 1-800-221-2647.

ISBN-13: 978-1-4967-3855-4 (ebook)

ISBN-13: 978-1-4967-3854-7
First Kensington Trade Paperback Printing: February 2023

10 9 8 7 6 5 4 3 2 1

Printed in the United States of America

For the librarians who went to war

PROLOGUE

WASHINGTON, DC—DECEMBER 22, 1941

Two weeks after the Japanese attack on Pearl Harbor, Colonel William "Wild Bill" Donovan—head of the Office of Coordinator of Information (COI), America's newly created centralized intelligence agency—entered the West Wing of the White House. The lobby was decorated with holiday wreaths and a lush, unlit Christmas tree, filling the air with a sweet scent of pine. Top American and British military leaders, as well as Franklin Delano Roosevelt and Winston Churchill, were soon to convene in Washington for the Arcadia Conference to develop military strategy for the war. But Donovan—a stalky, silver-haired World War I Medal of Honor recipient and prominent Wall Street lawyer who'd been placed on active duty—was not invited to the conference.

A deep determination burned within him. He squeezed the handle of his locked leather briefcase, which contained top-secret documents. Although he reported directly to FDR and had gained his trust and friendship, he wasn't a member of the president's inner circle. Regardless, he was committed to influencing US military strategy and obtaining support for his clandestine operations.

Grace Tully, a middle-aged secretary wearing a navy dress with a diamanté flower brooch, approached him. "Good day, Colonel Donovan."

"How are you, Grace?" Donovan asked.

"Well, thank you." She took his coat and hung it on a rack.

"And how is Missy?"

"Same," Grace said, a timbre of melancholy in her voice. "She's getting physical therapy in Warm Springs."

"I'm sure she's receiving the best of care," Donovan said, attempting to raise Grace's spirit. "If you speak with her, please give her my best wishes for a swift recovery."

"I will, sir."

Six months prior, Marguerite "Missy" LeHand, FDR's personal secretary, suffered a stroke that left her partially paralyzed with limited ability to speak. Donovan was shocked and saddened by the news. He'd grown fond of Miss LeHand, who—like him—was a New Yorker from Irish decent. Although Grace was cordial and competent, he revered Missy's gumption and gatekeeping skills, and he hoped that she'd somehow regain her health and return to her duties.

Grace accompanied Donovan to the Oval Office and knocked on the door.

"Come in," President Roosevelt's voice said.

"Have a good meeting, Colonel," she said.

"Thank you," he said.

Grace turned and left.

Donovan entered the room and closed the door behind him. "Hello, Mr. President."

"Good morning, Bill." Roosevelt wore a gray pinstripe suit and black tie, and was seated behind a veneer maple desk—cluttered with books, papers, pens, a telephone, and over a dozen figurines.

Donovan approached Roosevelt, who remained in his chair, and shook his hand.

"I suppose you purposely timed our meeting to influence the outcome of the Arcadia Conference," Roosevelt said.

"Indeed, sir," Donovan said.

"I appreciate your candor and counsel." Roosevelt gestured to an upholstered chair beside his desk.

Donovan sat, placing his briefcase on his lap. His eyes gravitated to two figurines on the president's desk—a Democratic donkey and Republican elephant, linked together with a metal chain. "New statuettes?"

Roosevelt nodded. "I thought the shackles might get them to work together."

He smiled.

Donovan admired the president's sense of humor in the most trying of times, as well as his willingness to collaborate with people who held opposing views. Although Donovan and Roosevelt had similar personalities, they had conflicting political views. A decade earlier, Donovan publicly criticized Roosevelt's record as governor of New York. Roosevelt never held a grudge and, when the war erupted in Europe, he'd enlisted Donovan to travel to England as an informal emissary to meet Churchill and the directors of British intelligence. FDR soon relied upon Donovan's insight and, five months earlier, had signed an order naming Donovan Coordinator of Information.

"What's on your mind, Bill?" Roosevelt asked.

"Now that we're at war, we need to establish a method for clandestine military measures against the enemy." Donovan unlocked his briefcase, removed a one-page memorandum, and gave it to the president. "My recommendations are brief."

The president read the memorandum. He rubbed his eyes and placed the paper facedown on his desk. Roosevelt—who downplayed the effects of his polio, except with his most trusted advisors and friends—labored to adjust the steel leg braces under his trousers and swiveled his chair toward Donovan. "Guerilla corps?"

"Yes, sir."

"Independent from the army and navy?"

"The coordination of spies and intelligence should be centralized." An image of his visit with Winston Churchill and his intelligence directors flashed in Donovan's head. "I recommend that our guerilla forces be similar to the British model."

"Special Operations Executive."

"Yes, sir."

Roosevelt paused, leaning back in his chair. "I'm sure you're aware that my appointment of you to head the COI has been received with animosity by the army and navy. Even J. Edgar Hoover views you as a threat to FBI authority."

Donovan nodded.

"Each branch previously led their own independent intelligence operations. You've taken their turf, and they're not happy about it. And now you want to create a combatant spy force that will steal away some of their best candidates."

"That's correct," Donovan said.

Roosevelt crossed his arms. "I agree with your proposal, but I have other urgent issues. Our armed forces are in no shape to fight. We're lucky to have two huge oceans separating us from our adversaries. It'll take time to ramp up our military personnel, arms production, and training."

Donovan straightened his back. "With all due respect, Mr. President, *time* is something neither we nor our allies have."

Roosevelt drew a deep breath. "All right, Bill. I'll include your recommendations in my discussions at the conference, but I cannot make promises."

"Thank you, sir."

A knock came from the door. Grace peeked her head inside and said, "Pardon me, Mr. President. Prime Minister Churchill has arrived early. He's on his way and will be here in thirty minutes."

"Thank you, Grace," Roosevelt said.

Grace slipped away and closed the door.

"I'm sorry you will not be joining us for the conference," Roosevelt said. "Churchill and I agreed to limit the attendance to heads of military. No intelligence chiefs will be at the meeting."

"I understand, sir," Donovan said, burying his disappointment.

"Churchill mentioned that he enjoyed your visit with him in England. He must have been quite impressed to grant you unlimited access to British classified information. Was it your sharing of war stories that won him over?"

"Perhaps," Donovan said. "But it might have been the poetry."

Roosevelt wrinkled his forehead.

Donovan, recalling the words, looked at the president. "'A steed, a steed of matchlesse speed, a sword of metal keene. All else to noble heartes is drosse, all else on earth is meane.'"

The president grinned.

"It's the beginning of a nineteenth-century poem, 'The Cavalier's Song' by William Motherwell. Churchill and I both knew the poem, which we recited together—word for word."

"What's it about?"

"Courage. Honor. And the calling to be a warrior."

Roosevelt's face turned somber. "I see why the poem resonates with you."

Donovan rubbed his knee, where he'd been hit by a bullet during the Great War. "The American public has been called upon to fight, Mr. President. And I have no doubt that—in the end—we'll win this war and liberate the world from fascist tyranny."

"Yes, we will," Roosevelt said.

Donovan adjusted the briefcase on his lap. "I have one more request, sir."

"I'm open to hearing it—as long as it doesn't take away resources from the army and navy."

"It won't."

"Good," Roosevelt said.

"With your approval, I'd like to establish a committee to acquire enemy newspapers, books, and periodicals for American war agencies. As you're aware, we're using the Library of Congress to support the intelligence needs of the COI, but we lack capabilities to acquire Axis documents."

"Do you have a name for this committee?" Roosevelt asked.

"IDC—it's short for the Interdepartmental Committee for the Acquisition of Foreign Publications."

"I can see why you shortened it," Roosevelt said. "And who will staff this special group?"

"Librarians."

Roosevelt's eyes widened.

"Microfilm specialists to be precise," Donovan said. "The agents will be deployed to neutral European cities, such as Lisbon and Stockholm. They'll pose as American officials collecting materials for the Library of Congress—which is attempting to preserve books and periodicals during the current world crisis. However, the agents will order Axis publications through bookstores and secret channels. Once publications are acquired, the agents will microfilm them—reducing size and weight—and they'll be transported to COI intelligence staff in either the US or London for analysis."

"I suppose you have someone in mind to lead this committee," Roosevelt said.

"Frederick G. Kilgour from Harvard University Library," Donovan said. "I believe he's well-suited for the job."

For the next several minutes Donovan explained details of his proposed committee, all the while fielding questions from the president.

"Librarians," Roosevelt muttered. He picked up a pen and rolled it between his fingers. "Are you sure about this?"

"They're precisely who we need to gain enemy intelligence." Donovan leaned in. "Sir, it's critical for us to station microfilm experts in Europe."

Roosevelt paused, retrieving a slip of paper. "Interdepartmental Committee—what's it called again?"

"Interdepartmental Committee for the Acquisition of Foreign Publications—IDC."

Roosevelt scribbled on his paper. "Deliver details of the proposal to Grace by this afternoon, and I'll sign an executive order by day's end. But in the future, I expect the names of your committees to be short enough for people to remember them."

"I'll do my best, sir. Thank you." A swell of triumph rose up within him. He removed a document from his briefcase and placed it on the president's desk. "I've taken the liberty of drafting an executive order."

"You're always one step ahead of me," Roosevelt said, setting aside his pen and paper.

"I like to be prepared," Donovan said. "And things get done faster by cutting out the red tape."

Roosevelt tilted his head. "Bill, you might be the most anti-bureaucratic person in Washington."

"I'll take that as a compliment, sir." Donovan stood and shook the president's hand. "Good luck with the Arcadia Conference."

"Godspeed with sending your microfilm experts to Europe," Roosevelt said.

Donovan left the White House and walked in the direction of his nearby office building. As he passed near the Lincoln Memorial, he gazed at the temple in honor of the sixteenth president of the United States, Abraham Lincoln. His patriotism surged. He quickened his pace and made mental notes for his plans to turn librarians into warriors.

PART 1

ENLISTMENT

CHAPTER 1

NEW YORK CITY, UNITED STATES—MAY 19, 1942

On the day librarians were recruited for the war, Maria Alves was microfilming historical newspapers in the Department of Microphotography of the New York Public Library. She peered through the viewer of a Leica 35mm camera, purchased by the library through a research grant, and adjusted the lens. A May 1933 article with an image of a Nazi book burning in Berlin's Opera Square came into focus. Gathered around a huge bonfire, fueled by over twenty thousand books, were scores of university students with their arms raised in a *Sieg Heil* salute. A wave of disgust rolled over her. She steadied her hands and pressed the shutter release, producing a soft metallic click.

"Our preservation of records will ensure that people never forget the wicked things that Nazism has done to the world," Maria said to Roy, a bespectacled thirty-year-old microfilm specialist working at an adjacent desk.

"I hope so," Roy said with an unlit pipe clenched in his mouth. He glanced at Maria's newspaper article and frowned. "I wish we could've saved all those books. It sickens me how much liberal and pacifist philosophy was lost in that fire."

"Me too," Maria said. "But I'm far more concerned about what might be happening to Jews in Europe."

Sadness filled his eyes. He nodded, then loaded a fresh roll of microfilm into his camera.

The Department of Microphotography—a small windowless room on the basement level of the library in Midtown Manhattan—contained two wooden desks, rows of film cabinets, a Valoy enlarger for printmaking, and a Recordak Library Film Reader that resembled a doctor's light box for viewing X-rays. The air was stagnant, due to inadequate ventilation, and it contained a faint, nutty scent of Roy's pipe tobacco, despite that he never smoked while inside the library. Although the room lacked airflow, the climate was cool and dry for storing film. And the isolated space permitted the team of two microfilm specialists, Maria and Roy, to work with little, if any, supervision—precisely the way they liked it.

Maria—a twenty-seven-year-old woman with wavy, golden-brown hair and hazel eyes—began working at the library as an archivist three years earlier. She'd obtained a bachelor's and master's degree in medieval studies from the University of California, Berkeley. With her experience of having attended a summer course at the University of Chicago, one of the country's first courses of instruction on microphotography, she was charged with cultivating the library's microfilm capabilities. And she was assigned to mentor Roy, a librarian and amateur photographer, to help create the unit.

The early days of working in the Department of Microphotography were frustrating for Maria. The library's budget for microfilming was miniscule, and much of her time was dedicated to lobbying Mr. Hopper—the library's director, who was reluctant to abandon traditional archival methods—to acquire expensive equipment.

"By converting printed material to microfilm, we'll save money on storage space," she'd told Mr. Hopper. "We could fit an entire wing of library documents in the space of a janitorial closet." But Hopper held firm, claiming that microphotography was in its early stage of development. Therefore, Maria's department was provided cheap, obsolete cameras and barely enough microfilm to archive a few local newspapers.

Undeterred, Maria stopped by Hopper's office each week to express her concerns about the library's lack of technology as compared to other leading institutions, like the Harvard University Library, which developed a program for microfilming foreign newspapers. Also, she informed him about a new company in Michigan that was specializing in microphotography to preserve library collections. Eventually, Hopper relented and shipments of equipment began to arrive. She'd wondered if it was her persistence, or if the director decided to invest in technology out of fear of being viewed as antiquated by the board of trustees. But to Maria, it didn't matter; the library had everything it needed to build a state-of-the-art microfilm department.

As days passed, Maria tutored Roy on the art of microfilm. He was a whip-smart yet humble graduate from Princeton, and he went out of his way to express his gratitude for Maria's mentorship, which she deeply appreciated. Within months, they were microfilming major American, Canadian, and British newspapers. They formed a close friendship despite having quite different interests and upbringings. Roy was a devoted family man with a lovely wife named Judith and a six-year-old daughter, Carol, whose drawings of pink cats filled the top drawer of her father's desk. He came from a large family and had six siblings. Also, he was born and raised in New York City, and he'd never been more than sixty miles from Manhattan, with the exception of a honeymoon in Niagara Falls.

Unlike Roy, Maria was happily single and quite comfortable with her independent life. Her immigrant photojournalist parents—Elise from Munich, Germany, and Gaspar from Coimbra, Portugal—had given her a life filled with travel and adventure. Maria was an only child and, until the age of six, she traveled almost continuously with her parents while they were on assignment in European cities. London. Lisbon. Berlin. Madrid. Barcelona. Paris. Rome. During her school-age years, she lived with a family friend in New Jersey and joined her parents in Europe for summer holidays. By the time she was a teenager, she'd become fluent in six languages. Her parents, who had limited financial means, had scraped to save money to send her away for college, and they'd spawned her desire for wanderlust. But her fight against fascism, even if limited to microfilming Nazi propaganda, was fueled by the death of her mother.

Elise was killed in 1937 while covering news of the Spanish Civil War. She and Gaspar were caught in cross fire between Republican and Nationalist troops while capturing photographs of the Battle of Brunete, fifteen miles west of Madrid. Elise was struck in the back by gunfire and died in her husband's arms. Maria, who was studying in Berkeley, received the news by telegram. She was devastated. After the funeral, her father gifted Elise's Art Deco sapphire engagement ring to Maria, which she placed on her right-hand ring finger. When Maria was feeling sorrowful, which happened more frequently than she liked to confess, she touched her mother's blue gemstone. *God, I miss you,* she would often say to herself. After fiddling with her ring, she would gather her composure, more determined than ever to find a way to honor her mother's sacrifice.

As Maria was inserting a new roll of film in her camera, a knock came from the door. A receptionist, wearing a wool skirt and white blouse, entered the room and approached Roy.

"A Western Union messenger left this for you at the front desk," the receptionist said, giving Roy an envelope. She turned and left.

Roy, his pipe stem clamped between his molars, stared at the envelope.

"Everything okay?" Maria asked, closing the back of her camera.

"Yeah." Roy opened the envelope and, as he read the message, a smile spread across his face. He set down his pipe and ran a hand through his receding brown hair. "I can't believe it."

"Believe what?" she asked.

"I suppose it's okay," he said, glancing at his telegram. "They said nothing about keeping it a secret."

She tilted her head.

"I've been accepted for a position to work overseas."

"Oh, my goodness!" She set aside her camera and approached him. "That's wonderful."

He nodded.

"How did this come about?"

"Frederick Kilgour recruited me," Roy said. "He's from Harvard, but he's recently taken on the role as head of the IDC—it's an acronym for Interdepartmental Committee for the Acquisition of Foreign Publications."

"I haven't heard of it," Maria said.

"It's a fledgling department that reports to the Office of the Coordinator of Information, the US government's new intelligence agency."

"Oh, my," she said, her eyes widening.

"Kilgour interviewed me last week." He lowered his head. "I'm sorry I lied about taking vacation days to spend with Judith and Carol. I didn't want to get my hopes up; I was worried that the IDC would declare me ineligible for service, like the army."

"It's all right," she said.

Roy had volunteered to join the army when the US entered the war, but he failed his physical examination. He was classified 4-F due to a high school knee injury that limited his range of motion and ability to run. Although he never complained about being branded a 4-F, Maria believed that Roy, a patriotic man, was deeply hurt by not being permitted to serve his country.

"Tell me more about where you're going and what you'll be doing," Maria said.

"I haven't been informed where I'll be stationed," he said. "I only know that I'll be serving as a microfilm specialist in a neutral European country to acquire foreign publications."

Maria clasped her arms. "Is everyone in the IDC a microfilm specialist?"

"Most are," he said, sounding apologetic. "But I think they're also considering librarians and scholars."

"I wish I could go with you," she said.

"Me too." He adjusted his glasses on the bridge of his nose. "During my interview, I told Kilgour that you taught me everything I know about microphotography, and I suggested that he speak with you."

"That was kind of you to say," Maria said. "I assume he told you that the IDC is not recruiting women."

"No. He said that he's seeking candidates with an Ivy League degree."

She furrowed her brow. "That's nearly the same thing."

His shoulders slumped. "Are you upset with me?"

"Of course not," she said, giving him a hug. "I'm happy for you. I truly am."

He released her. "This wouldn't have happened if it weren't for you."

She shook her head. "The IDC wanted you because you're a damn good librarian."

He grinned.

"I suppose you need to tell Hopper."

"Yeah."

"After you see him," Maria said, "go home and tell Judith and Carol the news. I'll cover for you."

"Thanks. I'll see you later." Roy placed his pipe in his mouth, swiftly cleared his desk, and left.

Maria, unable to concentrate, put away her camera and spent the afternoon organizing supplies. At 5:00 p.m., she left the library and walked eight blocks to Penn Station, where she boarded a train to Newark. Usually, she read a book during her commute to and from work. Instead, she leaned back in her seat and stared out the passenger car window. Although she was excited for Roy, a feeling of disappointment swelled within her. *I wish I could join the*

IDC. There's no good reason for them to require an Ivy League pedigree. She buried her thoughts and closed her eyes.

She disembarked at Newark Penn Station and walked a mile along Ferry Street to her three-story brick apartment building in the Ironbound, a working-class Portuguese neighborhood. She climbed the stairs to the second floor and entered her apartment, which she shared with her father.

"Hello," she called, placing her purse on the kitchen counter.

"I'm in the darkroom," a muffled voice said. "It's safe to come in. I'm finished."

She entered the darkroom, which had once been a miniscule spare bedroom, to a pungent metallic-like odor that Maria had grown fond of. The dim overhead light was on and Gaspar—a lean man with thick salt-and-pepper hair and a gray, stubble beard—was removing black-and-white photographs from clothespins on a draped cord.

"Hi, Dad," she said.

He turned and hugged her. "How was work?"

"Okay," Maria lied. "How about some fresh air?" She released him and opened a small window, its panes covered with black paint. A warm breeze and sunlight filled the room.

He looked at her. "What's wrong?"

You can always tell when something is bothering me. "It's nothing."

Gaspar rubbed his chin. "I'll make us a snack, and you tell me all about what's not troubling you."

"All right," she said reluctantly.

Minutes later, they sat at the kitchen table with a bowl of seasoned black olives. Gaspar poured two small glasses of port wine.

"*Saúde*," he said, clinking her glass.

She sipped her port, sweet with notes of blackberry and chocolate.

Gaspar patiently chewed an olive, then disposed of the pit on a plate.

Tension grew in her chest. "Roy was recruited to be an overseas microfilm specialist."

"Oh." He clasped the stem of his glass but made no effort to drink.

Maria drew a deep breath, and then told him everything, including that the IDC was seeking solely Ivy League candidates.

He took a drink and asked, "Are you envious of Roy?"

She shifted in her seat. "Maybe a little. He's my friend and I'm happy for him—he's become an expert with microfilm and he deserves to serve the IDC. But it's unfair that they're not considering people who didn't attend an elite school."

"I agree," he said. "You're as good as any Ivy Leaguer."

She smiled.

"Your mother suffered similar adversities in her career as a photojournalist," he said. "In fact, when newspapers refused to hire her because she was a woman, we created a plan where I claimed to be an agent of photographer William Sullivan, a fictitious person. Elise sold a lot of photographs under that name."

Maria had heard the story many times, but she made no effort to inform him. Instead, she glanced to one of several framed photographs on the wall—a black-and-white image of a military-uniformed woman with short hair and a rifle slung over her shoulder. Dark, defiant eyes peered toward the camera. "This is one of my favorites."

"Me too," he said. "That woman is a *miliciana*, a Spanish militia woman. There were hundreds of them fighting alongside the men. A week before Elise was killed, she captured that photograph in Madrid." He rubbed his eyes, then sipped wine.

"You miss her," she said.

"Every day."

Maria's heart ached. "Do you ever think you'll go back to working overseas?"

"Someday," he said. "For now, I plan to continue working for domestic newspapers. It's been nice being home after so many years away from you. I like to think that I'm making up for lost time."

Maria nodded, then nibbled an olive.

Gaspar finished his wine. "Selfishly, I would worry about you if you traveled abroad during a war. However, if you feel you must serve our country, I would never get in your way."

She straightened her spine. "How did you and Mom decide to cover news of the Spanish Civil War?"

"We both fled our homeland due to the rise of fascism," he said. "We thought it was important that Americans, as well as the rest of world, know about what was taking place in Europe."

Maria swirled her wine.

Gaspar slumped in his chair. "I regret that I'm a fatalist at heart. It's common in Portuguese culture to believe that people cannot change how events will unfold. Even so, there isn't a day that goes by that I don't wonder if there was something I could have done to have saved Elise."

"Oh, Dad," Maria said. She squeezed his hand.

"Your mother held quite different views. She was confident and optimistic, and she believed that she could shape her own future despite insurmountable odds." He looked into her eyes. "I see a lot of your mother in you."

Maria breathed deeply, fighting back tears.

He slipped his fingers away and stood. "I've got a bit of work to do. Would it be okay if we have a late dinner?"

She nodded.

He kissed the top of her head, made his way to the darkroom, and closed the door.

Maria, her heart aching, slumped in her chair. A memory of her mother packing a camera into a suitcase flashed in her head. She twisted the sapphire ring on her finger and gazed at the photograph of the *miliciana*, and she decided what she needed to do.

Chapter 2

Lisbon, Portugal—May 22, 1942

Tiago Soares—twenty-eight with nut-brown hair, a clean-shaven face, and a book tucked under his arm—walked along Rua do Crucifixo, a narrow cobblestone street in the historic center of Lisbon. As he approached his bookstore, Livraria Soares, he found Rosa, his store clerk, standing by the door with Artur, a gauche thirteen-year-old newspaper boy with weathered shoes.

"*Bom dia*," Tiago said.

"*Olá*, Senhor Soares." Artur removed a stuffed burlap sack from his shoulder and rubbed his arm.

Rosa—a sixty-seven-year-old woman with plump cheeks and gray, curly hair—tapped her wristwatch. "You're late."

"And you forgot your key," Tiago said.

She raised her chin. "I left it at home because I thought you'd arrive at work on time."

Tiago smiled. He placed his book inside Artur's sack and hoisted it over his shoulder. "How about I carry this inside for you?"

"*Obrigado*." Artur removed his cap, exposing unkempt hair and protruding ears.

Tiago unlocked the door and they entered the shop.

Livraria Soares in Baixa, the neighborhood that contained the Santa Justa Lift—a towering neo-Gothic iron elevator that connected the lower streets of downtown to the higher Rua do Carmo—was a ground-floor storefront of an eighteenth-century building. Worn blue and white tiles covered the floor. Although the shop had a high ornate plaster ceiling, it was a compact, three-meter-by-twenty-meter space. Holm oak bookshelves covered the walls, and two long tables, one of which had a thin piece of wood tucked under a leg to keep it from wobbling, were covered with stacks of books. A faint vanilla-like scent of aged paper and leather filled the air. And at the front of the shop was a checkout counter with a small radio and a crank-operated cash register.

Tiago removed a dozen newspapers from the sack, placed them on the counter, and then paid Artur with money from the cash register. "No skipping school today."

"I won't," Artur said, slipping the money into his pocket. He put on his cap and removed Tiago's book from the sack. "You forgot this."

"You can borrow it," Tiago said.

Rosa raised her brows. She placed her purse on the floor behind the counter and sat on a stool.

"What's it about?" Artur asked, examining the cover.

"It's a collection of poems by Luís de Camões," Tiago said. "After you read it, let me know which one is your favorite."

"All right," Artur said. He slipped the book in his sack and left.

Rosa swiveled on her stool and looked at Tiago. "He's going to skip school, and he won't read that book."

"Perhaps," Tiago said.

"His family needs money," she said. "He has no choice but to work."

"True," Tiago said. "But he's losing his childhood."

She ran her hands over her charcoal-colored dress and said, as if quoting scripture, "You shouldn't leave your flock of sheep in order to find the one that is lost."

Tiago shrugged. "I like to believe that they're all worth saving."

The lines in Rosa's face softened. "I suppose you're right."

Artur lived in Alfama, a poor neighborhood in Lisbon, with his mother and three siblings. His father was dead and Artur, the oldest child, worked before and after school as a newspaper boy to help support his family. Recently, Tiago discovered Artur shining shoes during school hours at the Rossio Railway Station. After lecturing Artur on the importance of education, he'd given him a bit of money and began buying more newspapers than his bookshop could sell. Artur had promised Tiago that his shoe shining was temporary, but given that the black stains on the boy's hands never faded, Tiago worried that the boy's truancy might be permanent.

"Would you like to tell me why you were late this morning?" Rosa asked.

"I was meeting with a French Jewish family in a café," Tiago said. "They arrived in Lisbon last night."

"Did your father courier them in from Porto?"

"Yes," he said. "They were stowed away on a wine delivery truck."

Tiago, who had a Portuguese Catholic father and a French Jewish mother, ran the final leg of his family's escape line for Jews fleeing German-occupied France. The route began at his grandparents' vineyard in Bordeaux, traveled through his parents' vineyard in Porto, and ended at his bookstore in Lisbon. Soon after the war began, Tiago's family—as well as Rosa—had begun aiding scores of Jewish refugees on their road to freedom.

"Where are they?" Rosa asked.

"They're in a boardinghouse. I was going to bring them here, but we nearly encountered a PVDE agent who was stopping refugees to check their papers, so we took a detour and walked in a park."

"Damn secret police," Rosa said, furrowing her brow. "There is no reason for refugees to be under surveillance. They're fleeing persecution and not hurting anyone."

An image of a throng of refugees, desperate to board the *Serpa Pinto* for a voyage to the United States, flashed in Tiago's head.

When the war erupted, Jews began fleeing Nazi-occupied

countries for neutral Portugal. Thousands of refugees were flooding Lisbon, the last gate out of Europe. Under direct orders of António de Oliveira Salazar, Portugal's prime minister and dictator, the Polícia de Vigilância e de Defesa do Estado (PVDE) controlled the entrance of refugees and the expulsion of undesirable immigrants. Wealthy Jewish refugees, often from Paris and the surrounding areas, had the money to obtain proper paperwork and passage to America. But most of the refugees had exhausted their life savings to reach Lisbon, and they had to rely on charity or support from Portuguese authorities. The American consulate and the British embassy were overwhelmed, and it often took many months for impoverished refugees to gather the correct stamps in passports and find a way to pay for ship passage.

"Tell me about them," Rosa said.

"It's a family of three from Bordeaux—Hubert, Irma, and their three-year-old-daughter, Violette." He ran a hand through his hair. "Irma's sister from Poitiers was supposed to join them but she was arrested by the Germans."

"I'm sorry," Rosa said. "Maybe she'll be let go and will make it to your grandparents' vineyard."

He nodded, despite knowing that those who were arrested rarely, if ever, were released.

"How's their paperwork?" she asked.

"Not good," he said, removing passports from his pocket. "Their transit visas are expired."

"How'd they make it through the border crossings?"

"They didn't," Tiago said. "They traveled through the mountains and backroads."

"They're fortunate not to have been spotted by the PVDE. Otherwise, they would have been arrested or sent back to Spain."

"You're right," he said. "The border patrols are stretched beyond capacity and more refugees are getting through. Also, Spain and Portugal are permitting the flow of some refugees, as long as they do not attempt to stay."

"If Salazar and Franco are allowing it to happen," Rosa said, "it's because they think it will help keep the Iberian Peninsula out of the war."

"You're quite astute."

Rosa tapped a finger to her temple. "Let me see their papers."

Tiago gave her the passports.

She retrieved a pair of reading glasses and placed them on the tip of her nose. "They're bad," she said, examining the documents, "but nothing I can't fix."

"If you don't have time, I'll work on them," he said. "It'll give me a chance to practice what you taught me."

"I'll handle it." Rosa opened her purse, removed a false bottom, and handed Tiago two passports. "My husband went to bed early last night, so I got caught up on my work."

Tiago glanced inside the passports of an elderly Jewish couple from Limoges, France, who were now hunkered in a Lisbon boardinghouse. All the dates and stamps were in order, giving the appearance that the couple had acquired passports and visas in France and successfully passed through Spanish and Portuguese border patrols. "They're perfect. Your acuity for detail is remarkable."

"It's the skills one acquires from working for the most scrupulous lawyer in Lisbon."

"It's a gift," Tiago said. "And now you're using your artistry to create hope for those who've lost everything."

Rosa nodded. She removed her glasses and rubbed her eyes.

Tiago had met Rosa, a retired secretary, shortly after the Fall of France. She'd entered the bookshop and overheard him, despite his whispers in French, consoling a distraught Jewish woman with an expired visa. As he was about to ask the woman to come back after business hours, Rosa approached them and said she could fix travel papers.

With the help of Tiago translating French to Portuguese, she'd convinced the woman to allow her to borrow the passport. The following day, Rosa returned it with a falsified expiration date that appeared to be authentic, even when held under a magnifying glass. Rosa wanted no money in exchange for her services. Tiago was impressed and, more importantly, believed that he could trust Rosa given that she'd committed a crime. He soon divulged details of his family's escape line for Jewish refugees, and that he was bribing stewards to smuggle refugees onto ships bound for the United States and Britain. In return, she'd told him about her twenty-five-year secretarial career for a prominent yet corrupt attorney, who required her to alter legal documents.

"We were desperate for money," Rosa had said. "With two young daughters and my husband, Jorge, struggling to hold a job with his rheumatoid arthritis, I did everything I could to support my family."

Tiago invited Rosa to join him at the bookshop. Despite the miniscule pay, because he was using most of his money to aid refugees, she accepted. Soon she was helping him with scores of escapees with invalid travel papers, and he learned that Rosa was far more than a clerk who'd learned a few forgery tricks. She was a fabrication maestro with the ability to erase and match ink, alter paper, and use dentistry tools to sculpt melted wax to mimic seals. And she worked day and night, as if she were seeking atonement for her decades of misdeeds.

Tiago slipped the forged documents into his pocket. "I have a bit of work to do in my office before I deliver the passports. Could you handle things for a while?"

"Sure." Rosa stashed the documents to be forged in the hidden compartment of her purse, and then turned a hanging sign in the window to signify the shop was open.

Tiago went to the back of the shop and entered a windowless office, which was little more than a broom closet. He pulled a long string, illuminating a bulb in the ceiling, and closed the door behind him. He removed a folded sheet of paper—given to him by his father the night before—from inside his wallet and sat at a small desk. Although letters could be sent between neutral Portugal and German-occupied territories, written communication was subject to censorship. Therefore, most of the messages between Tiago and his family were hand delivered.

He unfolded the paper, revealing a charcoal drawing of a windmill, and then lit a candle. He turned the picture over, exposing a blank side. As he carefully held the paper over the flame, he imagined the message's journey. It had been written in German-occupied Bordeaux by his grandfather, Laurent, using a fountain pen filled with onion juice. The message was carried by a fleeing French Jew on an arduous journey through the Pyrenees mountains, across the Spanish and Portuguese borders, to the sanctuary of his parents' vineyard in Porto, and eventually to Lisbon.

Tiago held the paper closer to the flame. His anticipation grew. And the words, the color of caramel from the dry juice oxidizing in the heat, gradually appeared.

My dear grandson,

I pray this letter finds you well. Your grand-mère and I are healthy and safe, and we long for the days when we are reunited.

Tiago squeezed the paper between his fingers. An image of his grandparents flashed in his head. Although he hadn't seen them since the Germans invaded France, he could recall every detail about them. The angelic timbre of his grandmother Odette's voice, reminiscent of an old violin, and the rich, nutty taste of her homemade hazelnut dacquoise. The sound of his grandfather's belly laughs, his gray felt beret, and the eucalyptus scent of his hair tonic that made him smell as if he'd come from a barbershop. *God, I miss them.*

The German occupiers permit us to operate our vineyard. They tolerate our ethnicity because of their thirst for our wine. We are fortunate to be permitted to work our land, as it allows us to host our guests. They stay in your favorite room. Do you remember it?

A childhood memory of playing in his grandparents' wine caves surged through his brain. Deep below the vineyard was a labyrinth of tunnels and cellars, hewn from limestone rock. His favorite place to play was a secret chamber that his grandfather constructed for him behind a wall of wine barrels. The room was accessed by removing a bottom barrel's chime loop and head cover, and then crawling through the empty barrel to the hidden space. What used to be an underground childhood hideout where Tiago read books by lamplight was now a refuge for Jews fleeing France, Belgium, and the Netherlands.

> *Like you, your parents have implored us to leave Bordeaux. But who will help asylum seekers reach freedom? Our family is their lifeline, and if any link in our chain is broken, countless lives could be at risk. Your grand-mère and I are compelled by our sense of duty to help who we can. We do not believe that we are in immediate peril and, for now, we plan to stay. I hope you understand.*

It's getting too dangerous. You need to leave. Tiago drew a long breath, attempting to relieve the tension in his shoulders. He shifted in his seat and continued reading.

> *We are proud of you and often think of the refugees whom you are helping to set sail for a new life. With the Americans in the war, we're optimistic that the Allies will liberate France and we'll be together.*
>
> *With love and hope,*
>
> *Grand-père*

Tiago's heart ached. *I'll continue to write them and, if necessary, I'll find a way to travel to Bordeaux and persuade them to leave.* But deep down, he knew that his grandparents would never abandon people in need. He crumpled the paper, ignited it with the candle, and placed it in an ashtray. As the letter burned, he lowered his head into his hands.

A cello concerto emanated from the front desk radio.

His adrenaline surged. *Damn it.* He grabbed a flip knife from a desk drawer, opened the blade, and pried up a loose tile from the floor. He tossed the passports into a small hole that contained an assortment of travel papers and forgery supplies, and covered it with the tile. He tamped the ashes, making certain there was no evidence of the message, and then folded his knife and slipped it into his pants pocket. With no way to air out the smell of burned paper, he plucked a cigar from a wooden box and lit it. He blew out the candle, and then exited his office to find a dark-suited man, his back to Tiago, browsing through a bookcase.

Agent Neves, Tiago thought, recognizing the man by his thick neck and bowler hat. He glanced at Rosa, who was straightening magazines near the checkout counter. *Good work alerting me of the PVDE by turning on the radio.*

Neves thumbed through a book.

"*Bom dia*," Tiago said.

The agent, ignoring Tiago, stroked his thick mustache and examined a row of books.

Agent Martim Neves was approximately forty years of age with a cleft chin, and he wore pinstripe pants with a solid black jacket that stretched over his barrel chest. Neves, who conducted surveillance on refugees and had a reputation as the most pro-German member of the PVDE, wasn't a customer of the bookshop. However, he did stop by last month to ask questions on the whereabouts of three Jewish refugees. Tiago had lied, telling him he hadn't seen them despite that he'd helped one of them gain ship passage to America.

"May I help you find something?" Tiago asked.

Neves turned and looked at Tiago. "Show me which books are attracting Jews to your bookshop."

Tiago gestured with his cigar to a table stacked with books. "I carry editions in foreign languages, including French, German, and English. Multilingual Lisboetas also buy them."

"Your establishment has become quite popular with refugees."

"Books are one of the few things they can afford," Tiago said. "Reading passes their time until they can leave the city."

Neves rubbed his jowls and approached Tiago. "If I were to order a raid on your shop, how many of your books would be in violation of censorship regulations?"

"None," Tiago said. *But many if you raided my apartment.* He shook away his thought and took a drag on his cigar, but found that the ember had gone out.

Neves slipped an engraved silver lighter from his pocket. He lit it and held the flame to the body of the cigar, nearly searing Tiago's chin.

He's trying to intimidate me. Tiago leaned back, lit the foot of his cigar, and removed it from his mouth. "*Obrigado.*"

Neves put away his lighter. "I suppose you wouldn't mind if I looked around."

Tiago puffed on his cigar. "Not at all."

While the agent conducted his inspection, Tiago joined Rosa at the counter. He unfolded a newspaper and pretended to read.

"Why is he here?" Rosa whispered.

Tiago eyed Neves, who was going through a shelf of books, and lowered his voice. "He's suspicious of why refugees congregate in the shop."

Rosa rubbed her hands, as if she were spreading ointment, and returned to tidying magazines.

Thirty minutes later, after Neves had conducted his perusal of inventory and rummaged in Tiago's office, he came to the front desk carrying a novel and a three-volume set of poetry. "I've found these publications to be perverse. I'm confiscating them to be examined by the Censorship Service."

Tiago's skin turned warm. He fought back his resentment and said, "I'm sorry. I endeavor to screen books for truth and morality. In the future, I'll do a more thorough job of scrutinizing our shipments from booksellers."

A smug smile formed on the agent's face.

"In the remote chance that the Censorship Service would deem the books to be moral," Tiago said, "I assume that you'll return them."

"Of course," Neves said.

Bullshit, Tiago thought but held his tongue.

Agent Neves tucked the books under his arm, tipped his hat to Rosa, and left.

"He stole those books for himself," Rosa said.

"You're probably right. But the secret police can do what they want—they don't need a warrant." He turned the radio off and looked at Rosa. "Thanks for alerting me about his arrival."

"It was nothing," she said.

"Do you mind running the shop today?"

"*Não*," she said. "Is everything all right?"

He nodded. "I'm going to deliver the passports you fixed, and then I'm going to find out how many cases of wine it will take to bribe a steward to stow away two passengers on the next ship bound for America."

Rosa grinned.

Tiago collected documents from the secret hole in his office and left the bookstore. As he made his way through the cobblestone streets of Lisbon, he scanned the area to make sure he wasn't being followed by Neves. He lengthened his stride and resolved to keep his family's escape line operating while he found a way to convince his grandparents to flee France before the last door to freedom closed.

CHAPTER 3

NEW YORK CITY, UNITED STATES—JUNE 23, 1942

Maria put away her camera, retrieved a metal mesh coin purse, and left the Department of Microphotography to take her lunch break. Instead of going to the New York Public Library's staff room or a nearby diner for a bite to eat, she walked along a basement hallway to a row of public telephones. She entered a wooden booth and closed the folding doors. She unsnapped her purse, full of coins, and placed it on a shelf below the payphone. With the handset pressed between her ear and shoulder, she inserted a nickel and dialed 0.

"Hello, this is the operator," a female voice said. "How may I direct your call?"

"Washington, DC," Maria said. "The Office of Coordinator of Information."

The operator instructed Maria on the amount of change to insert into the payphone.

Maria, who'd memorized the long-distance charge, swiftly inserted the coins.

"Please hold while I connect you," the operator said.

Maria sat on a stool and waited.

Each day over the past month, Maria had made telephone calls to Washington, DC, in an attempt to join the IDC. She'd begun her quest by calling Frederick G. Kilgour, the head of the newly created department. To Maria's surprise, Kilgour was easy to track down and he graciously accepted her initial phone call. But when she expressed her desire to join his team of overseas microphotography experts, he kindly but firmly said that the IDC was only considering Ivy League candidates. As Maria tried to inform Kilgour of her master's degree and microphotography experience, he thanked her for her interest and ended the conversation. She hung up the phone feeling rejected. However, she called him back the following day and, as she anticipated, he refused to take her call. So, she sent Kilgour a letter and résumé to which she didn't receive a reply.

Undeterred by Kilgour's declination, Maria wrote several letters and made daily telephone calls to Colonel William Donovan, head of the Office of Coordinator of Information. Donovan was the top person in charge and was likely, Maria believed, the boss of Kilgour's boss. She had little, if any, experience with the proper protocol of communicating up through a chain of command, and she disliked going over someone's head. *It feels like an underhanded method to get what I want*, Maria had thought while dropping a letter to Donovan in the mail. But it didn't matter. To date, she'd been unsuccessful with getting through to Donovan and time was running out, considering her coworker, Roy, was finishing his last day of work and leaving tomorrow for IDC training.

"I'm connecting you now," the operator said.

Maria listened to the phone ring. *I'm probably too foolish to know when to quit. But at least I'll be certain that I exhausted my efforts.* In an attempt to quell her tension, she clasped the shelf below the payphone and felt something sticky.

"C-O-I," a woman receptionist said.

"Yuck," Maria said, pulling back her hand.

"Is that you, Maria?"

"Yeah, Bertha," Maria said. "Sorry about that. Someone stuck gum under the payphone."

"Sounds disgusting."

"It is," Maria said, wishing she had a handkerchief. "How are you?"

"I'm fine, and you?"

"I'd be swell if you'd connect me to Colonel Donovan."

Bertha chuckled. "You know I can't do that. Donovan's personal secretary has told me not to transfer your calls. Each time I deliver her a telephone message slip, she lectures me on how busy the colonel is and that he's only accepting calls from people he knows or their referrals. No exceptions."

"Is she tossing my messages in the trash?" Maria asked.

"I think so," she said. "I'm sorry."

She is probably intercepting my letters, too. Maria slumped her shoulders. "Any chance you could put me in touch with one of the colonel's friends?"

"Honey, the colonel and I are not in the same social circle."

Neither am I.

"You don't like to give up, do you?" Bertha asked.

"I'm afraid not," Maria said.

"Being resolute is a good thing," Bertha said. "And I enjoy your calls."

Maria smiled. She fiddled with the phone cord. "How's your brother, Jim?"

"He leaves for army basic training next week," she said, the timbre of her voice turning somber. "He's barely nineteen. It makes me want to cry when I think of my baby brother going to war."

"I'm sure it's difficult for you to see him leave," Maria said. "I'll keep him in my thoughts and prayers."

"Thank you," Bertha said.

"Please insert sixty cents," the operator interrupted.

"I better go," Maria said, "or I won't have enough money to ring you tomorrow."

"All right," Bertha said. "You keep calling, and I'll keep delivering your messages. Eventually, you'll wear Donovan's secretary out and connect with the colonel."

"I appreciate you, Bertha."

Maria hung up the receiver, gathered her coin purse, and went to the restroom, where she washed gum residue from her fingers. She knew that she should try to eat something, but her stomach felt like she'd swallowed a hunk of clay. She went back to the Department of Microphotography where she found Roy cleaning out his desk.

"Any luck?" Roy asked, removing a stack of crumpled papers from a drawer.

"No." She put down her coin purse. "I could have purchased a new camera for what I spent this month in long-distance phone calls."

"I'm sorry," he said. "You should be in the IDC. You're a better microphotography specialist than me."

She looked at him. "Don't cut yourself short, Roy. You earned it."

He gave a faint smile. "When I get to training, I'll tell Kilgour—every chance I get—that he should recruit you. Maybe he'll reconsider."

"I appreciate you sticking up for me," she said. "But I don't want you to get in trouble or kicked out of the IDC before you go overseas. I'm counting on you to help us win the war."

Roy nodded. He picked up his unlit pipe from an ashtray but didn't place it in his mouth. "I gotta admit, I'm a bit worried about leaving."

"Why?"

"It might sound silly to you," he said.

"Try me."

"I've never traveled before."

"That's not true," she said. "I'm pretty sure that you've been to all five of the New York City boroughs."

Roy laughed.

"You'll do great," she said. "Whichever neutral country they send you to, you'll quickly pick up on the language and customs. You're the smartest person I know, and I have no doubt that you'll make a fine IDC agent."

Roy smiled.

"And when you're gone," Maria said, "my dad and I will check in from time to time with Judith and Carol to make sure they're getting along well."

"Thank you." He blinked his eyes, as if he were fighting back his emotions.

"Why don't you sneak out of here and spend the afternoon with your family?"

He adjusted his glasses. "I'm required to work until five."

"You're incorruptible and servile," she said.

"I can't help it," he said. "It's my parochial school upbringing."

She smiled. "It wouldn't hurt you to bend the rules. Besides, Mr. Hopper is tied up in meetings and I doubt that he'll dock your pay or terminate your employment for cutting out early on your last day of work. Gather your things, say goodbye to the librarians, and leave."

"Are you sure?"

"Yes," she said. "And pick up some flowers for Judith on your way home."

"All right." Roy cleaned out his desk, placed his personal items in a cardboard box, and approached Maria. "I'll see you after the war."

She hugged him. "I expect you to archive every European publication at risk of being destroyed in a Nazi book burning."

"I'll do my best," he said, releasing her.

"Take care of yourself, Roy."

"You too." He picked up his box of personal items and left.

Alone, a wave of melancholy rolled over her. *I'm going to miss him. He'll be overseas, and I'll be stuck here, training someone whom Mr. Hopper picks to be Roy's replacement.* To distract herself she microfilmed stacks of newspapers until 5:00 p.m. Afterward, she gathered her things, left the library, and walked to Penn Station, where she boarded a crowded train to Newark.

Due to a maintenance issue on the railway, she arrived at her apartment building in the Ironbound an hour later than usual. She entered the apartment and found her father in the kitchen.

"Hi, Dad," Maria said. "I would have been home sooner, but the train was delayed."

Gaspar stirred the contents of a skillet with a wooden spoon. "How was your day?"

She placed her purse on a counter. "Not so good. Roy left for the IDC, and I struck out again with getting through to the top brass in Washington."

"I'm sorry," he said. "Would you like to talk about it?"

"Maybe later." She inhaled, taking in a rich sent of sautéed onion. "Dinner smells great. What are you making?"

"Bacalhau à Brás," he said.

One of my favorite meals. She peeked into the skillet, sizzling with onion, shreds of salted cod, and finely diced fried potato. "I thought we were having sandwiches tonight. What gives?"

"Nothing," he said. "Can't a father make his daughter a nice meal once in a while?"

"Of course," she said. "I'm just a little surprised, given that we received our first ration book and we don't have a lot of money for food."

"I didn't use the Sugar Book to acquire ingredients." He looked at her. "With Roy leaving, I thought it might be a rough day for you. I've always found that a good meal takes the edge off of things."

"*Obrigada.*" She kissed him on the cheek.

He smiled and returned to sautéing food.

Maria set the table and, minutes later, Gaspar spooned Bacalhau à Brás onto a dish and garnished it with sliced black olives. He poured red wine into their glasses, and then sat across from her.

Maria sipped her wine, sweet with a hint of plum. "It's good. What kind is it?"

"The cheap kind," he said. "I spent most of the money on the food."

Maria's mind drifted to a memory of a microfilmed article about British shopkeepers and their protocol for canceling coupons in ration books. She shifted in her seat. "Do you think we'll endure severe food shortages like citizens of the United Kingdom?"

Gaspar rubbed his chin. "Americans will need to make sacrifices. We've already begun diverting sugar, butter, canned milk, and gasoline to the military. I do, however, think our country has enough agricultural resources to get us through the war."

Maria nodded. She took a bite of salted cod and potato, feeling grateful yet sad for Europeans who were struggling to survive.

During dinner Gaspar did most of the speaking, as if he was shielding his daughter from having to talk about her day. Maria, after eating some food and refilling her glass with wine, began to relax. *Dad is right. A good meal and company can soothe a painful day.*

"I'd like to show you something." Gaspar retrieved a newspaper from the counter and gave it to Maria. "One of my photographs made it in the *Times*."

Maria beamed. "Holy mackerel!"

"Don't get too excited," he said. "It's a small piece about the parade."

She opened the newspaper and found an image, which credited her father as the photographer, of a group of women—wearing skirted khaki uniforms and hats—who had joined the newly created Women's Army Auxiliary Corps. The women were smiling and, to Maria, their eyes were brimming with confidence. "It's a lovely snapshot. You captured their spirit."

"*Obrigado*," he said.

Maria's mind drifted to the recent New York at War parade, a military and civilian home front procession that was held to support mobilization efforts. The library had closed for a half day to allow employees to attend the event, which had over a half million participants—soldiers, police officers, nurses, civic groups, veterans of the Great War, Scottish bagpipers, high school marching bands, USO members, army corps, and hundreds of parade floats. To Maria, from her spot on Fifth Avenue, it looked like a patriotic version of the Macy's Thanksgiving Day Parade.

She stared at the uniformed women in the photograph. *No matter what it takes, I'll find a way to do more for the war effort.* Maria buried her thought and said, "Do you mind if I cut this out for our family scrapbook?"

"Not at all," he said.

Maria retrieved a pair of scissors from a kitchen drawer. As she cut out the piece, exposing the following page of the newspaper, her eyes locked on a headline.

COLONEL DONOVAN TO SPEAK
AT ASTOR MANSION

Her heartbeat accelerated. "Oh, my!"

Gaspar dropped his fork, clanging against his plate. "What's wrong?"

Maria scanned the page. "Donovan's coming to New York."

His eyebrows rose.

She read the article. While the piece announced Donovan's speaking engagement, three of the four paragraphs were focused on Vincent Astor, a prominent businessman and philanthropist, who was placed on active duty by the navy and given the assignment of area controller for New York.

Maria set aside the paper. "Donovan is going to give a speech at Vincent Astor's mansion."

"Goodness," Gaspar said. "Astor is one of the richest people in America."

She nodded. "All this time I was trying to connect with Donovan in Washington, and it turns out he'll be in Manhattan."

"When?"

"Next week."

"Who will attend the speech?"

"It didn't say," Maria said. "Most of the article is about Astor being called upon for naval service and the lending of his yacht, *Nourmahal*, to the coast guard. I assume it's a private event and the attendees will be affluent New Yorkers."

Gaspar took a gulp of wine. "Maybe you could try to have a word with Donovan when he arrives for the event."

"Perhaps." She imagined police and soldiers guarding streets on the Upper East Side, and her excitement waned. "Security will be high. It'll likely be difficult for an uninvited guest to approach Donovan, let alone step foot within a block of the Astor house."

Gaspar patted her hand. "No matter how things turn out, I'm proud of you for trying."

She forced a smile and picked at her food.

Maria cleared the table and washed the dishes. Afterward, she sat in the living room with her father and listened to *The Pepsodent Show*, a radio comedy program starring Bob Hope. Despite Hope's rapid-fire jokes that blossomed belly laughs from her father, her mood turned subdued. *It's worse knowing that Donovan will be a few miles away with nothing I can do to reach him.* Maria said good night to her father, went to her room, and settled into her bed. She prayed that Roy would avoid enemy conflict and safely return home to his wife and child, and that she'd somehow find a way to join the IDC.

Hours passed. Unable to sleep, Maria's mind raced. *One would need to be a millionaire or a socialite to get invited to the Astors' house.* Long after her apartment building turned silent, she got out of bed, sat at a writing desk, and flipped on a desk lamp. As she scribbled on a piece of paper, she resolved to risk everything to change her fate.

Chapter 4

New York City, United States—July 2, 1942

Maria raised the side zipper of her black taffeta evening gown and looked in a full-length mirror that was mounted on her bedroom door. She adjusted the sculpted ruffle collar and puffed sleeves, and ran her hands along the silky basque waistline and voluminous skirt. Her golden-brown hair was done in a sleek coiffure of ringlets and waves, thanks to a hairdresser who lived in her apartment building. She carefully applied red lipstick, and then retrieved a compact and dabbed rouge on her cheeks. *I barely recognize myself*, she thought, staring at her image. *But it'll take more than a glamorous facade to pass for a member of high society.*

Everything she was wearing—minus her newly purchased black patent leather pumps, which cost her a week's pay—was used or rented. Her pearl necklace and earrings were on loan from a pawn shop in the Ironbound that accepted two of her father's rare cameras as collateral, and her black beaded clutch purse was acquired from a boutique in Manhattan that specialized in upscale, secondhand accessories. Unable to afford luxury clothing from places like Bloomingdale's or Saks Fifth Avenue, she'd purchased the gown from an Upper East Side dry cleaners that had an array of formal wear that had gone unclaimed.

"They're barely worn," the store owner had said, showing her a rack of formal dresses. "You'd be shocked by how many rich people there are who don't pick up their stuff."

She'd bought the fanciest dress, despite being two sizes too big for her, for a fraction of its original cost. After four rounds of homemade alterations, one of which she accidentally stitched the hem tip to her clothing, the gown sculpted to her body as if it was fitted by a master seamstress.

"Your ride is here!" Gaspar called from the kitchen.

Maria's heart rate quickened. She tossed her makeup into her purse and went to the kitchen, where she found her father peering out a window. She clasped her purse to her stomach. "How do I look?"

Gaspar turned. A smile spread over his face. "Stunning."

"You really think so?"

"I do." He extended his arm. "I'll walk you outside."

She clasped her father's elbow. They left the apartment and descended the stairs, each of them being careful not to step on the hem of her gown, and exited the building. At the curb, a dark-suited man wearing a driving cap stood beside a Cadillac Fleetwood Imperial Limousine, its polished black paint gleaming like obsidian.

Butterflies swirled in Maria's stomach. She looked at her father. "Thank you for arranging the limo, and for pawning your cameras for the jewelry."

"You're welcome," he said. "I'm sorry that neither of us have enough money for the driver to bring you home."

"It's okay," she said. "It'll give me a chance to be the best dressed person on the train to Newark."

"Indeed."

She fidgeted with her purse. "Do you think I've gone bananas?"

"Of course not," he said. "You're pursuing your dreams, like your mother did."

Maria glanced at her bare ring finger. She hated not wearing her mother's sapphire ring, but she'd taken it off out of concern that a small gemstone would draw attention to her. "If I'm arrested, I don't want you hawking cameras to bail me out of jail. You need your photography equipment to work."

"I doubt that you'll end up in the big house." He patted her hand and grinned. "But if we need to hire a lawyer, I'll take up a collection from the neighbors."

She gave his elbow a squeeze and walked with him to the Cadillac.

The driver tipped his cap, and then opened the rear passenger door.

"Good luck." Gaspar blew her a kiss, as if he didn't want to risk smudging her makeup, and helped her into the limousine.

She tucked her gown over her legs. "Bye, Dad."

The driver shut the door, and then took his place behind the wheel. "Where to?"

"Upper East Side—130 East Eightieth Street," she said.

He glanced at her through the rearview mirror.

She leaned forward. "What's your name?"

"Harold," he said, "but my friends call me Harry."

Maria removed the last of her money from her purse and gave it to him. "Harry, I'm attending an event at the Astor house. If anyone should ask, my name is Miss Virginia Wilder and you picked me up at my aunt and uncle's home in Scarsdale."

The driver slipped the money inside his jacket pocket. "Of course, Miss Wilder." He started the engine and pulled away from the curb.

Maria looked out the rear window and watched her father, who remained standing outside the apartment building, disappear from sight. She leaned back in her seat and drew a deep breath. *I'll either gain entrance, be turned away, get kicked out, or arrested.* She closed her eyes and hoped it wasn't the latter. For the duration of the trip, she rehearsed her plan, over and over, in her head.

For the past week, Maria had worked on a scheme to gain entrance to Vincent Astor's house for Colonel Donovan's speaking engagement. With Roy's replacement yet to be filled, she used her time alone in the Department of Microphotography to research books, magazines, newspapers, and telephone directories. She learned everything she could about Vincent Astor and his second wife, Mary Benedict "Minnie" Cushing. In 1912, Vincent had become the richest young man in the world when his father, John Jacob Astor IV, a prominent business magnate and real estate developer, perished in the sinking of the *Titanic.* Minnie was a socialite and philanthropist, and the daughter of a famous neurosurgeon named Harvey Williams Cushing. Vincent and Minnie had married, shortly after Vincent's divorce from his first wife, a little over a year ago. And Maria hoped that the novelty of their marriage might increase her odds to blend into the crowd, given that the couple might be still getting to know each other's wide circle of friends and acquaintances.

Maria had tracked down the names and contact information for the event planner, caterer, and security firm that were hired for Donovan's speaking engagement. Additionally, she put together a list of likely invitees, based on newspaper articles and photographs of past Astor events. *The rich and influential make the papers far more than ordinary people*, Maria had thought, reading an article about an Astor ball that was attended by celebrities, British royalty, and politicians, including Vincent's boyhood friend Franklin Delano Roosevelt. Most importantly, she uncovered the names of both Vincent's and Minnie's personal assistants. And she put her plan into action with a telephone call—made during lunch hour to improve the chances that a person in charge would not be available—to the Astors' event planner.

"Goldman Event Services," a young female had said, answering the call.

"Good day," Maria said, peering through the glass panels of the library telephone booth. "This is Lillian Barclay, Vincent Astor's personal assistant. Mr. Astor would like to know the names of guests who have declined their invitation to Colonel Donovan's speaking engagement."

"Mr. Goldman is out of the office," the woman said. "I can take a message, and he'll get back with you this afternoon."

"Unfortunately, that will not work," Maria said. "Mr. Astor is leaving for a meeting in five minutes, and he wants the names to take with him."

"I wish I could—"

"I'm sorry," Maria interrupted. "I didn't catch your name."

"Miss Evans."

"Miss Evans," Maria said. "Between you and me, the last time Mr. Astor was kept waiting by a vendor, he discontinued their services—and so did his affluent friends."

"I—uh—"

"The way I see it, you can take a message and risk having to explain to Mr. Goldman why he lost his most important client. Or you can track down the list and read me the names."

"But—"

"The choice is yours, Miss Evans," Maria said calmly. "However, if I were you, I'd locate the list."

"Okay," she said. "But it might take me a few minutes."

"I'll hold."

Through the receiver, Maria listened to the receptionist rummage through a file cabinet, presumably in her boss's office. A moment later, the receptionist read the names of three couples, all of whom declined their invitation due to being out of town. Maria scribbled down the names, thanked the woman for her assistance, and ended the call.

Maria had conducted research, using the library's resources, on the couples and her attention was drawn to Albert and Ethel Wilder, prominent New Yorkers in their late fifties. Although they had no children, they had—between them—over a dozen siblings and scads of nieces and nephews spread across the country. Maria's second and last telephone call was to the Astor security firm. While claiming to be Minnie Astor's personal assistant, Maude, she'd requested the receptionist to add Albert and Ethel Wilder's niece—Miss Virginia Wilder, who was staying at the couple's Scarsdale estate while they were out of town—to the guest list. And she kindly asked the receptionist to inform the event planner of the change. Maria's confidence surged as she hung up the receiver. *It's incredible what one can accomplish with the power of a library card.*

Forty minutes after leaving the Ironbound, the limousine entered the Upper East Side of Manhattan. Maria, fidgeting with her purse, gazed at the majestic buildings on Madison Avenue. The driver turned onto East 80th Street, where there was a roadblock with policemen and a line of large, luxurious automobiles. At the front of the line, formal-dressed people were exiting vehicles and making their way to a palatial, neoclassic limestone townhome.

A police officer raised his hand and approached the vehicle.

The driver braked to a stop and lowered his window.

Maria clenched her hands.

"Are you here for the Astor event?" the officer asked.

"Yes, sir," the driver said.

"Follow the cars on the right."

The driver tipped his cap and pulled ahead.

As the procession of automobiles crept forward, Maria hugged her purse to her belly. Her anxiousness grew as she watched guests enter the residence. Soon, the driver stopped the car near a doorman, dressed in a royal blue jacket with tails and a black top hat.

I can do this. Maria drew a deep breath and leaned forward. "Thanks, Harry."

He looked at her through the rearview mirror. "Have a nice night, Miss Wilder."

The limousine's passenger door opened and the man in the blue jacket tipped his hat. "Good evening."

"Hello," Maria said, her mouth dry. She exited the limousine and was escorted by the doorman through the gate of an iron fence that spanned the front of the home. They traversed a stone portico that was bordered by two large pillars. Above the door, an ornate crystal chandelier glowed through a transom window. Her heart thudded against her rib cage.

The man opened the door and gestured for her to enter.

There's no turning back now. Maria gathered her composure and crossed the threshold.

"Welcome," a mustached host said, standing behind a podium in the vestibule.

"Thank you," Maria said.

"My apologies," he said, looking at Maria. "Your name slipped my mind."

"Virginia Wilder."

The host, a fountain pen in hand, scanned a piece of paper.

Please, let me be on the list.

A well-dressed couple entered the vestibule and stood behind Maria. Feeling pinned in, she glanced inside, where two broad-shouldered security guards were posted. Her skin turned cold.

"Wilder?" the host asked.

"Yes," she said.

"I'm afraid I don't see your name."

Oh, no! She fought away her fear and said, "I'm attending on behalf of my aunt and uncle—Ethel and Albert. It was a recent change."

He ran his finger to the bottom of the paper, and then flipped it over to expose a short list of handwritten names on the back. "Ah, yes, Miss Wilder. I'm deeply sorry for the confusion. Our latest changes are penciled in below the last names beginning with Z."

"It's quite all right," she said.

"The gathering will be held in the ballroom," he said, gesturing with his pen. "It's through the entrance hall and up the stairs. Have a lovely evening, Miss Wilder."

"Thank you."

Maria, a surge of adrenaline flowing through her veins, passed the guards and stepped into the entrance hall, where a group of guests were chatting near a fireplace that was large enough to roast wild game. She crossed a black-and-white-checkered marble floor, and then lifted her gown as she climbed a staircase. *I'll introduce myself to Colonel Donovan, make my pitch to join the IDC, and leave—hopefully of my own accord.*

Reaching the landing, she found that the entire second floor had been opened up to create a large ballroom. At the far end was a lectern, facing rows of chairs. A few guests were seated, but most people were mingling while servers, carrying silver platters, passed out hors d'oeuvres and champagne in fluted crystal glasses. She scanned the room but didn't see Colonel Donovan, whom she thought she could identify from his newspaper photographs. The people in attendance were lavishly dressed; the men were in fine tailored business suits or tuxedos, and the women sported evening dresses or gowns. She was relieved to see that her attire blended in, except that she wasn't wearing expensive gemstones. *There's more jewelry here than at Tiffany's*, she thought, glancing at a woman, her earlobes sagging with huge diamond drop earrings.

Rather than risk blowing her cover by talking with guests who might know the Wilders, she approached a server and selected a glass of champagne. While she waited for Donovan to arrive, she walked along a wall, viewing a series of gilt-frame paintings. Minutes passed and the crowd grew. She sipped champagne, citrusy with a hint of honey, but the alcohol did little to quell her apprehension. Soon, an elderly man, who was walking with an ivory-handle cane, stopped beside her. Before he could speak, Maria politely smiled and moved on to the next artwork.

She took a sip and stared at a painting of the Paris skyline. *It's now occupied by Hitler's army. God, I hope the French can hold out until the country is liberated.* She tried to imagine what it might be like if the United States was under German occupation. Images of Wehrmacht soldiers and swastika flags on New York City streets filled her head. She buried her thoughts and took a gulp of champagne.

"How do you like it?" a female voice asked.

Maria turned and saw Minnie Astor, whom she recognized from magazine photographs. She was in her mid-thirties with flawless alabaster-like skin and wavy, brown shoulder-length hair. Her silver silk gown accentuated her slender figure, and she wore a three-tier diamond bar necklace that matched the bracelet on her wrist.

"It's exquisite," Maria said, struggling to hide her shock.

"I don't believe we've met. I'm Minnie Astor."

Maria extended her hand. "Virginia Wilder. It's a pleasure to meet you, Mrs. Astor."

Minnie shook her hand. "Please, call me Minnie."

A strong scent of floral perfume filled Maria's nose. Her mind raced with what to say. "Your perfume is divine."

"Joy by Jean Patou," Minnie said. "Supposedly, it takes ten thousand jasmine flowers and twenty-eight dozen roses to make a one-ounce bottle."

Good, God! It must cost a fortune! "It's worth every petal."

"I agree," Minnie said.

Maria adjusted her clutch purse, dangling from a chain on her wrist. "You have a lovely home."

"Thank you." Minnie took a sip of her champagne and scanned the ballroom. "Despite its beauty, I'd love to sell it."

Maria, attempting to dispel her nervousness, wiggled her toes inside her shoes. "May I ask why?"

"Ghosts."

Maria straightened her spine. "It's haunted?"

Minnie laughed, nearly spilling her drink. "Of course not, darling."

Her face turned warm. *I'm such a fool.*

"It's not that kind of ghost I'm referring to." Minnie swirled her champagne. She leaned in and lowered her voice. "Let's just say that it's eerie for a bride to live in a home that was once inhabited by her husband's former wife."

"I see," Maria said, feeling surprised by the woman's candor. She looked at her. "If it doesn't feel like your home, perhaps it might be best to move."

Minnie sipped champagne. "The Astors never sell their houses."

"In this case," Maria said, her confidence building, "I think Mr. Astor should make an exception."

Minnie smiled. "I like your moxie."

Maria's shoulder muscles relaxed. *Maybe I can pull this off.*

"So, which gentleman accompanied you this evening?"

"I'm alone."

"Oh," Minnie said.

"My aunt Ethel and uncle Albert were unable to attend. I'm staying at their home in Scarsdale while they're out of town. I'm an admirer of Colonel Donovan, and they insisted that I come on their behalf."

"I'm delighted you're here," Minnie said. "I wish I could say that I know the Wilders well; they're my husband's friends. However, I did have the pleasure of meeting them at our holiday charity event. You must say hello to Vincent before you leave."

Maria squeezed the stem of her glass. "I will."

"Where do you live?"

"California."

Minnie looped her arm around Maria's elbow. "Well, Miss Wilder, allow me to introduce you to my East Coast friends."

"That would be lovely," Maria said, regretting that she hadn't chosen to hide in a coatroom.

Minnie walked her to a group of women, most of whom could pass for fashion models or Hollywood actresses. Maria hoped it would be a brief introduction, and that she could slip away to take a seat near the lectern before Donovan's speech. But it soon became clear, to Maria, that Minnie had little desire to make her rounds to other guests, the vast majority of whom were business associates of her husband. The group of women—which included Minnie's sister, Babe, who was a fashion editor for *Vogue*—were cordial and eager to hear about the latest social venues on the West Coast. For the next several minutes, Maria pretended to be Virginia Wilder, a socialite from California. Although she'd never visited a social club, or eaten outside of a school cafeteria or hot dog stand, she was able to recall the names of upscale restaurants and nightclubs in San Francisco. *Thank goodness I attended the University of California, Berkeley.*

A tall man with slicked-back hair and hooded eyes crossed the ballroom floor.

Oh, no—Mr. Astor! Maria's breath stalled in her chest. "If you will excuse me, ladies, I think I should visit the powder room before our guest of honor arrives."

"One moment," Minnie said, placing a hand on Maria's arm. She gestured to her husband.

Maria's legs felt weak.

"Colonel Donovan is in the entrance hall," Vincent said, approaching Minnie. "We should take our seats."

"Of course, darling," Minnie said. "But first, I want you to say hello to Albert Wilder's niece, Virginia."

Vincent looked at Maria.

"She's come all the way from California," Minnie said.

"It's a pleasure to meet you, Mr. Astor," Maria said, extending her hand.

Vincent, his face stoic, shook her hand.

I gotta get out of here. Her stomach turned nauseous, as if she'd drunk a pint of pickling juice.

"Ladies and gentlemen," a man at the front of the room announced. "Please take your seats."

Guests began to migrate toward chairs.

"Perhaps you two could chat after the colonel's speech," Minnie said.

"I look forward to it," Maria said, forcing a smile.

Vincent rubbed his chin and nodded.

Maria slipped away. She gave her champagne glass to a server, and then sat in a chair, between two elderly couples, in the middle of the third row.

Once everyone was seated, Vincent accompanied Minnie to a front row reserved seat. As he helped his wife into her chair, his eyes briefly locked on Maria. He leaned down to Minnie and whispered in her ear.

Minnie shifted in her seat. She glanced at Maria, and then faced forward.

They're talking about me. Goose bumps cropped up on Maria's arms.

Vincent made his way to the stairwell, where he spoke with a security guard. Seconds later, a second security guard accompanied Colonel Donovan, a silver-haired uniformed military officer, to the landing. Vincent greeted Donovan and they walked to the front of the room. Chatter faded as Vincent took a spot behind the lectern, while Donovan stood off to the side.

"Good evening, ladies and gentlemen," Vincent said, looking over the crowd.

Maria exhaled. *I'm overreacting; everything is okay. I'll meet Donovan before he leaves.*

Vincent delivered an introduction—providing an eloquent account of Donovan's business accomplishments and military service, including being awarded the Medal of Honor for his heroic acts in the Great War—and then extended his arm toward Donovan. "Please join me in welcoming the head of the Office of Strategic Services, Colonel William J. Donovan."

The audience applauded.

A wave of excitement surged through Maria.

Donovan stepped to the lectern, and Vincent took a seat beside Minnie.

"Thank you for the warm welcome, Vincent." Donovan placed his hands on the lectern and gazed over the audience. "When war erupted in Europe, I was a proponent of the United States joining the fight against Hitler. In fact, I was often accused by isolationists and neutralists of attempting to bring America into the fight. It is no secret that I was sent to London as Roosevelt's envoy to appraise Britain's power to withstand the German offensive, as well as to learn about British methods of unconventional warfare. And while doing so, I gained the trust of Prime Minister Winston Churchill and King George."

Maria clasped the seat of her chair.

"Since the Japanese bombing of Pearl Harbor, our country has become unified in the fight to conquer Nazi tyranny. We now stand with Britain and Allied forces. And to expand America's intelligence capabilities, President Roosevelt recently signed a presidential order for the Office of the Coordinator of Information—COI—to become the Office of Strategic Services—OSS."

For twenty minutes, Donovan explained the structure of the OSS, describing several of its branches, including a brief mention of librarians in the IDC. However, most of Donovan's time was spent describing the functions of intelligence, espionage, sabotage, and propaganda.

A woman, seated behind Maria, whispered to her husband, "I can't believe he's telling us all this."

"They don't call him Wild Bill for nothing," the husband said.

Maria shifted her weight.

"My plan for the OSS was inspired by Great Britain's SOE," Donovan said. "We are establishing training sites, and I expect our capabilities to be on par with the British within a few months. And, like the SOE, the OSS will have no gender restrictions. We will have both men and women agents in enemy-occupied territories."

Women as spies, Maria thought. A wave of patriotism swelled within her.

Two security guards walked forward and took positions along opposite walls, flanking the third row where Maria was seated.

Through the corners of Maria's eyes, she watched the guards, their hands clasped and peering in her direction. Her excitement evaporated. *Damn it—they know.* She expected the guards to call her aside, but they silently remained at their post. *They're keeping an eye on me until Donovan's finished speaking, then they'll remove me or have me arrested.* Her mind raced, determined to find a way to reach Donovan before they reached her.

"I'm seeking intelligent, independent thinkers who have the guts to serve behind enemy lines," Donovan said, looking over the crowd. "And I have faith that our clandestine warriors will lead us to victory."

Donovan stepped back from the lectern. The audience stood and applauded. Donovan, stopping to shake hands, gradually made his way forward.

Instead of exiting her row, Maria squeezed her way forward between chairs and guests. As she approached Donovan, the guards spotted her and sprang forward. Maria, refusing to give up, pressed ahead, sliding between two large men in tuxedos. But a few feet from Donovan, one of the guards stopped her.

"Come with me," the guard said, clasping her upper arm.

Maria's hopes sank. Pain shot through her bicep as the guard dug his fingers into muscle. "Okay," she said, her voice hushed. "I won't cause any trouble."

The second guard approached them and motioned for his comrade to exit, away from Donovan.

The guard gave a nod.

I can't give up when I'm this close. Her heartbeat thudded in her chest. Maria raised her leg and slammed the heel of her patent leather pump onto the guard's foot.

The guard winced and lost his grip.

Maria darted forward. "Colonel Donovan!"

Donovan turned.

She weaved through the crowd.

Vincent stepped to Donovan. "No need for alarm. We have an uninvited guest. Our security will remove her from the premises in short order."

Donovan nodded.

Reaching the colonel, Maria looked at him and said, "I have a volunteer for you, sir."

The security guards detained Maria, and guests backed away, as if attempting to avoid the disturbance.

"Please, Colonel," Maria said.

The lines in Donovan's face softened, and he waved off the guards. "It's all right."

Maria felt the guards release their hands from her arms. Her pulse pounded in her eardrums.

Donovan looked at Maria. "May I ask the name of your volunteer?"

Maria gathered her courage and said, "Me, sir. My name is Maria Alves. I'm a microfilm expert with the New York Public Library. I have a master's degree, I'm fluent in six languages with experience traveling overseas, and I believe that I can be of service to the IDC branch of the OSS."

Vincent frowned and leaned to Donovan. "She somehow gained entrance under the name of Virginia Wilder, claiming to be a niece of a guest who could not attend. Fortunately, I grew up with Albert Wilder and I know the names of all his family members."

Donovan rubbed his chin. "May I ask how you broke into the reception?"

I'm going to jail, and they'll throw away the key. With her scheme in shambles, she decided that further lies would only make matters worse, so she told Donovan how she impersonated the Astors' personal assistants to gain access to the guest list.

Wide-eyed visitors stared at Maria. Whispers grew from the crowd.

"I'm not normally a deceitful person, sir," Maria said. "My telephone calls and letters expressing my desire to serve in the IDC have been unsuccessful. When I found out that you were going to speak here, I saw it as my last chance to be recruited." She turned to Vincent. "Mr. Astor, I regret the trouble I've caused you."

Vincent crossed his arms.

"And I'm sorry about stomping your foot," Maria said, noticing the guard favoring his right leg.

"Take her away," Vincent said to the guards.

"Wait," Donovan said. "Wouldn't you agree, Vincent, that it would take someone quite cunning to gate-crash your event?"

Vincent shifted his weight. "It would."

"I have a policy to hire, on the spot, anyone who shows the skills and courage to serve in our intelligence services." Donovan extended his arm to her. "Welcome to the OSS."

Maria, her eyes wide, shook his hand. "Thank you, sir."

"Expect a telephone call from Frederick Kilgour of the IDC," Donovan said. "He'll reach you at the library to arrange for you to undergo training."

"Yes, sir," she said.

Donovan looked into Maria's eyes. "I'm counting on you."

Maria swallowed. "I won't let you down, sir."

Donovan stepped away with Vincent and greeted guests.

Maria was eager to leave, but she approached Minnie, who was standing alone with her arms crossed. "I regret not being truthful with you."

Minnie nodded. "Are you really joining the OSS?"

"Yes." Maria fiddled with her purse. "I'm deeply sorry for misleading you and your husband to get to Colonel Donovan."

Minnie's eyes softened. "You're welcome to stay. Guests will no doubt want to chat with a future secret agent."

"I appreciate the offer, but I think I've overstayed my welcome."

"Good luck to you," Minnie said.

"You too."

Maria, in a hurry to tell her father about her encounter with Donovan, left the Astor house and briskly walked to the train station. A mixture of resolve and trepidation swirled inside her. She hoped that Kilgour would follow through with Donovan's orders to have her undergo training for the IDC. And she prayed that she would have the prowess to serve her country overseas and not disappoint the colonel for taking a chance on her.

Chapter 5

Lisbon, Portugal—July 3, 1942

Tiago, carrying expired passports in a hidden pocket in the lining of his jacket, left a café in Praça do Comércio, a large plaza facing Lisbon's harbor. Morning sunlight shimmered over the stone blue water of the Tagus, the longest river in the Iberian Peninsula. His eyes gravitated to a group of refugees washing clothes along the riverbank. Behind them were tattered suitcases, blankets, and bags. *Thousands of Jews have poured into Portugal; most have no money and are sleeping in the streets.* He left the riverfront and made his way to his bookstore, all the while wishing he had the means to help them all.

Tiago arrived at his bookstore, Livraria Soares, and found the door unlocked and an *Open* sign posted in the window. A brass shopkeeper's bell, attached to the top of the door, jangled as he entered.

Rosa, who was sitting at the cashier desk with a newspaper, lowered her eyeglasses to the tip of her nose.

"*Olá*," Tiago said, placing his cap on a rack. "I see that you remembered your key."

She glanced at her wristwatch and frowned. "You're late again."

"I am." He gave her a grandmotherly peck on the cheek and grinned. "Good morning to you too, Rosa. How are you?"

The corners of Rosa's mouth twitched, as if she was fighting back a smile. "I'd be better if you'd timely arrive for work. Did you have a late night, or was it an early morning meeting?"

"Yes," Tiago said, intentionally being vague to fuel their banter. He looked forward to their robust morning conversations, but Rosa, he believed, enjoyed them even more.

She folded her newspaper. "So, which one was it?"

He removed a stack of passports from the hidden pocket in his jacket and placed them on the counter. "I was at a café this morning with a Jewish family from Rouen, France."

Rosa thumbed through the booklets. "How many children do they have?"

"Five," Tiago said. "And the mother is six months pregnant. I can't fathom how they trekked over the Pyrenees mountains, through northern Spain, and to my parents' vineyard in Porto."

"It's a miracle." Rosa touched her forehead, chest, and shoulders, making the sign of a cross.

"We're the last cog in the wheel to freedom," Tiago said, his voice turning somber. He looked at her, her eyes surrounded in dark circles from sleepless nights of forging documents.

She blinked, as if fighting back tears.

"I couldn't do this without you."

"True." She raised her chin. "And let's not forget that if it wasn't for me, you'd be even more tardy for work."

Tiago chuckled.

"When do you need their papers?"

"In a week, if possible."

She nodded, and then stashed the passports under the false bottom of her purse. "How are your grandparents?"

Tiago's chest tightened. "They're determined to stay in France, despite letters from me and my parents urging them to flee."

"They're protecting Jews from the Germans," Rosa said. "If you were in their shoes, would you abandon refugees in need of sanctuary?"

"No, but this is different."

"How so?" she asked.

Tiago shifted his weight. "Because they're my family, and I care about them."

"It's understandable to want to protect the ones you love," she said, "but it's also important to respect their wishes. Without your grandparents, there would be many refugees without the means to escape France."

The truth of her words stung Tiago. He drew a deep breath and nodded. A flash of his morning meeting in the café filled his head. "The family I met with this morning told me that my grandparents gave their children books to read and a cast-iron miniature horse to play with while they hid in the wine caves. Those were the same things that my grandparents spoiled me with as a child when I visited their vineyard."

"You must feel proud to have such courageous and compassionate grandparents."

"I do." *But I can't help worrying about them.*

"After the war is over," Rosa said, "I expect you to introduce me to them."

He smiled. "Nothing would make me happier."

A tall, rawboned man, and a woman wearing a headscarf, approached the glass window of the bookstore and peered inside.

Tiago stepped in front of the counter, blocking the couple's view of Rosa as she stashed her purse beneath the counter. He approached the door and opened it. "May I help you?"

The man glanced at his companion and stuffed his hands into his pocket. "*Parlez-vous français*?"

"*Oui*." Tiago gestured for them to come inside.

The couple, who appeared to be in their late sixties, given their gray hair and wrinkles around their eyes, shuffled inside. The man slid a cap from his head. "I'm Ephraim, and this is my wife, Helene," he said, clasping the woman's hand. "We're looking for a man named Tiago."

"I'm Tiago."

"We were told that you can help with travel papers," he said.

"Who told you that?"

"A man at the docks."

Hair rose on the back of Tiago's neck. It wasn't unusual for refugees, who hadn't traveled through his family's escape route, to be referred to him. But he had to be careful. In Lisbon, spies were everywhere, and even refugees were susceptible to bribes from the PVDE.

"I'm afraid you have me mistaken for another person," Tiago said. "I sell books. Perhaps I could interest you in something to read while you're in Lisbon."

Rosa, who didn't speak French, furrowed her brow as she struggled to understand the conversation.

"Please," Helene said, her jaw quivering. "Samuel Benda told us that you could help with acquiring a passport."

An image of Samuel and his wife, Pauline—whom he provided fake travel papers and temporary shelter at a boardinghouse—flashed in his head. He turned to Rosa. "I'll be in the back of the store. Turn on the radio if anyone enters."

She nodded.

He led Ephraim and Helene to the back of the bookshop, where he retrieved stools for them to sit. For several minutes, Tiago questioned them and, after he was sure he wasn't walking into a trap by the PVDE, he told them that he could help.

"My passport was stolen," Ephraim said.

"How?" Tiago asked.

"We arrived in Lisbon three days ago," Ephraim said. "With no place to stay, we've been spending much of our time in Rossio Square."

Where Jewish refugees congregate, Tiago thought. *And most asylum seekers are unaware that the PVDE is conducting surveillance on them.*

Ephraim rubbed his beard. "Helene was resting on a bench, so I decided to walk around the area. A street away, I was stopped by the Portuguese secret police to examine my papers. The agent, who spoke a bit of French, claimed that my visa was not properly issued—which was a lie—and he confiscated my passport."

"I'm sorry." Tiago looked at Helene. "Was your passport also taken?"

"*Non*," she said.

"Do you recall the name of the agent?" Tiago asked.

"I think his last name was something like Nuñez," Ephraim said.

"Did he have a mustache, cleft chin, and wear a suit with a bowler hat?"

"*Oui*," Ephraim said. "Do you know him?"

"Agent Martim Neves," Tiago said. "I recommend that you don't report what happened to the police. It will make matters worse for you."

Ephraim nodded.

"Where are you staying?" Tiago asked.

"For now, we're living on the streets," Helene said, lowering her eyes.

"Do you have any money?"

Helene slid a ruby ring from her finger and gave it to Ephraim, who removed his gold wedding band and held out his hand with the jewelry. "We have no money, but we can pay you with these."

Tiago's heart sank. "I don't charge for my services. But you'll need to trade the jewelry for escudos. It'll likely take months before you gain ship passage, and you'll need money to eat. Before you leave, I'll give you the address of a jeweler who will give you a fair price for the rings."

"*Merci*," Helene said.

"You can thank me when you acquire your tickets for your voyage," Tiago said. "Do you plan to go to America?"

"*Oui*," they said in unison.

Tiago leaned forward. "You should know your options before we proceed. You could choose to go to Portuguese authorities and tell them that you lost your passport, but there is the chance that they'll think you illegally entered the country and will deport you back to Spain, where you'll likely be sent back to France. Or I can create a fake passport for you. Most of my work is to alter existing passports, so there is a possibility that it might not pass inspection and you could be arrested." *And me, too, if they tell the PVDE where they acquired the phony papers.*

Ephraim glanced to his wife, who gave a nod. He turned to Tiago and said, "We'd like your help and promise not to tell anyone where we got the passport."

"Very well," Tiago said. Although he relied on Rosa for the forging of documents, he portrayed to refugees that he was acting alone. *If anyone is arrested, it will be me.* "Do you have any photographs of yourself, or other paperwork that I can work with?"

"*Non*," Ephraim said.

"Then we'll need to start from scratch." Tiago retrieved a pad of paper and pencil from his office. For several minutes he collected information from Ephraim. Full name. Date of birth. Nationality. Profession. "And where is your place of birth?"

"Libourne, France."

"That's close to my grandparents in Bordeaux."

Ephraim shifted on his stool. Helene chewed on her lower lip.

Tiago lowered his pencil. "Did I say something to upset you?"

Ephraim placed his arm around his wife. "Helene's sister, and her sister's family, were arrested in a village near Bordeaux."

Oh, God. "When?"

"Three weeks ago," Helene said.

"May I ask what happened?" Tiago asked.

Helene clasped her hands. "My sister, along with her husband and teenage daughter, complied with the order of the German occupation authorities to register as Jews. A week later, they—as well as a dozen members of their synagogue—were arrested by German soldiers."

Tiago's skin turned cold. "I'm sorry. Do you know where they were taken?"

"*Non*," Ephraim said. "But there are rumors in Libourne that Jews are being sent away to work camps."

Tiago, his mind and heart on the safety of his grandparents, struggled to concentrate while gathering information for Ephraim's travel papers. After they finished, he gave them a piece of paper with the address of a jeweler, walked them to the door, and said goodbye with plans to meet again in a couple weeks. He peered out the window and watched them travel down the street and disappear around a corner.

"What's their story?" Rosa asked.

"The man's passport was taken by Agent Neves."

"Bastard," Rosa muttered.

Tiago, his stomach in knots, turned to her.

"You look pale." Rosa approached him. "Are you okay?"

"No," he said. "The woman's sister, and her sister's family, were arrested in a German raid on a synagogue near Bordeaux."

"Oh, no," Rosa said.

Tiago ran a hand through his hair. "I appreciate your words about the virtue of selflessness, but things are getting worse for Jews in France. My grandparents are in peril, and I need to get them to Portugal."

"But you and your father have already written to them, and they declined to leave."

A burn grew in his chest. "I'm going to Bordeaux."

Her eyes widened. "No! It's impossible to get there and back without being arrested!"

"We've aided scores of Jews who've escaped from France," he said. "I know the route that the refugees take—from Bordeaux, through the Pyrenees mountains to Spain, and from Basque Country to Portugal. And I know the locations of the churches and monasteries that harbor Jews. I see no reason why I can't do the same trek, in reverse, to reach my grandparents."

"It's ludicrous," Rosa said.

"I must try," Tiago said. "And I'd like your assistance with travel papers."

She placed her hands on her hips. "I won't do it."

"Then I'll create the documents myself."

"Your novice forgery skills will get you captured," she said, as if to deter him.

"I'm going whether you assist me or not." He looked at her. "Please, Rosa. I need your help."

She nodded, reluctantly. "When do you leave?"

"Tomorrow."

They closed the bookstore for the day. Rosa telephoned her husband, who was unaware of his wife's clandestine work, and concocted a story that she was going to have dinner with a friend, which cleared the way for her to work late into the evening. In the back of the shop, they devised travel plans and papers for Tiago's journey. They finished at 10:00 p.m., stashed the forgery supplies in the hidden hole in Tiago's office, and left the bookstore. Despite Rosa wanting to walk home alone, Tiago accompanied her to the outskirts of her neighborhood.

"This is close enough," she said, stopping at a street corner.

He turned to her. "I'll see you in two weeks."

She removed a chain with a medallion from her neck, and handed it to him. "I want you to have this."

Under the dull glow of a streetlight, Tiago looked at a bronze St. Christopher medallion. *The patron saint of travelers.*

"It was Jorge's when he worked on a fishing boat. He gave it to me to wear on my walks to and from work. You might not want to wear it, because of your Jewish faith, but I think it might help you in France if you're stopped by the Germans."

"*Obrigado.*"

Tiago slipped the medallion into his pocket and watched her disappear into the night. As he made his way to his apartment, he passed a group of refugees, searching for a place to rest near a row of bushes in a public garden. *Thousands of Jews have reached Lisbon, but many have failed in their journey to reach freedom.* The odds of reaching Bordeaux, Tiago believed, were against him. And if he, a half-Jew, was apprehended in German-occupied France, it might cost him his life. Regardless, he was determined to save his grandparents at any price.

Chapter 6

Porto, Portugal—July 4, 1942

Tiago, carrying a canvas and leather duffel bag, exited the train at the Porto station and stretched his leg muscles, tight from sitting on the five-hour train ride from Lisbon. As he walked through the station, Rosa's St. Christopher medallion swung back and forth on the chain beneath his white button-down shirt. Outside, he made his way along narrow, cobblestone streets. Church bells rang throughout the city, filled with Baroque, Gothic, and Portuguese Romanesque buildings and cathedrals. At the riverfront, bustling with dockworkers, he hitched a ride on a *rabelo* boat, a wooden flat-bottomed cargo vessel, that was being towed upstream on the Douro River. As the boat traveled along the waterway, the city of Porto disappeared, giving way to lush valleys with vineyards cut into hillsides. Adolescent memories of helping his father load barrels of port wine onto *rabelo* boats flashed in Tiago's head, and he longed for the days when Europe was at peace.

An hour later, the boat docked at a riverbank, and he jumped out with his duffel bag. He hiked up a steep, dirt lane to a terraced vineyard where shoots and cordons of vines—comprised of Touriga Nacional, Tinta Cão, and Touriga Francesa grape varieties—grew along wires attached to posts. A hot breeze rustled the grape leaves. As his parents' two-story home came into view, an uneasiness grew in his chest. *How will they feel when I tell them about the raid on a French synagogue?* He shook away the thought and pressed upward, sending a burn through his thigh muscles.

Tiago had spent his entire life on the vineyard, until he'd left home to study modern languages and literature at the University of Coimbra. His father, Renato, had inherited the property as a young man when his parents died, within a week of each other, from influenza. Renato, who'd been more of a laborer than a winemaker, lacked scientific knowledge of grape cultivation and fermentation. However, he was committed to acquiring viticulture expertise and carrying on his family's business. Therefore, he became a mentee, in exchange for unpaid work, to a Douro Valley winemaker, and he embarked on a trip to the Bordeaux region in France, where he believed some of the best wines in the world were being made. While visiting a French vineyard, he met Lina, a beautiful and intelligent vintner who worked at her parents' winery. Despite their language barrier and different religions—Lina a Jew and Renato a Catholic—they fell in love and were married in a civil ceremony at the council office in Bordeaux. They moved to the Douro Valley and created a life together, eventually producing some of Portugal's best port wines. And when they had Tiago, their only child, they hoped that he would someday carry on the family wine tradition. But Tiago's passion for books, as well as his intolerance for fascism, had driven him away from home.

Tiago placed down his bag, rubbed an ache in his arm, and entered the house through an arched wooden door. "*Olá*!"

Footsteps came from the kitchen. His mother, Lina—a slender middle-aged woman with pronounced cheekbones and shoulder-length gray-and-auburn hair—appeared in the hallway.

"Tiago!" she said with a subtle French accent.

"It's good to see you, Maman." He kissed her on both cheeks.

"If I had known you were coming, I would have prepared a place for you to sleep." She glanced at the stairwell. "We have guests who are staying in the spare rooms."

Refugees, he thought. "How many?"

"Two families, a total of eight people, arrived last night."

He wondered, although briefly, if the refugees had mentioned anything about mass arrests taking place near Bordeaux, and decided that it was best to speak with his parents about it together. "How are they?"

She wrapped her arms around herself. "They had a difficult journey after they left your grandparents' vineyard. They're malnourished, and three of them have open sores on their feet. It might be a week before they're healthy enough to travel."

"I'm sure you'll make them well," he said. "If needed, I'll help them acquire papers when they make it to Lisbon."

She nodded.

He slid his hands into his pockets. "Where's Pai?"

"He's working in the wine cellar. I was about to join him."

"I'll come with you."

He stashed his duffel bag inside the house, and then walked with his mother to a stone-and-timber beam structure that was built into the hillside. As they entered the windowless building, he noted the cooler temperature, and a subtle scent of oak and aged port wine filled his nose. They traveled down a stone aisle, lined with oak barrels stacked three high, toward the glow of a lantern. They found his father repairing a wooden rack.

"*Olá*, Pai," Tiago said.

Renato—a tall, lean man with a receding gray hairline and the sleeves of his khaki work shirt rolled up to his biceps—placed down a hammer and hugged his son. "It's good to see you."

"You too," he said, releasing him.

"What brings you home?" Pai asked.

"There's something I need to talk to you and Maman about."

"Is everything all right?" Maman asked.

Tiago shook his head. "When did you receive your last message from Grand-père and Grand-mère?"

"A week ago," Maman said. "The refugees who arrived last night told me that your grandparents are doing well."

Thank God, Tiago thought. "Was there any mention about mass arrests of Jews?"

"*Não*," Pai said. "What's happened?"

"Yesterday, a Jewish couple—who did not travel through our family's escape line—visited my bookstore. While I was helping them with travel papers, they told me about a German raid on a synagogue near Bordeaux."

"Oh, God," Maman breathed.

"The couple is from Libourne, forty kilometers from Bordeaux," Tiago said. "The woman's sister, and her sister's family, were among the Jews who were arrested."

Pai placed his arm around his wife. "What did the Germans do with them?"

"The couple didn't know," Tiago said. "But they claim that there are rumors in Libourne about Jews being arrested and sent away to work camps." He looked into his mother's eyes, filled with fear. "It's become too dangerous for them. We need to get them out."

"They've ignored your father's and my requests to leave," she said. "I'll write them again to inform them of your news. I'll implore them to come here with the next group of refugees."

Tiago shifted his weight. "I've written to them, too. They're committed to helping Jews flee German-occupied France, and I have no reason to believe that another message will persuade them to abandon people in need. Also, letters to France are subject to censorship, and informing them about Jews being arrested might place them in more jeopardy."

"We must try," Pai said.

"Not by letters." Tiago's shoulder muscles tensed. "I'm going to Bordeaux."

Maman's eyes widened. "It's too dangerous."

Pai approached Tiago. "That is not an option. We'll find another way to get them out."

"I can do it," Tiago persisted. "I have forged travel papers that will get me across the Spain border, and another set of papers in the event that I'm stopped in France. Also, I have fake passports, with the proper stamps, for Grand-père and Grand-mère."

"*Não*," Pai said. "If you're arrested in Spain, they'll execute you if they find out that you fought against Franco in their civil war. And if the Germans arrest you in France, you might suffer dire consequences for being a half-Jew."

An image of fighting in the Spanish Civil War surged through Tiago's head. He was one of a few thousand Portuguese who'd fought against fascism, opposite the troops that Salazar sent to Franco. Most of the anti-fascist fighters who returned home were imprisoned. But Tiago had avoided arrest by his fake alibi of working—during the Spanish conflict—at his grandparents' vineyard in France, and the fact that most of the men in his unit, who could disclose Tiago's secret, were killed in combat. *I could be arrested or worse, but so could my grandparents if they stay in France.*

Tiago buried his thoughts and said, "My papers provide me with a new identity. No one will know about my history or being a Jew."

Pai crossed his arms.

"It's a day journey by automobile to San Sebastián, Spain," Tiago said. "And from there, it's a five-day journey by foot to Bordeaux, but my travel papers will allow me to board a train, which will get me there sooner. I can reach Grand-père and Grand-mère in less than three days from now."

Maman, as if contemplating her son's plan, rubbed her forehead.

"You don't have an automobile," Pai said.

"I was planning to use your truck," Tiago said.

"*Não*," Pai said.

"Then I'll steal one," Tiago said. "Either way, I'm going to Bordeaux."

Pai looked at his wife. "If anyone goes, it will be me. I'm a Portuguese Catholic, not a Jew. German soldiers will not view me as a threat, and neither will Spaniards."

"You don't have travel papers," Tiago said to his father.

"Then I'll arrange to get them," he said.

"That will take time, which we might not have," Tiago said. "It must be me who makes the journey."

"I don't want either of you to go," Maman said, a quaver in her voice.

After deliberating for several minutes, Tiago looked at his parents and said, "Please trust me. I'll get them out of France."

The concern on Pai's face softened.

Maman paused, wiping her eyes, and reluctantly nodded. "Promise me you'll be careful."

"I will," Tiago said.

Pai placed a hand on Tiago's shoulder. "I assume you have paperwork that provides a purpose for entering Spain."

"I do," Tiago said. "In addition to your truck, I'll need a case of port and boxes of unused wine corks."

Pai furrowed his brow. "Cork?"

He nodded.

First, Tiago met with the refugees who were staying at his parents' house. He gathered information about their journey, especially the locations of safe havens and areas in coastal, southwestern France that were patrolled by Wehrmacht soldiers. Afterward, he went to his father's truck and, while out of view of his parents, he opened his duffel bag and removed forged French paperwork, a box of ammunition, and an Astra 400 pistol that he'd used during the Spanish conflict. The cold steel of the weapon resurrected horrid images. Cannonade. The acrid smell of gunpowder. Wails of maimed men. He wondered, although briefly, if he would be required to kill to extricate his grandparents from Nazi-occupied France. He shook away his thoughts and hid the items under the seat.

For an hour, he and his parents loaded crates of cork, three large cans of *gasóleo*, and a case of unlabeled port wine into the bed of the truck and covered it with a tarp. Using a map, he showed his parents his travel route—from the Douro Valley to the Spain border, and to San Sebastián.

"I'll stow away the truck at the monastery in San Sebastián before hiking into France." Tiago folded the map. The name of the monk, whom he'd never met, flashed in his brain. "What can you tell me about Francisco?"

"He can be trusted," his mother said. "Your grandparents recruited him at the onset of the war to harbor Jewish refugees upon crossing the Pyrenees mountains into Spain. He gives them food and shelter before they embark on their journey here."

Tiago stashed the map, as well as a basket of food and a canteen of water, which was packed by his mother, in the cab and approached his parents.

"*Au revoir*," Maman said, hugging him.

He squeezed her tight.

Pai leaned in, wrapping his arms around them.

Tiago slipped away, got into the cab, and closed the door, its rusted hinges groaning. He started the engine and pulled away, watching his parents disappear in the rearview mirror. Reaching an unpaved road, he pressed the accelerator. The tires kicked up dust, and as the old truck's speed grew, the rear axle grinded like a millstone. He squeezed the steering wheel and hoped that the vehicle wouldn't break down before reaching the Pyrenees mountain range.

After three hours of driving over bone-jarring, rutted back roads, Tiago approached the Spanish border near the town of Alcañices. A fiery sun lowered over the Iberian Peninsula, painting the sky in streaks of orange and gold. Forty meters ahead were two Spanish border patrol agents, standing beside horses tethered to a tree on the side of the road. An angst spread through Tiago's abdomen. Although Spain and Portugal had a nonaggression pact, which provided mutual respect for borders, the agreement would be of no help to Tiago if he were identified as a former anti-fascist fighter. He glanced at his forged papers on the passenger seat. *I've evaded capture in Spain many times before. I will do it again.*

One of the border agents, wearing a khaki uniform with a holstered pistol, stepped into the road and raised his arm.

Tiago, his pulse rate accelerating, slowed the truck to a stop.

The agent, his shirt armpits stained with sweat, motioned to his comrade to inspect the bed of the truck. He approached the open driver's window and looked at Tiago. "*Hablas español*?"

"*Sí.*"

"Show me your papers," the agent said in Spanish.

Tiago handed him his identification and paperwork. Through the rearview mirror, he watched as the agent's companion—a stout, mustached man with fleshy jowls, giving him the appearance of having cotton stuffed inside his cheeks—pulled back the tarp and inspected crates. He lowered his hand to the seat, inches from his hidden Astra 400 pistol.

"Pedro Braga," the agent said, gazing over the paperwork. "What is your purpose in Spain?"

"I'm delivering cork to the Mendoza winery in Bilboa," Tiago said. "The shipment papers are included with the documents."

"I've never heard of Mendoza," the agent said.

Tiago inched his hand close to the pistol.

The agent thumbed through the papers, while his companion examined more boxes. He frowned and looked at Tiago. "Why doesn't the winery use Spanish cork?"

"Señor Mendoza is having trouble with cork taint from his supplier in Malaga," Tiago said calmly. "He claims that his bottles of Rioja wine, when opened, smell like a wet dog."

The agent wrinkled his nose.

Tiago rested his arm on the open window and leaned to the agent. "And, if I recall Señor Mendoza's words correctly, he said that he'd rather go to hell than buy cork from the communist bastards in Catalonia."

The agent grinned, revealing crooked teeth. "Most of the leftists have been shot or are rotting in prison. But they're like rats; they multiply and are hard to catch."

Tiago nodded, attempting to hide a burn rising from his stomach.

The comrade, holding a case of wine, exited the bed of the truck and approached the agent. "It's all cork and fuel, except for some *vino*."

The agent glanced at the bottles, and then looked at Tiago.

"Your papers permit the transport of cork, but there is no mention of wine."

"My employer, Señor Faria, uses the finest cork in Portugal for his port wine. He wanted to provide Señor Mendoza with bottles of port to show him the quality of cork."

"We're confiscating it," the agent said.

The comrade smirked.

"My boss might terminate my employment if I can't bring a sample," Tiago said, his confidence building. "Would you permit me to keep a few bottles?"

The agent handed Tiago his paperwork. He slipped a bottle from the case. "Because your employer hates communists, I'll permit you to keep a bottle."

"*Gracias.*" Tiago took the bottle and placed it on the passenger seat.

The agent motioned for him to leave.

Tiago, his adrenaline pumping through his veins, pressed the accelerator and pulled away. *The excitement of stealing Portuguese wine distracts them from searching the cab for contraband.* He drove into the Spanish countryside feeling grateful that he'd chosen to bring bottles of port as an offering to the border patrol.

He arrived in the Basque coastal city of San Sebastián at 2:30 a.m., according to his luminous dial watch. Under a moonlit sky, the Pyrenees mountains loomed over the town, which was silent except for the grinding of the truck's axle. Using directions he'd memorized from his conversation with refugees, he located the Benedictine monastery on the outskirts of the municipality. With no place to hide the truck, he parked it near a barn, and then placed his weapon, ammunition, and papers into his duffel bag. His boots crunched over gravel as he made his way to the abbey, a two-story stone structure with shuttered windows. He disliked having to disturb inhabitants of the monastery at this hour, but he didn't want to risk sleeping in a truck with Portuguese license plates, which might draw attention from Spanish patrols.

At the entrance, he knocked using a fist-size iron ring that was mounted on the door. Minutes passed and, as he was about to knock again, approaching footsteps came from within the abbey. A lock clicked and the door opened, revealing a bespectacled man wearing a black, hooded robe. A dull glow emanated from the man's candle lantern.

"My name is Tiago," he said in Spanish. "I'm here to see Francisco. He's friends with my grandparents, Laurent and Odette, in Bordeaux."

The monk nodded, as if he recognized the names, and ushered Tiago inside and closed the door. Without speaking, he led him down a long corridor and through a quadrangular cloister with twisted limestone columns. Reaching a connecting building, the monk opened the door to what appeared to be a dormitory cell, given the small bed and writing desk. Using his lantern, he lit a candle on the desk, and then motioned with his hand for Tiago to stay.

Vow of silence, he thought.

The monk left, closing the door behind him.

Tiago, exhausted from the trip, put down his sack and slumped in a chair. The candle flame flickered over the cell walls, absent decorations except for a crucifix above the bed. He drew a deep breath, taking in the scent of ancient timber and an earthy yet sweet aroma of burning beeswax. Several minutes passed and, as his eyelids grew heavy, the sound of footsteps came from the corridor. Fighting away his drowsiness, he rubbed his face and stood.

A soft tap on the door, and an elderly monk with white stubbled hair and beard entered the room. Dark, puffy bags hung under his eyes, making him appear stricken by insomnia. He wore a black robe with a scapular. A wooden cross dangled from his neck.

"I'm Tiago," he said, extending his hand.

"Francisco." He shook Tiago's hand and shifted his weight, as if he were uncomfortable conversing. "You're Laurent and Odette's grandson?"

"Yes," he said. "I've received news about a German raid on a synagogue, not far from my grandparents' vineyard in Bordeaux. It's becoming dangerous for them, and I need to get them out of France."

The monk clasped his cross. Tears welled up in his eyes.

A knot twisted in Tiago's stomach. "What's wrong?"

"German soldiers arrested your grandparents."

He stepped back. "No, it can't be. A group of refugees arrived two days ago at my parents' vineyard in Portugal. They reported that my grandparents were all right."

"I found out this afternoon, when a Jewish couple arrived at the monastery," Francisco said. "Your grandparents were arrested, a day after the couple's arrival at the vineyard. The couple avoided capture by hiding in a secret chamber of a wine cave."

An image of Tiago's childhood hideaway surged through his brain. A wave of nausea rose from his stomach, producing the urge to vomit.

"While fleeing Bordeaux, the couple discovered that the Germans were conducting scores of mass arrests of Jews in Bordeaux," Francisco said. "Your grandparents were among those who were taken away."

His legs felt like twigs about to snap. "Where?"

Francisco clasped his hands. "To a train station where hundreds were loaded into cattle cars and sent away."

"It must be a mistake," Tiago said, his head in denial of what his heart already knew.

"I'm sorry."

"May I speak with the couple," Tiago said.

"Of course. I've already woken them. They're waiting for you in the library." Francisco removed a folded piece of paper from a robe pocket and extended his hand. "Prior to your grandparents' arrest, the couple was given a message to deliver to you once they reached Lisbon."

Oh, God. Tiago took the message.

"When you're ready to speak with them, I'll be waiting outside in the corridor to lead you to the library."

Tiago stared at the folded message.

Francisco left and shut the door.

A wretched ache pierced Tiago's chest. He unfolded the piece of paper, revealing a charcoal drawing of a trellis with grapevines. *This can't be happening!* He flipped the paper over, exposing the blank side. He held it over the candle flame, all the while praying for a miracle. But the oxidized words—written with Grand-père's fountain pen filled with onion juice—slowly appeared on the page.

My dear grandson,

Your grand-mère and I are safe and well. There are rumors about German raids on synagogues in France. But due to the Germans' thirst for our wine, we have hope that we'll be spared from the anti-Semitic plague that has infected our homeland.

Tiago squeezed the paper. He sniffed, fighting back tears, and continued reading.

We have fully considered your pleas for us to leave France, but we've decided to stay. Each month that we remain, refugees from France, Belgium, and the Netherlands are given a chance of escape from Nazi persecution. Over the past weeks, more than a dozen Jewish refugees have found sanctuary in our home. There are few who will harbor them on their road to freedom. We cannot, and will not, abandon them. I hope you understand.

Tiago wiped tears from his eyes.

We're so proud of you. You are giving Jews a chance to set sail for a new life, far away from Nazi-occupied Europe. Please know that we love you, and that you've created an everlasting mark on our hearts.

With endless love and hope,

Grand-père

Tiago folded the paper. Devastated, he fell to his knees and wept.

Chapter 7

Washington, DC—August 9, 1942

Maria, carrying a purse, suitcase, and a tin of *biscoitos*—buttery, lemon-flavored Portuguese cookies made by her father—exited a train and made her way through the Washington Union Station. Towering, arched ceilings spanned over the Beaux Arts architecture of a grand interior hall, making Maria feel as if she'd entered a sacred monument. Thousands of people bustled through the station, many of whom appeared to be young men in transit to their military basic training. *They're on their way to war*, she thought, gripping the handle of her suitcase. *And so am I.* She worked her way through a dense, oncoming crowd, like a salmon swimming upstream. Reaching an exit, she went outside and hailed a taxi.

"Library of Congress," Maria said, taking a seat in the back of the cab. She adjusted her things on the space next to her.

The driver nodded and pulled away from the curb.

Maria fidgeted, tapping the lid of her cookie tin.

The driver's eyes peered at her through the rearview mirror.

"Would you like a *biscoito*?" she asked.

"What's that?"

"A Portuguese cookie," she said. "They're killer-diller."

"Sure."

She opened the lid, plucked out a cookie, and handed it to the driver.

"Thanks." He chewed the treat and maneuvered his way through traffic. "You're right. It's delicious."

"My father made them." A wistful feeling washed over her. *I'm at the start of my journey, and I already miss him.* She placed the lid on the tin and looked out the window, attempting to catch a glimpse of the Washington Monument.

Colonel William Donovan had told her to expect a telephone call from Frederick Kilgour, head of the IDC, and Donovan had been true to his word. The morning after she'd conned her way inside the Astor mansion to meet the colonel, she arrived at work at 8:30 a.m. to find a telephone message from Kilgour on her desk. She snatched coins from her purse and left the Department of Microphotography for a telephone booth, but on her way down the hall she was summoned by Mr. Hopper's receptionist to take a call from Kilgour in the library director's office. Unlike her past telephone conversation with Kilgour, who'd kindly but firmly told her that the IDC would only consider Ivy League candidates, there was no mention of education or his previous lack of interest in her candidacy. He'd simply informed her that Colonel Donovan wanted her recruited for the IDC, and that he would take care of her leave of absence with Mr. Hopper. With cordial and concise words, he'd told her to get her personal affairs in order and to expect to leave for Washington, DC, in thirty days.

She'd spent her final days at the New York Public Library training a new librarian named Evelyn—who would be her, as well as Roy's, replacement—on the duties of the microfilm department. In the evenings, she and her father cooked dinners together and took long walks in the Ironbound neighborhood. Before going to bed, they often sat in the living room and listened to *The Pepsodent Show* and big band music on the radio. And on the night before she left—while the sound of trumpets and trombones imitated a train whistle on a song called "Chattanooga Choo Choo" by Glenn Miller and His Orchestra—he'd turned to her and said, "God, I wish your mom was here to see you off at the train station. She'd be so proud of you." Maria, a mixture of melancholy swirling inside her, looked into her father's tear-filled eyes and said, "Me too."

Ten minutes after leaving the Washington Union Station, the cab stopped in front of the Library of Congress. The driver turned off the engine and carried her suitcase to the base of the library's palatial steps. She set down her cookie tin, removed money from her purse, and paid him.

His eyes wandered to the tin. "Do you need help carrying your things up the steps?"

"No, thank you. But you could lighten my load by taking a few cookies with you."

He smiled.

She opened her tin and he selected two cookies. As the driver left, Maria paused, taking in a view of the Capitol building, its dome crowned with the *Statue of Freedom*. Her mood turned somber. *I'll do everything I can to serve my country and win the war.* She gathered her things and scaled the steps, her resolve growing as she ascended to the entrance.

Inside, she waited on a lobby bench while a receptionist telephoned Frederick Kilgour, her new boss and head of the IDC section of the OSS. She fiddled with her mother's sapphire ring on her finger and admired the ornate building design of the largest library in the United States. Minutes later, a lean man in a dark pinstriped suit and tie crossed the lobby. He was in his late twenties with oiled brown hair combed close to his scalp, and he had a confident gait with a firm step. His polished, pointed-toe oxfords clacked on the floor.

Maria stood. *He's quite young to be head of the IDC.*

"Miss Alves?" he asked, approaching her.

"Yes."

He extended his hand. "Fred Kilgour."

She shook his hand. "It's a pleasure to meet you, sir."

"Follow me," he said. "We're going to the Annex Building. You can store your things there until you leave for your apartment. You'll be staying with Miss Ramirez."

"Yes, sir."

He turned and headed across the lobby.

Maria grabbed her things, nearly dropping her cookie tin, and rushed to catch up with him.

"How was your trip?" he asked, walking at a brisk pace.

"Good, sir." A flurry of questions buzzed in her head. *Who's Miss Ramirez? Where are we training? What country will I be deployed to? When will I leave?* Rather than inquire, she decided it was best to listen and follow orders, especially since he might be sore about her going over his head to be recruited to his team.

They traveled to the rear of the building and descended stairs to the cellar level, where they entered a long, concrete tunnel. An array of electrical conduit pipes covered the ceiling and caged lights were mounted on the walls, giving the space an appearance of a subterranean prison passage.

"The Annex Building is across the street," Kilgour said. "It's quicker to travel underground. The building was opened a few years ago, giving expansion space for the library. But with war efforts ramping up, Donovan acquired several thousand square feet of library space for the Research and Analysis branch of the Office of Strategic Services. A fraction of the area is dedicated to librarians and microfilm specialists of the IDC."

Her arm ached from the weight of her suitcase. She pressed ahead, struggling to keep up with him.

"In addition to the space at the library," Kilgour said, "Donovan is working to acquire weapons training grounds in Maryland and Virginia for OSS recruits."

Her skin prickled. "Do IDC agents undergo weapons training?"

"No. Combat training is for spies and saboteurs who will be deployed to enemy-occupied territories. IDC agents will work in a neutral country." He glanced at her. "Don't worry, Miss Alves, you won't be sent to the front lines."

"Yes, sir," she said, feeling foolish.

Upon reaching the cellar of the Annex Building, they took an elevator to the fifth and top floor of the building. At the end of the hallway, they entered through an unmarked door to a classroom with several men and one woman who were sitting at individual workstations. Maria, her arm muscles burning, put down her suitcase.

"May I have your attention," Kilgour said.

Heads turned.

Maria's angst faded upon seeing a familiar face.

Roy's jaw dropped open. His unlit pipe clanged onto his desk. He swiftly grabbed the pipe and tucked it inside his jacket.

Maria fought back a smile.

"Eugene, I'd like to introduce you to our newest IDC recruit—Maria Alves from the New York Public Library."

A bespectacled man in his late thirties, standing at the head of the class near a chalkboard, raised his hand. "Welcome, Maria."

"Thank you," she said.

"Mr. Power is our technical expert," Kilgour said to Maria. "He'll teach you everything you need to know about our microfilm processes and procedures."

Eugene Power, Maria thought. She immediately recognized the microfilm pioneer from newspaper articles and trade journals. Before the war, Power microfilmed materials for British libraries, and he helped create a program for the British Museum to microfilm rare books. Additionally, Power had founded a company in Michigan called University Microfilms International, which was transforming the way materials were copied and archived. It was clear, to Maria, that the OSS had brought in one of America's best minds to build an overseas microfilm team.

"I believe you know Roy," Kilgour said. He gestured with his hand to each of the recruits. "This is Matthew, Wilbur, Evan, Stephen, Henry, and Pilar."

Maria gave a wave. "Hello."

"You can get acquainted with everyone during breaks," Kilgour said. "Take the desk between Pilar and Roy. Our new microfilm equipment arrived this morning, and Mr. Power will be providing an overview of its functionality."

"Yes, sir," Maria said.

Kilgour joined Power at the front of the room. Using a hammer and pry bar, they removed the cover of a wood shipping crate and began unpacking cameras and film.

Maria sat at her workstation.

Roy leaned to her and in a soft voice said, "How in the world did you get here?"

"Taxi."

Pilar let out a stifled a laugh.

"It's good to see you, too, Roy," Maria said, unable to resist teasing her friend.

"Sorry," Roy said. "I'm dumfounded but glad you're here."

"I'll tell you everything later."

He nodded.

Kilgour and Power passed cameras to the recruits in the front row, and then dug through the crate for more equipment.

Maria turned to the woman named Pilar. She was petite and in her mid-twenties with nut-brown eyes and black hair, which was done in pin curls.

"Hi," Maria said, extending her hand.

Pilar shook Maria's hand. "It's nice to meet you," she said with a Spanish accent.

"Is your last name Ramirez?"

"Yes," Pilar said.

"I'm your new roommate."

Pilar nodded. "Mr. Kilgour mentioned that a new recruit would be staying with me, but he didn't provide a name. After work, I'll help you get settled in."

"That would be lovely."

Kilgour placed a boxy-shaped camera and film on Maria's desk. Once each of the recruits received their equipment, he took a seat facing the class and folded his arms, like a proctor monitoring an examination.

Maria and her classmates inspected their cameras.

"It's a Kodak Model D Microfile, otherwise known as a Recordak Thirty-Five Millimeter," Mr. Power said, standing in front of the chalkboard. "It's what you'll be using to microfilm Axis publications, as well as foreign books in need of preservation, once you've been deployed overseas."

Hair rose on the back of Maria's neck.

Mr. Power went over the camera specifications, as well as the protocol for labeling used canisters to store microfilm. Afterward, he instructed the group to load film into their cameras, and then gave each recruit a copy of *The Maltese Falcon* by Dashiell Hammett and a retractable, metal apparatus to hold the book in place while microfilming the pages.

It's a test, Maria thought, thumbing through the book. She hadn't read the novel. However, she did see the movie adaptation, staring Humphrey Bogart and Mary Astor, at a cinema last year.

"You have twenty minutes to microfilm the book," Power said.

Maria peeked at the last page. *Two hundred and twenty-four pages.* Her brain raced, doing the math in her head. *I'll need to average five seconds per page to finish on time. No problem.*

Power pulled a stopwatch from his pocket and pressed the start button with his thumb. "Begin."

The librarians stood, leaned over their desks, and peered through viewfinders. The sound of clicking cameras and flipping pages filled the air.

Maria pointed the camera over the first page of the book, adjusted the lens, and pressed the shutter release. She turned the page and continued microfilming. To Maria, the Recordak felt heavy and awkward to handle. She glanced at Roy, who was winding his camera.

"It's not as smooth to operate as our cameras at the library," she whispered.

"Indeed," Roy said, pressing an eye to the viewfinder. "Perhaps the developed photographs will be of higher quality."

Maria's microfilming was difficult. The camera felt cumbersome and clunky in her hands, and the metal contraption, which was supposed to hold the pages stationary, easily retracted, causing her to lose her place in the book. Her mind flashed to the old Leica—which had been her mother's camera while working as a photojournalist—that she'd packed in her suitcase. It was a departing gift from her father, who insisted that she take it with her for good luck. She fought away the urge to pluck it from her luggage and use it to microfilm the book. After all, it was a similar model to the one that she used at the New York Public Library. She buried her thoughts and continued microfilming, all the while struggling to improve her efficiency. But even after fifty pages of filming, her pace remained far slower than her typical production rate. And as the end of the time limit approached, she'd barely microfilmed half of the book.

"Stop." Mr. Power clicked his stopwatch.

The librarians lowered their cameras.

Maria looked at the desks of her classmates, all of whom had microfilmed far more pages than she had. And three of the recruits had microfilmed the entire book with time to spare. "I performed horribly," she breathed.

"You'll get the hang of it," Pilar said.

Maria nodded, feeling grateful for her encouragement.

Kilgour rose from his chair. With hands clasped behind his back, he walked from desk to desk, inspecting everyone's progress. He stopped at Maria and frowned. "Trouble with your equipment?"

"No, sir," Maria said. "It's my first time using a Recordak camera."

"You'll need to increase your pace if you expect to work overseas," Kilgour said.

"I will." Maria glanced at her suitcase. "I'm usually much faster at microfilming. At the New York Public Library, I used a Leica. I have a similar model in my suitcase, and I'd be happy to use it to demonstrate my productivity."

Kilgour tilted his head. "The OSS has no plans for their agents to use German manufactured equipment."

Gazes of classmates fell upon Maria.

A flush of embarrassment rose to her cheeks. "Of course, sir. I'll work on my technique with the Recordak."

"Carry on." Kilgour turned and continued his rounds.

For the remainder of the day—aside from restroom breaks and lunch in the library cafeteria, where Maria got acquainted with her classmates over coffee and egg salad sandwiches—they worked on getting accustomed to their new equipment. By evening, Maria had improved her microfilming pace; however, she lagged behind the other recruits. She wished that she could work late into the evening to gain proficiency with her new camera, but she didn't want to keep Pilar and Roy waiting. Therefore, she stashed away her equipment in a drawer under her desk and left the classroom. Outside the library, she walked with Pilar and Roy toward the Navy Yard, where Pilar's apartment was located.

Maria's mind raced, rehashing the day's events. "I'm such a knucklehead," she said, unable to contain her frustration.

"You'll get used to the Recordak," Roy said, carrying Maria's suitcase. "I've been using an old Kodak model since I arrived, and it took me some time to get comfortable with it."

"I'm not referring to the camera," Maria said. "It was foolish of me to suggest using my German camera when we're at war with Hitler."

"Oh, that." Roy removed his pipe from his jacket and clamped the stem between his molars.

"I have a Leica, too," Pilar said. "And I prefer it to the Recordak."

"Did you tell Kilgour that you liked it better?" Maria asked.

"Oh, hell no," Pilar said, laughing.

Maria chuckled. She admired Pilar's candidness. And, despite knowing her for less than a day, she felt that Pilar was someone she could trust. "I hope Kilgour doesn't hold a grudge about me having a Leica."

"He won't," Pilar said. "He's focused on one thing—to have a top-notch microfilm team ready to be deployed as soon as possible."

And I intend to be one of them, Maria vowed to herself.

Roy nudged Maria with his elbow. "So, I've been waiting all day to hear how you managed to get recruited for the IDC. How did you do it?"

Maria shifted her purse and cookie tin in her hands. For several blocks, she told them about her telephone calls and letters to Colonel Donovan's office that received no reply, and about her impersonating the Astors' personal assistants and pretending to be a socialite from California to gain entrance to the Astor mansion for Donovan's speaking engagement.

Roy furrowed his brow. "You're pulling my leg."

"Not this time," Maria said. "I spent nearly all of my money to look the part—dress, shoes, limousine, jewelry."

"Jeepers," Roy said.

Pilar's eyes widened.

"At first, everything went well," Maria said. "I got through security and was chatting with Minnie Astor and her friends while I waited for Donovan to arrive. Unfortunately, I was introduced to Vincent Astor, who has a photographic memory with names. He deduced that I was a fraud, but I managed to get to Donovan before I was removed from the mansion by security guards."

"What did you say to Donovan?" Pilar asked.

"The truth," Maria said. "I admitted to deceiving the Astors in a last-ditch attempt to speak with him about joining the IDC. I thought I might be arrested, but Donovan was impressed with me gate-crashing the event and he told me to expect a call from Kilgour."

"Good God," Roy said. "You might be the luckiest—and most stubborn—person I've ever met."

Maria smiled. "I'll take that as a compliment."

Minutes later, they arrived at Barracks Row, a commercial strip in the Navy Yard neighborhood. They entered a brick building, climbed stairs to the third floor, and entered Pilar's apartment.

Roy put down the suitcase. "I'm sure you're exhausted from travel and work, and you need to unpack. My apartment is down the street. How about we meet up for an early breakfast?"

"Perfect," Maria said.

Roy left and Pilar gave Maria a brief tour of the furnished, two-bedroom apartment, which was far more spacious than her place in the Ironbound. After unpacking her things, Maria was drawn to the kitchen by the aroma of brewed coffee. With her tin of *biscoitos* in hand, she joined Pilar, who was sitting at a table with two steaming cups.

"Here," Pilar said, sliding a cup to Maria.

"Thanks. It smells wonderful." She opened her tin. "These will go well with the cups of joe."

Pilar selected a *biscoito* and took a bite. "Yummy."

"My dad would be happy to hear that."

"Is he a baker?"

"Photojournalist."

Pilar chewed her cookie. "He might want to consider a change in profession."

Maria chuckled and took a sip of coffee.

"Why did you join the IDC?" Pilar asked.

"To help win the war—I cannot be a bystander while a Nazi dictator tries to conquer Europe." Maria swirled her coffee. "Despite my horrid performance today, I'm actually a good microfilm specialist. I have experience traveling overseas, due to my parents being photojournalists, and I'm fluent in six languages. I thought that I might be useful to the IDC."

"Your parents must be proud of you."

"My dad is." She glanced at the sapphire ring on her finger. "My mom is dead."

"I'm sorry," Pilar said. "Was it recent?"

Maria shook her head. "It happened when I was in college. While they were in Spain, covering news of the Spanish Civil War, my mom was killed by military crossfire."

"Oh, God," Pilar breathed. "I'm deeply sorry."

"Thank you." An ache rose in Maria's chest. She ran a finger over the rim of her cup. "I think about her all the time. A big part of me wants to honor my mom by serving our country."

"She'd be proud of you."

Maria nodded, and then nibbled a *biscoito*. "Enough about me. Why did you join the IDC?"

"Like you, I hate the rise of Nazism and dictatorships in Europe," Pilar said. "I'm originally from Madrid, Spain. I'm guessing that you've noticed my accent."

"I have, and it's lovely."

Pilar smiled. "My family left Spain for the United States before the civil war. My father was a librarian at the Biblioteca Nacional de España, and he now works at the Library of Congress. After I graduated from Pembroke College, I got a job in the microfilm department of the Library of Congress."

"Oh," Maria said. "Did the IDC recruit you?"

"No," Pilar said. "When I learned about the microfilm specialists in the Annex Building who were training to go overseas, I approached Kilgour and talked my way in, claiming that my father and I had connections with librarians in Spain that could provide access to Axis publications."

"I like your moxie."

Pilar grinned.

"How does your family feel about you potentially going back to Spain?"

"My mom is worried about me," she said. "But my dad often says that if he knew something about microfilm, he'd find a way to go with me."

"You'll do great," Maria said.

"You too."

For an hour, they chatted over coffee and *biscoitos*. Rather than go out for dinner, they prepared leftovers from what was in the refrigerator, which amounted to cold meatloaf sandwiches, carrot sticks, and three bottles of Pabst beer. With full bellies, mainly from the empty cookie tin, they settled in the living room. They turned on the radio and listened to a broadcast of *They Burned the Books*, a radio play about the destruction of publications that the Nazis banned for nationalistic, political, and anti-Semitic reasons. Images of book bonfires and men with their arms raised in a *Sieg Heil* salute flashed in Maria's mind. Goose bumps cropped up on her arms.

"The fate of humanity is at stake," Maria said, turning to Pilar. "And we're going to do our part to save it."

CHAPTER 8

WASHINGTON, DC—AUGUST 10, 1942

Maria and Pilar joined Roy at a diner for an early breakfast of scrambled eggs, toast, and coffee, and they walked to the Library of Congress Annex Building. The classroom was empty, due to arriving forty minutes before they were scheduled to work. Maria removed her Recordak camera from her workstation drawer and, with instruction from Pilar and Roy, she practiced microfilming a two-day-old edition of the *Washington Post* that she'd brought with her from the diner. To Maria, it felt odd to be tutored. Since being charged to develop the New York Public Library's microfilm capabilities, she'd been relied upon to be the expert to teach others, including Roy, the art of microphotography. Regardless, she was humble and grateful for their help to accelerate her learning curve with a new type of camera.

Minutes passed and the other recruits arrived, one by one, to the classroom. They congregated near a bookshelf and chatted about their evening.

Maria, in one swift motion, snapped the shutter release and advanced the film. She repeated the sequence and turned a page of the newspaper.

"You're an ace," Roy mumbled, a pipe clenched between his teeth.

"Yeah," Pilar said. "You've got the hang of it."

Maria put down her camera. "Thank you both."

"Anytime," Roy said.

Kilgour and Mr. Power entered the classroom and walked to the front of the room.

"Good morning," Kilgour said, holding a clipboard. "Take your seats."

The recruits took their places at their workstations, and Mr. Power sat on a stool near the chalkboard.

"Before Mr. Power begins his technical instruction," Kilgour said, "I want to cover expectations for if, and when, you are deployed."

Maria straightened her back. *I thought we were all going overseas.*

Kilgour glanced at his clipboard. "Upon arrival in a neutral country, you will pose as an American official collecting materials for the Library of Congress, which is, of course, interested in preserving records of the present world crisis. However, your primary objective will be to acquire Axis publications."

She fidgeted with her ring.

"You will visit bookstores and newsstands to buy Axis publications," Kilgour said. "Also, you will attempt to persuade store proprietors to order Axis information for you through their purchasing channels. And to acquire the publications, you'll use foreign currency, which we will provide you with. Additionally, you'll be supplied with American magazines, such as *Life*, *Newsweek*, *Time*, and *Vogue* to use to barter with. However, some of the neutral countries have censorship laws that ban the magazines, so you'll need to be extraordinarily discreet to avoid arrest and deportation."

We're going to do far more than save books from Nazi bonfires, she thought.

"Once you acquire enemy publications," Kilgour said, "You'll microfilm them and place the film canisters on a weekly plane route for either the US or Britain. No printed materials will be flown—they'll take up too much weight and space on the plane." He paused, looking over notes on his clipboard.

A flurry of questions swirled in Maria's mind. She raised her hand.

"Yes, Miss Alves," Kilgour said.

"Sir, will IDC agents be required to develop any of the film?"

"No," he said. "Our role will be limited to three things—acquiring, microfilming, and shipping. A team of OSS agents, either in London or Washington, DC, will handle developing the film and scouring the documents for intelligence."

For thirty minutes, Kilgour lectured the group on processes and expectations—or, more precisely, what they were *not* permitted to do. Recruits scribbled on pads of paper while Maria, her fingers pressed together, made mental notes.

"You're not spies, and at no time will you attempt to engage in espionage," Kilgour said. "Your job is to simply acquire as much Axis-published material as possible, and send it back in the form of microfilm."

Maria shifted in her seat. *We're being sent on a fishing expedition.*

Kilgour lowered his clipboard. "Are there any questions?"

Maria raised her hand.

"Yes, Miss Alves."

"Sir, may I ask what type of Axis publications we should be searching for?"

"Everything—books, newspapers, directories, magazines—anything you can get your hands on. Each agent will receive a detailed briefing on Axis publications before their deployment." Kilgour looked over the classroom. "Are there any other questions?"

Classmates glanced to one another, but no one raised their hand.

Maria looked at Roy, who locked eyes with her and subtly shook his head, as if he was suggesting that it was best for her to keep quiet. *The recruits are afraid to ask questions. Maybe they're worried that challenging authority might adversely impact their assignment.* Her restlessness grew.

"Mr. Power," Kilgour said, "they're all yours for technical training."

Maria raised her hand.

Kilgour frowned. "Okay, Miss Alves. What's your question?"

"Sir, if an IDC agent should discover non-published enemy intelligence while performing their duties, what is the protocol for relaying the information?"

"I'm not sure that I understand your question," Kilgour said. "Could you be more specific or provide an example?"

"Yes, sir." She clasped her hands. "The IDC will be in neutral countries searching for Axis information, so I would expect that our enemies will also be in the same venues attempting to dig up intelligence on Allied nations. How would you like us to relay anything we hear or observe that we think might be useful for military intelligence?"

"The agent can report it to me," Kilgour said. "But—under no circumstances—will IDC agents engage in spying. Espionage is the duty of uniquely trained OSS agents, who will soon be deployed to Europe." He adjusted his glasses on the bridge of his nose. "You are librarians, not spies. Your role is to acquire Axis publications, microfilm them, and place the undeveloped film on a plane to Allied headquarters—nothing more."

If we are expected to bribe bookstore owners to acquire information on our enemies, Maria thought, *we're complicit in espionage whether we're calling the shots or not.* Rather than challenge the issue, she looked at him and said, "Yes, sir. Thank you for the clarification."

Kilgour ran a hand over his necktie. "All right, Mr. Power. They're all yours."

For the day, they microfilmed stacks of old magazines and newspapers. Mr. Power administered a series of timed tests, like he did the day before. But unlike the previous day, Maria performed as well as the other candidates. And by late afternoon, she was outpacing most of the class.

"Let's take a break," Power said, clicking his stopwatch. "Be back in fifteen minutes."

The recruits put down their cameras.

Power approached Maria. "Your speed is much better today."

"Yes, sir," Maria said. "Pilar and Roy gave me pointers on the Recordak."

"Good teamwork." Power gave a nod and left the room.

Maria turned to Pilar and Roy. "How about joining me in the cafeteria for a cup of coffee. I'm buying."

Roy wrinkled his forehead. "The coffee is free."

"I know," Maria said. "That's why I'm inviting you."

Pilar chuckled.

In the cafeteria, they each drank a cup of coffee and ate a piece of apple pie, courtesy of Maria, who purchased the desserts with change from her purse as a thank-you for their help with the Recordak. Fueled with caffeine and sugar, they returned to the classroom, expecting to work with Power for the remainder of the day. Instead, they found Kilgour writing on the chalkboard.

"Take your seats," Kilgour said, turning to the recruits entering the room.

Maria sat. Her eyes gravitated to a list on the chalkboard.

Portugal

Spain

Sweden

Switzerland

Lichtenstein

Andorra

Mr. Power entered and sat on a stool near Kilgour.

"I've made decisions on our first wave of deployment," he said, dusting chalk from his hands. "What you see on the board is a list of neutral European countries, some of which will be locations for IDC agents."

Maria's adrenaline surged. She hoped to be one of the first agents sent overseas.

"Initially, we'll focus our efforts in Lisbon, Stockholm, and Bern. Once things are up and running, we'll deploy more agents and expand into other neutral European cities." Kilgour turned and drew a horizontal line the length of the chalkboard. Along the line, he wrote in milestone dates, the first of which was September 1942.

Maria's eyes widened. *Goodness! That's next month!*

Kilgour faced the class. "Roy, we're sending you to Lisbon."

"Yes, sir," Roy said.

Pride surged through Maria. *Way to go, Roy!*

"Stephen," Kilgour said.

A mustached man straightened his spine, as if he'd been given a mild electrical shock. "Yes, sir."

"We're sending you to Bern, Switzerland, but it'll depend on our ability to smuggle you in."

"I'll be ready, sir," Stephen said.

For several minutes, Kilgour discussed plans to deploy two more recruits, neither of whom was Maria or Pilar.

"Our plans will continue to evolve in the coming weeks, and I'll keep you apprised of my decisions." Kilgour looked at his wristwatch. "You're dismissed."

Recruits stood and began to leave the room.

Maria, burying her personal disappointment, approached Roy and Pilar outside the door. "Congratulations."

"Thanks." Roy looked at her. "You'll get your chance. I'm sure of it."

"We will," Maria said, nudging Pilar.

"Indeed," Pilar said.

Maria glanced inside the classroom, where Kilgour was alone and wiping the chalkboard with an eraser. "I left something at my workstation. Go on ahead. I'll catch up with you on the route home."

"Are you sure?" Pilar asked.

Maria nodded. She entered the classroom and retrieved her

two-day-old newspaper, which she folded and placed under her arm. Her shoulder muscles tightened as she approached Kilgour.

"Excuse me, sir," Maria said. "May I have a word?"

Kilgour placed the eraser on the chalkboard tray and turned. "If it's about your performance, Miss Alves, Mr. Power has already informed me that your microfilming speed has improved."

"It's not about my performance," she said. "It's about the deployments."

He crossed his arms. "Very well. What's on your mind?"

"I've gotten to know the recruits. The men you are planning to send in the first wave are not multilingual."

"I'm aware," Kilgour said. "They're smart Ivy League men. They'll pick up on language and customs when they arrive."

She shifted her weight. "May I speak candidly, sir?"

He nodded.

"The first wave will be more effective if you accompany the agents with someone who is fluent in the native language."

"I assume you are referring to yourself."

"And Pilar," she said. "I'm fluent in six languages, including Portuguese, French, and German. Pilar is fluent in Spanish and her family has connections in Madrid. Knowing the local language and culture will build trust with booksellers, which will enable the IDC to be more effective with acquiring Axis material."

"I appreciate your eagerness to serve," Kilgour said. "Donovan said he was impressed with your tenacity, and I can see why he recommended you. But you've only been here two days; you need more training. As for Pilar, we're not yet prepared to deploy an agent to Madrid." He paused, adjusting his shirtsleeve. "I need to see that you're worthy of serving overseas. In the meantime, you'll need to be patient."

"With all due respect, sir, time is something our country might not have."

Kilgour rubbed his jaw. "My decisions stand."

"Yes, sir. Thank you for allowing me to say my piece."

Maria left the library and walked toward her apartment. As she quickened her pace, her mind drifted to her favorite photograph—taken by her mother shortly before her death—of a Spanish militia woman with dark, defiant eyes and a rifle slung over her shoulder. Maria's veins pumped with determination. *I'll do everything I can to prove my mettle. Somehow, I'll find a way to join the fight.*

Part 2

Mission

Chapter 9

New York City, NY—February 21, 1943

Maria, her nerves surging like electrified wire, entered a grand, Art Deco lobby of the Marine Air Terminal (MAT) at La-Guardia Airport, a new seaplane base that was America's foremost aerial gateway to Europe. Her father, who'd taken the afternoon off from work to accompany his daughter to the terminal, carried her luggage. Around the rotunda was an enormous mural depicting humankind's quest to conquer the skies, from ancient mythology to the flying boat.

She stopped and stared at the artwork. "It's beautiful. I've always wondered what it would be like to fly."

Gaspar put down Maria's suitcase. "I'm sure it will be much better than the third-class accommodations we had on the ships that we took with your mother to Europe."

A childhood memory of holding her mother's hand on a crowded steerage deck flashed in her head. *God, I wish she was here.*

"After the war," he said, "maybe we'll get to fly on a plane together."

She turned to him. "We will."

His bottom lip quivered. "I promised myself not to cry."

A lump formed in her throat. "Me too."

He drew a deep breath, as if he was struggling to contain his emotions. "I'm glad that your travel brought you through New York. It gives me the chance to give you a proper send-off for your journey."

She nodded, regretting that the OSS limited her to twenty-four hours at home before her departure. "I don't know how long I'll be gone, but I'll write you every chance I get."

He placed a hand on her shoulder. "I'm so proud of you."

Tears welled up in her eyes. She wrapped her arms around him. "I love you, Dad."

"I love you, too." He hugged her tight. "Promise me you'll be careful, and that you won't do anything to put yourself in danger."

He's thinking about what happened to Mom. Her heart ached. "I promise."

Gaspar released her.

"Bye, Dad."

He kissed her on the cheek. "Take care of yourself."

"I will."

He wiped his eyes with the back of his hand, and then walked across the lobby and exited the terminal.

Alone, a strange mixture of sadness and anticipation swirled inside her. She picked up her suitcase and approached a Pan American World Airways kiosk. She gave her luggage to a porter, and then removed a ticket and passport from her purse and gave it to a female airline attendant.

The attendant reviewed the documents and returned them to Maria. "Enjoy your flight to Lisbon."

"Thank you." She slipped her papers into her purse.

Maria traveled along an ornately tiled corridor and exited the rear of the terminal building. A frigid wind, gusting over the leaden water of Bowery Bay, stung her cheeks. Docked at the end of a jetty was a huge, four-engine boat plane with the name *Yankee Clipper* emblazoned on the side. Behind the windshield of the bridge—located on the upper level of the vessel—a pilot and copilot were seated behind control wheels. Male and female passengers, most of whom were wearing elegant wool coats and hats, formed a line on the jetty. One by one, they entered through a door under the wing of the boat plane. *There's no turning back now.* She pressed her purse to her stomach and stepped onto the dock.

For the past six months, Maria was stationed at the Library of Congress. Her skills had matched or surpassed her classmates, yet Mr. Kilgour had not granted her an overseas assignment. While several of the male recruits had left for deployment in Europe, she and Pilar remained at the library. With their training complete, they were assigned positions in the library's microfilm department. Maria, unwavering in her pursuit to serve her country overseas, made numerous unannounced visits to Kilgour's office to inquire as to when she and Pilar would be given their posts.

"You'll go when our European operations are safe and running smoothly," Kilgour had said, sitting with his arms crossed behind a rosewood desk.

As time passed, Maria began to think that she might be stuck working at the Library of Congress for the duration of the war. But, two days after Thanksgiving, Kilgour summoned her and Pilar to his office.

"Pilar," he'd said, pressing the tips of his fingers together, "I'm sending you to Lisbon, Portugal, next month to join Roy. And Maria, you'll be deployed to Lisbon in February—which will free up Roy to travel with Pilar to Madrid, Spain, to establish a new outpost."

Maria, shocked and elated, had left his office with Pilar to plan for their departure. They made telephone calls to their families and, after work, they went to a diner for a celebratory meal of pancakes and sweet potato pie. Maria wondered if her impromptu visits to Kilgour's office had influenced his decision, or if Kilgour had grown concerned that—if he kept her stateside for too long—she might, once again, find a way to go over his head to Colonel Donovan. But it didn't matter. She and Pilar were going overseas to serve their country.

Maria traveled down the jetty and stepped onto one of the boat plane's sponsons, lateral extensions at the waterline on both sides of the hull, which appeared to stabilize the craft while floating as well as serve as a gangway for passengers. Pan Am stewards, posted on both sides of the door, greeted Maria. Her excitement grew as she stepped inside the sleek, massive vessel.

A steward, wearing a white jacket with black trousers and tie, glanced at her ticket and guided her through the aircraft, which resembled a compact, luxury hotel. At the front of the plane, stairs led to an upper level that housed the pilot and crew. Moving back from the nose of the vessel, there was a passenger compartment, followed by a galley, a lounge and dining area with pressed white linen tablecloths, and several more passenger compartments. As Maria made her way through the aircraft, it became clear that every person on board was a first-class passenger. *The tickets must cost a fortune. The OSS is sparing no expense to transport me to Lisbon.*

The steward took Maria's coat. He gestured to a wide, wool-upholstered seat next to a window.

Maria sat and placed her purse on her lap. "The chair is comfy. I feel like I'm sitting in a living room."

"It's designed to be converted into a bunk, miss," the steward said. "Tonight, the passenger compartments will transform into sleeper cabins."

Holy mackerel.

"I'll stow away your coat." He gestured to the tail section of the plane. "In the back are dressing rooms and separate bathrooms for women and men. If you should need your luggage, let me know and I'll retrieve it from the upper cargo hold."

"Thank you."

"Welcome aboard, miss." The steward left the compartment.

Maria, peering out the window, watched a group of passengers cross the jetty and board the plane.

"Hi," a man said with a Southern accent.

Maria turned. "Hello."

The man—wearing a gray double-breasted suit with a white pin collar shirt and maroon tie—sat next to her. He was about forty years of age, Maria believed, given a smidge of gray in the sideburns of his brown hair.

He smiled and extended his hand. "I'm Ben, the guy you'll be stuck sitting next to for the next eighteen hours and thirty minutes."

Maria chuckled and shook his hand. "I'm Maria. It's hard to believe we can get to Lisbon that fast. The last time I traveled to Europe, it took me over a week on a passenger ship."

"Have you flown before?"

Maria shook her head.

"You'll love it, especially a flight in this luxurious fortress. It's a Boeing 314 Clipper—and this particular one was christened by Eleanor Roosevelt."

An image of the First Lady, smashing a bottle of champagne over the bow of the vessel, flashed in her head.

"It cruises at one hundred eighty miles per hour and can travel over three thousand miles on a tank of fuel. It can hold thirty-six sleeping passengers and a dozen crew. But I heard from a steward that this is a USO flight and, due to extra cargo, the plane will have a few less passengers."

"It sounds marvelous." She looked at him, attempting to determine if he was a member of the USO. "Are you an entertainer?"

He laughed. "Goodness, no. I can't sing, act, or deliver a good punch line. But I'm not a bad writer."

"What do you write?"

"I've published a few books, but now I'm a journalist and war correspondent. After I arrive in Lisbon, I'm taking a British plane to England. I have a new job as the chief of the *New York Herald Tribune*'s London bureau."

"Congratulations."

"Much obliged," he said.

"What are the titles of your books?"

"My latest is *Red Hills and Cotton*. It's about my boyhood in Pickens County, South Carolina."

Maria rubbed her chin. "Are you Ben Robertson?"

His eyes brightened. "Yes, I am. Did you read my book?"

"Unfortunately, no. But I promise to pick up a copy."

"How did you know my name?"

"I'm a librarian," Maria said. "It's a requisite for my job to be familiar with authors and books."

He ran a hand over his tie. "What brings you to Lisbon?"

"I work for the Library of Congress," she said, using her cover story. "I'm collecting materials for the library, which is interested in preserving records of the world crisis."

His face turned somber. "Damn Nazi book burnings."

"Precisely."

For several minutes, while passengers got seated, they discussed their careers. And, considering Ben's experience of working in the newspaper business, she told him about her photojournalist parents who covered the Spanish Civil War. However, she didn't bring up her mother's death. *There's no need to dampen his spirits when he's eager to begin a new job as a war correspondent.*

A woman in her late thirties with coiffed, brown hair and dark exotic eyes entered the passenger compartment and stopped near Maria's row. She placed her purse on a seat and adjusted a silver flower brooch, studded with amber gemstones, that was pinned to her navy dress.

Maria's eyes widened, recognizing the famous singer and actress—from magazines and Broadway musical posters—named Tamara Drasin.

Tamara looked at Maria and smiled. "What's buzzin', cousin?"

"Hopefully the propellers," Maria blurted, instantly regretting her response. Her face flushed with embarrassment.

Tamara laughed. "I'm Tamara."

"My name is Maria," she said, regaining her composure. She gestured with her hand. "And this is Ben."

"It's a pleasure to meet you," Ben said.

"Delighted," Tamara said.

A glamorous woman with shoulder-length, brunette hair and

ruby-red lipstick entered the passenger compartment and greeted Tamara with a hug. The two chatted about the seating assignments, and then took places in a row on the opposite side of the aisle.

Maria, feeling a bit starstruck, leaned to Ben. "I think that's Jane Froman."

Ben glanced across the aisle. "Yeah, I think you're right."

"I love her singing voice."

"Me too," he said. "She was terrific in the movie musical *Stars Over Broadway*. Have you seen it?"

Maria nodded.

Two men, both of whom were carrying musical instrument cases, given their odd sizes and shapes, sat in front of Maria and Ben.

Maria watched a steward stow away the men's cases. *Guitar? Clarinet?*

"I'm thinking that we won't get much shut-eye," Ben said.

"Why do you say that?" Maria asked.

"It's a USO flight, and I'm betting that there'll be lots of entertainment."

Maria struggled to recall the last time she'd heard live music, other than on the radio. She turned to Ben and said, "I hope I don't sleep a wink."

Stewards walked through the plane and prepared the passengers for departure. Chatter filled the cabin.

Maria buckled her seat belt and looked through her window. Outside, a dockworker untied a rope from the boat plane and stepped onto the jetty. The engines coughed, and then roared to life. The plane vibrated. Goose bumps cropped up on her arms. *Here we go.*

Ben removed a silver case from his jacket. "Cigarette?"

"No, thank you."

Ben lit a cigarette and took a drag.

A scent of burnt tobacco filled her nose. She fought back the urge to cough.

The boat plane pulled away from the jetty. Propellers buzzed as they sailed for several minutes through the East River. Water lapped against the belly of the boat. Conversations dwindled. Passengers stared out the windows. Reaching Long Island Sound, the grinding of engines grew. Gradually picking up speed, the vessel bounced over the water like a mammoth racing boat.

Maria, her adrenaline surging, squeezed the armrests of her seat. The aircraft shimmied and rumbled as waves lashed the hull. Acceleration grew. The nose of the plane tilted upward, and she felt the weight of gravity press her into the seat. She said a silent prayer and, seconds later, the boat plane was airborne. The aircraft banked to the right, turning toward the open Atlantic, and then leveled off.

Maria peered down at the ocean. "This is incredible."

Ben puffed his cigarette. "Once you fly, you'll never want to go back to traveling on a passenger ship."

As minutes passed, the *Yankee Clipper* gained altitude. Several thousand feet in the air, a steward announced that passengers were free to walk about the plane.

Maria unfastened her seat belt. Instead of mingling, she reached inside her purse and removed a map of Portugal and a notebook that contained a lengthy list of bookstores. She attempted to chart her first week's itinerary but soon discovered that she was too exhilarated to hold a thought in her head. She set aside her material and watched clouds pass by her window.

Soon, the sound of ice cubes clinking in glasses emanated from the lounge. Passengers, holding cocktails and glasses of beer, milled about the aircraft. After sunset, when nothing was visible outside her window, Maria joined Ben in the dining area. As part of the airfare, they were served a six-course meal that included an entrée of sliced ham, buttered peas, and bread rolls, all of which was served on fine china. Although she was thrilled to be on her way to serve her country, a wave of guilt washed over her. *Our country is rationing, people around the world are dying from war and starvation, and I'm eating like a queen.* With her appetite gone, she passed on the hors d'oeuvre and dessert and, instead of having a cocktail, she drank black coffee.

Ben had been right. A few hours into the flight, members of the USO, including Tamara Drasin and Jane Froman, settled in the lounge. The two women—accompanied by a guitarist, clarinetist, and a drummer who tapped his drumsticks on an instrument case—sang for the passengers.

Maria squeezed her way into the lounge and stood. Although a war raged over Europe, which was getting closer by the second, the passengers of the *Yankee Clipper* celebrated through music. Tamara and Jane alternated with singing Broadway tunes and big band hits. For the moment, the war was forgotten and everyone was joyful. She admired the USO volunteers, who'd left their friends and families to entertain military servicemen stationed abroad. She imagined them performing for crowds of Allied soldiers in Great Britain. To Maria, the USO members were far more than entertainers; they were givers of hope.

As the show came to a close, Tamara sang the final song, a ballad called "I'll Be Seeing You." The lyrics, which Maria had heard many times before, resonated in her heart. She thought of her mom, who'd died far too young, and her dad, who'd lost the love of his life. Her mind drifted to the millions of soldiers who'd gone off to battle, the countless souls who would inevitably perish in the fight for freedom, and the families that would be ravaged by war. An ache twisted inside her chest. She'd once assumed that the song was simply about missing a loved one. But now, eleven thousand feet above a dark Atlantic Ocean and on her way to an uncertain future, the lyrics took on a new meaning—the power of love to transcend time and space.

Tamara sang the last verse with her angelic vibrato. She touched her fingers to her lips and slowly bowed her head.

Passengers applauded. Maria wiped tears from her cheeks. Looking at the crowd, she discovered that she wasn't alone. There wasn't a dry eye on the plane.

CHAPTER 10

HORTA, AZORES—FEBRUARY 22, 1943

Maria gripped the armrests of her seat as the *Yankee Clipper* glided to a landing in a bay at Horta, an island town in the Portuguese archipelago of the Azores. Water splashed against the hull, creating a sea mist over the cabin windows. The buzz of the propellers decreased and the boat plane sailed toward a harbor.

"We landed like a goose on a pond," she said, turning to Ben.

He nodded. "Only four more hours until we arrive in Lisbon. How do you feel about passenger ships now?"

"I used to be fond of voyages," she said. "But I think air travel has spoiled me."

"Me too." He took out a cigarette and lit it.

As the vessel entered the harbor, Maria peered out her window. Oared fishing boats sat empty above the shore's high tide line, and three-story stone buildings lined the waterfront. Beyond the town, steep grassy hills covered the volcanic island of Faial. With few trees, the lush yet rock-strewn landscape reminded Maria of Jules Verne's novel *Journey to the Center of the Earth*.

The engines stopped. A few passengers unbuckled their seat belts.

"Are we getting off?" she asked.

"I'm afraid not," Ben said. "Only passengers with the Azores as their final destination will deboard."

A steward opened the door to the aircraft. A fresh breeze flowed through the compartments, lessening the smell of cigarette smoke. Minutes later, a motorized fishing boat, with a gray-bearded man in a rain jacket at the helm, pulled alongside the aircraft. Two male passengers, each carrying a suitcase and a duffel bag, exited the plane and got onto the boat. The captain gave a wave to the steward and ferried the men to shore.

As the crew was preparing the boat plane for departure, Maria noticed Ben hunkering forward to look through her window.

"Would you like to trade seats?" she asked.

"That's very thoughtful of you, but I'd feel bad about taking your view."

Maria unbuckled her seat belt. "Please, I insist. I've had plenty of time to gaze at the sea. Besides, I'd like to get a few hours of rest before arriving in Lisbon."

"Are you sure?"

"Absolutely."

"Much obliged." He stood and exchanged seats.

Within minutes the plane was airborne, and Maria leaned back and closed her eyes.

She'd barely slept during the night. After the impromptu musical show by members of the USO, Maria had gathered her nerve to speak with Tamara Drasin and Jane Froman to compliment them on their performances. She found that, despite their fame, they were quite humble and easy to speak with. And, like Maria, the women were eager to serve their country. For over an hour, the trio remained in the lounge chatting over tea and biscuits. Afterward, they went to their cabin where a steward had transformed their seats into sleeping bunks. In the women's changing room, Tamara and Jane slipped into satin nightgowns with quilted bed jackets. And Maria had laughed at herself as she put on a worn pair of pink flannel pajamas, which had once been white before she had accidentally washed them with a red sock. Despite the comfort of her bunk, which included a soft pillow and warm blanket, she was unable to relax. With the humming of propellers in her ears, she remained awake rehearsing her mission plans, over and over, in her head.

Maria was stirred by a gentle nudge to her arm.

"Sorry to disturb you," Ben said. "But I thought you might want to see this."

Maria rubbed her eyes and looked at Ben, who pointed to the window. The sun had set, painting the horizon in warm hues of orange, red, and gold. In the distance, a dark blue sea crashed against a rugged coastline.

Her heart rate quickened. "I must have slept for hours—we're here?"

He nodded.

Nearing the coast, the plane banked to the right and gradually descended to several hundred feet above the mouth of the Tagus River. Lights twinkled throughout the city of Lisbon, which was filled with buildings and cathedrals of Pombaline and Manueline architectural styles.

"It's beautiful," she said. "Most of Europe is under strict blackout rules, but Lisbon remains a city of light."

"It'll stay lit," Ben said, "as long as the country can keep out of the war."

The plane flew upriver. Approaching strings of water landing lights, the aircraft made a descending turn to the left.

Maria's weight tilted to Ben, their shoulders nearly touching. She clasped her armrests. "When's your flight to London?"

"Tomorrow afternoon," Ben said, smiling. "It gives me a day to explore Lisbon. Do you begin work immediately?"

"Yes. My colleagues should be—" She gasped as the left wingtip skimmed the surface of the river.

Ben pressed a hand to the window. "Oh, Lord!"

Passengers screamed. The wing dug into the water. A screech of tearing metal.

Maria's body slammed forward as the aircraft crashed into the river. Piercing pain shot through her hip. Frigid water, gushing in through a hole in the fuselage, flooded the cabin. She inhaled and choked. Absent light, she blindly reached for Ben. Her hand struck what felt like a bulkhead, and she discovered that her seat had been ripped away from the floor.

Moans and cries permeated the stygian wreckage.

The water level rose, covering her chest, chin, and mouth. She strained her head upward and clawed at her seat belt.

The fuselage creaked, like a submarine under immense pressure. A woman whimpered.

Nearly submerged, Maria drew a breath and curled underwater. She tugged on her seat belt, but it didn't budge. She wriggled her body, sending a sharp pang through her hip and pelvis. Her diaphragm contracted, attempting to recycle used air in her lungs. Her pulse pounded her eardrums. With her body nearly depleted of oxygen, she pried at her seat belt. The buckle unfastened. She shot up, striking her head on the fuselage, and located an air pocket, the size of a shallow upside-down pail. Pressing her mouth and nose to the ceiling, she sucked in deep, rasping inhales. The water level continued to rise. As the air pocket was about to vanish, she took a final breath and went under. Using her arms and dragging her useless right leg, she propelled herself through the submerged fuselage, maneuvering through debris and lifeless bodies. *Oh, God, no!*

Her eyes, burning from the brackish water, scanned for an opening but found only blackness. With each stroke, her oxygen faded. Her heart hammered her rib cage. As she was about to give up, her hand touched a jagged opening in the fuselage. She twisted through the hole, its sharp edge lacerating her back, and swam through the murk. Breaking the surface, she gasped for air.

Moonlight shimmered over a remote section of the vast river, several miles north of the city center. The boat plane—its wings sheared away—lay submerged except for the tip of its tail. The closest shore was a mile away, Maria estimated, and given the lack of shore lights and sirens, there was no indication that rescuers from the Cabo Ruivo Seaplane Base would arrive anytime soon.

Using her arms to tread water, Maria scanned for survivors. Several yards away, a crew member was struggling to help a woman onto a floating piece of wreckage. Disregarding the throbbing in her hip, she swam to them.

"Can you help me to get her up?" the man asked, struggling to hold a woman afloat. "She's badly hurt, and I think my back might be broken."

"I'll try." Maria, with one hand on the makeshift raft, wrapped an arm around the woman, whom she recognized to be the singer and actress Jane Froman. She felt the woman's rapid, shallow breathing, as if she was going into shock. "I got you. You're going to be all right."

Jane leaned her head on Maria. "Where's Tamara?"

She strained to see through the night. Nearby, a patch of debris floated in the water. "I—I don't know." *Oh, no—where's Ben!*

The crewman—who was a copilot, given the wings on the breast of his jacket—struggled to pull himself onto the makeshift raft and roll onto his side. Groaning in pain, he labored to slide Jane onto the wreckage, and as the woman came out of the water, Maria witnessed the extent of her injuries. Jane's left leg was nearly severed below the knee, and her right leg had a compound fracture.

Fear flooded Maria's veins. "She needs a tourniquet."

The copilot removed his necktie and, with Maria's help, wrapped it around Jane's left leg.

With the raft too small for three people, Maria floated alongside the wreckage. She removed her cardigan, struggled to squeeze out some of the water, and draped it over Jane.

Moans emanated from the darkness.

"Where are you?" Maria called.

Seconds passed. "Help," a distant voice whimpered.

Thirty yards? Forty yards? She looked at the copilot. "I'm going."

"I'll go." He winced as he struggled to sit up, and then lowered his body to the raft.

"One of us needs to keep her tourniquet tight," she said. "You should stay—you're worse off than me."

"How badly are you injured?"

She placed a hand to her right leg, which was turned inward. "My hip is out of place."

"You can't go," he said.

Cries penetrated the night.

"I must. I'll swim with my arms, and I can float if I have to." Maria slipped from the raft. "Hold on—I'm coming!"

Maria swam—her hip flaring with pain—in the direction of the voice. Thirty yards into her journey, her lungs burned and her muscles grew tired. She paused, treading water, and called out. Following the sounds of distress, she continued her swim despite pangs shooting down her leg. She swallowed water and gagged. Soon, her stokes turned feeble. The moans faded, then disappeared. Too weak to return to the raft, she floated on her back while the river's current carried her toward the sea. Her temperature plummeted and her teeth chattered. She prayed to find survivors and for help to arrive. But, as minutes passed, neither had come.

Chapter 11

Lisbon, Portugal—February 22, 1943

Tiago closed the bookstore for the evening and walked to the Rossio, a large square and meeting place for the people of Lisbon since the Middle Ages. But with Hitler's army conquering much of Europe, the square had become a gathering area for Jewish refugees. Baroque fountains stood at opposite ends of the square, and in the center was a towering marble monument topped with a bronze statue of King Peter IV of Portugal. Bustling streets—lined with automobiles, taxis, and streetcars—surrounded the Rossio. Dozens of cafés and shops were filled with patrons. On the rooftop of a neoclassical building was a huge neon sign—*Medicamentos*—with a Bayer Cross logo, which gave the appearance that the German drug company was, in additional to advertising their medicines, displaying pro-German propaganda. The electrified glass tube signage, combined with streetlamps and a multitude of bulbs strung over the streets, illuminated the square like daylight.

On the sidewalk, Tiago weaved past a group of well-dressed people who were entering Café Chave d'Ouro, the largest establishment in the Rossio. Chatter in several languages—Portuguese, French, English, and German—emanated through the open door. An aroma of garlic and grilled sardines penetrated his nose. He raised the collar of his wool coat, crossed the street, and entered the square. Unlike the cafés, where wealthy people feasted on succulent meats and wine, the public area was filled with underprivileged Lisboetas and refugees. Despite the cold temperature, children in haggard clothing played with paper boats in a fountain. A woman, sitting on a bench, covered herself with a scarf as she nuzzled a crying baby to her breast. An elderly couple, who were sharing a blanket, nibbled raw potatoes. *They have nowhere to go and feel safe in groups.* His mind drifted to his grandparents, resurrecting an ache in his heart.

He'd been devastated by the news of his grandparents' arrest. Instead of leaving the monastery in San Sebastián and returning to Porto to inform his parents, he'd continued his journey to Bordeaux. He had no reason to doubt the stories of the Jewish escapees, who witnessed his grandparents being loaded onto railway cattle cars and sent away, but he had to know for certain. Fueled by grief and armed with a pistol and fake papers, he'd made the journey through the Pyrenees mountains and into France. Days later, after hiding in Catholic churches and avoiding German checkpoints, he arrived at his grandparents' vineyard. He'd prayed for a miracle as he approached the two-story stone farmhouse. But the sound of an approaching vehicle sent him scurrying into the woods. Crouched behind an oak tree, he'd watched two German Wehrmacht officers, wearing field-gray uniforms and jackboots, exit a Kübelwagen and enter the house. He'd hunkered in the forest until nightfall, and then sneaked through fields to the home of a man named Paul, an elderly vineyard worker and friend of his grandparents. Paul had confirmed what he already knew—that his grandparents were gone and German officers were using the vineyard house as their living quarters. But Tiago was shocked to learn that the French police did nothing to stop Gestapo agents and Wehrmacht soldiers from rounding up Bordeaux Jews, and that all of the arrested were no longer in France.

"My brother works at the railway station," Paul had said, wiping his eyes with a handkerchief. "He overheard a German soldier say that the Jews were sent to a labor camp in Poland."

Tiago, feeling helpless and gutted, had left Bordeaux and journeyed to his parents' home in Porto. His mother, upon hearing the news, collapsed to her knees and sobbed. And as he and his father consoled her, Tiago's heart ached with regret. *If I had left sooner, I might have convinced them to leave France.* His parents lit a candle and placed it in a window. Together, they prayed that Grand-mère and Grand-père would survive their captivity, and that they'd be reunited after the war. But Tiago feared that he'd never see them again.

Tiago mingled through the crowd in Rossio Square. Eventually, he spotted Ephraim and Helene, the couple who'd informed him about arrests of Jews near Bordeaux, sitting on an iron bench. Since their arrival in Lisbon last summer, they'd struggled to acquire the means to gain ship passage to the United States. With their money exhausted, they were living on the streets, except for when they stayed in a boardinghouse—arranged and paid for by Tiago—during bouts of inclement weather.

"Pretend that you don't know me," Tiago said softly in French.

The couple turned to him.

"Make room for me to sit on the bench," he said. "And focus your attention on the children playing by the fountain."

The couple scooched over.

Tiago sat. With his eyes, he scanned the crowed. "We need to be careful—the PVDE are everywhere."

"Of course," Ephraim said, his voice low.

"I've come with news," Tiago said. "And I want you to refrain from displaying any emotion. Can you do that for me?"

Helene clasped her husband's hand. "*Oui*."

Sirens blared on a nearby street.

Tiago's skin prickled.

Two ambulances and a police car passed by the square and traveled in a northeast direction.

Tiago's angst faded. He removed a small, leather-bound book from his coat pocket and placed it next to him. "In a moment, I'm going to get up and leave. There will be a book on the bench.

Inside it you'll find tickets to board the *Serpa Pinto*. You leave on your voyage to America in the morning."

"God bless you," Ephraim said, his voice quavering.

Helene blinked tears from her eyes. "How can we ever repay you?"

"There's no need," Tiago said, looking in the direction of a child folding a newspaper into a boat. "But when you reach New York, please tell people about what is happening here."

"We will," Ephraim said.

Early in the war, Tiago was able bribe ship stewards and dock-workers, using a modest amount of money and cases of port wine, to smuggle refugees onto boats. But with the increased demand due to asylum seekers flooding Lisbon, the cost of bribes had soared. Despite that the couple had travel papers, thanks to Rosa's forgery skills, they had no financial means to leave Portugal and were surviving on charity. It had taken Tiago months, given that his finances were drained from aiding scores of refugees, to acquire the money to purchase their tickets.

"I wish I could have arranged for your passage sooner."

"We're grateful for everything you've done," Ephraim said.

Helene dabbed her eyes with the sleeve of her coat. "We'll never forget you."

"Nor I." Tiago stood, leaving the book on the bench. He walked into the crowd and left the square.

Tiago had assumed, after the arrest of his grandparents, that his family's escape line would collapse. However, he'd underestimated the resiliency of Jewish underground networks. Despite that his grandparents' vineyard in Bordeaux was billeted by German officers, French Jews—through word of mouth and creating their own means of escape through the Pyrenees mountains—were finding their way to his parents' vineyard in Porto and his bookstore in Lisbon. The number of refugees with expired or missing travel documents increased. He and Rosa were overwhelmed with work and the bookstore was on the verge of bankruptcy. Regardless, they carried on, day after day, forging passports and visas for asylum seekers who—if caught by the PVDE without travel papers—were at risk of being exiled to the Spanish border.

Arriving in the Chiado neighborhood, Tiago approached his apartment complex, its facade covered in azulejos—blue, tin-glazed ceramic tiles. He entered the front door and climbed to the fourth and top floor of the building. He reached for his apartment door and froze. He stared at a dull glow, coming from beneath his apartment door.

Did I leave a lamp on?

Rather than insert the key, he gently turned the doorknob and found it to be unlocked. His pulse quickened. He pressed his ear to the door but heard nothing. He entered, expecting to find his apartment ransacked from a burglary. However, everything in the kitchen appeared to be in place, except for a stench of cigar smoke and lamplight coming from the living room.

"Come in, Tiago," a deep voice said.

He turned, his adrenaline surging, and entered the living room. On the sofa was Agent Martim Neves of the PVDE. On a side table was an uncorked bottle of his family's port wine and a partially filled glass.

Neves, wearing a knee-length wool coat and bowler hat, puffed on a cigar.

A wave of anger surged through him. "What are you doing here?"

"I want to speak with you," Neves said. "I found the door unlocked, so I came inside to wait for you to arrive."

"I bolted the door when I left for work."

"You must have forgotten." Neves flicked ash and placed his cigar on a side table, the ember singeing the wood. He rose from the sofa and approached him.

Tiago held his ground. "May I see your search warrant?"

"Certainly." Neves shot his arms, shoving Tiago.

Caught off guard, he stumbled into a wall.

Neves, in one swift motion, slid a stiletto from his coat and placed it to Tiago's neck. His nostrils flared. "*This* is my authorization to enter your home."

Tiago felt the long, slender blade dig into his skin. His breath stalled in his chest.

"I'm an agent of the PVDE, and I can do what I goddamn want." Neves eased back, but kept the needlelike point of the dagger pressed to Tiago's larynx. He patted his cheek. "Don't worry. If I wanted to kill you, your throat would already be slit."

You're a lunatic. Anger boiled up inside him. "What do you want?"

"Sit down." Neves stepped back and gestured to the sofa with the stiletto.

Tiago sat. He rubbed his neck, and then looked at his hand, smeared with a bit of blood. *Bastard.*

"It's a scratch," Neves said.

An image of his pistol, hidden under a floorboard in the kitchen, flashed in Tiago's head. He fought back the urge to snatch it, knowing that he'd be stabbed if he darted from the sofa.

"I'm searching for someone," Neves said.

Tiago clenched his hands.

"He's a Jew named Henri Levin."

"I've never heard of him."

"He might be using an alias. He's a German journalist who was exiled before the war for his criticism of his country's militarism. He's fled Marseille, France, for Portugal, and he's wanted by the Gestapo." He removed a photograph from his pocket and held it to Tiago.

He looked at the image of a man in his forties with dark, slicked-back hair and a goatee with mustache. "I don't recognize him."

"Remember his face," Neves said, slipping the photograph into his pocket. "It'll help you identify him if he enters your bookstore."

"What makes you think that he'll enter my store?"

"Because you consort with Jews."

He doesn't know that I'm forging government papers, otherwise I would have already been arrested. A wave of defiance surged through him. "Consorting isn't a crime. I'm breaking no laws by providing books or charity to refugees."

"Perhaps. But Levin is a communist, and Salazar and the secret police despise communists as much as the Germans do. If I discover that you collaborated with Levin, I'll have you arrested. You'll spend the rest of your life rotting away in prison." Neves, still holding his stiletto, poured port into the glass and swirled it. "If you see or hear of him, I expect that you'll contact me."

Tiago nodded, despite having no intention of being an informant for Neves.

The agent gulped port and placed the empty glass on the table. "I'm surprised it's drinkable, considering the winemaker's wife is a Jew."

Tiago's skin turned hot. *He's investigating me, and he knows about my parents.*

"Yes—I'm aware that you're a half-Jew," Neves said. "But I'm willing to look past that, as long as you do what I ask of you."

"I've done nothing wrong," Tiago lied. "But I will keep you apprised if I encounter Levin."

"See that you do." Neves slipped his stiletto into a sheath inside his coat. He slid his fingers, thick as sausages, over the brim of his bowler hat and left.

Tiago bolted the door. He inspected his apartment, including the hidden space under the floorboard that contained his pistol. Other than the wine, a disheveled bookshelf, and partially open drawers, nothing was missing. Looking in the bathroom mirror, he used a washcloth and soap to clean a two-inch shallow laceration to his neck. As he applied pressure to his wound, he reflected on the sacrifices of his family and the refugees fleeing France. A boldness burned within him. *I'll never cower to fascists. As long as my lungs breathe and my heart beats, I'll aid anyone who seeks freedom from persecution.* He placed a bandage over his cut. Refusing to allow Neves's mark on his Adam's apple to worry Rosa, he rummaged through a chest of drawers in search of a roll-neck shirt to wear to work.

Chapter 12

Lisbon, Portugal—February 23, 1943

Tiago woke early, had a breakfast of stale, toasted bread and milky coffee, and arrived at the bookstore before sunrise. Refusing to allow his encounter with Agent Neves to impact his pursuit of helping refugees, he went to his office and meticulously labored to alter an expired visa for a Jewish woman from Nantes, France, who'd arrived last week in Lisbon. A few hours later, while he was waiting for the ink to dry on his forgery, the bell above the door rang. He placed the paperwork, being careful not to smear the ink, in his secret hole in the floor and covered it with a tile. As he traveled to the front of the store, Rosa was hanging up her coat.

"*Bom dia*," Tiago said.

"Ah!" Rosa, her eyes wide, dropped her coat and turned. "You nearly scared me to death! What are you doing here?"

"Sorry. I work here, remember?"

"Don't sneak up on me like that."

"I didn't mean to." He picked up her coat and hung it on the rack. "Didn't you see my office light on?"

"I did," she said, "but I assumed that you'd forgotten to turn it off when you closed up last night—you're typically late for work."

"I am, but it's because I usually make morning rounds to see refugees in parks and cafés. Today, my meetings are in the afternoon." He scratched his head. "I thought you'd be happy about my early arrival."

"I don't like when people are tardy—and I don't like when they arrive early, either." Her bottom lip quivered, as if she were fighting back a smile. She tapped her watch. "You should be on time. I don't like surprises—who'll run this place if you kill me with a heart attack?"

"I'm sure your heart is fine. You've got more energy than me."

"True," she said, raising her chin.

"All right, Rosa. From now on, I'll do my best to be on time."

"I'll believe it when I see it." She adjusted her glasses and squinted. "What's with the turtleneck?"

He touched his neck, making sure his bandage was covered. *There's no need for her to fret about my safety.* "I thought I'd try out a new look."

"It doesn't suit you," she said, furrowing her brow. "You look like you're trying to hide a love bite."

Tiago chuckled.

"While we're on this topic," Rosa said, placing her purse behind the front counter, "when was the last time you wooed someone?"

He shifted his weight. Although he was glad to move away from the subject of his roll-neck shirt, he dreaded having to discuss his lack of personal life. He'd dated little since the war, and his last serious relationship was with a woman named Leonor, whom he'd fallen for while studying at the University of Coimbra. Leonor was beautiful and outgoing, and she loved literature, which was the catalyst of their blossoming relationship. He thought that Leonor might be the woman he would spend his life with. But things changed when the Spanish Civil War erupted and he confided in her that he planned to join the conflict to help fight the spread of fascism. Leonor, who supported Salazar's dictatorship of Portugal, abruptly ended their affair. Blinded by her beauty, he'd failed to see that their beliefs—beyond art and books—did not match. He was heartbroken. However, as time passed, he realized that he wanted to be with someone who dreamed of a world that was free from authoritarian rule and, most importantly, was willing to do something about it.

Tiago looked at Rosa. "I'll have plenty of time for personal endeavors after the war."

Rosa frowned. "It isn't healthy for you to endlessly work, especially with an old woman who complains about your timeliness and the way you dress. You should be planning your future."

"I'll think of myself when there are no longer refugees struggling to flee persecution."

Rosa drew a deep breath and nodded.

He approached the front counter. "I have something important to tell you."

For several minutes, he told Rosa about his encounter with Agent Martim Neves—leaving out that Neves had broken into his apartment and held a stiletto to his neck. Also, he provided her with a description of Henri Levin based on the photograph.

"If Neves thinks that Levin might show up here," Tiago said, "there will likely be secret police conducting surveillance on the bookstore. It's becoming more dangerous, and my business is in near financial ruin. Soon, I'll have nothing left to fund aid for refugees. I'll understand if you decide to leave."

She sat on a stool and propped her elbows on the counter. "To hell with Agent Neves. I'm staying."

"Good," he said. "It'd be near impossible to operate this place without the best forger in Lisbon."

Rosa grinned. "*That*, Tiago, is the smartest thing you've said this morning."

The bell rang as the door opened. Artur, the newspaper boy, entered carrying a burlap sack.

"*Olá*," Artur said.

"*Bom dia*," Rosa said.

Artur put down his sack and rubbed his shoulder.

"How are you?" Tiago asked.

Artur removed his cap from his head. "I'm well, Senhor Soares."

"I assume you're going to school after you finish your deliveries."

Artur slipped his hands, stained with black shoe polish, into his pockets. "Oh, yes, *senhor*."

He disliked that Artur was skipping school, and that he was not forthright about his truancy. However, he admired the boy's work ethic and commitment to help support his family. Since the death of Artur's father, he'd been working two jobs. Tiago hoped that his prodding would encourage Artur to someday continue his schooling. Until then, he was determined to supply him with loads of books to augment his education.

Tiago went to a bookshelf. He scanned the rows and selected *Legends and Narratives*, a collection of novellas by Alexandre Herculano. "Here," he said, giving the book to Artur.

"*Obrigado*." Artur thumbed through the pages.

Tiago removed a small stack of newspapers from Artur's sack and placed them on the counter. With little money in the cash register, he removed change from his pocket and gave it to Artur. "You've done well today. It looks like you've sold most of your newspapers."

"I did," Artur said. "Everyone wants to read about the disaster."

"What disaster?" Tiago asked.

"A flying boat crashed in the river last night," Artur said.

Rosa's eyes widened.

Tiago unfolded a newspaper on the counter.

AMERICAN CLIPPER CRASHES IN TAGUS RIVER!
4 KILLED; 20 MISSING; MOST OF OTHER
15 PASSENGERS AND CREW INJURED

"Oh, God," Rosa said.

A memory of wailing sirens flashed in Tiago's head. A knot formed in his stomach. "Last night in the Rossio, I saw ambulances and a police car speeding in the direction of the river."

Her face turned pale.

Together, they read the short article about a Pan Am flying boat from the United States called the *Yankee Clipper* that crashed in the Tagus River while landing at the Cabo Ruivo Seaplane Base in Lisbon. The names of passengers were not provided, and there was no indication about the cause of the disaster.

Rosa touched her forehead, chest, and shoulders, making the sign of a cross. "Those poor people."

"It's tragic." Tiago set aside the newspaper and placed his hand on the boy's shoulder. "Take care of yourself, Artur. Perhaps tomorrow's paper will have better news."

Artur nodded. He picked up his burlap sack and left.

For the morning, Tiago struggled to concentrate on his work. His mind drifted, like a boat caught in a current, to the news of the tragedy. He hoped that the passengers who perished didn't suffer, and that the missing people would be found alive.

Chapter 13

Lisbon, Portugal—February 23, 1943

Maria, her brain foggy from anesthetic, opened her eyes to a hospital room with bare gray walls and matching tile floor. Layers of white sheets covered her body, which lay on a black, metal frame bed. Her tongue was dry, making it difficult to swallow. A malodor of antiseptic and pine cleaner penetrated her nostrils. Moans emanated from behind a curtain that divided the room. She attempted to move and a sharp pain shot through her hip and down her leg. Nausea rose from her stomach. She grabbed a metal, kidney-shaped basin on a stand next to her bed, held it under her chin, and vomited.

A woman, wearing a nursing cap that looked like a starched, white towel that was folded into a swan, entered the room. "It's the side effects of the anesthesia," she said in Portuguese. "Do you think you could drink water?"

"I'll try," she said, her voice hoarse.

The nurse set aside the basin, and then raised the top of the bed by cranking a handle under the frame. She retrieved a pitcher of water, poured some into a glass, and gave it to Maria.

She sipped.

"Not too much," the nurse said.

Maria gave her the glass and lowered her head to her pillow. A memory of floating debris and bodies flashed in her brain. Tears welled up in her eyes.

"The doctor will be in to examine you," the nurse said.

"There was a man named Ben Robertson seated next to me on the plane. Did he survive?"

She lowered her eyes. "There's no one here by that name."

Maria swallowed. "Tamara Drasin?"

The nurse shook her head. "I'll get the doctor." She grabbed the dirty basin and left, her heals clacking over the tile floor.

Maria, her heart aching, covered her face with her hands and wept.

Maria had been one of the last survivors pulled aboard a rescue boat. She'd been in the frigid water for thirty minutes before a Pan Am crew that launched from the Cabo Ruivo Seaplane Base arrived on the scene. Two men lifted her, shivering and incoherent, from the river as she was beginning to go under. Suffering from hypothermia, she was wrapped in blankets and rushed ashore where she was placed in an ambulance. By the time she reached the hospital, her numbness was replaced by agonizing pain in her hip and leg that were badly out of place. She was injected with morphine and examined by an elderly surgeon with small, child-like hands.

"Your hip joint is pushed out of the socket," the doctor had said. "I'm going to put you under anesthesia and try to put it back in place."

She was placed on a gurney and wheeled into an operating room, where the doctor was accompanied by a nurse and two broad-shouldered hospital attendants. Her eyes glanced from the frail doctor to the muscular men. *He's going to have the orderlies pop my leg into place.* A thick, rubber mask was placed over her nose and mouth. Eager to get it over with, she took deep inhales of a sweet, musky-smelling gas and everything went black.

"*Bom dia*," the doctor said, entering the room. He glanced at a chart attached to the footboard of the bed. "How are you feeling?"

"Groggy." She rubbed her temples. "Do you know how many survived the crash?"

"They're still searching the river." He clasped his hands over his belly. "Let's take a look at you first. Once you are feeling better, we can—"

"Please, Doctor," she interrupted. "I want to know."

His face turned somber. He glanced over his shoulder, as if he was worried that someone might hear him. "You're one of fifteen survivors."

Oh, God. There were thirty-nine passengers and crew on board. Horrid images of people, strapped to their seats in a sunken fuselage, filled her head. "Is Jane Froman among the survivors?"

"She made it through surgery."

Maria pressed her cheek into the pillow.

"You're fortunate to be alive." He approached her bedside and placed a hand on her shoulder. "May I examine you?"

She nodded.

The doctor lowered the sheets and inched up a white hospital gown to expose her upper right leg and hip, swollen and bruised the color of beetroot. He gently raised her leg.

She winced.

"The ball of your hip joint is back in the socket. You'll be on crutches for a month, and it might take two to three months to completely heal. Until then, you'll need to be careful to avoid dislocating it again." He bent her knee and tested moving her thighbone.

She drew a sharp breath, attempting to dispel the pain shooting through her hip.

The doctor lowered her leg and covered her with the sheets. "You also had a deep laceration on your back. It required twenty-four stitches."

With the pain in her leg, she'd barely noticed the discomfort beneath a bandage between her shoulder blades. "When can I leave the hospital?"

"In a few days, assuming your hip remains in place." He picked up the chart and scribbled on it with a pen from his pocket. "I'll ask the nurse to bring you ice packs for the swelling. I want you to keep it on for as long as you can handle the cold."

"Okay."

He hung the chart on the end of the bed and looked at her. "You have visitors; they spent the night in the waiting area. Are you feeling well enough to see them?"

"Yes, please."

Moans and labored breathing grew from behind the curtain. The doctor stepped around the divider and examined a patient. Sunlight, streaming through a window, cast a silhouette of the doctor administering an injection. Groans dissipated and the doctor left.

The nurse placed ice packs on Maria's hip, sending chills over her skin. Her alertness grew. Several minutes after the nurse had left, Pilar and Roy entered the room.

"Oh, Maria," Pilar said, her voice quavering.

Maria blinked back tears. "I'm so happy to see you."

Roy placed a hand on the base of the bed. "How are you?"

"My hip was dislocated and I received stitches to a cut on my back, but I'll be all right." She clasped her hands and noticed that her mother's sapphire ring was still on her finger. A wave of vulnerability surged through her. "I could really use a hug."

They approached the bed and held her.

She squeezed them, disregarding the pain in her hip.

They slipped away. Roy sat in a wooden chair, while Pilar remained on the edge of the bed.

Maria gathered her courage and told them everything that she could remember about the crash—the wing of the plane slicing into the water, a bone-jarring impact and her seat breaking from the floor, holding her breath and swimming blindly through a submerged fuselage, and fighting to stay afloat until help arrived. "It was a USO flight. The entertainers were selfless and optimistic about supporting the troops." She drew a jagged breath. "Most on board perished in the crash."

Pilar squeezed Maria's hand. "I'm so sorry."

Roy placed his palms together. "We were at the seaplane base waiting for your arrival."

"You saw it happen?" Maria asked.

"No," Pilar said. "There was an emergency announcement, and a Pan Am ground crew scrambled to locate a boat."

"The responders weren't prepared," Roy said. "It took them too long to leave the dock. I wish there was something I could have done. I felt helpless."

"There was nothing you could have done," Maria said.

Roy removed his pipe from his jacket but made no effort to place it in his mouth.

"I need to let my dad know that I'm okay," Maria said. "I'm sure the news has reached the States and he's worried sick."

"We've sent him a telegram," Roy said. "He knows that you're safe."

"Thank you so much." The tension in her chest eased. She smoothed the sheets over her legs. "Have you communicated with Kilgour?"

"We have," Roy said. "He was shocked by the news and relieved to know that you're all right."

Pilar shifted her weight and glanced at Roy.

"Is there something that you're not telling me?" Maria asked.

Roy fiddled with his pipe, as if he was pondering what to say.

"Kilgour wants to send you home," Pilar said. "Once you're well enough to leave the hospital, he expects you to board a passenger ship for the States."

Maria struggled to sit up. A twinge shot through her back. "I'm not leaving."

"You have no choice in the matter," Roy said.

"Yes, I do," Maria said. "I've worked far too hard to get here."

"I know you're upset," Roy said. "But it might be easier for you to regain your health back home."

"You're damn right I'm upset," Maria said. "Most of the people who were on that plane are dead. They gave their lives while supporting our country, and I will not allow their sacrifice to go in vain. I'm not giving up. As soon as I'm out of this bed, I'm going to work as an IDC agent. And I'm not going home until this war is over."

Pilar looked at Roy. "Maria's right—she should have a choice in the matter. We need to stick together and tell Kilgour that we're in support of Maria remaining in Lisbon. He's in no position to reprimand all of his agents in the Iberian Peninsula."

Roy rubbed his forehead.

Maria patted Pilar's arm. "Thanks for having my back, but I don't want to risk getting either of you into trouble. I'll handle things with Kilgour. Could you fetch me something to write with?"

Pilar left the room and returned with a pad of stationery and a pencil.

Maria placed the paper against her good leg and scribbled.

Mr. Kilgour,

My colleagues have relayed your request for me to return home. I deeply appreciate your concern for my welfare, but I must respectfully decline your offer. I've received splendid medical care and an excellent prognosis. A mild hip dislocation will have me sidelined for no more than forty-eight hours. Afterward, I plan to begin my duties in Lisbon.

Thank you for your interest in my well-being. You should expect my first shipment in the coming weeks.

Respectfully,

Maria Alves

Pilar peeked at the message. "I like it."

"Roy," Maria said, "could you please send a telegram to Kilgour?"

"Sure."

She gave the paper to Roy.

He looked at the note. "Don't be surprised if Kilgour sends a reply demanding that you return home on the next ship."

"You bring up a good point." Maria scribbled another note on her pad and handed him the paper. "If he does reply with a demand for me to leave, telegram this one."

Roy's eyes widened as he read the message.

Mr. Kilgour,

I'm aware that you have full authority to remove me from the IDC. However, you should know that I plan to stay in Lisbon to acquire foreign publications, regardless if I'm relieved from my duties. If you do not want my microfilm, then I will arrange to provide it to the British embassy. I'm quite certain that our allies will be receptive to acquiring the information.

Respectfully,

Maria Alves

"You can't be serious," Roy said.

"I am," Maria said.

Pilar approached Roy and read the message. She looked at Maria and grinned.

"All right," Roy said. "I'll send the telegram, and I'm hoping that I don't have to send the second one." He placed the messages in his pocket and left.

"He can be quite stubborn when it comes to following protocol," Pilar said.

"He'll come around; he always does." She looked at Pilar. "It's not easy for him to challenge authority. He's gotten here by following the rules. I, on the other hand, have gotten here by breaking them."

"I'm glad you did."

Pilar stayed with Maria while she ate a bowl of bone broth. Soon after, the nurse requested for her to leave.

"I'll be back this evening," Pilar said, hugging Maria. "And I'll buy you some things to wear for when you're released from the hospital."

"Thank you." She imagined her luggage—that contained her

clothes, microphotography equipment, and her mother's Leica camera—submerged in the cargo hold of what was left of the *Yankee Clipper*.

Alone, Maria wrote a two-page letter to her father describing the tragedy and her injuries, but most of all to reassure him that she would be all right. Afterward, she asked the nurse if she could visit with survivors of the crash, but the woman insisted that she needed to remain in bed. So, when the nurse was on her break, Maria purposely spilled a glass of water on her bed. While an orderly placed her in a wheelchair so that he could change the sheets, she rolled herself down the hall. She spoke with three survivors, including a badly injured USO dancer named Jean Lorraine, whose husband and dance partner, Roy Rognan, was killed in the crash. It was heartbreaking for Maria to see the woman mourn the death of her husband from a hospital bed. She held Jean's hand until neither of them had tears left to shed.

She located Jane Froman but she was too heavily sedated to communicate. Jane's right arm was in a cast and her right leg was in traction. Although Jane's injuries were serious, Maria was relieved to see that her left leg, bundled in bandages, had not been amputated given that it had been nearly severed below the knee. She whispered a prayer for Jane, and then wheeled herself back to the room, where the nurse chided her for disobeying orders to remain in bed. With her hip throbbing, she was given another injection of morphine. And she wished that drug could—in addition to relieving pain—erase macabre memories.

Chapter 14

Lisbon, Portugal—March 2, 1943

Maria, using crutches with her right leg raised to avoid pressure on her hip, leaned over a table and positioned a Recordak 35mm camera over the front page of a German newspaper. A wave of disgust rose from her stomach as she peered through the viewfinder at an article written by Joseph Goebbels, Hitler's chief propagandist. She pressed the shutter release, producing a soft metallic click, and then turned the page and repeated the microfilm process.

Kilgour had permitted Maria to remain as an agent in Lisbon based on her claim of an excellent medical prognosis, and Roy had been relieved that he didn't need to send Maria's backup telegram that threatened to deliver her microfilm to the British embassy. She'd left the hospital two days after the plane crash and moved into Pilar's two-bedroom flat, down the hall from Roy's apartment. Their homes were on the top floor of a four-story building near Avenida da Liberdade, a ninety-meter-wide boulevard lined with trees, palatial homes, residential buildings, luxury hotels, banks, and cafés. Although Maria had visited Lisbon with her parents as a child, she'd spent little time in the upscale areas, considering they stayed in cheap hostels and boardinghouses in the less affluent areas of the city. And upon entering her new residence—fully furnished and with the dining room converted into a miniature microfilm department—it was clear, to Maria, that the OSS had spared no expense in providing them everything they needed to perform their duties.

Instead of allowing herself time to recuperate from her hip injury, she'd gone straight to work, microfilming German newspapers that included the likes of *Das Reich*, *Der Angriff*, and *Völkischer Beobachter*—the official newspaper of the Nazi party. The publications, stacked knee-high in the corner of the dining room, had been acquired from newsstands by Roy and Pilar prior to her arrival. Maria was astonished by how readily available Axis publications were in neutral Portugal, and she was eager to begin exploring newsstands and bookstores on her own. But with the risk of reinjuring her hip due to the challenges of using crutches on Lisbon's steep hills and cobblestone sidewalks, she'd remained in the apartment while Pilar and Roy made their rounds. Within a few days, Maria had accumulated enough used microfilm to be shipped to the OSS. Her comrades had been sending weekly cargo of undeveloped film aboard the *Yankee Clipper*. Until another American boat plane route was established to Lisbon, Kilgour had arranged for them to ship microfilm aboard a British Overseas Airways Corporation (BOAC) plane to OSS headquarters in London, where a team of agents would develop the film and scour it for intelligence.

"Good morning," Pilar said, entering the room.

"Hi." Maria snapped a photograph and lowered her camera. "Sleep well?"

Pilar nodded. "What time did you wake?"

"Four thirty," Maria said.

"That's too early. You need more rest."

Maria leaned on her crutches. "I couldn't sleep."

"Another bad dream?"

"Yeah."

"I'm sorry," Pilar said.

"Thanks."

Since the accident, Maria was plagued with night terrors. In predawn hours, she'd awakened—gasping for air with the sensation of drowning. With visions of submerged corpses still reeling in her head, she'd hobble to the dining room to microfilm papers. The only remedy to keep the nightmares at bay, it seemed, was to bury herself in work.

Maria shifted her weight on one leg. "One benefit of not sleeping is that it allows me to be productive. I like to think of it as making up for lost time. While I was sitting idle for months in Washington, the two of you were hard at work."

Pilar pointed to a box of used microfilm. "You're doing a bang-up job, and you're making me and Roy look bad."

Maria smiled.

"How about some breakfast before I leave?"

"Sure." Maria set aside her microfilm equipment and hobbled to the kitchen.

They prepared a meal of black coffee and buttered toast, and then sat at a small wooden table.

Pilar sipped her coffee. "Will you be all right while Roy and I are gone?"

"Of course, we're stocked with plenty of food." Maria took a bite of toast, crisp and buttery. "Are you all packed?"

Pilar nodded.

With Pilar's assignment to establish an outpost in Madrid on hold until Maria's health improved, Kilgour had requested Pilar and Roy to expand their search for Axis publications outside of Lisbon. In a few hours, the pair would board a train for an overnight trip to Coimbra, a city in central Portugal.

"I wish I was coming with you," Maria said. "Coimbra is a beautiful city that's rich in history. Try to gain access to the library at the University of Coimbra. It's one of the oldest universities in the world."

"I will." Pilar chewed a bit of toast. "Please be careful if you decide to venture outside while we're gone."

Maria swirled her coffee. "What makes you think that I'm going to leave the apartment?"

"Because I know you," Pilar said.

"The building doesn't have an elevator, and there are few flat places in Lisbon to walk with crutches."

"I doubt that would stop you."

Maria chuckled.

"It'll be good to have you in the bookstores. Acquiring German newspapers has been relatively easy, but acquiring books has been a challenge. Unlike you, Roy and I aren't fluent in German and Portuguese. You'll be able to sift through publications that might be of value, and you'll more easily gain the trust of proprietors because you can speak like a local. I'm thinking that you'll have better success than us."

"You've done an incredible job," Maria said. "And you'll do even better when you return to your homeland of Spain. I'm counting on you to win us the war."

Pilar grinned.

A knock on the door. Pilar left the kitchen and returned with Roy, holding a leather suitcase.

"Good morning," Roy said.

"Hi." Maria pointed to a pot on the stove. "Would you like some coffee?"

"With pleasure. My joe tastes like tar." He put down his suitcase, retrieved a cup from a cabinet, and poured himself a coffee. "How you feeling?"

"Better," Maria said. "I'm able to put a little weight on the leg."

"That's good to hear." He took a sip. "Things are going well with you dedicated to microfilming our acquisitions. I know you're anxious to canvass bookstores, but it might be best for you to ease into things. There's nothing wrong with taking more time to avoid a setback with your health."

Maria straightened her back. "Each day that the war goes on, more soldiers will die in battle. They aren't getting a break. Why should we?"

Roy swallowed. "I see your point."

Pilar finished her coffee and placed her cup in the sink. She turned to Maria. "This will be our first trip outside of Lisbon. Since you've traveled in Portugal, do you have any suggestions for us?"

Maria ran a finger over the edge of her cup. "There's a greater chance of being stopped by the PVDE at train stations. Make sure that you have your travel papers stored someplace for easy access. And if you're stopped, remain calm and stick to our script about collecting materials for the Library of Congress."

They nodded.

"You're not breaking any laws, unless they search your luggage and find publications in violation of Portugal's censorship. I realize that the bartering of American magazines has worked well for you to acquire Axis newspapers. However, I wouldn't take them with you. There will be checkpoints in the train stations, and the secret police might view them as immoral. I recommend purchasing everything with escudos."

Roy ran a hand through his hair. He placed his suitcase on his lap and removed a bundle of magazines, comprised of *Vogue*, *Life*, *Newsweek*, and *Time*.

Maria peeked inside his luggage. Her eyes locked on stacks of escudos. "Jeez, Roy! How much money are you taking?"

"I wanted to make sure we have enough for the trip."

"Take a modest amount of escudos. You can always travel back to the source for another purchase. Too much money will raise suspicion. The last thing you want is to be interrogated by the PVDE about why you're carrying an excessive amount of cash."

Roy removed most of the money from his suitcase and placed it on the table. He looked at Pilar. "How's your luggage?"

"Mine's good—no magazines. I have escudos in my purse, but not an amount to create alarm."

Roy closed his suitcase and placed it by his feet.

Maria's mind drifted to their stashes of escudos, amounting to more than most Portuguese citizens earn in years, which were hidden in a pillowcase, a cookie tin, and a water-tight jar taped inside a toilet tank. With the seemingly endless funds provided by the

OSS, it was easy for one, Maria believed, to become desensitized to money, and she hoped that it would never happen to her.

Maria, hobbling on her crutches, accompanied them to the door, hugged them goodbye, and watched them disappear down the stairs. She locked the door and went to the dining room. Rather than return to microfilming, she eased weight onto her bad leg. A dull ache radiated from her hip. *To hell with it.* Before she changed her mind, she hobbled to the bathroom to wash and put on clean clothes.

Thirty minutes later, Maria draped a large cloth bag, which contained her purse and Roy's handwritten list of bookstore addresses, over her shoulder and left the apartment. Using a handrail, she awkwardly descended the stairs while holding her crutches in her free hand. She paused in the lobby to catch her breath, and then hobbled outside and hailed a taxi. Rather than take a direct route to a bookstore, she requested the driver to tour her around the city.

As the taxi traveled on Avenida da Liberdade, she rolled down her window and breathed fresh air. The temperature was in the high fifties with a bright sun and cloudless blue sky. Outside cafés, people sat at sidewalk tables while they smoked cigarettes and sipped espresso. Leaving the main thoroughfare, the taxi traveled along Rossio Square. Maria's eyes were drawn to throngs of people, wearing layers of clothes despite the mild weather. Bags and luggage were stacked near the base of a fountain, where women and small children were resting on blankets. She knew, from American newspaper and radio reports, that refugees from German-occupied territories were flooding into Lisbon. But the reports, which did not provide specific tallies, had done little to prepare her for witnessing the vast numbers of asylum seekers.

Maria's heart sank. "Can you tell me about the refugees?" she asked in Portuguese.

The driver peered through the rearview mirror. "There are too many of them. Each day, more enter the city."

"Where are they coming from?"

"Everywhere." The driver lit a cigarette and veered off the square.

For an hour, she toured the city. It looked much the same as it did when she'd visited years ago with her parents, except for the refugees, who congregated in the city's squares, especially the Rossio and Praça do Comércio. And upon reaching the waterfront docks, she was shocked by the masses of people who were waiting to board a passenger ship.

"All those people cannot possibly fit on that ship," Maria said, looking out her open window.

The driver took a drag on his cigarette. "They show up each day in hopes that they'll be permitted to board. Those without money wait many months, sometimes a year, before they leave Lisbon."

"Why so long?"

"The Portuguese government doesn't allow them to work, so they need to rely on charity."

Maria, having seen enough, leaned forward and said, "Take me to Baixa."

Soon, she paid the driver and exited the taxi in the heart of downtown Lisbon. She carefully crutched her way along the sidewalk, made of smooth limestone paving stones. For the remainder of the morning, she visited newsstands but found little of interest. After a lunch of grilled sardines at a kiosk café, which looked like a gazebo with an inserted concession stand, she reviewed Roy's list and found a nearby bookstore—Livraria Soares, located on Rua do Crucifixo. And next to the name of the store was a note in Roy's handwriting:

Crummy shop - few newspapers, lots of poetry books.

Eager to search through something other than newspapers, she disregarded Roy's note and traveled down a narrow cobblestone street until she located the sign. A bell above the door rang as she entered. An elderly woman with curly gray hair and plump cheeks was seated on a stool behind the counter.

Maria smiled. "*Olá*."

"*Boa tarde*." The woman lowered her eyes to an open magazine on the counter.

Maria hobbled along a wall of bookshelves and examined books. Most were of poetry, but as she moved deeper into the shop, she discovered a table filled with French-, German-, and Polish-language books. A door hinge squeaked as she lifted a book.

"May I help you," a man's voice said.

Maria turned, nearly losing her balance, and dropped the book. She clasped the handles of her crutches to steady herself.

"My apologies," he said, picking up the book from the floor. "I should be more careful not to startle customers when exiting my office."

The man, in his late twenties, was tall with a muscular build. He wore a gray wool suit with a white button shirt. His hair, the color of chestnut, was neatly combed and his face was clean-shaven. And near his Adam's apple was a slight scar, as if he'd nicked himself while using a straight razor.

"That's quite all right," she said.

He handed her the book. "Welcome to my bookstore. Is there anything that I can help you find?"

"Yes," she said. "I'm an American collecting publications for the Library of Congress, which is interested in preserving records of the present world crisis."

"Your Portuguese is excellent."

"Thank you," she said. "As I was saying, I'm with the Library of Congress and we're of particular interest in books that—"

His lips formed a smile.

"Have you heard this before?"

"Yes, but in English from a pipe-smoking man."

"I see," she said. "Would it be okay if I looked around?"

"Of course. Everything here is for sale and, in my opinion, worth preserving." He extended his hand. "I'm Tiago."

"Maria." She shook his hand.

"I'll be up front if you should need assistance."

"*Obrigada*."

He turned and left.

Maria examined the foreign-language books on the table, most of which were poetry. She was tempted to leave, considering Roy had already looked around the store. But her hip was beginning to ache and she decided it might be best not to canvass more stores for the day. So, she browsed deeper into the back of the shop, going bookcase by bookcase, shelf by shelf, until she discovered a small reference section. Her eyes widened upon seeing a thick, leather-bound book titled *Die Industriekultur Deutschlands* (*The Industrial Heritage of Germany*). She removed the book from the shelf and thumbed through it. In addition to the country's manufacturing history, the book provided a lengthy index with names and addresses of companies by business sector. She ran her finger down the list—clock manufacturers, cycle manufacturers, engine manufacturers, firearm manufacturers . . .

Holy mackerel! She glanced to the front of the store, where Tiago was conversing with the woman seated at the counter. She turned to the copyright page of the book and discovered that it was published in 1936, and she suspected that many of the factory addresses would still be accurate. She imagined squadrons of Allied bombers dropping their payloads and destroying engine plants used to build Hitler's Panzer tanks. She searched the remaining bookshelves but found nothing further of interest. In an attempt to camouflage her purchase, she added several French books of poetry, a Hungarian novel, and a Polish cookbook. She placed the items in her cloth bag and lugged them to the counter.

"Find everything you need?" Tiago asked.

"Yes."

He gestured to the woman at the counter. "This is Rosa."

"It's nice to meet you. I'm Maria."

"Tiago tells me that you're a librarian from America," Rosa said with a timbre of suspicion. "Where did you learn Portuguese?"

"My father. He was born in Coimbra."

The lines on the woman's face softened. "Do you have family in Portugal?"

"Not anymore," Maria said. "Except for my father, who lives in New Jersey, the Portuguese side of my family is deceased."

"I'm sorry," Rosa said.

"*Obrigada*." Maria leaned on a crutch and placed the books onto the counter.

"You have an eclectic taste in books," Tiago said.

"We're acquiring a wide array of publications."

"Why no Portuguese books?" he asked.

"We're interested in preserving books from countries who are at war. Portugal is neutral." She gripped the handles of her crutches. "Are you able to order more books from foreign suppliers?"

"It depends," Tiago said. "What type of books are you interested in?"

"Books of cultural, religious, or political opposition—such as publications by Jewish authors. And I would be highly interested in any German or Italian reference material."

Tiago rubbed his chin. "I'll see what I can do. What's the best way for me to reach you?"

"I'll stop by in a week or two," she said, deciding it was best not to reveal her contact information.

He nodded.

Rosa rang up the books on the cash register.

Maria paid with escudos and placed the books in her bag.

"Do you need help carrying your things?" Tiago asked.

"I can manage. I'm taking a taxi home." She looped the handles of her bag over her shoulder.

"Do you mind if I ask what happened to your leg?" Tiago asked.

"No," she said. "I was injured in a plane accident."

Rosa gasped. "Were you on the boat plane that crashed in the river?"

A knot formed in her stomach. "Yes."

Rosa made the sign of a cross over her head and chest.

"I'm so sorry," Tiago said.

"Me too," Maria said.

Rosa got off her stool and approached Maria. She looked into her eyes. "God must have a purpose for you. There's a reason you survived. *You* have destiny to fulfill."

Maria swallowed, feeling surprised and moved by the woman's emotional words. "I hope so."

Tiago extended his hand. "The books are heavy. Please allow me to carry your bag to a taxi."

"All right."

He lifted the bag from her shoulder and accompanied her outside. At the end of the street, he hailed a taxi and helped her into the back seat.

The driver pulled away. Although she was eager to microfilm the German publication, she reflected on Rosa's words about purpose and destiny. Instead of going back to the apartment, she instructed the driver to take her to the Rossio.

For the remainder of the afternoon, Maria sat under a jacaranda tree on the outskirts of the square. The area was filled with throngs of refugees, who appeared to have no place to stay. It saddened her to see people who'd fled their homelands in search of freedom. And she hoped that her duties would in some way play a part in ending the suffering in Europe.

At sunset, a tall man wearing a black coat over a gray suit crossed the square and sat on a bench next to a long-bearded refugee with a rolled blanket at his feet.

Maria's eyes locked on the well-dressed man, fifteen yards away from her spot under the tree. *That's Tiago.*

Tiago slipped a book from his coat and placed it next to him on the bench. He briefly conversed with the bearded man, and then sat in silence. A moment later, Tiago walked away, leaving the book.

She stood, gathered her bag, and hobbled toward the bench. As she neared the man, he lifted the book's cover, exposing what appeared to be a passport and escudos. The man closed the book and stashed it under his blanket.

Maria, curiosity burning within her, changed her course and followed Tiago across the street. She struggled to reach him due to her hindered pace and the crowd on the sidewalk. She called his name, but he didn't hear her over the chatter and street traffic. She hobbled faster. Her crutches dug into her armpits.

He turned onto a side street.

Reaching the corner, she turned and the tip of her crutch caught on a raised paving stone. She stumbled forward, falling to the ground and spilling books from her bag. A pang shot through her hip.

Tiago turned. His eyes widened with recognition and he darted to her. "Are you hurt?"

Maria ran a hand over her hip and was relieved to find it in place. "I'm okay." She took in deep breaths and gathered her composure.

He helped her onto her crutches.

She felt a twinge between her shoulder blades and a trickle down her spine. "I think the stitches on my back have come loose."

"How bad is it?"

"I can't tell," she said. "Do you mind taking a look?"

He helped her to slide her jacket below her shoulders. "There's blood on your blouse."

Darn it.

"I'll take you to a doctor."

"No," she said. "I'll tend to it when I get home."

"Do you have someone who can clean and patch your wound?"

"No. I'll handle it myself."

"You won't be able to reach it. Let me take you to a hospital."

Maria shook her head.

"I'm not going to leave you like this. Either allow me to take you to a doctor, or let me help you with tending to your wound with bandages and antiseptic. I live in Chiado, a five-minute walk from here."

He looked safe enough, but she barely knew him. Most of all, she dreaded having to return to the hospital unless she had no other choice. "Okay. Let's go to your place."

"Stay here. I'll get a taxi."

Before she could reply, he darted to the corner and waved down a driver. Minutes later, they arrived at an apartment building, its front covered in blue ceramic tiles. Inside, he helped her with climbing the stairs. He unbolted his door, flipped on a light, and led her to a table, where he turned around a chair so that she could sit with her back exposed.

Maria eased onto the chair and leaned her crutches against a wall. She glanced over the apartment, sparsely decorated with antique furniture and old books. "Do you live alone?"

"Yes." Tiago stepped away and returned with bandages, gauze, medical tape, and a bottle of rubbing alcohol. Over a kitchen sink, he sterilized his hands with alcohol and dried them with a clean towel.

She removed her jacket. "Does it look bad?"

He stepped behind her. "Your shirt has a blood spot, the diameter of a plum. You'll need to expose your back for me to examine the wound."

I must be crazy. She unbuttoned her blouse. "No peeping at my unmentionables."

"What's that?"

"Undergarments."

"Oh," he said. "I promise to keep my eyes on your wound."

She slid down her blouse to expose her back.

"A couple of stitches are pulled away, but the remaining ones are secure. I think we can forgo a visit to the hospital."

Thank goodness.

"This might sting." He soaked gauze in rubbing alcohol and applied it to the laceration.

She felt a cold burn—yet beyond the discomfort, she noticed his gentle touch.

He cleaned away the blood and dabbed on more rubbing alcohol. "Most of the bleeding has stopped."

She ran a finger over a blemish on the table. "I'm grateful for your help."

"You're welcome." He applied light pressure to the laceration. "I was stunned by the news of the boat plane accident. I cannot begin to imagine what you went through. I'm deeply sorry."

"*Obrigada*."

"Are you in pain?"

"Some. My hip was dislocated, but it's getting better and I hope to be off crutches soon. A doctor will remove my stitches next week." An image of water gushing into a plane fuselage flashed in her brain. "The visions of the crash are worse than my physical injuries."

"With time, the bad memories will fade," Tiago said, as if he'd experienced tragedy.

Eager to change the subject to something other than her health, she asked, "Is Rosa your grandmother?"

"No, but she's a wonderful surrogate grandparent—aside from her stubbornness and demands for punctuality."

"She's sweet." Maria smiled. "It sounds to me like you've been tardy for work."

He chuckled. "You're quite perceptive. But in my defense, I sometimes conduct business before going into the bookstore."

"You mentioned surrogate grandparent—are your grandparents deceased?"

"My grandparents on my father's side of the family died before I was born. I don't know if my mother's parents are alive."

"Have you lost touch with them?"

"No, it's nothing like that, our family is quite close." He placed a clean piece of gauze on her back. "My mother's side of the family is Jewish. My grandparents have a vineyard in Bordeaux, France."

Maria's skin prickled.

"My grandparents were among the hundreds of Bordeaux Jews who were arrested by German soldiers and shipped away in cattle cars."

"Oh, God. I'm so sorry."

"*Obrigado*."

"Where were they sent to?"

"A labor camp in Poland."

Her mouth turned dry.

"My parents and I had written them, imploring to flee France, but they refused to leave."

"Why?"

"My grandparents were committed to aiding Jewish refugees," he said. "They hid them in their wine caves and helped them escape the country through a network of Catholic churches to reach my parents' vineyard in Portugal's Douro Valley, and eventually to Lisbon."

"Your family created an escape line."

"Yes," he said. "Last summer, a refugee couple told me that German soldiers had arrested Jews in a raid on a synagogue near Bordeaux. Fearing for my grandparents' safety, I journeyed to their vineyard with the intent to convince them to leave. But I was too late; they were apprehended and sent away, days before my arrival."

"It's not your fault. You did everything you could to help them."

He nodded. "I haven't given up hope, but there are days when I feel like I'll never see them again."

"You will."

He drew a deep breath. "Enough about me. I thought your plans were to take a taxi home from the bookstore. Why were you walking around the city on crutches?"

"I've been stuck in my apartment since leaving the hospital, and I wanted to get some fresh air." She covered her chest with her arms and turned slightly to him. "I was in the Rossio and saw you leave a book for a man on a bench. It contained a passport and money."

He retrieved a bandage and a strip of tape. "You're quite observant."

"Are you helping him to flee Lisbon?"

"I am."

"Did he come through your family's escape line?"

"Yes. He's a Jewish refugee who's been living on the streets for nearly a year while trying to collect enough money for ship passage to America. I'm helping to fund his transport."

"That is very kind of you," she said. "But why did you give him a passport?"

"I was holding it in safekeeping for him."

"Do you expect me to believe that?"

"No, I don't." He placed the bandage over her wound, and then applied a strip of tape to hold it in place. "Tell me more about why you're interested in acquiring foreign publications."

"The Library of Congress wants to preserve records that might perish in the war. Many works, if destroyed, would be lost forever."

"You seem particularly interested in German records," he said.

"We're interested in all publications that might be at risk of destruction."

"Do you expect me to believe that?"

"I guess not." *It looks like we're both not willing to divulge all of our secrets.*

He finished covering her bandage with strips of tape. "How does it feel?"

"Much better. Thank you."

He stepped away and returned with a white button dress shirt. "Wear this home."

"That won't be necessary," she said.

"You have a clean bandage. How about we keep it that way?" He placed the shirt on the table and turned his back to her.

Maria set aside her bloodied blouse. She slipped on his shirt, buttoned it, and tucked the bottom underneath her wool skirt. "All right."

He faced her. "Do you have stairs or a lift at your apartment building?"

"A lift," she lied. *He'll want to accompany me home, and I've inconvenienced him enough.*

Together, they left his apartment. Step by step, she slowly descended the stairs. Rather than use the banister for support, she held Tiago's arm. Outside, he helped her into the back seat of a taxi, and then loaded her crutches and bag into the vehicle.

"I'll return your shirt," she said.

"There's no need. Take care, Maria." He closed the taxi door.

The driver pulled away. She peered out the window and watched Tiago disappear from sight.

At her building, she labored up flights of stairs and entered her apartment. Despite her fatigue and aches, she was determined to microfilm her German book purchase, *Die Industriekultur Deutschlands*, before allowing herself to rest. Rather than change her clothing, she rolled up the sleeves of Tiago's shirt and began filming the book. Several pages in, her mind drifted to their time together. *He's tender and kind, and he and his family are risking everything to aid refugees.* She was grateful for his care, and she wished that she would have made an effort to talk about her own family, especially the loss of her mother. *Both of us have loved ones who were taken from us during times of war.* She buried her thoughts, resolving to get to know him better when she returned to his bookstore.

Maria finished microfilming the book. Too tired to cook food, she ate a dry slice of bread, olives, and a glass of wine. She hobbled to a sofa and slumped onto the cushions. Instead of reading a book, she pulled his shirt tightly around her. Soon, she fell into a deep sleep. And for the first time since the plane accident, she wasn't awoken by night terrors.

Chapter 15

Lisbon, Portugal—March 10, 1943

Tiago, hunkered in his office at the bookstore, retrieved a small stack of passports and travel papers from his secret hole under a floor tile. He sorted through the documents, categorizing them based on expiration dates, improper visas, missing photographs, and damaged pages. They had far more work than he and Rosa could handle, and they were laboring day and night to keep up with the demand. The money in his bank account was nearly evaporated, and Rosa had insisted on helping to subsidize their operation by using her retirement money to purchase forgery supplies. He'd promised to pay her back, but considering his store's sluggish book sales and the escalating numbers of refugees in need of aid, he doubted that he'd be able to repay her anytime soon.

He hadn't seen Maria since he'd bandaged her wound and watched her depart in a taxi. But he had, as promised, contacted his book suppliers to order foreign publications based on her interests. Within weeks, books would be arriving to the shop. He hoped that he'd have the money to pay for them and, even more, that Maria would return to his bookstore.

Since his encounter with Maria, he'd reflected on their conversation. He hadn't discussed what had happened to his grandparents with anyone, except his parents and Rosa. However, Maria had made him feel comfortable and, for reasons he couldn't quite explain, he trusted her. Like him, she was passionate about books, and he suspected that she was harboring secrets, given her interest in Axis publications. *She may be trying to preserve books that could be destroyed in the conflict, but her country is at war and will no doubt use any intelligence that can be obtained.* Also, he regretted not asking about her family and reasons for leaving the safety of her homeland to acquire books for the Library of Congress.

Classical music emanated from the radio on Rosa's counter.

His pulse quickened. He stashed the passports and papers into the hole and sealed it over with the tile. He brushed his hands over his clothing, smoothing out wrinkles, and exited his office. A burn rose in his chest as he approached two men, one of whom he recognized by the bowler hat.

"*Bom dia*, Agent Neves," Tiago said, approaching the men.

Neves turned but spoke to his comrade, a pinstripe-suited young man with a cauliflower ear that gave him the appearance of a boxer. "Look around."

The young man nodded, approached a shelf, and browsed through books, some of which he tipped from their shelves onto the floor.

Rosa, seated behind her counter, looked at Tiago.

"How may I help you?" Tiago asked.

"I'm training a new recruit," Neves said. "I brought him here to search for books that should be examined by the Censorship Service."

"He'll find no banned publications," Tiago said. "You've inspected my shop before. I'm sure you missed nothing."

"That was quite some time ago," Neves said. "Even if he finds nothing, it'll give him practice with identifying immoral books."

The young agent plucked a book from a table, flipped through the pages, and tossed it to the floor.

"I assume your comrade will clean up his mess."

Neves stepped to Tiago. "Are you still vexed about my visit to your apartment?"

Rosa's eyes widened.

Tiago held his ground.

"I see that my visit left a scar," Neves said, pointing at Tiago's neck.

Anger pulsed through his veins. Since his encounter with Neves, he kept a sheathed fillet knife in the interior pocket of his jacket. He'd considered carrying his Astra 400 pistol, but if he were caught with a concealed firearm, he'd be arrested and interrogated as to how he acquired a Spanish service weapon. A fillet knife, however, was a common tool owned by most Lisboetas, since fish was a primary source of meat. He dreaded the thought of sticking a man, even someone as vile as Neves, but he would defend himself if he had to. *The next time Neves attempts to cut me with his stiletto, he'll receive a blade to his ribs.*

The bell over the door jangled. Artur entered with a sack of newspapers. The boy's eyes locked on the books, strewn over the floor, and froze.

"*Olá*, Artur," Tiago said, hoping to calm the boy. "I'd like a dozen newspapers today."

The boy slid his cap from his head and pulled papers from his sack.

Neves looked at Tiago. "Do you know the whereabouts of Henri Levin?"

"*Não*," Tiago said, recalling the photograph that Neves had shown him.

"How about this man?" Neves slid a newspaper clipping from his pocket that contained a blurred photograph of a thin-haired man in his fifties. "His name is Karl Bregman."

He shook his head.

The comrade tossed a book to the floor.

Tiago's skin turned hot.

Neves approached the counter, where Artur was giving Rosa a stack of newspapers, and held up the clipping. "Have either of you seen this man?"

Rosa and Artur shook their heads.

Neves retrieved another photograph from his pocket. "How about this man? His name is Henri Levin."

"*Não*, *senhor*," Artur said, his face pale.

"I never forget a face," Rosa said. "I've never seen that man before."

Neves slipped his photographs into his suit jacket.

Tiago paid Artur for the newspapers with change from his pocket. "I expect you to go to school as soon as you finish your deliveries."

"I will." Artur stuffed the money into his pocket, slung his sack over his shoulder, and left.

Neves turned to his comrade, who returned to the front of the shop. "Find anything?"

"These." The young agent handed Neves two books of poetry by Luís de Camões. "I think this is the poet banned by Salazar."

"You're thinking of Fernando Pessoa," Tiago said.

The young agent furrowed his brows.

"You might be right," Neves said. "But we'll take them to be examined by the Censorship Service to make sure the content is moral." He tipped his hat to Rosa and then left the bookshop with his companion.

The door jangled shut.

"That son of a bitch," Rosa said, rising from her stool. "He came to your apartment, didn't he?"

"Yes." Tiago picked a book off the floor and placed it on a shelf.

"When?"

"A few weeks ago."

"Why didn't you tell me?"

"I didn't want to worry you," Tiago said.

"Tell me what happened."

He ran a hand through his hair and, for the next few minutes, he told her about how Neves had broken into his apartment and held a dagger to his neck.

Rosa clenched her hands. "We should inform the head of the PVDE, Captain Agostinho Lourenço."

"You and I both know that nothing good will come from complaining to the secret police."

"We need to do something," she said.

"We are," Tiago said. "We're giving refugees a chance to rebuild their lives."

"Yes, but—"

"I can handle Neves and his harassment." He approached her and looked into her eyes. "We might be losing a few battles to Neves, but we're winning the war with helping refugees find freedom."

Rosa's eyes welled with tears.

"Hell," Tiago said, smiling, "if Neves's protégé isn't smart enough to search my office—or know the difference between Luís de Camões and Fernando Pessoa—we've got nothing to worry about."

Rosa smiled and wiped her eyes. "Help me clean up this mess. You don't pay me enough to do it by myself."

"The last time I checked, I wasn't paying you at all."

She chuckled. "True."

Together, they picked up books from the floor and placed them on shelves. Afterward, Tiago went to his office, removed two passports from the hidden hole in the floor, and gave them to Rosa.

"How about you go home for the day?"

"There's no reason for me to leave. I can't work on passports until my husband, Jorge, is asleep."

"Then take the afternoon off to relax," he said. "It'll help you be fresh to work tonight."

"What will you do?"

"I'm taking the afternoon off, too," he said. "We haven't taken some time off in ages."

"All right." She placed the passports in the hidden compartment in her purse and left.

Tiago watched her disappear around a street corner, and then placed a *Closed* sign in the front window. He locked the door and returned to his office. Instead of going home, he worked on forging travel papers until the early hours of the next morning.

CHAPTER 16

LISBON, PORTUGAL—MARCH 17, 1943

Tiago walked along the harbor and docks at Alcântara, filled with refugees who were patiently waiting to board a ship. Near an idle crane that was used to load cargo onto vessels, he located a French Jewish couple, Edmond and Blanche, with their six-month-old baby, Elisa, bundled in a blanket.

"How are you?" Tiago asked, approaching them.

"We're well." Edmond wrapped an arm around his wife, who was holding their baby.

Tiago smiled. "I have Elisa's travel papers."

Tears welled up in Blanche's eyes. "God bless you."

"*Merci*," Edmond said.

Tiago, after making sure no one was watching him, removed papers from his jacket and gave them to Edmond. He pointed to a gangplank, where people were going through a checkpoint to enter the ship. "It looks like I arrived on the dot. You should get in line."

The couple hugged him. They picked up their bags and weaved their way through the crowd.

Tiago sat at the base of the crane and waited for the family to safely board the ship. The couple had fled Tours while Blanche was pregnant. During their arduous escape through the Pyrenees mountains, Blanche had gone into labor a month early and delivered their baby under the canopy of a black pine tree. Rather than seek the help of a consul in Spain, the couple—fearing deportation back to France—hitched a ride on a farm truck to a remote area of the border, where they crossed into Portugal without being detected. Although the couple had travel papers and enough money sewn into the hems of their clothing to acquire ship passage, their baby had no birth certificate, let alone a passport. But things changed for the couple when they arrived in Lisbon and were instructed by a woman, who received a fake visa from Tiago, to visit Livraria Soares on Rua do Crucifixo.

Tiago watched the couple clear authorities and board the ship, and then left the docks. On his journey to the bookstore, the ship's horn gave a long blast, signaling its departure. A mixture of pride and sadness surged through him. *They're on their way to a new life. God, I wish my grandparents could be here to see refugees bound for freedom.*

He arrived at the bookstore shortly before noon. As he entered the front door, he expected to banter with Rosa about his late arrival. Instead, he found her sitting on her stool and chatting with the American woman from the Library of Congress.

"*Olá*," Maria said, turning to Tiago.

"Welcome back," he said. "How are you feeling?"

"Much better." Maria gestured to a crutch that was leaned against the counter. "I'm down to using one of these instead of two, and my stitches have been removed."

"That is good news," he said. "How long have you been here?"

"A little while," Maria said. "Rosa and I were having a splendid conversation."

Rosa tapped her wristwatch. "She's been waiting a long time for you. You're fortunate I'm good company, otherwise she might have left."

"*Obrigado*, Rosa." He looked at Maria. "My apologies for running late."

"It's quite all right," Maria said. "I stopped in to see if you've had any luck with acquiring more books. But before I forget, I washed and pressed your shirt. Thank you again for letting me wear it." She removed a folded white dress shirt and placed it on the counter.

Rosa grinned.

Tiago's faced turned flush. "It's not what you think, Rosa."

Rosa raised her palms. "I wasn't thinking anything."

Maria's eyes widened, as if realizing her gaffe. "Oh, it's nothing like that. Tiago rebandaged the wound on my back and let me borrow a shirt."

Rosa leaned forward on the edge of her seat, like a theatergoer watching a show.

"I obtained some books that might be of interest to you," Tiago said, attempting to divert the conversation.

"That's terrific," Maria said.

He glanced to the back of the shop to make certain there were no customers. "The books are at my apartment. The PVDE routinely inspect bookstores to confiscate publications that they think might be in violation of censorship laws. Given the nature of the books, I thought it would be best not to have them stored in the shop. I can retrieve the books and be back in fifteen minutes, assuming you have time."

"I'll go with you." Maria placed her crutch under her right arm.

"Are you sure?" he asked.

"Yes," Maria said. "My leg isn't hurting and I could use a little exercise."

"All right." Tiago retrieved his shirt from the counter.

Maria turned to Rosa. "I enjoyed our conversation. *Obrigada*."

"Me too," Rosa said.

Maria and Tiago walked to the door.

"Tiago," Rosa said. "May I have a word with you?"

He looked at Maria. "I'll meet you outside."

Maria nodded and left.

Rosa approached Tiago and placed her hands on her hips. "I like her."

"I'm relieved," he said. "I thought you were going to tell me something bad."

"I'm being serious," she said. "Don't mess things up with her."

"There isn't anything to ruin, Rosa. I'm selling her books—nothing more. We need the money, remember?"

She lowered her glasses to the tip of her nose. "You know what I mean."

"I need to go."

"Take your time coming back to work."

He leaned to her and pretended to inspect her face. "Who are you, and what have you done with Rosa Ribeiro?"

Rosa bit her lip, as if she was fighting back a smile.

Minutes later, Tiago and Maria arrived at his apartment in Chiado. It was clear, to Tiago, that Maria's health had improved, considering she was placing weight on her bad leg and needed no assistance to ascend the stairs.

He set his shirt on a table and gestured to a living room sofa. "I'll get the books."

Maria sat.

Tiago retrieved an old vacuum cleaner from a closet and joined her on the sofa.

She raised her brows.

He unzipped the vacuum's cloth bag and removed several books.

"Clever."

He tapped his shoe on the hardwood floor. "It's not a brilliant hiding place if an intruder discerns that I don't have a rug to clean."

"I doubt anyone would notice."

He placed the books between them on the sofa. "They're from my supplier in Braga. Prior to the war, he had a business relationship with a Dutch publisher of German writers in exile from Nazi Germany."

She examined the books, which included a directory of manufacturers in Hamburg, Germany, and a novel called *Mephisto* by Klaus Mann.

"They're excellent," Maria said. "How many books does your supplier have like these?"

"Many," he said.

"Order them—I'll buy them all."

"Perhaps we should discuss a price for these books first."

"How much do you want?"

"It'll cost more than the ones in my store, since some of these will be in violation of Portuguese censorship laws." He rubbed his chin as he contemplated a price.

Maria reached into her purse and gave him a stack of escudos. "This should cover it."

"That's far too much money."

"Consider it a retainer," she said.

He thumbed through the currency, which he estimated to be enough to buy freedom for several refugees, and placed it on a stand next to the sofa. "Portuguese libraries aren't known to have exorbitant funds to acquire books. How did the Library of Congress get so much money?"

"Taxpayers. The United States is a populous country."

Tiago nodded despite believing there was more to her explanation. "If you need a place to hide books at the shipyard before sending them to America, I have a dockworker friend who is trustworthy."

"That won't be necessary," she said. "We're not shipping the books."

He tilted his head. "What will you do with them?"

"We're converting them to microfilm to transport on a plane. It's a fast and permanent method to preserve the publications, and the film takes up far less cargo space."

"It sounds like the speed of getting the contents of the books to your superiors is important."

"It is."

Her nation's library is using her as a pawn to gather intelligence, he thought, but held his tongue. Although he expected that Maria would likely not disclose the true purpose of her role in Lisbon, he desired to know more about her. "I make it a point to get to know my business partners. Would you feel offended if I asked how you became a microfilm librarian?"

"It's a rather long story."

"I have time," he said. "Rosa insisted that I take my time returning to work, which is unlike her. You made quite an impression on her."

"That's nice to hear," she said. "Rosa spoke highly of you."

"About my punctuality?"

She smiled. "Everything but that."

"When we last met, you were kind and compassionate about my grandparents," he said. "I'd like to know more about you, if you're willing to tell me."

She fiddled with the sleeve of her blouse that protruded from her wool jacket. "I was an only child who was raised by photojournalist parents. My mom was born in Munich, Germany, and my father was born in Coimbra, Portugal. They emigrated to the United States on the eve of the Great War. They met at a boardinghouse in New York City, fell in love, and eventually had me."

"You grew up in New York?"

"Partly," she said. "As photojournalists, my parents often traveled to Europe for work. When I wasn't in school, they took me with them on business trips, mostly to France, England, Italy, Portugal, Spain, and Belgium. Some of my fondest childhood memories are of holding my parents' hands while we walked along Champs-Élysées in Paris."

"It sounds like you had a wonderful childhood."

"I did. We had little money, but we felt rich. My parents were affectionate, incredible listeners, and they taught me to be independent. I'm grateful for their gift of adventure; it enabled me to learn six languages and master the use of a thirty-five millimeter camera. And while they were working, I spent much of my time in libraries, where I fell in love with books."

"Your parents fostered your interest in libraries and photography."

"Yes," she said. "After college, I landed a job at the New York Public Library and, since I'd completed a course on microphotography, the library charged me with helping build their microfilm department."

"How did you end up serving overseas with the Library of Congress?"

"Part of my duties in New York was to microfilm foreign newspapers, which included photographs and articles of Nazi book burnings taking place all over Germany. I was infuriated and sickened by the images, and I wanted to do something to save the books and fight against Nazism." She drew a deep breath. "Let's just say I found a way to be recruited by the Library of Congress to serve abroad."

"I'm impressed."

"*Obrigada.*"

"Your parents must be proud of you."

"My dad spoils me with praise. He tells me he's proud of me, seemingly every chance he gets." She clasped her hands. "My mom is dead."

"I'm sorry."

She nodded. "She was killed in Spain while I was in college."

His heart sank. "May I ask how it happened?"

"My parents were on assignment covering news of the Spanish Civil War. While capturing photographs of a battle, they were caught in cross fire between Republican and Nationalist troops." She took a deep breath. "My mom was struck by gunfire and died in Dad's arms. I was notified at college by telegram."

He extended his hand toward her arm, but stopped shy of touching her. "It must have been devastating for you."

Maria nodded. "A week before Mom was killed, she captured a photograph of a brave, Spanish militia woman holding a rifle. It's displayed in our apartment in New Jersey and reminds me of my mom's spirit." She looked at the ceiling, as if she were searching through her memories. "It took time for me and my dad to work through our grief. There's not a day that goes by that I don't think about her, and I worry about my dad being lonely. She was the love of his life. Since her death, he's worked solely in the US on freelance assignments. I hope he'll someday regain his ardor to work overseas."

"He will."

"What makes you so sure?"

"If he's anything like you, he'll be on the first boat to Europe when peace is declared."

She smiled and tucked strands of hair behind an ear.

Tiago rubbed his chin, reflecting on her story. "Do you know the name of the battle your parents were covering in Spain?"

"The Battle of Brunete."

A dull ache spread through his chest. "I know it well."

"How?"

"I was nearby in the Siege of Madrid."

Her eyes widened. "Did you fight in the Spanish Civil War?"

He nodded.

"You don't seem like the kind of person who would have willingly fought for the Francoist dictatorship. Were you part of the troops that Salazar sent to Spain to support Franco?"

"No." He ran a hand through his hair. "I was an anti-fascist fighter."

She straightened her back. "If the Portuguese government knew, you'd surely be imprisoned. How did you keep it a secret?"

"My passport and visa records indicate that I was in France during the time of the Spanish conflict. I claimed to be working at my grandparents' vineyard in Bordeaux, but I slipped over the border to fight with the international brigade."

"It's risky to disclose such information," she said. "Perhaps you should refrain from telling people, especially ones you recently met, that you combatted fascism."

"I could also be arrested by the PVDE for smuggling you banned books," he said. "If one can't trust a librarian, who can one trust?"

"I like to think you're right." She smoothed her hands over her skirt. "May I ask you a question?"

"Of course."

"Since we last spoke, I've been thinking about your family. It's obvious that you care deeply for your parents and grandparents, all of whom have deep roots in winemaking. Why did you choose to leave the vineyards and become a bookseller?"

"It wasn't necessarily an easy decision to make," he said. "Like you, I have no siblings and, in a strange way, I felt like I was abandoning my family by going away to the university to obtain a degree in modern languages and literature. But my passion has always been books, and my family eventually accepted my decision, although I think my father hopes that someday I'll come to my senses and return to the Douro Valley to take over the family business. I doubt that it will happen. I cannot see myself doing anything that wasn't surrounded by books."

"Me too."

"Speaking of wine," he said, "would you like a bottle of my parents' port to take with you?"

"Only if you sample it with me before I leave."

He stepped away and returned with two glasses of port wine.

"What shall we toast to?" he asked, giving her a glass.

She looked at him. "To our families and a swift end to the war."

"*Saúde.*" He clinked her glass and sipped wine, rich with hints of blackberry and bitter chocolate.

She took a drink. "It's magnificent. Your dad is right; you've gone mad. One would need to be crazy for not wanting to be part of a vineyard that makes wine this good."

He laughed.

She swirled her wine. "So, what does your girlfriend think about you bringing women book buyers to your apartment?"

"I don't have a girlfriend." He sipped wine. "What does your fiancé think about you being in Lisbon?"

She ran a finger over the rim of her glass. "I don't have a fiancé."

They chatted for several minutes about their favorite books, foods, and music, and she told him about her coworkers, Pilar and Roy, who would be leaving on assignment in Madrid as soon as she was fully recovered. They finished their wine and set aside their glasses.

He stood and extended his hand. "I should let you get back to work."

"Unfortunately, yes." She clasped his hand and stood.

Tiago placed her books in a paper sack, and then added in two bottles of port, tomatoes, and a cabbage to give it the appearance of a grocery bag. He carried it for her as he accompanied her outside. With her improved stamina, she insisted on taking a tram instead of a taxi, so they walked two streets away to a tram stop.

Tiago scanned the area and lowered his voice. "You can't be too careful. Lisbon is filled with informants for the secret police."

She nodded.

A yellow electric tram approached and slowed to a stop.

"*Obrigada* for the books," Maria said. "I enjoyed our conversation."

"Me too."

Using one crutch, she climbed onto the tram.

He got on board and handed her the sack. Their fingers met and lingered. "Goodbye, Maria."

"*Adeus*."

Tiago, his skin tingling from her touch, slipped away. He exited to the curb and watched the tram rumble forward and disappear down the street.

Chapter 17

Estoril, Portugal—May 10, 1943

Maria, wearing a black cocktail dress with an asymmetric V-neckline, plucked a satin clutch purse from a dressing table and left her bedroom. Her peep-toe high-heeled shoes clicked over the hardwood floor as she entered the living room, where Pilar and Roy—who were dressed in semiformal evening attire—were examining stacks of newly acquired books.

Roy turned. His eyes widened.

"Spin around," Pilar said.

Maria did a twirl and ran a hand over her diamanté-covered bodice. "How do I look?"

"Like a Hollywood starlet," Pilar said.

Maria smiled. "I love that olive-green color on you."

"Really?" Pilar said.

"I do," Maria.

Roy buttoned his double-breasted suit jacket. "What about me?"

Maria placed a finger to her chin. "Are sure you want to wear that paisley tie?"

"What's wrong with it?" he asked, looking down at his tie.

"Yeah," Pilar said, glancing to Maria. "I was thinking the same thing. It clashes with the suit."

He furrowed his forehead. "I'll go put on another one. I'll be back in a minute."

"Roy," Maria said. "We're pulling your leg. You look swell."

Roy chuckled. "You had me worried. I'm not good at matching colors. Judith usually picks out my tie when we go someplace fancy."

It was their first night out since Maria had arrived in Lisbon. Despite her ailing hip, she'd canvassed newsstands and bookstores by day, and microfilmed acquisitions by night. Even Pilar and Roy had taken little, if any, time off from work. Maria had gradually regained her health. She no longer needed crutches and the pain in her hip had disappeared, except for a dull ache after being on her feet all day. Pilar and Roy suggested that they take an evening to celebrate Maria's recovery, but she'd delayed their invitation by making excuses about the amount of microfilming she had to finish, or that she needed to write a letter to her dad. *It feels wrong to celebrate me when twenty-four of the people on board the* Yankee Clipper *are dead.*

Three days ago, Maria's justifications for avoiding a night on the town became void when Roy was summoned to the American embassy for a telegram message from Kilgour, giving orders for Pilar and Roy to establish their operation in Madrid, which would leave Maria temporarily running things in Lisbon. Additionally, Kilgour provided a date and time for the trio to attend a meeting with the OSS operations head for the Iberian Peninsula—code name "Argus"—in the bar at the Hotel Palácio Estoril.

None of the three had visited Estoril, fifteen miles west of Lisbon on the Portuguese Riviera. It was an affluent seaside town with luxury hotels and the Casino Estoril. From what they knew, Estoril and the adjacent town of Cascais were home to the well-to-do and royalty in exile from German-occupied countries. Given the posh venue for their rendezvous with Argus, they'd purchased suitable attire using a bit of their OSS funds. Although it was important that they blend in with the crowd for their meeting, Maria disliked using money for clothing that could have gone to the war effort.

"What can you tell us about Argus?" Maria asked.

"Not much," Roy said. "I destroyed the telegram after reading it, per our protocol. Kilgour's message only provided a code name, and that Argus would be traveling to Spain to be the station chief in Madrid."

"I assume Argus wants to meet to discuss arrangements for you and Pilar to establish microfilm operations in Madrid."

"You're probably right," Roy said.

"I have to admit," Maria said, "I'm a smidge envious of this person having a code name."

"Me too," Pilar said.

"We're not performing a clandestine function like the other OSS agents," Roy said. "Our job is to openly pose as representatives of the Library of Congress. It's the way things are set up, and I'm sure there's a reason for the rules."

A memory of Kilgour's words ran through Maria's head. *Under no circumstance will IDC agents engage in spying. Espionage is the duty of highly trained OSS agents.* "I understand that Kilgour has limited our roles to the acquisition of foreign publications, but we're at war, and we need to defeat our enemies at any cost. I would not hesitate to break regulations if it improved our chances of bringing the bloodshed to an end."

"It's hard to argue with that," Pilar said.

Roy fidgeted with his tie and nodded. "Pilar was showing me your new shipment," he said, as if eager to change the subject. "It's impressive. Where did you get it?"

"Livraria Soares on Rua do Crucifixo," Maria said.

"Is that the crummy shop with all the poetry?"

"It is, and it's the best bookstore in Lisbon," Maria said. "The owner, Tiago, is finding us exactly what we're looking for."

"Jeez," Roy said. "I really misread that place."

Maria had been meeting weekly with Tiago, but she was disappointed that their length of interaction was curtailed by their commitment to duties—hers with acquiring publications and his with aiding refugees. However, the absence of time between them only fueled Maria's desire to see him. Aside from smuggling books for her, he'd confided in her by revealing details of his family's escape line for Jews and his military service to fight the spread of fascism. He'd been empathetic about the death of her mother, and she admired his selfless acts of service to aid freedom seekers. She trusted him and felt at ease in his presence. And although her commitment to her duties came first, she hoped to someday find a way to nurture their relationship.

Roy glanced at his watch. "We should go downstairs. Our driver will be picking us up soon."

"We have time for a photograph," Maria said. "It'll be nice to have something to remember our time together in Lisbon."

"I'll use my camera," Pilar said. "It has a self-timer so we can all be in it."

Pilar attached her camera to a tripod and, like a school photographer, she directed her friends on where and how to stand. She set the timer and dashed to her spot with Roy between her and Maria. The women smiled. Roy grinned with his pipe clasped between his molars. The camera clicked, and their moment of zeal faded.

Thirty minutes after leaving Lisbon, their vehicle pulled into the entrance of the Hotel Palácio. The front of the grand hotel had a white facade, and the grounds surrounding the complex were filled with lush gardens that were illuminated by electric lanterns and a moonlit sky. They paid the driver, exited the vehicle, and entered the front door, which was held open by a white-gloved attendant wearing a navy suit with gold buttons and a short red cape.

A glittering two-tier chandelier hung from an ornate, plaster ceiling in the lobby, and the walls were adorned with candle-like wall sconces, placed between large gilt-framed paintings. They walked along a travertine tile corridor, passing exquisitely dressed guests, including a woman wearing a princess ballgown with a diamond and ruby tiara. To Maria, it felt like she'd been transported to the Astors' mansion, filled with socialites for Colonel Donovan's speaking engagement.

They entered the hotel bar and took a seat at a corner table to allow privacy and a clear view to observe guests. A black-and-white-checkered stone floor covered the lounge, and the room was dimly lit with small table candles, twin brass lamps at opposite ends of the bar, and illuminated liquor bottle display shelves. The air smelled of leather, burnt cigars, and stale champagne. Two men with slicked-back hair and wearing tuxedos were seated on barstools, and a group of men in dark suits were chatting at a table on the opposite side of the room.

A waiter took their order and returned with drinks, a whisky for Roy and gin and tonics for Maria and Pilar.

"It might take us some time to recognize him," Roy said.

Maria sipped her drink, citrusy with a strong pine-like taste. "We won't have to. He'll easily recognize us—one man and two women."

Halfway through their cocktails, a tall man wearing a black suit and hat entered the bar. His eyes locked on them and he approached the table. "Good evening."

Roy swallowed. "Hello."

"Argus, I presume," Maria said confidently.

The man nodded.

"I'm Maria. This is Roy and Pilar."

Argus shook their hands, removed his hat, and sat. The man was in his mid-to-late-thirties with a receding hairline, upswept eyebrows, and meaty jowls. He smelled of expensive cologne with a hint of bergamot, and his silk tie was perfectly done with a dimple below the knot.

"Have you been waiting long?" Argus asked in a baritone voice.

"No," Roy said.

Argus looked at the waiter, who gave a nod and headed to the bar.

Maria sipped her drink.

Argus glanced over the room, as if to make certain they were out of earshot of guests. "I hear good things from headquarters about the microfilm work that you're doing."

Roy straightened his back. "Thank you, sir."

"I assume you're aware that I've the been appointed operations head of the Iberian Peninsula."

They nodded.

"I'll be in charge of things in Portugal and Spain," Argus said, "but I want to assure you that my being here will not interfere with your duties or reporting relationship to Kilgour."

A little change might have been nice, Maria thought, but held her tongue.

"I'm sure Kilgour is giving you proper assistance, and I'll be available to support you if the need should arise."

"Much obliged, sir," Roy said.

The waiter came to the table with a tray containing a bottle of white wine and four glasses. He uncorked the bottle, poured a splash into a glass, and gave it to Argus.

Argus took a sip and nodded to the waiter.

"It's Château d'Yquem," Argus said as the waiter poured wine. "It's one of the finest varietals of the Bordeaux region. The hotel's cellar was well stocked with French wine before the war erupted."

Maria thought of Tiago's Jewish grandparents, who were arrested by German soldiers at their vineyard. An image of people being forced into cattle railway cars flashed in her head. Her chest tightened. She looked at Argus and said, "The wine sounds lovely, sir, but I will pass on having some. I've chosen not to indulge in French wine until Allied forces liberate France from their German captors."

Roy and Pilar looked at Maria.

Argus raised his hand.

The waiter ceased pouring wine.

"I admire your principles," Argus said. "Will you drink Portuguese or Spanish wine instead?"

"Either would be splendid," Maria said.

Argus looked at the waiter. "Take this away and bring us a bottle of your finest Portuguese wine."

The waiter cleared the table and left.

Roy rubbed his unlit pipe, as if it were a worry stone.

"I leave tomorrow for Madrid," Argus said, seemingly unfazed by the wine selection change. "A small team has arrived in Lisbon, and I'm taking some of them with me to establish our Spanish intelligence operation. Roy, Pilar—how soon can you be there?"

"Our papers are in order," Pilar said. "We can leave immediately, if needed."

"I agree," Roy said.

"Very well. Take the train in the morning." Argus intertwined his fingers and turned to Maria. "I heard about you being on the *Yankee Clipper*. I'm sorry."

"Thank you," she said.

"Is there anything you need while your colleagues are in Madrid?"

"No, sir." Maria said.

"Good," Argus said. "If anything should come up, you can leave a message for me at the embassy."

The waiter returned and poured four glasses of red Portuguese wine. With the travel plans out of the way, they sipped their drinks and discussed the Allied war efforts taking place in Europe. Maria observed Argus's word choices, pronunciation, and familiarity of European cities and landmarks, and she deduced that he was well educated—likely overseas—and that he spoke several languages. *He's probably a wealthy business executive turned spy*, she thought, swirling her wine. Although she was disappointed that her friends would be leaving, she was glad, yet not surprised, that Colonel William Donovan had recruited a top-notch person to head OSS operations on the Iberian Peninsula.

"Have you been to Estoril?" Argus asked, topping off their glasses with more wine.

"No," Roy said.

"I've been here a week," Argus said, "and I've gotten the lay of the land. Hotel Palácio is considered a hotel for the Allies." He gestured with his eyes. "The men at the other end of the bar are British MI6."

Maria squeezed the stem of her glass.

"The Germans typically haunt the Hotel Atlântico, which is also in Estoril. But it's not unusual to see them in here having drinks. Yesterday, I recognized two Abwehr agents eating at a table across from British MI6 and some of my OSS agents."

Pilar shifted in her seat and took a drink of her wine.

"It's not necessarily easy to recognize Abwehr," Argus said. "The German military-intelligence service has some agents who speak English better than you or I."

Maria wondered, although briefly, if she could identify an Abwehr agent by means other than dialect.

"There are German spies everywhere, and Estoril is filled with rumors and counter-rumors. Don't trust hotel or bar staff—they could be paid informants. Everyone, it seems, is greasing their pockets by feeding stories of overheard conversation to spies."

Roy gulped his drink.

They finished their wine and their conversation dwindled. Argus paid the waiter for the wine and cocktails.

"Since it's your last night as a group in Portugal," Argus said, "I suggest going to Casino Estoril for some entertainment. It's a short walk from here."

"I appreciate the recommendation, sir," Maria said. "But I have work to do tonight, and Pilar and Roy have packing to—"

"I insist," Argus said. "I'm aware of your microfilm production. It's outstanding. I think it will be good for all of you to have a night off."

"Yes, sir," Maria said.

Argus stood and put on his hat. "I'll see the two of you in Madrid. Best of luck to you, Maria."

"Thank you, sir," Maria said.

Argus left the bar and disappeared down the hallway.

"Well, you heard the boss," Roy said. "Let's go to the casino."

They left the hotel and entered a manicured garden with a sloping, panoramic view of the Atlantic Ocean, its water shimmering with moonlight. The crashing of waves, mixed with laughter from a nearby champagne-drinking couple, penetrated the salty air. Maria, her head buzzing from alcohol, felt an urge to kick off her shoes and walk barefoot on the beach. Instead, she followed her friends to Casino Estoril, its entrance covered in bright lights like a Broadway theater.

Entering the casino, they were greeted by crowd noise and tobacco smoke. Throngs of well-dressed men and women were gathered at gaming tables of blackjack, roulette, craps, and baccarat. Bow-tied waiters, balancing trays of champagne and cocktails, maneuvered through the masses. Maria gazed over the casino, filled with blithe people drinking and gambling while much of the world was in turmoil. *To wealthy Europeans, Estoril is a war-free Shangri-la.*

"Do you know how to play blackjack?" Roy asked.

Maria and Pilar shook their heads.

"Come and watch me play," he said. "You'll pick it up in no time."

"Okay," Pilar said. "I've always wanted to learn how to play blackjack."

"Go on ahead," Maria said. "I'm going to mingle a bit."

"Are you sure?" Pilar asked.

Maria nodded. "I'll catch up with you later."

Pilar and Roy left, heading to a blackjack table with an open seat.

Maria, people-watching and eavesdropping, wandered through the casino. Conversations were spoken in Portuguese, English, French, Romanian, Hungarian, Polish, and Dutch. And as she neared a card table, filled with cigar-smoking men in fine tailored suits speaking in German, hairs rose on the back of her neck. Her heart thudded in her chest. In an attempt to clear the alcohol buzz from her head, she purchased a tonic water with lime at a bar, and then stood a few feet behind the Germans. She pretended to observe their game, all the while attempting to make out their words, mostly spoken while the dealer was shuffling cards. But after she listened for a few minutes to one of the Germans complain to his comrades that they were late for their dinner reservations, the men tossed in their cards and left.

Maria, disappointed with learning little about the men, other than they were headed to the Hotel Atlântico, scanned the casino for another group on which to eavesdrop.

"*Boa noite*," a male voice said from behind her.

Maria turned to a tall, blond-haired man wearing an ash suit, white shirt, and steel-blue satin necktie. "*Olá*"

"*Você é português*?"

She shook her head. "American."

"Forgive me," the man said in English. "I thought you might be Portuguese."

French? Swiss? she thought, attempting to identify his accent. "You're half right. My dad was born in Portugal."

He smiled and extended his hand. "I'm Lars Steiger."

"Maria Alves." She shook his hand. "Where do you call home, Lars?"

"Bern, Switzerland."

She took a sip of tonic water. "And what brings you to Portugal?"

"I'm a banker," he said. "I do business in Lisbon."

"Your English is excellent," she said.

"Thank you. It's from years of working in international banking, and from doing a stint in London." He removed a silver case from the inside pocket of his jacket. "Cigarette?"

"No, thank you. I don't smoke."

"Do you mind if I do?"

"No."

As he lit a cigarette, she got a better look at Lars. He was in his late forties, given his V-shape hairline and slight wrinkles at the corners of his blue eyes. His physique was muscular and fit, like someone who spent their leisure time on a tennis court. A gold wedding band adorned his left hand.

He puffed on his cigarette. "What brings you to Portugal?"

"I'm a librarian with the Library of Congress," she said. "We're working to preserve books and records during the world crisis."

"A noble endeavor," he said. "Are you having any success?"

She sipped her drink. "Some, but not as much as I would like."

He took a drag and exhaled smoke through his nose. "Are you here alone?"

"I'm with friends. They're playing blackjack or, more likely, losing all their money, which will require me to pay for our fare back to Lisbon."

He laughed. "It sounds like you're wise with your money."

"If you're on a librarian's salary, you pinch pennies, not bet them on games of chance."

"I see." He gestured to a roulette table. "If you don't like to gamble your own money, would you like to join me to wager some of mine?"

"That's an enticing offer." She swirled her drink. "What would your wife think about you inviting a woman to the gaming tables?"

He glanced at the ring on his finger. "I'm a widower."

"I'm sorry," she said, wondering if he was being truthful. "How long ago did it happen?"

"Three years." He shifted his weight. "My wife, Gisela, and my children—Perrine and Nilo—were killed in a car accident."

She swallowed. "I'm deeply sorry."

"Thank you," he said. "I wear the ring to remind me of her and what we had together."

Maria noticed a deep sadness in his eyes, and she felt a twinge of guilt for initially being skeptical of his story.

He adjusted his gold cuff links. "The roulette wheel is whispering my name. It was a pleasure meeting you, Maria. I hope that your work in Lisbon is fruitful." He tamped out his cigarette in a nearby ashtray and walked toward a gaming table.

A decision stirred inside her. "One game."

He stopped and turned.

She approached him. "I'll play one game of whatever it is that you're playing. But if your intentions are to entice me to your room, you'll be disappointed. I'm not interested in anything more than conversation."

"Are you always this candid?"

"Yes."

"I like your honesty; it's an admirable trait." He placed his cigarette to his lips and inhaled. "If you're wondering why I spoke to you, it's because you were alone and appeared in need of a bit of company. And to be forthright, you're too young for me."

"Good," she said. "We should get along splendidly."

Lars led her to a table, where a croupier, who was running the roulette game, signaled with his hand to a floor supervisor. Soon, a casino employee arrived with a leather briefcase, which he opened to reveal a large stash of casino tokens. The employee stacked the tokens on the table in front of Lars.

Maria noticed that the other players were placing money on the table for the croupier to exchange for tokens. *Lars must be a high roller at the casino.*

Lars briefly explained to Maria the game of roulette with the odds and payouts. "Tell me what you'd like to do and I'll place the bets."

"I barely know what I'm doing. I'll lose your money."

He patted a stack of tokens. "I'll earn more."

"All right. Don't say that I didn't warn you." She gazed over the squares on the roulette table. "Let's place a bet on black."

Lars placed a stack of tokens on a square with a black diamond. "How about picking four straight up number bets?"

"Okay," she said. "Let's go with nineteen, twenty-one, twenty-four, and thirty-two."

He placed large stacks of tokens on the table to mark their bets.

That's far too much to wager. She clasped her drink between her hands.

"No more bets!" the croupier called. He spun the wheel and rolled the ball on a circular running rail.

Her tension grew as the wheel whirled. Seconds later, the ball—losing momentum on the running rail—dropped into the center of the wheel, where it bounced several times and settled into a slot.

The croupier looked at the wheel. "Twenty-four, black, even!"

Maria turned to Lars. "What does that mean?"

"It means we won."

"Holy mackerel."

The croupier cleared the losing bets and placed an equal stack of tokens next to their bet on black, and a huge stack of tokens for their straight up bet on the number twenty-four.

Her eyes widened. "That's a lot."

"A winning straight up bet pays thirty-five to one," he said.

"Then we should quit while we're ahead."

"Let's play some more," he said.

"I promised one game," she said.

"What will you do while you wait for your friends to finish gambling?"

"Mingle."

"You'll have more fun here," he said. "What do you have to lose, besides my money?"

Maria pondered his offer. *Maybe a little entertainment will be good for me.* "All right. I'll stay."

For over an hour, they played roulette. Maria picked the numbers, and Lars placed the bets. The stack grew and shrank as they won and lost their wagers. To Maria, the game was thrilling despite that she was risking nothing. She wondered if Lars gambled because he was a rich banker and enjoyed the entertainment, or if it was a means to distract himself from the loss of his family. She decided it was the latter when she picked up on his habit of fidgeting with his wedding band while the roulette wheel whirled round and round.

"This was fun," Maria said, "but I need to go."

"One moment." Lars motioned to the croupier. Soon, the casino employee with the briefcase returned.

Lars slid a large stack of tokens to the edge of the table and turned to the employee. "Take these to the cashier to exchange for money, and see that the proceeds are given to Maria."

The employee nodded.

"Oh, no," Maria said, raising her palms. "I don't want your money."

"It's the casino's money," Lars said. "And it's half of the winnings from the bets that you picked."

"I can't," Maria said.

The employee placed the tokens in the briefcase.

"It's yours to keep," Lars said.

"Then I'll give it away," she said.

"As you wish." Lars reached into his pocket, removed a business card, and gave it to her. "Thank you for the delightful evening—and your good luck. Look me up if you plan to return to the casino. These days, I'm spending more time in Portugal than Switzerland."

Maria slipped the card into her purse. "Goodbye."

He bowed his head, and then turned to the roulette table and placed a bet.

Maria followed the casino employee to a cashier station. The tokens were tallied and she was given several bundles of escudos. Since there was too much money to fit inside her clutch purse, the cashier gave her a cloth money bag to carry her winnings. She left the cashier and caught up with Pilar and Roy, who were leaving their blackjack table.

"How'd you do?" Maria asked.

"Terrible," Roy said.

"I did well." Pilar smiled and held out a handful of tokens. "Dinner is on me tonight."

"Congratulations. But I want you to save it to spend in Madrid." Maria lifted her cloth bag.

Roy's mouth dropped open.

"What'd you do," Pilar asked, "rob a bank?"

"A Swiss bank, to be precise."

"I'm confused," Roy said.

"I'll tell you all about it on the way home," Maria said. "It's probably not a good idea to be walking around here with a bag of money. Let's cash in Pilar's winnings and get a bite to eat in Lisbon."

At the cashier station, they exchanged Pilar's tokens for escudos. While making their way to the exit, Maria glanced at Lars, who was still at the roulette table. His plentiful stacks of tokens had dwindled to a few miniature piles, but a casino employee was unloading another briefcase full of tokens. *Goodness. How much money does he have to gamble?* She buried her thought and left the casino feeling pleased to treat her friends—by virtue of a chance meeting with a Swiss banker—to a good meal on their last night together in Lisbon.

CHAPTER 18

LISBON, PORTUGAL—MAY 11, 1943

Maria gripped the handle of a shipping trunk, opposite from Pilar, that was filled with camera equipment and microfilm. Together, they carried it to the front door of their apartment and placed it next to Pilar's suitcase. While they waited for Roy to arrive, they sat in the kitchen and ate a breakfast of black coffee and toasted bread with pear jam.

"What are you going to do with the money you won at the casino?" Pilar asked.

"Give it to charity," Maria said.

"Which one?"

Maria's mind raced. She trusted Pilar implicitly. Equally, she didn't want to breach Tiago's confidence in her by revealing his secretive work. "A charity that will aid Jewish refugees. Tiago, the bookseller on Rua do Crucifixo, is knowledgeable about their plight. I plan to talk with him about how to make a donation."

"That would be a good use of the money. It breaks my heart to see so many desperate people fleeing Europe to escape persecution." Pilar looked at Maria. "When are you going to see him?"

"Today."

A slim smile formed on Pilar's face.

"What are you thinking?"

"You fancy Tiago."

Maria's skin turned warm. "He's delivering us superior Axis publications to microfilm. His bookstore is the best source for our acquisitions, and his salesclerk, Rosa, is quite entertaining to speak with."

"I've noticed that you refer to him as Tiago, rather than his bookstore, Livraria Soares. When you discuss other proprietors, you typically use the name of the shop."

"I hadn't noticed," she said.

Pilar set aside her empty cup. "I've been meaning to tell you—I was in Tiago's bookstore yesterday."

Maria perked her head.

"I was in the area, so I stopped in to pick up a morning newspaper."

"Did you see Tiago?" Maria asked.

"I did."

"What did he say?"

"He asked how you were doing."

Maria picked at crumbs on her plate. "And what did you tell him?"

"I told him you were well." Pilar leaned forward. "You *are* fond of him, aren't you?"

"Maybe I am." Maria ran her hands over her skirt. "But I have no time for a personal life. My duties come first."

"You're going to be alone," Pilar said. "It might be good to have a friend while Roy and I are in Madrid."

Maria drew a deep breath and nodded. An emptiness spread through her chest. "I'm going to miss you."

"Me too."

"How are you feeling about going back to Spain?"

"I'm worried," Pilar said. "It's no longer the country that my parents and I left before the civil war. It'll be difficult to see Spaniards living under a dictatorship."

"I'm sure it will be." She looked at Pilar, her eyes filled with apprehension. "I believe in you. You'll do great things in Madrid."

"Do you really think so?"

"I know so," Maria said. "And I'm expecting you to uncover an enemy publication that will help us win the war."

Pilar smiled. "I'll do my best."

A knock came from the door.

"I'll get it." Maria left the table and opened the door.

Roy entered and placed two pieces of luggage on the floor. He looked at Pilar, who was stacking plates in the sink. "Ready to go?"

"Yeah," Pilar said. "Give me a minute to wash a few dishes."

"Leave it—I'll take care of it later," Maria said. "Would you like me to come with you to the train station?"

"That's very kind of you to offer, but it's not necessary," Pilar said.

"We'll send you a telegram to let you know when we arrive in Madrid," Roy said. "I'll keep you informed of when I'm cleared to return to Lisbon."

Maria helped them carry their luggage to the curb, where a driver loaded items into the trunk of a taxi. She hugged them goodbye and, as the taxi pulled away, a wave of loneliness washed over her. She returned to the apartment, locked the door behind her, and began microfilming a book that she'd procured from Tiago. Several pages into the document, a knock came from the door.

Pilar must have forgot something. Maria put down her camera and approached the door. *But why isn't she using her key?* She peeked through a peephole. Her eyes widened as she recognized the man by his upswept eyebrows. She flipped open the lock and opened the door.

Argus removed his hat from his head. "*Bom dia.*"

"*Olá*," Maria said. "You missed Pilar and Roy. They're on their way to the train station."

"I'm aware," Argus said. "I was waiting for them to leave so I could speak privately with you. May I come in?"

Maria's skin prickled. She gestured for him to enter.

He stepped inside and closed the door. "Do you have coffee?"

"There's some leftover on the stove," she said. "I'll warm it up."

"No need. I'll drink it as is."

They sat at the kitchen table with lukewarm cups of coffee. Maria's brain buzzed with reasons why Argus might want to speak with her alone. *Is it about the books that I've acquired? Did I say something last night to upset him? Does Kilgour want to reassign me?* She took a sip of her coffee, acidic and bitter.

"I thought you were going to Madrid?" Maria asked.

"I've delayed my trip."

"May I ask why?"

He took a gulp of coffee. "I was informed that you were spending time with a man at Casino Estoril. I want to know details about your encounter and what you discussed."

Maria straightened her spine. "Everything?"

"Yes."

For several minutes she told him about meeting a Swiss banker named Lars Steiger, joining him at the roulette table, and him insisting on sharing their winnings.

"Did he discuss anything personal or business related?" he asked.

"He mentioned that he's a widower, and that his family was killed in a car crash. He spends much of his time in Portugal on banking business." She retrieved her clutch purse from the counter, removed a business card, and gave it to Argus. "I made it clear that I had no interest in him, but he gave me his card and told me to look him up if I returned to Estoril."

Argus eyed the business card and placed it on the table. "What did you tell him about yourself?"

"I told him who I was, and that I was here on behalf of the Library of Congress—I followed the protocol script that was given to us by Kilgour."

He nodded and swirled his coffee.

"What's this all about?" Maria asked, her patience waning.

"Lars Steiger is under the surveillance of Britain's intelligence services," Argus said.

"Did an MI6 agent inform you about seeing me and Lars together?"

"Yes," he said. "Lars is no ordinary Swiss banker. We believe he's laundering Nazi gold for Germany to acquire Portugal's wolfram."

Maria's eyebrows rose.

"Are you familiar with wolfram?"

"A little," she said, gathering her composure. "I know it's a metal that is crucial for the making of hard steel, like in armor-piercing shells and tanks."

"That's correct," Argus said, appearing impressed. "Portugal is the largest European source of wolfram. Most of it is mined in the mountains near Covilhã, and the country has been selling it to both Germany and Britain in an attempt to appease both powers. Without wolfram, Hitler's military would collapse. Germany is doing everything that it can to secure it by either working through Portugal's dictator, Salazar, or by buying it on the black market and smuggling it through the mountains to Spain."

"How involved is Lars Steiger with this?"

"Steiger appears to be the mastermind of the gold-laundering operation."

Her mouth turned dry.

"We think he's using a complex scheme between German, Swiss, and Portuguese banks. It's believed that Portugal's Salazar wants to keep his financial dealings with the Germans a secret, so there is no direct transfer of gold from Germany to Portugal."

Maria rubbed her forehead. "Instead, the gold flows through Swiss banks."

"Precisely." He took a gulp of coffee. "It's also believed that most, if not all, of the Nazi gold used to acquire wolfram was stolen from the central banks and citizens of German-occupied countries."

Oh, dear God.

"Steiger is well connected," Argus said. "He has frequent interaction with Salazar's banker and the German ambassador to Portugal. Also, he's linked to German military intelligence services. MI6 surveillance has observed him, on more than one occasion, in the company of Admiral Wilhelm Canaris, head of the Abwehr."

Maria felt sick to her stomach. Her head ached, attempting to take in everything that Argus had told her. She pushed aside her cup. "Why are you revealing all of this to me?"

"I want you to get to know Lars Steiger."

She shifted in her seat.

"Any knowledge we obtain about Steiger's gold laundering, as well as the amount of wolfram being smuggled on the black market, would be advantageous to the Allied fight. Also, if you're able to gain Steiger's confidence, it might prove useful for intelligence or counterintelligence purposes."

"Are you asking me to be a spy?"

"Yes."

Adrenaline surged through her veins. "How do you expect me to gain his trust?" she asked.

"We'll leave that up to you."

"I won't sleep with him," she said, firmly.

"That's not what I was referring to," he said. "You're a resourceful person. You've managed to obtain vital Axis information, including the location of arms factories in Germany. And I know about how you conned your way into the Astor mansion to get yourself recruited by Colonel Donovan. In fact, the colonel likes to tell the story as an example of the ingenuity and guts that are needed by someone worthy of serving in the OSS. If you can break into the home of the richest man in America, I'm thinking that you might be cunning enough to obtain intelligence on a Swiss banker—without the means of seduction."

Maria drew a deep breath and exhaled.

"If you accept my proposal, you would need to continue the front of being a representative of the Library of Congress, and you would need to keep your surveillance on Steiger a secret from Pilar and Roy. Only you, OSS headquarters, and I would know about your espionage."

"What about Kilgour?"

"He won't be informed, unless Colonel Donovan deems it's necessary."

"Is there anything else I should know?"

He placed the tips of his fingers together. "If you agree to spy on Steiger, it would come at great risk. If you're discovered, you could be arrested by the PVDE for acts against Salazar's regime, and there's the possibility that the Germans will want to have you assassinated. We would, of course, get you out of Portugal if we became aware that your cover was broken."

She clasped the table to keep her hands from trembling. "What if I decline?"

"You'll continue your role in Lisbon, acquiring and microfilming Axis publications."

"So, I have a choice in the matter."

Argus nodded. He stood and put on his hat. "I've given you much to consider. Take a day to weigh my offer. You can reach me at the Hotel Palácio. I'm staying as a guest under an alias—Howard Davies."

Maria, a flurry of emotions swirling inside her, rose from her chair. She accompanied him to the door, all the while praying for the strength to make the right decision. But as she clasped the doorknob, an image of her mother's photograph of a Spanish militia woman flashed in her head. A surge of patriotism flowed through her veins. Despite Argus's warning that her life would be at stake, she turned to him and said, "I can give you my answer now, sir. My decision is yes."

Chapter 19

Lisbon, Portugal—May 11, 1943

Tiago, running late for work due to delivering a forged passport to a refugee at Rossio train station, lengthened his stride in an attempt to make up for lost time. He traversed side streets and, as he rounded the street corner to Rua do Crucifixo, his bookstore came into view. A black sedan was parked at the curb, and Agent Neves and his cauliflower-eared protégé were standing on the sidewalk smoking cigars. *Damn it.* His shoulder muscles tensed. Refusing to give in to their intimidation, he approached the men.

"*Bom dia,*" Neves said, blocking the sidewalk. He puffed on his cigar. "You lack a routine."

"I've never been one to adhere to a schedule," Tiago said.

Neves flicked ash.

Tiago looked through the store window. Inside, Rosa and Artur were stacking newspapers onto the counter. "Are you interested in buying a morning paper?"

Neves picked a fleck of tobacco from his lip. "I don't buy goods or services from Jews."

The protégé snickered.

"Excuse me," Tiago said, fighting back his irritation, "I need to get to work."

Tiago brushed by them and entered his store. He expected the agents to follow him, but they remained outside, smoking their cigars.

Artur hoisted his newspaper sack onto his shoulder. "*Olá*, Senhor Soares."

"How are you, Artur?" Tiago asked, forcing a smile.

"I'm well, sir," the boy said.

Rosa opened the cash register. "It's nearly empty. Do you have money to pay him?"

Tiago removed escudos from his pocket. "How many newspapers?"

"Twelve," Artur said.

Tiago did the math in his head and paid him.

"*Obrigado*." The boy left, darted past the PVDE agents on the sidewalk, and scurried down the street.

Tiago looked at Rosa. "How long have they been outside?"

"They were here when I arrived for work."

"I'm sorry. Maybe I should schedule my meetings in the evenings instead of mornings."

"*Não*. I can handle them." Rosa glared at the agents through the window. "It's the third day this week that they've been skulking about our street. They're scaring away our customers."

"Maybe I should have chosen a bookstore location that wasn't within walking distance to PVDE headquarters."

"True," Rosa chuckled. "But it wouldn't have mattered today—Neves arrived by automobile."

Tiago nodded. "I've got a few things to do in my office."

Rosa stood and motioned for him to walk to the rear of the shop. She picked up a book and pretended to show it to Tiago. "Last night on my way home, I was approached by a refugee named Henri Levin."

Tiago leaned in. "Was it the same man in the photo that Agent Neves showed us?"

"Yes," she said. "Except he's changed his appearance."

"What did he want?"

"He tried to come here to speak with you, but he feared being seen by the PVDE. He'd spotted me entering the store and he waited a few streets away until I left work."

"What did he say?"

"He's on the run and needs papers."

"Did you gather the information we need?"

Rosa shook her head.

"Why not?"

"This is far more dangerous than the other forgeries we've done. He's wanted by the PVDE and the Gestapo, and I didn't want to commit you to helping him unless you were on board."

"Of course I am," Tiago said.

"That's what I thought you would say. I told Levin to be at the Carmo church at noon today, and that you would show up if you were willing to help him."

"Are you sure that you're okay with this?" Tiago asked.

She glanced to the men outside. "To hell with them. Let's do this."

Tiago, anticipating that he might be trailed by the secret police, left early for his rendezvous with Levin. Neves had left in his automobile shortly after Tiago arrived for work, but his young protégé had remained at his post, presumably on Neves's orders to observe who entered and left the bookstore. And as Tiago expected, the young PVDE agent followed him. Instead of heading to his meeting place, Tiago took a detour to a nearby café. He stood at the bar and sipped an espresso while the agent waited outside. After finishing his drink, Tiago went to the water closet, opened a window, and climbed through to a side street. He wiped wrinkles from his clothes and walked away, wondering if the agent would admit to Neves that a bookish proprietor gave him the slip.

At noon, he arrived at the medieval ruins of the Carmo Convent, located in the Chiado neighborhood on a hill overlooking the Rossio Square. The convent was destroyed in the Great Lisbon Earthquake of 1755; however, its church remained in partial ruins. The stone ceiling above the nave had collapsed, leaving pointed arches and pillars that resembled the rib cage of a giant carcass. He entered the remains of the church, his shoes crunching over ancient rubble. He caught movement through the corner of his eye and turned.

A bearded man with dark, sunken eyes raised his hands.

"Levin?"

The man nodded.

"I'm Tiago." He approached him and shook his hand.

Levin was barely recognizable from the man in Neves's photograph. Instead of having slicked-back hair with a neatly trimmed goatee and mustache, he had a mane of unkempt salt-and-pepper hair and a chest-length beard. His clothes sagged on his body, giving him the appearance of someone who'd lost a significant amount of weight.

"I understand you're looking for me," Tiago said.

"There are refugees at the docks who say you can provide travel papers."

"Perhaps," Tiago said. "Let's start with you telling me why the PVDE and the Gestapo are searching for you."

Levin slipped his hands into his pockets. "I'm a former German journalist from Berlin. Prior to the war, I was exiled for my criticism of Germany's Nazism and militarism. I fled with my family to Marseille, France, where I set up an independent press to report on events taking place in Germany. I'm viewed as a radical critic of Hitler, and when France was invaded by the Germans, I again became a fugitive." He paused, stroking his beard. "I guess you could say that I've run out of places to hide."

"I understand why the Gestapo wants you arrested," Tiago said. "But I was recently approached by Agent Neves of the PVDE, requesting me to inform him of your whereabouts. Why is Neves determined to find you?"

"I'm aware of Neves," Levin said. "He's pro-Nazi fanatic, and I think he's being paid by the Gestapo to help kidnap me. If I'm apprehended, I'll be handed over to the Gestapo and sent to a Germany prison, or worse."

Tiago felt pity for him. "Neves won't catch you. I'll have you out of Portugal before he can find you."

"Thank you."

"Do you have any identification, passports, or travel papers to give me something to work with?"

Levin removed papers from the inside pocket of his jacket and gave them to him.

Tiago examined the documents, all of which were expired. "I see that you have a wife, Estelle, and a daughter, Albertine."

Levin nodded. "Albertine turned ten years old last week."

"I'm sure it hasn't been easy for her and your family," Tiago said. "How's everyone's spirits?"

"To be honest, not so good." Levin's bottom lip quivered.

Tiago placed a hand on his shoulder. "Tell them freedom is near, and that Albertine will celebrate her eleventh birthday in America."

"I will." He wiped his eyes with his sleeve. "I probably should have told you this first—I don't have much money."

"None is needed," Tiago said. "Do you have a place to stay in Lisbon?"

"We're hiding in the home of a Jewish fisherman."

"Good," Tiago said. "What is the address?"

Levin shifted his weight.

"I'll need to know where to find you, especially if I need to reach you on short notice."

Levin provided the address.

"It'll take time to create forged passports and documents," Tiago said. "Each of you will have a new name and identity. Also, new photographs will need to be taken."

Levin ran a hand over his beard. "I look quite different from the picture in my old passport. My wife looks the same, but my daughter has grown several inches since her old passport was issued."

"It'll be safer if we use new photographs for everyone."

Tiago led Levin to a section of rubble, overgrown with weeds.

He lifted a flat stone the size of a dinner plate. "We'll use this as a dead drop. Leave a note under this if you need to reach me and don't feel it's safe to come to my bookstore. I'll check it every other day. You do the same."

Levin nodded.

They left the ruins of the Carmo Convent in opposite directions. Normally, Tiago would immediately make arrangements for photographs to be taken. But this was, by far, the most perilous forgery he and Rosa had embarked upon, and the person he'd been using for portraits had become wary of helping him, due to the growing number of refugee referrals. On his way back to the bookstore, he thought through names of photographers and people he knew who owned professional-grade cameras. And he decided that he trusted none of them more than Maria.

Chapter 20

Lisbon, Portugal—May 12, 1943

Tiago didn't have to wait days for Maria to stop by his bookstore. After closing the shop for the evening, he went to his apartment building and found her, sitting on the fourth-floor landing near his door.

"Maria," he said, feeling surprised.

"*Olá*." She stood and dusted her skirt.

"Is everything all right?"

She nodded and picked up a grocery bag. "I need to speak with you."

"Of course."

Tiago unlocked the door and they entered. He turned on a light and bolted the door.

"Were you waiting long?" he asked.

"An hour."

"Why didn't you come to the bookstore?"

"Because of this." She held out the grocery bag. "I meant to give it to you sooner. I've been sidetracked with work."

Tiago took the bag, which was light in weight, and placed it on the kitchen table. He reached inside and removed a cloth sack. "What's this?"

"Something to help refugees reach America."

He loosened the bag's string and looked inside. His eyes widened. "Where did you get this money?"

"Casino Estoril," she said. "I won it playing roulette."

He sifted through stacks of bills. "There must be a couple thousand escudos in here."

She smiled. "There's more than that."

He ran a hand through his hair. "Why are you doing this?"

"I have all of the funds I need from my government to acquire Axis publications, and I can think of nothing better than using this money to buy someone's freedom."

"I'm stunned—and grateful. Your gift will change lives." He set aside the money, approached her, and gently clasped her hand.

Her eyes met his.

"*Obrigado*."

She swallowed. Her fingers intertwined with his. "*De nada*."

He felt her slip away.

She approached a window and looked outside. "My colleagues have left for an assignment in Madrid."

"How long will they be gone?"

She turned to him. "I don't know."

He shifted his weight. "How would you feel about spending more time with me?"

"That would be lovely," she said. "Unfortunately, I'll be doing the job of three librarians while my colleagues are out of town. I'll be working more hours than ever and will have little free time."

Tiago nodded. He buried his disappointment and said, "While we're on the topic of work, I received a small shipment from my supplier in Braga. Would you like to see it?"

"Yes."

Maria sat on the living room sofa and Tiago stepped away. He returned with six books, two German magazines, and a leather-bound directory.

Maria picked up the directory titled *Vereinigte Suhl-Zella-Mehlisser Waffenfabriken* (*United Suhl-Zella-Mehlisser Arms Factories*). Her jaw dropped open. "Holy mackerel."

"It was published in 1937," he said, sitting beside her.

She thumbed through the pages. "Incredible. It's an association of arms manufacturers that supply the Wehrmacht."

"You look pleased."

"I am."

He watched her examine the German publications, and a memory of meeting with Henri Levin entered his head. His shoulder muscles tensed. "May I ask a favor of you?"

"Of course."

"Would you be willing to take some photographs for me?"

She set aside a book and turned to him. "Sure. What are they for?"

I need to tell her. She might discover the true purpose when she photographs Levin and his family, and I'd rather her find out from me. "Passports."

"Why not seek help from Portuguese emigration authorities?"

He looked at her. "I'm forging travel documents for a Jewish family hiding from the PVDE and the Gestapo."

Her eyebrows rose. "Tell me about them."

For several minutes he told her about Levin, a pacifist and former German journalist, who was struggling to stay one step ahead of being captured by German and Portuguese secret police. Also, he revealed details of his clandestine work, forging travel papers and bribing stewards, to smuggle Jewish refugees onto ships bound for America.

"Some asylum seekers arrive in Lisbon with expired visas and improper paperwork," Tiago said. "They're at risk of being deported, so I help them by creating fake or altered papers."

"Levin might be on wanted lists with the PVDE and emigration authorities," she said. "I assume you'll need to create a new identity for him and his family, as well as supporting documents to verify who they are."

"Correct," he said. "I will also fabricate birth certificates and visa applications."

"Where did you learn how to counterfeit documents?" she asked.

"I'm self-taught," he lied.

She tilted her head. "You're protecting someone, aren't you?"

He nodded. "I hate placing you in this predicament. My photographer has become unwilling to help me, and I need someone whom I can trust. I'll understand if you don't want to do this. If so, I'll find another—"

"I'll help you."

"Are you sure?"

"I am."

"*Obrigado*."

They agreed on a date and time for the photography session, which Maria insisted would be easier and safer if done in her apartment. He would have preferred a remote location for the session, but he relented to her request.

"I should go," Maria said, rising from the sofa.

Tiago stood. He retrieved her grocery bag, loaded it with the Axis publications, and carried it to the door.

She took the bag from him and placed it at her feet. "Before I go, I want you to know that I value your openness and trust in me, and it pains me that I haven't reciprocated the same to you. I've been rather guarded and you might be thinking that I have no interest in you, other than as a purveyor of Axis books."

"I don't think that about you."

"There are things that I want to tell you, but I can't right now. I hope you understand."

"It's all right."

She drew a deep breath. "You might be seeing less of me in the coming weeks and months, and I don't want you to get the impression that you've said or done something wrong, or that I'm avoiding you."

"I won't." He looked into her eyes. "I promise."

She leaned in and wrapped her arms around him.

He pulled her tight and pressed his cheek to her hair. His heartbeat quickened.

"When I'm away, please know that you'll be in my thoughts."

"And you'll be in mine," he breathed.

Maria stood on her toes and kissed him on the cheek. She slipped away, picked up her bag of books, and left.

As the clack of her footsteps faded down the stairs, conflicting emotions surged through him. His heart urged him to run after her, confess his feelings for her, and tell her that they could find a way to be together. But his brain told him to respect her wishes of placing her job first. *We're fighting a war on different fronts.* An overwhelming feeling of *saudade* washed over him. He closed the door and slumped onto the sofa, and prayed that Maria's duties wouldn't place her in jeopardy.

CHAPTER 21

ESTORIL, PORTUGAL—MAY 18, 1943

Maria, wearing a navy evening dress with a pearl necklace and earrings, stood outside her apartment building as a black Mercedes-Benz with flared front fenders stopped at the curb. She pressed her purse to her stomach, attempting to suppress her disquietude. A portly man in a dark suit and driver's cap exited the vehicle.

"Maria Alves?"

"Yes," she said.

"I'm Heitor," he said, tipping his cap. "I'm your chauffeur to take you to Estoril." He opened the rear door and gestured with his hand.

Maria sat in the back seat and tucked her dress around her legs.

The driver took his place behind the wheel and pulled away. "Senhor Steiger is running late with an out-of-town business meeting. He requested that I bring you to his home. He thought you would be more comfortable waiting there than at the casino."

"That's very considerate of him." Maria twisted her mother's sapphire ring on her finger. "Where's his meeting?"

The driver's eyes peered through the rearview mirror. "I'm not sure."

He might know and not be permitted to say.

Maria rolled down her window in hopes that sea air would calm her nerves, surging like electrified wire. She drew in an elongated breath and leaned back in her seat. For the duration of the trip, she rehearsed her plan, over and over, in her head.

Soon after accepting Argus's request to spy on Lars Steiger, she'd fetched his business card from her purse and telephoned him. She'd left a message with a receptionist and he called her back within an hour. She'd thanked him for the delightful evening and his generosity, and she informed him that, with her colleagues out of town, she would like to take him up on his offer to join him at the casino. They set a date and Lars insisted on arranging for a driver to transport her to and from Estoril. She'd hung up the receiver, determined to gain Lars's trust and obtain intelligence on his banking and wolfram dealings. But Maria knew, if successful, she wouldn't stop there. *If Lars is acquainted with Admiral Wilhelm Canaris, head of the Abwehr, I might be able to use Lars as a steppingstone to get to him.*

In the days leading up to her evening with Lars, she'd attempted to learn everything she could about the Portuguese banking system and wolfram mines. Although Argus had briefed her on the subjects before leaving for Madrid, much of her knowledge was obtained by reading books and periodicals at the National Library of Portugal. But regardless how well versed she became with wolfram mining and international banking, it would mean nothing if she was unable build Lars's confidence in her.

Forty minutes after leaving Lisbon, she arrived in Estoril at an imposing, two-story mansion perched on a hill overlooking the sea. The driver stopped the vehicle on a stone rotunda lined with bloomed pink oleander trees. He helped her from the back seat, and she walked alone to the entrance and rang a mechanical brass doorbell that was mounted to the side of an arched door with carved panels. The sound of footsteps grew and the door opened to reveal a middle-aged woman wearing a maid uniform.

"Senhorita Alves?"

"Yes," Maria said.

"Welcome," she said, ushering Maria inside the home.

"Senhor Steiger should be arriving within the hour," the woman said. "Would you prefer to wait for him in the parlor or on the patio?"

"The patio would be lovely," Maria said. "It might be a good evening to watch the sunset."

"Splendid choice."

The woman led Maria down a wide hallway, its walls covered in hand-painted, cobalt blue and white tiles. They traveled through a parquet floor ballroom with an Empire-style crystal chandelier, and then exited through French doors to a stone patio, surrounded by a magnificent garden, pool, and tennis court—all of which had a view to the sea.

"Would you like to sit at a chaise lounge or table?" the woman asked.

"A table, please."

The woman slid back a cushion chair from an iron table with seating for ten.

Maria sat, placing her purse on her lap. "Thank you."

"Would you like an aperitif?"

Maria had planned to keep a clear head, but she decided that a smidge of alcohol might help her to relax. "A gin and tonic—light on the gin—would be splendid."

The woman left and, within a few minutes, delivered the drink, along with mixed nuts and an assortment of crackers.

For an hour, Maria sat alone on the patio. She nursed her gin and tonic and watched the sun, painting the sky in hues of orange and red, gradually set below the ocean. As the first stars began to appear, Maria heard a sound of a vehicle engine, followed by the closing of a car door. Her heart rate quickened. Seconds passed and Lars—dressed in a tailored gray suit and carrying a leather briefcase—emerged from a pathway on the side of the house.

"I thought you'd be out here," Lars said, approaching her.

She stood and smiled. "You guessed right."

He put down his briefcase and greeted her with alternating kisses on her cheeks. "I'm sorry about the delay."

"It's no problem at all. It gave me a chance to enjoy an aperitif and a glorious sunset."

"I'm glad." He glanced at his watch. "Would you like to have dinner before we go to the casino?"

"Sure."

He raised his hand, signaling the housekeeper, who was standing vigil at the French doors.

She approached them. "Yes, sir."

"Have Tomás prepare dinner for two on the patio," he said.

"Oh," Maria said. "I thought you were implying that we would go out for dinner. There's no need for anyone to fuss over me."

"It's no trouble at all," Lars said. "What would you like?"

"Whatever is easy," she said.

"What's your favorite dish?"

"A bowl of seasoned black olives."

He smiled. "I'm not letting you get off that easy. Tomás loves a challenge. Tell me your favorite meal."

A memory of her father cooking dinner flashed in her head. *God, I miss him*. She buried her thought and said, "Bacalhau à Brás."

Lars turned to the housekeeper. "We'll have two orders of Bacalhau à Brás and, in the meantime, bring us a bottle of champagne and a bowl of seasoned olives."

"Yes, sir." The housekeeper went inside and turned on the outdoor lights, illuminating the patio and garden.

Lars slid back a chair for Maria and helped her into her seat. He sat next to her, at the corner of the table, and smoothed his silk blue tie.

"How was your business meeting?" she asked.

"It went well," he said. "It's the five hours in an automobile on potholed roads that I could have done without."

She glanced at his wingtip dress shoes, coated with a layer of dust. "Where was your meeting?"

"Covilhã. I expected to come back yesterday, but my stay was prolonged."

Maria folded her hands in her lap. *Wolfram is mined in the mountains near Covilhã,* she thought, recalling her conversation with Argus.

"We could have rescheduled for another night."

"No," he said. "I was looking forward to seeing you."

The housekeeper delivered a bottle of champagne, fluted crystal glasses, and a bowl of seasoned black olives.

Lars popped the champagne cork and filled their glasses. "What shall we toast to?"

"To new friendships," she said, raising her drink.

"To friendship." He clinked her glass.

She sipped champagne, dry with almond and citrus notes. "You have a beautiful home."

"Thank you," he said. "With the amount of time I spend in Portugal, I decided to purchase a second home here."

"It's grand," she said. "Do you mind me asking how many bedrooms it has?"

He took a gulp of champagne. "Nine bedrooms and seven bathrooms."

"Goodness, that's like an apartment building in my neighborhood in New Jersey."

He laughed. "Where do you live in New Jersey?"

"The Ironbound. It's a working-class Portuguese neighborhood in the city of Newark." She gazed over the grounds. "We don't have homes like this where I grew up."

"Neither did I," he said. "My family was poor."

"Oh," she said. "I would have guessed that you had an affluent upbringing."

"Quite the opposite," he said. "My father was a railroad worker who was seldom sober, and my mother was a seamstress. They struggled to support me and my five brothers and sisters. We never had enough to eat, and my clothes were tattered pieces, passed down to me from my older brothers."

"I'm sorry."

"Don't be," he said. "It made me who I am today."

"How so?"

"It motivated me to get out of poverty," he said. "In grammar school, I envied wealthy children whose parents had high-paying jobs or owned businesses. Their families seemed to have everything that mine did not—a warm home, good clothing, and plenty to eat. And I knew that the only way I could be like them was through education. I worked hard in school and went on to attend the University of Bern, where I studied economics and business with the intent of becoming a banker."

"Most bankers don't do as well as you," she said, her confidence building. "The ones I know pass out piggy banks with new savings accounts, and they don't have a mansion overlooking the sea and high-roller status at a casino."

He grinned. "I like to compete and win."

"You're obviously good at it." She chewed an olive—flavored with oregano, garlic, and lemon—and deposited the pit into a silver dish.

He lit a cigarette and took a long drag. "I'd like to hear more about your background. I know little about you, other than your father is Portuguese and you work for the Library of Congress."

"And that I'm good at picking roulette numbers."

"Indeed." He leaned forward. "Please, tell me about yourself."

"All right." Her mind raced with falsehoods yet she remained calm and confident. *I can do this.* "Like you, I grew up without money. My father is a struggling photojournalist, who never achieved his dream of gaining critical acclaim. My mother married him because he convinced her that he'd someday become a successful writer. She served as his assistant, developing his camera film and proofreading his articles."

"What newspaper does he work for?" Lars asked.

"He's a freelance photojournalist, and he accepts assignments from any newspaper willing to pay him. One of the few good things about growing up with a photojournalist father is that it provided me and my mother the opportunity to live part-time in Europe."

"Where?"

"London, Paris, Lisbon, Rome, Madrid. We spent quite a bit of time in England and Scotland. Many of my lasting friendships were created while traveling abroad."

He flicked ash from his cigarette. "Do your parents travel with the war?"

"No. My father is working solely in the US, and my mother is dead."

"My condolences."

She nodded.

"Did she die recently?"

"It happened when I was in college." She took a long sip of champagne, fabricating a story in her head. "My father went to Madrid with my mother to cover the Spanish Civil War. He promised her that covering the conflict would be his big break in journalism. Instead, he got my mom killed by placing her in military crossfire. I've never forgiven him."

"That must have been horrible for you to endure. I'm sorry."

"Thank you."

He rolled his cigarette between his fingers. "Is your mother from Portugal, like your father?"

She shook her head. "Germany."

He took a drag and blew smoke through his nose.

"She emigrated to New York after the Great War." Maria swirled champagne in her glass. "After her death, I managed to finish my studies and earn a master's degree. But women—even ones who are highly educated and fluent in several languages—have few career paths."

"So, you became a librarian."

"Yes, but it's temporary. I accepted the overseas position in Lisbon to get a change in scenery and time to plan my future."

"I see," he said.

The housekeeper set the table with silverware, napkins, and

candles, and then delivered two plates of Bacalhau à Brás and a bottle of *vinho verde.*

Maria took a bite of salted cod with bits of potato and egg. "It's wonderful. I can see why you insisted on eating here rather than a restaurant. Please pass along my compliments to Tomás."

"I will," Lars said.

For several minutes, they chatted while eating their meal. But soon Lars moved the conversation from family and travel to more sensitive topics of politics. Maria felt as if she were entering a mine field. Her stomach turned nauseous, but she forced herself to eat her food and pretend to enjoy his company. Although Lars was subtle with his questions and comments, it became increasingly clear, to Maria, that she was being interviewed.

"What are your thoughts on America being in the war?"

"In my opinion, we should have never entered the conflict," she lied. "The Japanese attacked Pearl Harbor because the United States prevented Japan from purchasing oil. After the bombing, America should have negotiated a peace treaty instead of declaring war."

"Are you an isolationist?"

"No. I believe countries should interact with each other. I do, however, think the United States should have remained neutral."

"Like Switzerland."

"And Portugal."

A slim smile formed on his face. He refilled their glasses with wine.

"On our telephone call," he said, lighting his third cigarette of the evening, "you mentioned that your colleagues were out of town and you wanted to take me up on an evening at the casino." He took a deep drag. "Are there any other reasons for wanting to see me?"

"Several."

He leaned back in his seat. "Please tell."

"First and foremost, I had a delightful evening with you. It felt like ages since I'd had that much fun."

"Me too." he said. "What else?"

Her eyes gravitated to the ring on his hand. "I was moved by your commitment to wear your wedding band in memory of your wife and children. I can see that you loved them deeply, and I'm sorry for your loss."

"Thank you."

"Your act of remembrance resonated with me." She held up her hand, displaying her sapphire ring. "It's my mother's wedding ring. I never take it off."

His face softened.

"Also," she said, "I'm grateful for the casino winnings that you shared with me. It might not seem like a lot to you, but a bag of money is a windfall for a librarian. Having a taste of something that eludes you can be intoxicating. It got me thinking that I want to live a different life than the one I have, and I'm not talking about handouts or marrying someone for their wealth."

He shifted in his seat.

"Does this disappoint you?"

"Not at all," he said. "You're too young for me, remember?"

Maria smiled. She smoothed her dress over her legs. "Someday, I'm going to break the cycle of poverty in my family, too. And I'm going to do it on my own."

"I admire your determination," he said. "But in order to win at something, one usually needs a wager. What are you willing to risk to get what you want?"

She looked into his eyes. "Everything."

CHAPTER 22

LISBON, PORTUGAL—JUNE 2, 1943

Maria, feeling groggy from a late night at Casino Estoril, rubbed sleep dust from her eyes, slipped on a robe, and went to the kitchen, where she placed a pot of coffee on the stove. While she waited for the brew to percolate, she retrieved her 35mm camera and microfilmed a recent edition of *Völkischer Beobachter*, the official newspaper of the Nazi party.

Over the past two weeks, she had five evenings with Lars. Their nights typically began with cocktails and dinner on his patio. While eating delectable meals prepared by Lars's private chef, they'd gradually gotten to know each other. She'd twisted her stories to create an illusion that she was dissatisfied with her government duties, and that she aspired to have a better life than the one she was living. She did, however, include many truths about herself that could be verified if Lars had the means and desire to investigate her background. After each dinner, a driver drove them to Casino Estoril, where they played roulette until the wee hours of the morning. She'd never repeated her luck with picking winning numbers, like she did on their first night together. But it didn't matter to Lars. He displayed no displeasure with losing hordes of money, and whenever their gaming chips dwindled, a casino employee arrived with a briefcase full of tokens.

Maria had gained little intelligence on Lars. But the more time they spent together, the more he eased his guard. On their last rendezvous, Lars had commented—after consuming several glasses of champagne—that he needed to wake early for a trip to Covilhã to see a client. "What's your client's business?" she'd asked, expecting him to dodge her question. Instead, he drained his drink and said, "A mining company." She was surprised by his admission, but it provided her with nothing that the OSS didn't already know about him. She hoped that with time he'd eventually divulge something of significance.

Throughout their interludes, Lars had been kind and generous, and he appeared genuinely excited to see her when she arrived at his home. He'd been a good listener, and he'd empathized with her about having been aboard the *Yankee Clipper* that crashed into the river. Also, he'd respected her wishes of keeping their relationship purely platonic, although his eyes gravitated to her calves when she crossed her legs. He portrayed the role of a friend, except for his subtle, yet persistent, inquiries about acquaintances and confidants that she had in Washington and London. To fuel his interest, she'd fabricated people she knew, including a Liverpool woman named Vera who served as a wireless telegraph operator for the Women's Royal Naval Service (aka Wrens), a man named Niles who landed a job in the mail room of the London branch of the OSS, and a secretary named Gladys who worked for the US Department of Defense in the newly constructed Pentagon. To keep track of her conversations with Lars, she'd recorded details of the people she'd conjured in a journal that she kept hidden in the cloth bag of a vacuum cleaner—a trick she learned from Tiago.

When she wasn't with Lars, she labored to acquire and microfilm Axis materials, and she made biweekly trips to the Lisbon Portela Airport, where Allied and German planes were often parked near each other on the tarmac. *People back home would never believe it*, she'd thought while walking past an airplane with an iron-cross insignia. She gave a box of undeveloped film to a

British Overseas Airways Corporation (BOAC) baggage attendant, and she waited by a perimeter fence until the plane flew away en route to London. She'd shipped what she knew to be valuable microfilm, especially the directories of weapons manufacturers and a German newspaper article that unwittingly disclosed the strength of Wehrmacht troops in Le Havre, France. But she received little feedback from Kilgour, other than his routine check-in telegrams through the US embassy. Also, she had yet to receive contact from Argus or hear news when Roy and Pilar would return to Lisbon. She felt isolated and lonely, and she missed her father. She hoped that he was getting along well, and that her letters—sent with her microfilm shipments—would eventually reach him and quell his worry about her serving in the war.

Maria's solitude was compounded by not seeing Tiago in weeks. With her microfilm duties and time with Lars, she'd had few opportunities to visit his bookstore. When she did stop in, Tiago was out on appointments. In his absence, Rosa had given her a stash of Portuguese poetry books that he'd left for her in his office. Arriving home, Maria discovered that the books had fake dust jackets that covered works of Nazi-banned Jewish authors. She cherished his help with procuring books, and she admired his resolve to aid refugees. But selfishly, she missed the comforting timbre of his voice, and the joy she felt in his presence.

Per her promise to Tiago, she'd taken photographs of Henri Levin and his family. They'd arrived at her apartment under the cover of darkness. Her heart ached for them, especially Henri's daughter, Albertine, who avoided eye contact and appeared traumatized from months of hiding from the Gestapo. She'd lightened the girl's spirits by serving her a *pastel de nata*, a Portuguese custard tart, and gifting her a February 15, 1943 edition of *Life* magazine with Princess Elizabeth on the cover. She'd hugged the family goodbye and assured them that they'd have a beautiful life in America.

To develop the film, she'd converted Pilar's bedroom into a darkroom by blocking out a window with cardboard and tape. Because she had no film developing supplies, due to her role being limited to microfilming, she'd purchased an enlarger, chemicals, and paper at a photography shop in Lisbon. Despite her makeshift operation, the pictures turned out well, which she attributed to her father for teaching her the art of developing film. She'd gone to Tiago's apartment with an envelope of photographs tucked inside her purse. When he didn't answer after repeated knocks, she'd slipped the envelope under his door and left, feeling sad by having missed him again.

Maria put down her camera and went to the kitchen. She removed the pot of coffee from the stove and, as she poured herself a cup, the telephone rang.

She jerked, spilling coffee over the counter and burning the back of her hand. She shot to the sink and ran cold water over her skin.

The phone rang again.

Her heart raced. Few people had her telephone number. It was unlikely that Roy or Pilar would call her from Madrid, and Argus avoided telephone communication due to potential wiretapping by German spies or PVDE. The only other person she'd spoken with on the phone was Lars, but it was much earlier than he typically rang her. She poured water over a dishtowel, wrapped her hand—prickling with pain—and darted to the telephone as it rang for the fifth time.

"*Olá*," she said in a composed voice.

"Did I wake you?" Lars asked.

"No. I was working. You're up awful early, especially with how late we were out last night."

"I could say the same thing about you," he said.

She forced a chuckle.

"I had fun."

"Me too." She peeked at a red mark on the back of her hand and wondered if it would turn into a blister.

"What are you doing this afternoon?"

"Working."

"Take the afternoon off," he said.

"Why?"

"I have a meeting that has come up in Lisbon."

She straightened her spine. "Would you like to get together someplace after your meeting?"

"No," he said. "I want you to come with me."

She fidgeted with the telephone cord.

"The banker I'll be meeting with is bringing his wife, due to family plans in the city. I thought you could spend time with her while I attend to business. Afterward, we'll get a drink."

"All right—tell me the time and the address and I'll be there."

"I'll pick you up at your apartment," he said. "I'd like to see your place."

Her eyes locked on stacks of Axis publications. She swallowed. "It's a bit messy at the moment. I'll meet you outside."

"I insist," he said. "It's not fair that you've been to my house several times and I've never seen your apartment."

She wanted to hold her ground but feared that refusing to allow him inside might cause suspicion. "Okay. But don't be disappointed that it isn't swank like your place."

"I won't."

"What time?"

"One o'clock."

"See you then."

She hung up the receiver and tended to her burn by soaking her hand in cold water. She hated giving Lars a glimpse into her world, but there was no way around it if she expected to fully gain his trust. *The OSS might not approve, but I need to give up something to get something greater.* As she waited for the pain in her hand to fade, she thought through options in her head and decided on the pieces of intelligence that could be relinquished without jeopardizing her mission.

Maria spent the morning staging her apartment. She hid the most sensitive Axis publications under Pilar's bed, but she couldn't stow away everything, given that she'd told Lars about her work to save European publications that were at risk of destruction. The dining room remained a miniature microfilm department, and she decorated the space with a wide range of books, magazines, and newspapers.

She bathed, applied makeup and perfume, and slipped on a form-fitting blue dress. As she clasped the backs of her pearl earrings, a knock came from the door. A knot formed in the pit of her stomach. She looked at her reflection in the bathroom mirror. *Everything is going to be okay.*

She went to the door and peeked through the peephole to see Lars, wearing a charcoal suit with a maroon tie and holding a bouquet of purple flowers. Her tension eased and she undid the latch.

Lars entered and gave her a kiss on each cheek. He handed her the bouquet. "I thought you might like some fresh cut lavender."

"Thank you." She sniffed the flowers. "They smell lovely. Make yourself comfortable while I put these in water."

He nodded.

Maria went to the kitchen, filled a ceramic pitcher with water, and inserted the lavender. She carried it to show Lars, whom she found in the dining room.

"I don't have a proper vase," she said, raising the pitcher. "What do you think?"

"I like your style."

She smiled.

His eyes gravitated to a table, covered with publications and a camera. "Is this your work?"

"Yes." She cleared away a stack of magazines and placed the pitcher on the table.

He picked up a French book, *Belle de Jour* by Joseph Kessel, and flipped through the pages. "What does the Library of Congress want you to obtain for them?"

"Any foreign newspaper or magazine I can get my hands on, and any books written in German, French, Dutch, or Polish. They have me casting a wide net. Most days, I feel like I'm searching for butterflies but catching bugs."

He nodded. "What happens to your film when it reaches the United States?"

She wondered, although briefly, if he had knowledge of airline routes or her visits to the airport. "Since the crash of the *Yankee Clipper*, the film is being shipped on a plane to London. It's supposed to be forwarded to the Library of Congress in the US for preservation, but I suspect it's being inspected for intelligence."

"I think your intuition is right." Lars put down the book and approached her. "Does your country's library pay you a reward when you deliver something of importance?"

"No."

He adjusted a gold cuff link. "Such a pity."

"It's not all bad," she said. "I receive a budget allocation in escudos to purchase books, and I do my own accounting." She tucked hair behind her ear. "Would you think less of me if I told you that I skim a little something for myself?"

"No," he said. "You're not hurting anyone. You're simply making sure that you are adequately compensated for your worth."

"Precisely."

Twenty minutes later, Lars's driver stopped the vehicle in front of São Bento Palace, located in the historic district of Lisbon. Lars, carrying a monogrammed leather briefcase, helped Maria from the back seat.

She gazed at the stately, neoclassical building with towering columns. "I thought you said that you were meeting with a banker."

"I am," he said.

"In the palace?"

"In the adjacent mansion."

"But isn't that the prime minister's residence?"

"It is." He looked at her. "My meeting is with Prime Minister Salazar and his banker, Ricardo Espírito Santo."

Her eyebrows rose. "It would have been nice to know that we were coming here."

"I didn't tell you whom I was meeting with because I was afraid you might decline my invitation. Also, I didn't want you to worry all morning about it."

"I wouldn't have fretted about this," she lied. "But I would have put on something more formal to wear."

"You look perfect. My meeting will be brief, and I appreciate you keeping Ricardo's wife, Mary, company." He placed a hand on her arm and smiled. "When you return to America, you'll get to tell everyone that you met Salazar."

She drew a deep breath, gathering her nerve. "All right."

They walked to an adjacent white stone mansion and ascended stairs to the entrance. The door swung open and they were greeted by a housekeeper. Inside, the air smelled of vinegar, like the home had undergone a thorough cleaning. Maria's legs felt weak as the woman led them down a corridor.

The housekeeper stopped at a door and knocked.

"Come in," a male voice said.

The woman opened the door and gestured for them to enter.

Maria and Lars stepped inside a dimly lit office with glass door bookcases. Floor-length black curtains covered the windows, and the only light source was from an Art Deco brass desk lamp. She recognized the dictator, António de Oliveira Salazar, from photographs in newspapers. Salazar—seated at his desk and writing on a piece of paper—was in his mid-fifties with slicked-back, salt-and-pepper hair. He wore a three-piece black suit, and his skin was pale and free of wrinkles, as if he went to great lengths to avoid exposure to the sun.

"Prime Minister," Lars said. "It's good to see you."

"You too." Salazar finished scribbling and set aside his pen. He rose from his chair and shook Lars's hand.

Lars turned. "This is Maria Alves. She'll be keeping Ricardo's wife company while we meet."

Salazar looked at Maria and clasped his hands in front of himself. "Good afternoon."

"It's a pleasure to meet you, sir," Maria said. She felt awkward and tried to appear relaxed.

The sound of approaching footsteps grew in the hallway, and a man and woman entered the office. Salazar moved past Maria and shook the man's hand.

Maria stepped back, giving space for the others to greet Salazar. She glanced at the prime minister's desk, which had stacks of paper and a large framed photograph of the Italian dictator, Benito Mussolini. *Good Lord!*

"Maria," Lars said, "this is Ricardo."

Maria faced him and smiled.

The banker was in his forties and fit, like an avid golfer, and he wore a double-breasted plaid gray suit with a polka-dot bowtie. He approached Maria and shook her hand.

"And this is Mary," Lars said, gesturing to an attractive woman in an ivory-colored dress and matching shoes. Her sleek black hair was pulled back and tied with ribbon.

Maria shook her hand. "It's lovely to meet you."

"Delighted to make your acquaintance," the woman said.

The housekeeper appeared in the doorway. "Ladies, if you will follow me, I've prepared coffee for you in the garden."

Maria and Mary were ushered out of the house and into a manicured courtyard, where a table for two was set with a porcelain coffeepot, cups with saucers, and a plate of pastries. After pouring and preparing the coffee to their liking, the housekeeper left.

"Ricardo tells me that Lars has been spending time with you," the woman said, lifting her cup to her lips.

"Yes," Maria said. "We met a few weeks ago."

The woman sipped her coffee. "At the casino, I assume."

"Yes," Maria said.

"Ricard mentioned to me that Lars enjoys your company."

"The feeling is mutual." Maria's mind raced. "How did you and Ricardo meet Lars?"

The woman took a bite of a pastry. "Through business at my husband's bank."

"Which bank is that?"

"Banco Espírito Santo," she said, sounding annoyed that Maria didn't know the name. "It's the most important bank in Portugal."

"Of course," Maria said.

The woman looked in the direction of a chirping bird on the limb of a jacaranda tree, bloomed with violet flowers.

"Do you see Lars often?" Maria asked, attempting to generate conversation.

"Ricardo does. They meet at least once a week and they talk daily on the telephone. I see Lars about once a month, usually at our home in Cascais." The woman looked over the grounds. "You'd love our garden in Cascais. The plants and flowers are spectacular. It's every bit as nice as this one."

"It sounds grand," Maria said.

For an hour, Maria chatted with Mary, who monopolized much of the conversation by talking about her home, four daughters, friends, and social functions at the Sporting Club of Cascais. And her eyes lit up while telling Maria about her special guests, the Duke and Duchess of Windsor, whom she hosted at her home for a month at the onset of the war. The woman asked little about Maria. And each time Maria attempted to veer the conversation to gain information about Lars or her husband, Mary turned the topic back to her herself.

"Did you have a nice visit?" Lars asked, entering the garden.

"Oh, yes," Mary said. "You'll need to bring Maria with you the next time you're over to the house."

"I will," Lars said. "Ricardo is speaking with the prime minister. He'll be here in a few minutes. I'd like to stay, but we have another engagement."

Maria stood. "I enjoyed getting to know you, Mary."

"Thank you, darling," the woman said.

Maria and Lars left São Bento Mansion and got into their car. The driver pressed the accelerator and pulled away from the curb.

"Are you ready for a drink?" Lars asked.

"Yes."

"I thought we could go to Hotel Tivoli. It's on Avenida da Liberdade, not far from your apartment."

That's where Germans are rumored to stay in Lisbon, she thought. "That would be splendid."

Minutes later, they arrived at the hotel. Maria glanced at the briefcase in Lars's hand and thought it was odd that he'd brought it with him. She wondered if the case contained something he wanted to show her, or if there was something inside it from his meeting with Salazar and his banker that was too important to be left with his driver. She buried her thoughts and walked with him through a two-story lobby with an Art Deco glass skylight. They entered a bar, which also appeared to serve as a restaurant, given the white tablecloths, napkins, and silverware on the tables. It was early for cocktail hour and the place was sparsely crowded. Lars stepped away and spoke with a maître d', and they were seated at a window table that overlooked Avenida da Liberdade. As a waiter left with their drink orders, a group of employees removed the neighboring tables and chairs.

"Did you request that?" Maria asked.

"Yes," he said. "It gives us privacy."

She glanced through the window to where pedestrians walked along a tree-lined street. "Lovely view."

"Indeed."

Maria crossed her legs, bumping his briefcase with her foot. "Sorry."

"It's all right." He moved his case next to his chair.

The waiter delivered their drinks, a gin and tonic for Maria, and a schnapps for Lars.

"How was your meeting with the prime minister?" Maria asked.

"It went well."

She raised her glass. "To your successful meeting."

He clinked her glass and took a gulp of schnapps.

Maria sipped her drink, more gin than tonic. A warmth flowed down her throat and into her stomach.

"I'm curious," Lars said. "Why haven't you asked me about my banking affairs?"

"Because I already know what you do," she said without hesitation.

"Tell me your assumption," he said.

She fought back her trepidation. "You arrange the sale of wolfram."

He swirled his drink. "Why do you think that?"

"I suspected it when you mentioned a trip to Covilhã to meet with a mining company. Now that I know you're working with Salazar and his banker, I'm fairly certain of it." She looked at him. "It's no secret that Portugal is selling wolfram to the Allies and Germans, and I doubt that any negotiations on trade would take place without Salazar."

He took a sip of schnapps. "You're perceptive."

"Thanks," she said, feeling relieved by his calm reaction.

Lars put down his glass and intertwined his fingers. "The wolfram war is Salazar's most challenging dilemma. London and Washington are pressuring him to embargo sales of wolfram to Germany. And Germany is coercing him to sell them higher quantities. But the prime minister is attempting to appease both sides by selling wolfram in equal amounts to Allied and Axis powers."

What about the wolfram on the black market? she wanted to ask but held her silence.

"Salazar is buying Portugal's neutrality with wolfram," Lars said. "If he stops selling wolfram to Germany, Hitler will invade Portugal or force Spain to do it for him. And if he ceases sales to the Allies, they'll take over Portugal's Azores Islands and perhaps the mainland."

"So, to keep out of the war, Salazar needs a Swiss banking partner to transfer funds for the sale of wolfram."

He nodded.

She ran a finger over the rim of her glass. "Are you going to tell me which country you're working for?"

"I think you know the answer to that question."

Maria nodded.

"Does this offend you?"

"No," she said, hiding her disgust. "I suppose Switzerland and Portugal are in similar predicaments. To remain independent, they need to cooperate with Germany. If I were a Swiss banker with powerful connections, I'd do the same thing if it meant that I could make a lot of money and keep my country out of the war. The way I see it—it's better to be rich than poor when the conflict ends."

His lips formed a slim smile.

Maria, hoping the alcohol would steady her nerves, finished off her gin and tonic.

Lars signaled to the waiter, who swiftly brought them another round of drinks. He waited until the server was out of earshot and said, "There's something I'd like to discuss with you."

"If it's about whether I'll continue to be your gambling buddy, the answer is yes."

He laughed. "I'm glad to hear it, but that's not what I want to talk about."

"Tell me what's on your mind."

He leaned forward and lowered his voice. "What would you say if I told you that I know someone who will pay handsomely for Allied military intelligence?"

An ache grew in her abdomen. "I'd say that I'm listening."

He removed a silver case from his suit pocket and lit a cigarette. He took a long drag. "This person is seeking information out of London and Washington."

"What kind of information?"

"Troop movements. Locations of ships and submarines. Military plans. Quantities of armament." He flicked ash into an ashtray. "Anything related to Allied forces."

"I assume your contact is with the Abwehr," she said.

He puffed his cigarette. "My contact wishes to remain anonymous."

Maria sipped her drink. "How much is this person willing to pay for intelligence?"

"It'll depend on the quality. But one could become wealthy if they proved to be a reliable source of intelligence."

"What makes you think that I'm capable of obtaining Allied information?"

"I don't know that you can. But you are clever and have connections in London and Washington. You can accept or deny the offer—it doesn't matter to me. I simply wanted to let you know that the opportunity exists."

She paused, rubbing her chin. "Let's suppose that I did decide to do this. What would be the next step?"

"Garner the intelligence and deliver it to me. In the interim, my contact has instructed me to pay you the equivalent of one thousand dollars in escudos as a good faith payment."

Maria wondered if his contact was Admiral Wilhelm Canaris, head of the Abwehr. *Oh, God! This is really happening!* She clasped her glass to keep her hands from trembling.

"Would you like time to consider the proposal?"

"No," she said, looking into his eyes. "I accept."

He smiled and raised his drink. "To your future."

Maria clinked his glass and sipped her drink. Her mind and heart raced. She wondered what Argus would do when she told him about accepting an offer to spy for the enemy, and if she'd be reprimanded or deployed back to the United States. However, her fears of a rebuke from the OSS were soon replaced with suspicion. She wanted to believe that Lars had disclosed his wolfram dealings with Salazar, as well as his Swiss banking connections with Germany, because of her ability to gain his confidence. But deep down, she suspected that Lars was too ingenious to be entirely manipulated, and that he was using a tactic similar to hers—giving up information to gain something greater. Lars, she believed, was giving her a test with dire consequences if she failed. Not only did she plan to pass his scrutiny, she intended to infiltrate the Abwehr and win the intelligence advantage.

Chapter 23

Lisbon, Portugal—June 4, 1943

Tiago, sitting in the office of his bookstore, looked at his wristwatch, which read 6:20 p.m. Anticipation grew inside him. Using a knife, he pried up a loose floor tile and removed passports and birth certificates—which fabricated new identities for Henri Levin and his family—from the secret hole. He replaced the tile, stashed the documents in a hidden pocket in the lining of his sports jacket, and left his office. He made his way toward the cashier's counter, where Rosa was ringing up the sole customer in the store.

"It has a surprise ending," Rosa said, handing a book and a bit of change to an elderly woman wearing a headscarf.

The woman gave a nod. She put the change in a coin purse and slipped it, along with her book, into a canvas tote bag.

Rosa leaned over the counter. "Want a hint about what happens?"

Tiago fought back a smile.

"*Não, obrigada.*" The woman slung her bag over her shoulder and left.

Rosa shrugged.

"I'm surprised she didn't run away with her fingers plugged in her ears."

"I didn't ruin the story for her," she said. "I was merely offering my insight on the book."

"Of course you were."

She pointed to an empty rack, as if she was eager to change the subject. "We've run out of newspapers again."

"That's the third time this week," he said. "Perhaps we should ask Artur to give us a bigger supply."

She lowered her glasses to the tip of her nose. "I interpret that to mean that I should tell Artur, since you're not always here when the boy makes his newspaper deliveries."

"Yes," he said. "I was trying to be polite."

"And I was being forthright."

"I like your candor, Rosa. I never have to guess what's on your mind."

"As it should be," she said, raising her chin.

Tiago chuckled.

Rosa glanced to the storefront window. "Business has picked up since Agent Neves and his henchman stopped skulking outside our door."

"It's likely temporary," Tiago said. "The PVDE will resume surveillance when they have nothing better to do."

"You're probably right." Rosa shifted her weight on her stool. "How are your parents?"

"Their heartbreak is still raw," he said, recalling his recent trip to Porto to see them. "They keep a candle in the window and haven't given up hope that my grandparents will survive the German labor camp."

Rosa drooped her shoulders.

"They're carrying on to help Jews who arrive at their vineyard. Clergy on the escape lines in France continue to route refugees to my parents' home. In a way, it feels as if my grandparents are still aiding people to flee Bordeaux for Portugal."

"They've created an enduring path of hope."

"I like to think so," Tiago said. A sadness welled up within him. "I pray that they're alive and not suffering."

"You'll see them again." She lifted her purse from the floor and removed rosary beads with an attached crucifix made of wood. "I pray for them, too."

"I'm grateful for you, Rosa."

She set down her beads and rubbed her eyes.

"I need to leave," he said, burying his sorrow. "I'm meeting Henri Levin to deliver his and his family's travel documents. Because of your masterful forgeries, they have new identities to get them on the *Serpa Pinto* for America."

"It's some of my best work," she said proudly. "But I can't take all the credit."

Tiago raised his brows.

"We're fortunate that Maria took the photographs. She provided the correct size images for the passports, and the quality was better than our last photographer."

"I agree," he said.

She leaned forward. "When was the last time you saw her?"

"Last month."

"Not good," she said waving a finger. "She's been in the store to see you and you've been out."

"I've been busy."

"You must make an effort to see her, otherwise your paths might never cross."

"I'll see what I can do," he said, stepping to the door.

She stood and placed her hands on her hips. "Remember what I said."

"I will. Have a good night, Rosa."

Tiago left the bookstore and made his way toward the Rossio, where Levin had requested to meet per his dead drop message. Along the route, he thought about his last encounter with Maria. She'd wanted to open up to him, Tiago believed, and he hoped with time that she'd be able to tell him the things that she was keeping locked inside herself. He'd been surprised by her embrace and kiss to his cheek, and he wished that their visit hadn't come to an abrupt end. Despite weeks of separation, she'd remained on his mind and in his heart. *Maybe after the war there will be time for us.* He set aside his thoughts and quickened his pace over an uneven stone sidewalk.

He reached the Rossio at twilight and the square was illuminated in lights. Groups of refugees were congregated near the fountains, and a yellow electric tram clamored over rails on its route through the city. As he walked by Café Chave d'Ouro, an aroma of grilled sardines filled his nose. The streets surrounding the Rossio had a modest amount of traffic, given that rush hour was over. He crossed into the square and mingled through the crowd in search of Levin. Minutes later, he spotted him—by his overgrown, chest-length beard—standing on the opposite side of the street. Rather than signal with his hand, which might garner attention, Tiago lowered his head and walked to the curb.

A black sedan, parked in front of a hotel, roared to life. The vehicle accelerated into the street, cutting off a taxi. A horn blared.

Tiago turned as the sedan, containing four men in dark suits, raced past him.

Levin's eyes widened as the sedan sped toward him. He turned and dashed down a narrow, one-way street.

Tiago's adrenaline surged. He sprinted toward the intersection.

The automobile's tires screeched as it rounded the corner and continued onto the side street.

Tiago pushed past men smoking cigarettes. He darted to the corner and ran down the street, void of pedestrians. Ahead, the vehicle braked and skidded to a stop. The passenger and rear doors flung open, and three men jumped out and gave chase on foot. Within seconds, one of the men tackled Levin to the ground.

Levin screamed.

"Stop!" Tiago shouted.

One of the assailants punched Levin in the face, while the others repeatedly kicked his ribs and legs.

Tiago, running toward them, struggled to remove a sheathed knife from his jacket.

The men dragged Levin, bleeding from his nose and mouth, toward the sedan.

Tiago pulled out his knife. "Leave him alone!"

One of the attackers, a blond-haired man with round-lens eyeglasses, locked eyes with Tiago. He slipped a pistol from a holster beneath his suit jacket.

Fear flooded Tiago's veins. He bolted to a doorway as a bullet ricocheted off a stone wall.

The driver shifted the sedan into reverse and accelerated.

Tiago's heart rate soared as the sedan shot toward him. He dived toward the sidewalk. The rear bumper grazed his left foot, and then slammed into the door, ripping it from its hinges. He tumbled onto the pavement, jamming his right shoulder. Pain flooded his arm. The blade slipped from his hand and clanged over cobblestone.

"*Schnell*!" one of the men shouted.

His pulse pounded his eardrums. With no place to hide, he expected the gunman to round the vehicle and fire a bullet into him. Refusing to go down without a fight, he scrambled on his hands and knees to retrieve his knife.

A crowd gathered at the end of the street. A siren sounded.

The driver shot the vehicle forward and stopped. "*Steig ins Auto*!"

Levin was pushed into the back seat and was pinned in by two of the men. The gunman got into the passenger seat, slammed the door shut, and the sedan sped away.

Tiago rolled onto his side and sucked in air.

The wail of the siren grew. Pedestrians from the Rossio cautiously made their way toward him.

He stood, pain flaring down his arm, and slipped the knife into his pocket. A wave of dread surged through him. He ran away from the crowd. His leg muscles burned as he willed himself to move faster, all the while determined to reach Levin's wife and daughter before they met the same fate.

CHAPTER 24

LISBON, PORTUGAL—JUNE 4, 1943

Several streets away from the Rossio, Tiago waved down a taxi. With his shoulder throbbing, he got into the back seat and instructed the driver to take him to the riverfront in Alfama. Minutes later, he paid the driver, exited the vehicle, and hurried through the confined streets and stairways of the ancient fishing neighborhood of Lisbon. The area was dimly lit and lacked signage. After some backtracking, he found the home address that Levin had given him when they first met.

He glanced behind him to make sure he hadn't been followed and knocked on the door. He wiped sweat from his forehead and took deep inhales to catch his breath.

Seconds passed and the door partially opened to reveal an old man with weathered cheeks and a gray stubble beard. He wrinkled his forehead. "Who are you?"

"I'm Tiago. I've come to speak with Estelle Levin."

"There's no one here by that name." The man began to close the door.

He wedged his foot between the door and frame. "I'm Henri's friend. Tell Estelle that it's urgent that I speak with her."

The man glanced over his shoulder.

"Please, there's little time."

The man ushered him inside and bolted the door. "Wait here." He disappeared down a hallway. A moment later, he emerged with Estelle and her daughter, Albertine, whom Tiago recognized from their passport photographs.

"I'm Tiago," he said. "I've been helping Henri with your travel papers."

"He went to meet you." The woman, her eyes filled with fear, placed her arm around her daughter. "Where is he?"

His heart ached. "He was abducted."

"Oh, God," she said, her voice quavering.

The girl whimpered. Tears pooled in her eyes.

"I tried to stop them," Tiago said. "He was taken away by four men in an automobile."

Estelle's face turned pale. "PVDE?"

The voice of the driver flashed in Tiago's brain. "The men spoke German. They might be Gestapo."

Estelle collapsed to her knees. Her daughter fell to her side and wept.

Tiago approached them and kneeled. "I'm so sorry. I'll do everything I can to find him, but for now we must leave. If these men were following Henri, they might know of this place. They might come for you and Albertine."

"Maybe there's someone in Portuguese law enforcement who can help us," Estelle said.

"It's too risky," Tiago said. "Agent Neves of the secret police has been searching for Henri. Your husband told me that he thought Neves was being paid by the Gestapo to help locate him. The PVDE has pro-Nazi agents in their ranks, and if you were to go to them for help, they'd likely deport you, given that you entered Portugal illegally. You'd be sent back to the Spanish border, where the Gestapo might be waiting for you."

The woman pressed her lips to her daughter's hair. Her body trembled.

"We must go." Tiago placed a hand on Estelle's shoulder. "I'll take you to a boardinghouse. The owner is sympathetic to Jews. You and Albertine will be safe there."

The woman wiped her eyes and nodded.

"I'll gather your things," the old man said.

"There's no time; I'll come back for them later." Tiago looked at the man, wringing his hands. "I suggest that you leave for a week or two. Do you have someplace to go, or would you like to come with them to the boardinghouse?"

"I have a brother who lives in Setúbal," he said.

"Go now," Tiago said.

The man nodded.

Tiago helped Estelle and Albertine to their feet and they left the home. At the riverfront, they got into a taxi and twenty minutes later they arrived at a boardinghouse in the parish of Ajuda. He arranged for their stay, using their new identities, and then walked them to their room. He sat with them while they wept, and he tried to console them with words of hope and promises that he would do everything possible to find Henri. When neither of them could shed any more tears, he gave Estelle money from his wallet and hugged them goodbye.

"Bless you," Estelle said, her voice hoarse from crying.

Albertine nuzzled to her mother's side.

"I'll return in the morning," he said.

The woman nodded.

Tiago left the boardinghouse. As he walked through the streets of Ajuda, a twinge of regret pricked at his conscience. *This wouldn't have happened if I refuted his dead drop message to meet in the Rossio. I should have insisted on meeting someplace discreet.* Levin was likely on his way back to Germany to be imprisoned or worse. Anguish chewed at his gut. Instead of taking a taxi, he walked toward home, hoping the time would allow him to clear his head and find a way to undo the undoable.

At his apartment building, he scanned the street but saw no onlookers. He entered, rubbed the ache in his right shoulder, and began his climb on the stairs. Halfway through his ascent, the entrance door squeaked open and closed. Hairs rose on the back of his neck. He eased his way upward, listening to the clack of footsteps two floors below him. At the third-floor landing, floorboards creaked above him. He stopped. An image of Agent Neves holding a stiletto to his throat echoed in his brain. His pulse rate spiked. Using his left, nondominant hand, he slipped the knife from his jacket. Footsteps grew from below him. With nowhere to hide, he ascended the stairs to meet his fate.

Chapter 25

Lisbon, Portugal—June 4, 1943

Maria scribbled a note on a piece of paper, folded it in half, and slid it under the door. She tossed her pencil into her purse and turned. Her eyes widened at the sight of Tiago holding a blade.

Tiago, standing near the top of the staircase, placed a finger to his lips.

Her breath stalled in her lungs. She nodded.

The clack of footsteps resounded through the stairwell.

He peeked over the banister. Seconds passed, a door opened on the floor below them, and the footsteps disappeared into an apartment. He motioned for Maria to approach him.

She crept forward.

He gestured for her to remain on the stairs, and he slowly inched his way to the door. While holding his knife, he unlocked the bolt, slipped inside, and flipped on a light.

She listened to the creak of his weight on the floor as he searched the rooms. Her heart raced.

A moment later, Tiago appeared in the doorway and tucked his blade into his jacket. "I'm sorry to alarm you. It's safe to come in."

She drew a deep breath and exhaled. Tension eased from her shoulders and she entered his apartment.

He shut the door and bolted the lock.

"What's going on?" she asked.

"Henri Levin was abducted."

Her heart sank. "Oh, no. Where's Estelle and Albertine?"

"I moved them to a safe house."

"Thank goodness." She looked at him, his faced filled with sadness. "Tell me what happened."

They sat at a kitchen table and, for several minutes, Tiago provided her the details of Levin's kidnapping by four German-speaking men on a street near the Rossio, nearly being shot and run over by their automobile, and how he raced to hide Levin's wife and daughter in a boardinghouse.

"I think they were Gestapo," Tiago said. "Levin believed that Agent Neves of the PVDE was working with the Gestapo to apprehend him."

"Did you see Neves?"

He shook his head.

She wrapped her arms around herself. "Estelle and Albertine must be devastated."

He nodded.

"What are they going to do?" she asked.

"There's nothing they, or we, can do for Henri. His abductors are either driving him to the Spanish border and onward to German-occupied France, or they're flying him back to Germany. Either way, Levin is en route to a German prison." He rubbed his jaw. "In the morning, I hope to convince Estelle to flee with her daughter to America."

"It'll be heartrending for them to leave," she said. "They might be reluctant to depart from Lisbon without knowing where he's imprisoned."

"Perhaps," he said. "But if they stay and report Henri's abduction to Portuguese authorities, they'll likely be deported due to their illegal immigration status. I expect Estelle, after given time to work through her shock of the tragedy, will place her daughter's welfare first and set sail for America under their new identities."

Maria's chest ached for the Levin family—and for Tiago. She could tell, by the hurt in his voice and the gloom in his face, that he was shaken by Henri's abduction. The pain that Estelle and Albertine were experiencing was similar to what Tiago suffered when his grandparents were arrested and sent away to a German prison camp. She wished that there was something that she could do to ease his sorrow.

"I'm so sorry," she said.

"Me too." He looked to the ceiling, as if he was reliving the events in his head. "I should never have agreed to meet Levin in the Rossio. If I would have insisted on a more secure location, or delivered his travel papers to the home where he was hiding, he'd be on his path to freedom."

"It's not your fault." She clasped his hand. "If it was the Gestapo, they were likely tracking him and looking for the right location to apprehend him. You've done everything you could to help him. You cannot blame yourself for the acts of evil men."

He squeezed her fingers.

"How soon can you get Estelle and Albertine on a boat to the United States?"

"It will take a couple months," he said, "unless I'm able to pay off someone to expedite their ticket purchase and boarding date."

Maria slipped her hand away. She removed stacks of escudos, bound with rubber bands, from her purse and placed them on the table. "Will this help?"

His eyes widened. "Yes."

She slid the money to him.

He flipped through the bundles. "This is too much money for a librarian to purchase books. Where did you get it?"

An image of Lars, giving her bribe money from his briefcase, flashed in her head. "It doesn't matter where I got it. What's important is that you use it to aid refugees. I'm thinking that there is more than enough money there to expedite Estelle's and Albertine's voyage to freedom."

"There is," he said. "*Obrigado*."

"I'm glad to help." An angst grew inside her. She shifted her weight in her chair. "I have a favor to ask of you."

He set aside the money. "Of course."

"I don't want you to accept my request before you know what it is," she said. "The timing to discuss this is terrible, considering everything that's happened this evening. But I don't know when I'll see you again."

"It's all right," he said. "You may ask me anything."

"Would you be willing to forge some documents for me?"

"What kind of documents?"

She swallowed. "Royal Navy operations lists."

He rubbed stubble on his chin.

"The list shows the locations and movements of Allied and Royal naval ships. They're referred to as pink lists and are usually printed every three or four days."

"Why do you need to create them?" he asked.

Tension grew in her chest. "To feed misinformation to someone."

"Why doesn't the US government help you with creating the documents?"

She thought about her conversation with Argus, and her agreement to spy on Lars. "I'm a long way from Allied support, and my role requires me to work autonomously."

He tilted his head. "To whom are you giving these deceptive lists?"

"It's best that you don't know the name of my contact."

"You can trust me," he said.

"I do," she said. "But I don't want you implicated if my plan should fail. There's no need for you to be exposed to this any more than you need to be." She placed her hands on the table. "The lists will be red herrings to mislead German intelligence. To pull it off, I'll need your help. If you don't want to do it, I'll understand."

"I'll help you."

"*Obrigada*."

"Do you have a sample of a pink list?"

She patted her purse. "I do. It's several years old, but the format of the list likely hasn't changed. The Board of Admiralty has been using the same form to track ships since the Great War."

"I suppose you're not going to tell me how you acquired it."

"In a book," she said. "You'd be surprised by how much information one can acquire in Portugal's national library."

He raised his brows.

She removed a book from her purse and showed him a page with a blurred image of a pink list, which categorized information by class of ship, place, date of arrival, and date of departure. Afterward, she gave him a piece of paper with fabricated fleet movements from the port of Liverpool. "This is what I want the list to contain."

He eyed the handwritten notes. "You schemed this?"

"I did."

"Why Liverpool?" he asked.

Because I told Lars that I have a friend there who works in the Women's Royal Naval Service, she thought. "The port of Liverpool is the main link between Britain and North America."

He nodded. "We'll need to use British paper to make it look authentic."

"Will it be difficult to obtain?"

"No, but it will be a challenge to match the color, considering that we're using a black-and-white image as a model."

"Do you think you can replicate it?"

"Yes. To ensure the paper is the right shade, we can take photographs of it with your camera to see how it looks in comparison to the book image."

"Excellent." Maria set aside her purse. "Do you have any questions?"

"Yes," Tiago said. "Have you eaten dinner?"

Surprised, she straightened her back. "No."

"I'll make you something to eat."

"That's okay. I'll get something to eat when I get home."

He rose from his chair. "For the rest of the evening, let's forget about the war. We can pick up with our work in the morning. For now, let's be two people who are enjoying each other's company over a meal."

She felt conflicted. Her sense of duty prodded her to leave, but her heart longed to stay. *I feel good when I'm with him and I don't want to leave.* "All right."

Tiago slipped off his sports jacket and rolled up his sleeves. He rummaged through his kitchen and produced a half loaf of bread, a tin of sardines, a ripe tomato, a red onion, olive oil, and half of a lemon.

"What are we having?" she asked, looking at the items on the counter.

"Sardine toasts with tomato and sweet onion," he said. "I hope you like it."

"It sounds perfect. What can I do?"

"You can pick out the wine. It's in the lower left side cabinet."

Maria opened the cabinet. Inside were identical bottles of his family's port wine. She chuckled and selected a bottle.

Minutes later, Tiago served the sardine toasts, poured two glasses of wine, and lit a candle in the center of the table. He helped her into her chair and took a seat next to her.

"It looks lovely," she said. "This is something my dad would make for dinner."

"Do you approve?"

She tucked hair behind her ear. "Very much so."

He raised his glass. "*Saúde*."

She clinked his glass and sipped wine, full-bodied with notes of chocolate and blackberry.

Tiago took a drink and put down his glass. He squeezed a lemon wedge over the shared platter of food. "Tell me what you think."

Maria took a bite of sardine toast, salty and rich with olive oil. "Goodness—this is incredible."

He smiled.

She chewed her food and thought of their conversation at their last rendezvous. Curiosity grew inside her. "You mentioned that you don't have a girlfriend. Was there ever someone special for you?"

"A woman named Leonor. We met while studying at the university in Coimbra." He took a sip of wine. "Our relationship didn't last."

"Why not?"

"She opposed my decision to join the Spanish Civil War to fight the spread of fascism."

"It's a good thing that it didn't work out," she said.

He nodded. "Was there ever anyone special for you?"

"I dated some in college," Maria said. "But I never met anyone I could see myself spending a lifetime with."

"You will."

"What makes you so certain?"

"Any man would feel fortunate to be with you."

She smiled.

"After the war, you'll have many admirers seeking to gain your affection," he said. "Eventually, you'll meet the one for you."

Maybe I already have. She took a gulp of wine, attempting to lull her emotions. *Tiago is caring, handsome, and sincere. He's committed to fighting fascism and helping refugees. I feel true to myself when I'm with him, and he gives me hope that the world will have a better future.*

"What are your plans after the war?" he asked.

"I haven't given it much thought."

He moved his chair close. "You must have dreams—they make life worth living."

She paused, twisting her mom's sapphire ring on her finger. "I hope to have a life like my parents. They adored each other."

"I'm truly sorry about your mother. From what you've told me about her, she was a courageous woman."

She nodded, feeling grateful for his kind words.

Tiago nibbled a piece of toast.

"What do you want after the war?" she asked.

"My wishes are similar to yours," he said. "My parents' and grandparents' homes were filled with love and laughter. Someday, I'd like to have a family of my own."

She smiled. "Do you want children?"

"Yes."

"How many?"

"If possible, more than one. Being an only child, I've always wanted to have a sibling."

"Same."

He gently touched her arm. "You've barely eaten."

Her skin tingled. "It's delectable. I was distracted by our conversation."

For an hour they chatted while finishing off their meal. Afterward, he topped off her glass with wine and insisted that she enjoy her drink while he washed the dishes.

"You're a wonderful host," she said. "And you're spoiling me."

"Good." Tiago dried the plates with a towel and placed them on the counter. He raised his elbow and winced.

"What's wrong?"

"I hurt my shoulder in the scuffle at the Rossio."

"You should have said something." She put down her glass and stood. "Take a seat and let me have a look at it."

"It's not necessary."

"You're being stubborn, like when I was reluctant to let you care for my pulled stitches." She touched his arm. "Please, sit."

He pulled a chair from the table and sat.

"I'm going to need to see your injury."

He unbuttoned his dress shirt and placed it over his lap.

She stood behind him and gently slid down the shoulder strap of his ribbed, cotton undershirt to reveal a large black-and-blue mark.

"How bad is it?" he asked.

"You have a bruise the size of a pear." Maria glanced over the kitchen, absent an icebox. She made a substitute cold pack by soaking a dish towel with cold water from a faucet and placing it to his shoulder. Water dribbled between her fingers and ran down his back, broad and muscular. Her heartbeat accelerated. "Is it helping?"

"Yes," he said, his voice soft.

Maria applied the compress for a few minutes, and then set it aside. She caressed his shoulder. As if by reflex, she lowered her forehead to his hair and whispered, "Better?"

"Much." Using his good arm, he clasped her hand and their fingers intertwined.

Her breath deepened. She felt him slip away as he rose from the chair.

He approached her and placed a hand to her cheek, caressing her skin with his thumb.

She leaned into him and his arms wrapped around her. Butterflies swirled in her stomach. She looked up at him, their eyes met, and his lips approached her own.

Tiago gently kissed her. His lips drifted from her parted mouth, to her cheek, and settled against her neck. "Will you stay?"

Her heartbeat thumped against her rib cage. "Yes."

He lifted her hand and kissed her palm. He walked with her to his bedroom, where he placed the candle—burned to a nub—on a dresser.

Candlelight flickered over Tiago's face. "I would never do anything to hurt you."

"Nor I." Maria slowly unbuttoned her blouse. She gently clasped his fingers and placed his hand to her chest.

Patiently, they undressed each other, undoing buttons, buckles, and zippers. Their clothing fell to the floor and they slipped into the bed. As their bodies molded to one, Maria's passion soared, and she wished that their embrace would never end.

Chapter 26

Lisbon, Portugal—June 5, 1943

Tiago awoke to the sensation of Maria's breath, flowing in tranquil waves over his bare chest. She was nuzzled to him with an arm and leg draped over his body. Sunlight streamed through an opening in the curtains, creating a dull glow over the room. For minutes, he remained still, taking in her warmth and listening to the cadence of her breath.

Maria stirred and opened her eyes.

"*Bom dia*," he said.

"Hi."

He pressed his lips to her hair. A faint scent of lilac perfume filled his nose, resurrecting images of their night together.

She glided a finger over his sternum. "Last night was lovely."

His skin tingled. "It was."

"Unfortunately, I need to go."

"Let me make you coffee."

"Another time." Maria gave him a squeeze and slipped out of bed. She collected her underwear and clothing, strewn over the floor. "No peeping at my unmentionables."

He chuckled. "A little too late for that, don't you think?"

She turned, covering herself with her clothes, and smiled.

He held out his hand.

She shuffled to him.

He clasped her hand, pulled her into the bed, and wrapped her in his arms.

She laughed.

He squeezed her tight, ignoring the ache in his shoulder.

She placed a hand to his cheek and kissed him long and soft, and when she eased away she whispered, "I want to stay but I have to go."

"May I see you tonight?"

"I can't," she said. "But I promise to find a way to see you later in the week."

Tiago felt their embrace fade as she slipped from the bed.

Maria dressed and fixed her hair with her fingers. He put on a pair of trousers and walked her to the door, where they kissed goodbye. He watched her descend the stairs and closed the door.

A deep longing to be with her swelled inside him. Since his grandparents were arrested and sent to a prison camp, he'd felt little more than sadness, but Maria had resurrected his joy and zest for life. She'd given him friendship, warmth, and—most of all—hope. But regardless of his desire to be with her, he knew that their relationship would need to wait. He was committed to aiding refugees, who were continuing to pour into Lisbon, and she was dedicated to serving her country. The only chance for them to be together, Tiago believed, would be for the war to end.

To complicate matters, Maria's duties were more perilous than he originally thought. She wasn't a librarian whose role was limited to the acquisition of books for intelligence purposes; she was a spy who pretended to serve Germany while actually serving the Allies. Now, he was conspiring with her to mislead the enemy. And if his fake documents didn't appear to be authentic, it could place Maria's life at risk. He hoped and prayed that he wouldn't fail her.

Tiago showered, dressed, and gathered Maria's book and instructions, which he hid in the lining of his sports jacket, and then left his apartment. He skipped his usual morning visit to a café and arrived at the bookstore as the newspaper boy was exiting the door.

"*Olá*, Senhor Soares." Artur adjusted his sack on his shoulder. "I left extra newspapers. You should have enough to last the day."

"Much appreciated," Tiago said. "Have a good day at school."

"I will." The boy turned and walked down the sidewalk.

"Your school is the other way," Tiago called.

"Yes, *senhor*. I—I have one more delivery to make." The boy quickened his pace.

Tiago frowned. He entered the store and found Rosa at her counter reading a newspaper.

"Prodding Artur to get an education won't change the fact that he needs to work to help support his family," she said, her eyes focused on her paper.

"I must try," Tiago said.

She turned a page. "You're quite an idealist."

"And what are you?"

"A realist," she said. "You should try to be one. The world would be easier for you to navigate."

Tiago scanned the bookstore to make sure it was free of customers and approached her counter. A heaviness grew in his chest. "I have bad news."

She looked up and swallowed.

"Henri Levin was abducted last night."

Her face went pale. She touched her forehead, chest, and shoulders, making the sign of a cross.

For several minutes, he told her about Levin's kidnapping by the Gestapo, and him racing to hide Levin's wife and daughter in a safe house.

Rosa removed her glasses and rubbed her eyes. "How are Estelle and Albertine?"

"They're shattered," he said. "I'm going to see them this morning, and I hope that I can convince them to set sail for America."

Rosa jutted her jaw. "Damn PVDE are allowing the Germans

to have free rein in Lisbon. Their Gestapo, spies, and informants are everywhere."

Tiago nodded.

"Agent Neves was searching for Henri. Even though he wasn't present at the time of the kidnapping, I'm sure he was involved with helping the Gestapo to track him down."

"I agree." He slipped off his jacket and removed the book and handwritten notes.

"What's that?"

"A new scheme for us to work on." He placed the items on her counter.

She raised her brows. "That doesn't look like travel papers."

"You're correct."

He told her about meeting with Maria, minus their romantic interlude, and her work to feed misleading information to the Germans. Although he disliked having to reveal Maria's secrets, he didn't feel like he was breaking her trust, since she knew that he had someone whom he relied on to help with forgeries. He would have preferred to create this high-risk, fake document himself, but to pull off a realistic forgery, one that may undergo great scrutiny, he needed the talents of the best counterfeit artist in Lisbon—Rosa.

"Our Maria is a spy," Rosa said, beaming.

More like a double spy. He opened the book to the page with the sample pink list, which was used to identify the locations and movements of Allied and Royal Naval ships. He slid the handwritten notes to her.

She examined the information.

"Is this something you would be willing to do?" he asked.

"Hell, yes."

He smiled. "Do you think that you could find matching British paper for the forgery?"

"I think so." She turned to Tiago. "Does Maria know that I'll be doing this?"

"No," Tiago said.

"I don't mind if you reveal to Maria my role in this."

He shook his head. "We'll handle this like all of our other forgeries. I'll be the person of contact. There is no reason to place two people at risk. We agreed on this when we started working together, remember?"

"I do." She thrummed her fingers on the counter. "When do you need it finished?"

"As soon as possible."

She closed the book. "I'll need to take some time away from the bookstore to find the proper paper."

"Of course." He slipped on his jacket. "How about leaving when I get back from checking on Estelle and Albertine?"

She nodded. "Give them a hug for me, and tell them that they are in my prayers."

"I will."

Tiago left the bookstore. As he made his way to the boardinghouse, a strange mixture of hope and dread swirled inside him. He was optimistic that he could persuade Estelle to flee with her daughter for America, and he was confident that Rosa could create a flawless forgery that could fool a German intelligence agent. But he worried about Maria. If her Axis contacts discovered that she was betraying them, she'd be abducted or killed. Despite his overwhelming desire to protect her, he would never interfere in her pursuit to fight Nazi tyranny. Like her, he was devoted to combat the spread of fascism, even if it cost him his life. He resolved to do everything he could to aid Maria's success as a double agent, and to overcome any obstacle that prevented them from being together.

Chapter 27

Estoril, Portugal—July 1, 1943

Maria's shoulder muscles tensed as the taxi driver slowed the automobile to a stop in front of the Hotel Atlântico, a gathering ground for German spies. She took in a deep breath and exhaled. *I can do this*, she thought, twisting the sapphire ring on her finger. *If I appear credible, my lies will be truths.*

She paid the driver, got out of the taxi, and entered the hotel lobby. Her high-heeled shoes clicked over the white marble floor as she made her way to the bar, where Lars had requested her to meet him. She passed a group of men who were speaking German and discussing where to eat dinner. Their conversation paused as the men's eyes gravitated to the sway of Maria's hips. She continued her pace, confident and steady, and rehearsed her plan in her head.

At the end of the lobby, she entered the bar, and a hotel employee wearing a tuxedo escorted her to a private table where Lars was smoking a cigarette.

"*Olá*," Maria said, putting on a fake smile.

Lars tamped out his cigarette in a crystal ashtray. He stood and greeted her with alternating kisses on her cheeks.

They sat and Lars looked at the employee. "A gin and tonic and a schnapps."

The man gave a nod and left.

"You know me well," she said.

"Of course."

Maria glanced to a window with a view of a starless, twilight sky over the Atlantic Ocean. "Beautiful seascape."

"It's much better during the day," he said. "At night, it's difficult to see the garden that leads to the shore. I'm not much of a flower person, but the hotel has a reputation of having one of the most beautiful grounds in Estoril."

"Then you'll need to invite me back during the day."

He smoothed his tie. "It's good to see you."

"You too," she said, hiding her consternation.

"I'm disappointed that I'm unable to join you for dinner." He glanced at his watch. "I have a business engagement in forty minutes."

"I understand," she said. "I appreciate you making time to meet with me on short notice."

He adjusted a cuff link. "You mentioned on the telephone that you have good news that was best to be discussed in person."

"Yes." She lowered her voice, despite being out of earshot of guests. "I've been in communication with a friend, who works for the Women's Royal Naval Service. She's agreed to provide me with Allied military intelligence."

A slim smile spread over his face.

"Also—to create a channel to receive her information—I've recruited a friend, who works in the London branch of the OSS. He will smuggle the intelligence to me on board the British plane that is used to transport my supplies to Lisbon." She leaned toward him. "I received my first shipment."

Lars placed his fingers together. "I'm impressed."

Maria opened her purse. She removed Tiago's fake pink list and placed it facedown on the table. "The document contains details of an Allied naval convoy that traveled from Halifax Harbor to the port of Liverpool."

Lars peeked at the list and placed it inside his briefcase, which was stowed under the table.

A waiter delivered their drinks and stepped away.

Maria sipped her gin and tonic. "I have a few requests that will need to be met before your contact person receives further intelligence. First, I would like to reach an agreement on a fair payment. My price has gone up, now that I have two people on my payroll."

"I'll give the intelligence to my contact to examine," he said. "Afterward, I'll act as an intermediary between you and him to reach an agreement on compensation. I will do my best to get you a high price for your work."

"I'm sure you will."

He took a gulp of schnapps. "In case he asks, what are the names and roles of your friends?"

"They would like to remain anonymous. For now, let's call the Liverpool woman Vera, and the London man Niles."

"Understandable." He swirled his schnapps. "May I ask why your friends agreed to smuggle the information to you?"

Maria rubbed her thumb and forefinger together. "Money."

"Of course, but what is their underlying motivation?"

Maria's brain raced. "Vera's a widower with two children under the age of five, and she's desperate for money. Also, she's sympathetic to Germany—her parents emigrated from Berlin after the Great War." She sipped her gin and tonic. "As for Niles, he'd sell his mother for a pint of beer."

"I see," Lars said. "What are your other requests?"

"Vera will forward most, if not all, of her future reports in handwritten notes. If she continues to steal original documents, she'll likely get caught."

"That would be wise," he said. "Anything else?"

"I'd like to meet the person who is buying my intelligence."

"In due time," Lars said. "Like your Vera and Niles, my contact wishes to remain incognito."

"All right."

He raised his glass. "Well done. You're on your way to becoming a rich woman."

Maria clinked his glass.

"What are your plans this evening?"

"I'm going to get a bite to eat and take a taxi home."

"How about meeting me at ten o'clock at Casino Estoril? My business will be finished by then. We can celebrate your accomplishment over champagne and roulette."

"That sounds lovely." She rose from her seat and picked up her purse. "I'll see you there."

Maria, adrenaline pumping through her veins, left the bar and exited the hotel. She strolled around the building and made her way toward the shore in hopes that the fresh sea air would calm her nerves. Entering the unlit garden, she glanced back to the hotel, its interior brightly illuminated. Lars's comment echoed in her head. *At night, it's difficult to see the garden that leads to the shore.* She changed direction and crept toward the hotel.

Maria hid behind a jacaranda tree. Poking her head around the trunk, she scanned the windows of the bar and located Lars, puffing on a cigarette. She waited for several minutes and, as she was about to leave, a man walked across the room and sat at Lars's table. She struggled to identify the man because of her distance from the hotel. A choice burned in her gut. Before she changed her mind, she made her way to a row of hedges, ten yards from the window. She crouched and peered through the glass, all the while praying that glare from the lights inside the building would prevent the men from spotting her. She'd expected Lars to be joined by Salazar's banker, Ricardo Espírito Santo. But the man was older with gray, slicked-back hair and thick eyebrows. She inched closer and recognized him—by his photographs in Axis newspapers—to be Admiral Wilhelm Canaris, the chief of the Abwehr. *Oh, dear God.* A chill ran through her body as Lars reached into his briefcase and gave Canaris her phony pink list.

Chapter 28

Lisbon, Portugal—July 15, 1943

Maria entered Jardim do Príncipe Real, a garden in central Lisbon, and was greeted by a predawn chorus of chirping swallows. The green space was a maze of inky shadows, created by the pale glimmer of a crescent moon. She traveled along an earthen path to the center of the garden, where she saw the silhouette of a tall figure standing under the canopy of an ancient cypress tree.

"Tiago?"

"Yes." He approached her.

His face came into view and she wrapped her arms around him.

"I've missed you," he said, holding her tight.

"Me too. I'm sorry that I haven't been able to see you."

"It's temporary."

She nuzzled to him and took in his warmth.

Maria hadn't seen Tiago since their brief interlude. She'd arranged to meet him at Príncipe Real Garden by leaving a message with Rosa at the bookstore. She felt horrible for not seeing him, but her life had been irreversibly altered since delivering the fake Allied intelligence to Lars.

"How are you?" he asked.

"I'm okay," she said, not wanting to worry him.

"Are there concerns with the veracity of the forged document I provided you?" he asked, as if he could sense her disquietude.

"No," she said. "Much has happened in the past few weeks. At some point, I'll tell you everything, but I can't right now. Please know that I am safe, and that you are in my thoughts when we're apart."

He squeezed her.

"Do you trust me?"

"With my life."

Tears welled up in her eyes. She leaned her head to his chest. "Tell me something good."

He looked at her and caressed her cheek with his thumb. "Tomorrow, Estelle and Albertine board the *Serpa Pinto* for America."

She smiled. "That's glorious news."

"It wouldn't have happened without your funding for their tickets and bribes to ship stewards."

"I'm glad the money helped, but it was you who created their path to freedom."

"We both played a part in their future."

He led her to a wooden bench, where they sat and held hands. They spoke nothing more of the war. Instead, they discussed their hopes and dreams until night turned to dawn.

"Someday," he said, "we'll spend every morning together, watching the sun rise."

She leaned to him. "Nothing would make me happier."

He gently lifted her chin and pressed his lips to hers.

She kissed him deeply and her troubles melted away.

The grinding of a car engine grew on a nearby street. A church bell rang.

Maria eased back. "I need to go."

"When will I see you again?"

"I don't know." She rose from her seat.

Tiago, remaining seated, pulled her to him and pressed his cheek to her chest. "Please be careful."

It's too late for that, she thought, running her fingers through his hair. She kissed the top of his head and slipped away.

At her apartment building, she scanned the area to make sure there were no onlookers. Inside the building, she climbed the stairs and entered her apartment.

The floorboards in the living room creaked.

Her adrenaline surged. She darted to the kitchen, grabbed a knife from a drawer, and turned.

"Easy!" Argus said, raising his hands.

"You nearly scared me to death," Maria said, her heart racing. She placed the knife on the counter. "How did you get in here?"

"The message that you left at the embassy instructed me to use the fire escape to enter through the window. It was locked, so I had to break the glass."

"That was two weeks ago," she said. "Much has changed since then. I thought you would be here sooner. What took you so long?"

"I was stuck in Madrid," he said. "I left as soon as I could."

Maria shook away her angst and pointed to a pot on the stove. "Would you like some coffee?"

"Yes, please."

Minutes later, they sat at the kitchen table with cups of reheated coffee. Maria's head buzzed with the events of the past weeks and the welfare of her friends.

"How are Pilar and Roy?" she asked.

"Well," he said. "But they might be returning to Lisbon."

"I thought Pilar would be staying in Madrid?"

"They've discovered that Axis information is more challenging to acquire in Spain than Portugal, and Kilgour is weighing the option of redeploying them."

"That's unfortunate."

He nodded. "How is your spying on Lars Steiger coming along?"

Maria took a drink of day-old coffee, acidic and bitter. "Better than expected."

"How so?"

She drew a deep breath, gathering her nerve. She told him about spending time with Lars at his home and Casino Estoril, and how he gradually revealed to her bits and pieces of his Swiss bank dealings with Portugal to provide wolfram to Germany.

"He's acquiring wolfram two ways," she said. "Through the black market and through transactions with Salazar and his personal banker. He spends lots of time in the mountains of Covilhã, where the wolfram is being mined. Given how much money he spends at the casino, he's probably smuggling more on the black market than through the Portuguese government."

"That's what we suspected all along," he said. "Have you gained any intelligence on the tonnage of wolfram or the amount of gold and escudos that is changing hands?"

"I'm working on it." She sipped coffee. "I accompanied Lars to São Bento Mansion for a business meeting with Salazar and his personal banker."

His eyes widened. "You're kidding."

She shook her head. "I didn't sit in on their discussion, of course, but I got to meet Salazar and his banker." An image of her visit flashed in her head. "In Salazar's office, he has a framed photograph of the Italian dictator, Benito Mussolini, on his desk."

"I'll be damned."

She swirled her coffee. "I suppose that Salazar and his banker thought that I was using Lars as a sugar daddy."

He swallowed. "I assume you're still spending time with Steiger."

"Several nights a week."

"Good work. I'd like for you to draft a report with everything you can recall from your meetings and conversations."

Tension grew in her chest. "There's more that I need to tell you."

He leaned forward in his chair.

"Over drinks, Lars told me that he knew someone who will

pay handsomely for Allied military intelligence, and he asked if I would be interested in supplying the information."

Lines formed on Argus's forehead. "What did you say?"

"I said yes."

He shifted in his seat.

"If I would have said no, Lars's confidence in me might have been broken."

"It's all right," he said. "We'll work around it. We can devise a plan to stall and—"

"I've already implemented a plan," she blurted.

He rubbed his meaty jowls. "You should have consulted with me first."

"I didn't have the time to check with you. I seized the opportunity when it arose."

He loosened his tie. "Very well. Tell me what you did."

She refilled their coffees and told him about conjuring a story about two people—Vera with the Women's Royal Naval Service and Niles with the London branch of the OSS—who stole and smuggled information to her on the British plane used for her supplies.

"I gave Lars fictitious information about an Allied naval convoy," she said, leaving out that Tiago forged a document for her. "And I witnessed Lars passing along the information to Admiral Canaris, head of the Abwehr."

"Good God, Maria," he said, running a hand over his hair. "You're going to get yourself killed."

"Initially, I thought the same thing. The day after delivering the fake information, I noticed two men in an automobile that was parked outside my building. They surveilled me for days. I presumed that they were Abwehr agents observing my whereabouts as a prospective spy for the Germans." She glanced to the broken window. "That's why my message instructed you to use the fire escape. I didn't want them to spot you."

He set aside his coffee.

"After a week, the surveillance stopped and I received a call from Lars to inform me that a man would be stopping by my apartment to deliver a gift." She looked at him. "It was an Abwehr agent. He gave me a German codebook, invisible ink, and the location of a dead drop."

"You're in over your head, Maria. I'm sending you home on the next ship back to the States."

She rose from her seat. "I'm staying."

"Your scam will never work. You'll be dead in a month."

Maria opened a cabinet, removed a biscuit tin, and placed it on the table. She opened the lid, revealing mounds of cash and a small bar of gold.

Argus's jaw dropped open. He lifted the bar of gold and examined its swastika and Reichsbank stamp.

"My plan is working. The Abwehr believes I'm spying for Germany. Why else would they pay me in escudos and Nazi gold?" She looked into his eyes. "We can use my misinformation to the Allies' advantage and—with all due respect, sir—I'm not leaving Lisbon until we win the damn war."

Part 3

Operation Fortitude

Chapter 29

Lisbon, Portugal—December 10, 1943

Maria, her fountain pen filled with invisible ink, scribbled a note in German code that provided a fake account of a Gato-class submarine called the USS *Stonefish* that had been launched from the Portsmouth Naval Shipyard in Kittery, Maine. She blew on the ink to accelerate its drying time, and then stashed the message in her purse. She looked at a wall clock, which read 10:07 a.m. With plenty of time to deliver her message to the Abwehr dead drop before her rendezvous with Argus, she retrieved her camera and began to microfilm a weekly newspaper edition of *Das Reich*.

Not only had Argus permitted Maria to remain in Lisbon, the OSS had given her full support to supply misinformation to German intelligence. Over the past several months, she'd created a team of seven fake subagents in Britain and the United States. In addition to Vera in Liverpool and Niles in London, her imaginary team consisted of Malcolm—a fisherman in Glasgow, Ruby—a cleaning woman who worked at the US War Department in Washington, Daniel—a bartender in Portsmouth who served drinks to shipyard workers, Raymond—a cargo handler at the New York Port of Embarkation, and Hazel—a birdwatcher and amateur photographer in South East England. She'd delivered over twenty secret messages to an Abwehr dead drop, a cavity behind a loose brick in an alley near the German embassy. To date, her intelligence hadn't been refuted by the Abwehr, but she suspected that it was only a matter of time before German intelligence agents discovered a flaw in her facts. And if this were to happen, she hoped that she could redeem herself by blaming her subagents for false information and mistakes.

In addition to fake reports, Maria provided the Abwehr with real information of low military worth, and important intelligence that was intentionally postponed. In September, shortly prior to the Allied invasion of Italy, Maria's subagent in Glasgow reported a convoy of Allied troop ships and amphibious landing vessels—painted in Mediterranean camouflage. Although the letter was sent by airmail and postmarked before the invasion, it was intentionally stalled by OSS and British intelligence and it arrived too late to be of value for the Germans. Soon after, Maria received a coded message in her Abwehr dead drop that—when deciphered—read: "We're disappointed that your news was received late, but the intelligence was superb."

Maria never met directly with Admiral Wilhelm Canaris or his Abwehr agents, with the exception of a German spy, code name Wolf, who delivered invisible ink and a codebook, and gave her a crash course on espionage. The Abwehr referred to her as Codex, a term for ancient manuscript books, and the OSS called her Virginia, which was the name Maria used to gate-crash the Astor mansion and meet Colonel Donovan. All of her communications with the Abwehr were done through a dead drop, and her payments—for her and her subagents—were hand-delivered to her by Lars. In less than six months, she'd been paid the equivalent of over $115,000 in escudos and Nazi gold. She'd kept no payments for herself. Instead, she'd turned the bribe money over to the OSS, but not before giving sizable donations to Tiago to aid refugees.

The tide of the war was leaning toward the Allies. Italy had signed an armistice and ousted its dictator, Benito Mussolini, although he remained in northern Italy as a puppet leader under

Hitler. Allied troops, battling their way north from the "toe" of Italy, were halted south of Rome by strong German defensive lines. Despite the stalled progress, and the possibility that fighting could linger for years, Maria was hopeful that Allied forces would eventually liberate Europe. With an end to the conflict, she'd reunite with her father, whom she dearly missed, and she'd be free to build a future with Tiago. But for now, she refused to think about herself. She resolved to do her duties until the world was at peace.

A knock came from the door.

Maria cautiously crept to the door and peered through the peephole. Her eyes widened at the sight of Pilar and Roy, and a wave of joy surged through her. She undid the latch and threw open the door, and wrapped her arms around them.

Pilar squeezed her. "I'm so happy to see you."

"Me too," Maria said, releasing them. "I've missed you terribly."

Roy grinned. "You look surprised."

"I am," Maria said. "I thought you were arriving in a few days."

"We finished up early in Madrid," Pilar said. "We took the overnight train to Lisbon."

Maria ushered them inside to sit at the kitchen table while she made a fresh pot of coffee. She filled their cups and, with little food in the apartment, she served a plate of week-old *biscoitos.*

"The cookies are a bit stale," Maria said. "I recommend that you dunk them in your joe."

Roy dipped a cookie into his coffee and took a bite. "You're right—it's good."

"Where's your luggage?" Maria asked, despite knowing what they would say.

"We dropped it off at our new apartments," Pilar said with a timbre of disappointment. "I think it's wasteful that Kilgour has moved me to a separate apartment when there's plenty of room here with you."

"Kilgour has his reasons," Roy said, sticking up for his boss.

"He wants us to have storage space for the books that we microfilm."

Although Maria continued her book acquisition role as a cover story, she infrequently communicated with Kilgour since she began reporting to Argus, the OSS operations head for the Iberian Peninsula. Last week, Argus informed Maria that her comrades, upon their return to Lisbon, would have separate living quarters, which would allow her privacy to conduct her clandestine work. Maria hated keeping secrets from them, but she agreed with the OSS's decision. Most of all, she wanted to shield her friends from danger in the event that the Abwehr discovered that her loyalties remained with the Allies and they came to kill her.

"It won't be the same without you here," Maria said. "Where are your new apartments?"

"Near Estrela Basilica," Roy said.

Pilar frowned. "It's a thirty-minute walk from here."

"At least you'll be close to the embassy," Maria said. "I'll visit you every chance I get."

For thirty minutes, Pilar and Roy filled her in on their time in Madrid. They'd had minimal success with acquiring Axis publications, due to the reluctance of bookshops and libraries to source enemy material. Most of the acquisitions were German newspapers, which they could obtain in Lisbon.

"Although Spain is neutral, the country is aligned with Germany," Roy said. "I think it stems from when dictator Franco called upon Hitler to help him win the Spanish Civil War."

Sadness filled Pilar's eyes. She picked at cookie crumbs.

Maria reached across the table and gave a gentle squeeze to Pilar's hand. "You did everything you could. After this war, things will change. Someday, your Spain and my Portugal will be democracies."

"I hope so," she said.

"I have faith that it will happen," Maria said. "When the dictators are gone, I expect all three of us to be here to celebrate with the people of the Iberian Peninsula."

Roy slipped a pipe from his jacket pocket. "It might take generations for things to change."

Maria looked at him. "Then you better live a long time. You're not getting out of this, Roy. You're going to join us when it happens, and it *will* happen."

"If I'm alive," he said, "I'll be here."

"It's a deal," Maria said.

Pilar smiled and took a sip of coffee. "Enough about us. How are you?"

"I'm good," Maria said, an uneasiness rising inside her. *I hate keeping secrets from them*. She refilled her cup and told them about her book acquisitions and microfilming.

"How's Tiago?" Pilar asked.

"He's well," Maria said.

"Who's Tiago?" Roy asked, packing tobacco into his pipe.

Pilar nudged him. "The bookseller on Rua do Crucifixo."

"Oh, yes," Roy said. "He has the store with all the poetry."

Maria nodded. "He's our best supplier of Axis publications in Lisbon."

Pilar looked at Maria. "Maybe we could take a walk sometime after work this week. I'd like to hear about the books you got from Tiago."

She knows that I care for him. "That would be lovely." Maria glanced at the clock. "I hate to run off when you just got here, but I have an appointment to pick up books."

"I'll come with you," Pilar said.

Maria stood. "I would enjoy your company, but you need to get some rest. I doubt that you slept much on the train. Get settled into your new place, and I'll be over for a visit."

"All right," Pilar said.

They cleared the table, and Maria wrote down their addresses and telephone numbers. They left the apartment building and headed in separate directions.

Near the German embassy, Maria entered a narrow, pedestrian alleyway. She located the loose brick in the wall of an old building.

She kneeled and pretended to adjust her shoe until the area was clear of people. She removed the brick and inserted her note into a cavity in the stone. After securing the brick back into its place, she made her way toward the riverfront.

At the docks in Alcântara, she approached an old man with a wind-weathered face who was standing near a wooden dinghy. The man gave a nod, helped her into the boat, and gestured to take a seat on a bench in the bow. He sat in the stern, pulled a cord on an outboard motor, and the propeller buzzed to life. The motor whined as the dinghy pulled away from the dock. The bow bobbed up and down as they traveled across the Tagus River. The smell of the briny water resurrected macabre memories of the *Yankee Clipper*. Her heart ached for the fallen and injured passengers. Images of Ben Robertson, Tamara Drasin, and Jane Froman flashed in her head. She buried her thoughts and gripped the side of the dinghy as water sprayed over the bow.

Minutes later, they arrived at an anchored fishing boat near the south side of the Tagus River. A rowboat, which Maria presumed was Argus's mode of transport, was tied to the back of the vessel. The dinghy pulled close and Argus emerged from the wheelhouse. Maria grabbed the rung of a metal ladder that was placed over the side of the boat, and she labored upward.

Argus helped her onto the boat and looked at the dinghy captain. "Return in an hour," he said in Portuguese.

The man revved the throttle of his outboard motor and left.

They went inside the wheelhouse, where they sat on overturned wooden crates emblazoned with the word *sardinha*. A faint yet pungent smell of old fish filled the air.

"Pilar and Roy arrived this morning," Maria said, breaking the silence.

"I'm aware," he said.

"Is that why we are meeting here?"

"No," he said. "I have something important to discuss."

She straightened her back. "Everything we talk about is confidential."

"Yes, but for this meeting I wanted to take extra precaution that we wouldn't be seen or overheard."

She swallowed.

He leaned forward and intertwined his fingers. "Allied intelligence services are confident that the Abwehr believes you are working for them."

She smoothed her wool skirt. "I think so, too. Otherwise, I'd be dead."

He nodded.

Maria drew a deep breath, attempting to ease a tightness in her chest.

"You've been chosen as a double agent to participate in a special operation. It's part of an overall Allied deception strategy."

Her heart rate quickened. "What kind of deception?"

He looked at her. "The location of the Allied invasion of France."

A mixture of fervor and fear surged through Maria's veins.

"Over the coming months, you'll be supplied with disinformation about the buildup of troops and transport vessels. Your role will be to supply the fake intelligence to the Abwehr to create an impression of where the invasion will take place."

"And where might that be?"

"I don't know," he said. "At some point, I expect you'll be informed of where we want the Germans to think we'll invade. But I doubt that either of us will know the true location of the land invasion."

Her mind raced. "When will the invasion occur?"

"I wasn't provided a date," he said. "But I suspect it will be within a year. It'll depend on when Italy is liberated."

"Does this plan have a code name?"

"Operation Fortitude."

For an hour, they discussed her role in the operation and made plans on how she and Argus would communicate, which they agreed would be through a dead drop rather than leaving messages at the embassy. Their meeting was brought to a close by the growing buzz of the dinghy's outboard motor.

Argus shook Maria's hand. "Godspeed."

"Thank you, sir."

Maria left the wheelhouse and climbed down into the dinghy. As the craft was crossing the river, she glanced back and saw Argus, rowing a boat toward Almada, a town on the south shore. She faced forward. A cold, damp wind nipped at her cheeks. As the city of Lisbon neared, a will to fight burned inside her. For the first time since the war began, she felt that victory was within reach.

CHAPTER 30

LISBON, PORTUGAL—JANUARY 7, 1944

Maria, wearing a sleek black evening dress that was hidden beneath her wool coat, quickened her pace on the smooth, limestone sidewalk of Rua do Crucifixo. She reached Tiago's bookstore as Rosa was locking the door for the evening.

"*Olá*," Maria said.

Rosa turned and smiled. "It's good to see you."

"You too." She took in a deep inhale, attempting to catch her breath. She glanced through the front window at the dark interior of the store. Her shoulders slumped. "I've missed him again, haven't I?"

"Yes. You and Tiago have divergent schedules." Rosa slipped her key into the lock and opened the door. "Come inside for a moment."

"It is kind of you to offer," she said. "But you were on your way home. I'll stop back another time."

Rosa entered and turned on the lights. She removed her coat and placed it on a rack.

Maria, feeling obligated, entered and shut the door.

"May I take your coat?" Rosa asked.

"That's okay," she said, not wanting to reveal her attire.

Rosa slid a stool from behind her counter and tapped the seat. "Sit."

"I feel bad taking the only chair," she said. "I can stand."

"I insist," Rosa said. "I've been on that stool all day. It's good for my blood flow to stretch my legs."

Maria sat and placed her purse on her lap.

"How are you?" Rosa asked.

"Okay," she lied.

Rosa lowered her glasses on the bridge of her nose. "Tiago refuses to burden others, and he rarely tells me if something is troubling him. But I can tell that he's lonely and sad, much like what I see when I look at you."

Maria shifted in her seat.

"He cares for you."

"I'm fond of him, too."

Rosa fixed her glasses. "Someday, the conflict and suffering will end, and so will your duties in Lisbon. Eventually, you and Tiago will have time for each other."

"I hope so."

Rosa picked up her purse and removed rosary beads. "I pray for you."

A wave of emotion rolled over Maria. She blinked her eyes, fighting back tears. "*Obrigada*."

She slipped the beads into her purse and placed a hand on Maria's shoulder. "There's something that I would like you to remember."

Maria looked at Rosa, her aged, brown eyes magnified by her thick lenses.

"It might feel like the war has created a mountain between you and Tiago, but with diligence and faith, anything is possible."

Maria nodded and wiped her eyes.

Rosa patted Maria's shoulder and then put on her coat. "I should let you go. No need for me to make you late for an engagement."

She gathered her composure. "What makes you think that I have someplace to be?"

"You're wearing nice shoes. The quality of the dress material, peeking from the hem of your coat, tells me that you're going someplace lavish. You're wearing a smidge of makeup, absent lipstick, which I assume you'll put on prior to your arrival. If I had to guess, I'd say you're going to an expensive restaurant in Lisbon, or to Estoril where all the posh people eat."

"You'd make a good detective."

Rosa tapped a finger to her temple. "My eyesight isn't what it used to be, but I still see everything."

Maria smiled. *Indeed, you do.*

They exited the bookstore and Rosa locked the door.

Maria watched Rosa disappear around a street corner, and then made her way to Praça do Comércio. She was sorry to have missed Tiago, but was grateful for Rosa's words of encouragement. She hailed a taxi and got into the back seat.

"Where to?" the driver asked.

"Estoril."

A half hour later, Maria arrived at Lars's mansion overlooking the sea. Inside, a maid took her coat and led her to a dining room with lit candles and a chilled bottle of white wine.

"Senhor Steiger will be down in a moment," the woman said. "Would you care for an aperitif?"

"No, thank you."

The woman turned and left.

Maria sat at one of the two place settings at the end of an Art Deco rosewood table, large enough to seat a dozen guests. Minutes passed and footsteps grew in the corridor.

"Good evening," Lars said entering the room.

Maria stood and exchanged kisses to their cheeks. His face was freshly shaven, and he smelled of lavender-scented soap. She glanced to the candles. "It looks like your chef, Tomás, is making us dinner."

"His meals are better than any restaurant in town," he said. "Also, I wanted to talk in privacy."

She forced a smile. "Dinner here is perfect."

He poured two glasses of white wine.

Maria took a sip. "Is there something in particular that you wanted to discuss?"

"A couple of things," he said. "One is business and the other is personal. Where would you like to start?"

"Let's get business out of the way."

He lit a cigarette from a silver case in his suit jacket. He took a drag and exhaled. "I've heard a concerning rumor."

Her skin prickled. "What about?" she asked calmly.

"A reliable source informed me that Admiral Canaris might be on his way out as head of the Abwehr."

Holy mackerel! She swirled her wine. "Do you mind if I ask who told you this?"

He took a swig. "A Swiss banker, especially one with German clients, never discloses their sources. I hope you understand."

"I do," she said. "Forgive me for asking."

"It's all right," he said. "I don't blame you for inquiring. I'd do the same thing if I were you."

"Are you sure about Canaris possibly being removed?"

"Yes," he said. "I didn't want you to be surprised by the change. Canaris spends a good deal of time in Portugal. His removal, or sudden unknown whereabouts, might make the newspapers."

"Thank you. I appreciate you keeping me informed."

Maria's mind flashed to her last coded message to the Abwehr. It contained a fake report, supplied to her by Allied intelligence in London, about the sighting of eight marine landing craft in an estuary near Dover, England. *The Allies might want the Germans to believe they will invade at Pas-de-Calais, France, which is across the Channel from Dover. But how effective will my misinformation be if Abwehr leadership is disrupted?* She buried her thought and asked, "Do you have any suggestions on how I should navigate things if Canaris is ousted?"

"Carry on with supplying your intelligence to the Abwehr, and I'll continue to deliver their payments to you. If I learn of Canaris's successor, I will let you know."

She nodded. "Is there any other business to tell me about?"

"No." He flicked ash into an ashtray.

"What is the personal item that you wanted to talk to me about?"

He smoothed his black tie over a crisp, white dress shirt. "I'm flying to Switzerland for a wedding. It's several months away, but I was wondering if you would like to accompany me."

"Oh," she said, feeling surprised. "Who is getting married?"

"A family friend. Her name is Margarete."

She looked at him and put on a fake smile. "Are you asking me to be your date? I thought you said that I was too young for you."

"You still are," he said. "I enjoy your company, and I thought you might like to get out of Lisbon for a weekend, assuming you're comfortable with being on an airplane."

"Is it safe to fly to Switzerland?"

"Yes. I fly often between Lisbon and Bern. We'd be traveling from one neutral country to another neutral country, and the flight path over Spain and Vichy France is secure for Swiss flights."

Maria wiggled her toes inside her shoes. She had no intentions of going on a trip with him, but she wanted to let him down gracefully to avoid damaging their relationship and her access to the Abwehr. "After what I experienced in the crash of the *Yankee Clipper*, I'm not sure if I can bring myself to get on a plane. May I think about it?"

"Of course." He touched her hand.

She fought the urge to pull away from him.

"I know it will be difficult for you. You'll have months to consider the invitation. I don't plan on asking anyone else to join me."

She looked at his wedding ring. A memory of him confiding in her about the death of his wife and children echoed in her brain. "I hope you don't think that I'm being intrusive. But do you think Gisela would have wanted you to move on with your life?"

He lowered his hand and stared into his drink. "Yes."

"Why don't you?"

"I'm not ready to leave the past."

"You must try."

His eyes filled with sorrow. "Maybe someday."

Maria felt pity for him. Despite that she detested his collaboration with the enemy, she understood the lingering pain of losing family. Unlike Maria, Lars had been unable to work through his sorrow. He'd chosen to numb his heartache by acquiring riches and gambling them away, as if he were avoiding the process of coming to terms with the death of his family. She wondered, although briefly, if his grief played a factor in his decision to conspire with Germany and launder its Nazi gold. She set aside her emotions and resolved to keep her sympathy for him at bay.

They spoke little during dinner. Afterward, they went to the casino, where Lars lost huge sums of money at roulette. Maria stood by his side and pretended to enjoy the evening, all the while brainstorming plans for Operation Fortitude in her head.

CHAPTER 31

LISBON, PORTUGAL—JANUARY 10, 1944

Tiago entered the office of his bookstore, closed the door, and sat behind his desk. He removed an envelope with United States postage from his jacket. His anticipation grew as he opened the envelope and unfolded the stationery.

Dear Tiago,

There are no words to express my indebtedness for all that you have done to protect me and my daughter. Because of you, we no longer live in a constant state of fear and oppression. I am forever grateful for your gift of freedom.

A smile spread over Tiago's face. *Estelle and Albertine.*

I wish I had news to report about my husband. American authorities are working to determine where he might be imprisoned. I hold hope that, after the war, he will be released by his captors and find his way back to us.

Tiago's mind drifted to his grandparents and Henri Levin. He prayed that they were alive and not suffering, but a sense of foreboding lingered in his gut.

Like me, my daughter is heartbroken. She misses her father, and I long for my husband. We are gradually adapting to our new lives. My daughter is making friends at her school, and I've found work as a seamstress. With the money you gifted us, we've moved into a boardinghouse in Brooklyn. Someday, I hope to repay you for your kindness. May God bless you with the means to allow asylum seekers to reach America.

Your beholden friend

Tiago glanced at the envelope's return address. He thought it was shrewd of Estelle to not provide names, considering that letters, especially ones from outside the country, were often inspected by Portugal's Censorship Service. He was relieved to know that Estelle and her daughter were safe, and her words reaffirmed his commitment to aid Jewish refugees. *Grand-père and Grand-mère would be overjoyed by this news*, he thought. A wave of optimism surged through him. Eager to send a reply to Estelle, he took out a piece of paper and retrieved a fountain pen.

A classical piano concerto sounded from the radio on Rosa's counter.

Hairs rose on the back of his neck. He stashed the letter in his secret hole under a floor tile and stood. As he reached for the doorknob, a loud crash came from the front of the store. His adrenaline surged. He darted from his office to find Agent Neves and three men at the counter with Rosa. Artur, his eyes wide and clutching his sack of newspapers, stared at a pile of broken wood and shattered vacuum tubes.

"I was trying to turn it off for you!" Rosa glared at Neves. "You're going to buy me a new radio!"

Neves, ignoring Rosa, locked his eyes on Tiago.

"What's going on?" Tiago said, approaching him.

"I have authorization to conduct a search." Neves motioned to one of the men, who brushed past Tiago and made his way to the office.

"I'd like to see the warrant," Tiago said.

Neves removed a folded paper from his coat and extended his hand. As Tiago reached, Neves cocked back his arm and landed a fierce punch to Tiago's stomach.

Pain shot through his abdomen and he buckled over.

Rosa screamed.

Artur's face went pale. He pressed his back to a magazine rack.

"Search him," Neves said.

Two agents lifted Tiago by his arms and slammed him against a bookcase. Rows of books tumbled to the floor. One agent removed a baton from his coat and pressed it over Tiago's larynx, while the other man searched through his clothing.

Tiago, unable to breathe, fought to push the baton from his neck. His pulse pounded in his eardrums.

"Stop!" Rosa clawed at the men but was pushed aside by Neves.

An agent removed Tiago's wallet and a sheathed knife from the interior pocket of his jacket. His comrade lowered the baton.

Tiago fell to his knees and gasped for air.

Rustling came from Tiago's office. Seconds later, an agent—carrying his hat like a basket—approached his comrades.

Neves took the man's hat and rummaged through the contents—forgery supplies, three expired passports, a roll of escudos, and a small gold bar. He picked up the gold and eyed its swastika and Reichsbank stamp.

Neves grabbed Tiago's hair, yanked his head back, and held the bar inches from his face. "Where did you get this?"

Tiago stared at the Nazi gold, given to him by Maria. Defiance burned in his chest. He clenched his jaw.

"Handcuff him," Neves said.

"Leave him alone!" Rosa shouted.

The agents placed handcuffs on Tiago, tightened them to gouge into his wrists, and lifted him to his feet.

"Take the woman to headquarters for questioning," Neves said.

"Tiago!" Rosa cried.

"Everything will be all right," Tiago called.

An agent clasped her arm and led her out of the store.

Neves grabbed the back of Tiago's collar and forced him toward the door.

Tiago glanced at Artur. He felt sick about the boy having to witness his arrest. "Run along now."

Artur looked down and away. "I'm sorry, Senhor Soares."

Neves paused, placing a hand on the boy's shoulder. "Well done, my boy."

Tiago lowered his head. *Oh, God. How could I have been so blind?*

CHAPTER 32

LISBON, PORTUGAL—JANUARY 10, 1944

Tiago was taken to PVDE headquarters, led to the basement level of the building, and placed in a windowless interrogation cell. Two of Neves's comrades shackled him to a metal chair. The bindings were tightened, cutting off the circulation to his hands and feet. The room was dark, except for a desk lamp that was pointed at his face. He squinted, attempting to shield his eyes from the intense light. The agents left and closed a solid steel door behind them. He listened for Rosa but heard nothing, except for a high-pitch buzz coming from the filaments of a high wattage lightbulb.

Regret gnawed at his soul. Informants were everywhere in Lisbon, yet he'd taken little, if any, precaution with Artur. With his focus on Artur's education, he'd failed to consider that the boy, struggling to earn money for his family, could be susceptible to bribes from the secret police. It had taken little time for Neves's comrade to locate his secret hole. The agent, Tiago believed, must have known precisely where to look. He imagined Artur, while in his bookstore for his daily delivery, detecting the sound of a clinking floor tile in his office.

His carelessness, Tiago believed, would result in dire ramifications for him and Rosa. He prayed that she wasn't undergoing the same kind of treatment in her holding cell. There was nothing that he could do to save himself, but he was determined to find a way to absolve Rosa from any crimes, regardless of the consequences to him.

His miscalculation about Artur wasn't his only blunder. He'd been preoccupied with work, and he'd failed to take the Nazi gold bar—a donation by Maria to aid refugees—to his trusted jeweler to melt down and sell. In addition to the gold that Neves confiscated in his bookstore, there were several other palm-size gold bars hidden in his apartment. He gathered his resolve. *No matter what they do to me, I'll never reveal Maria's name.*

Hours later, the cell door opened and Agent Neves entered.

Tiago raised his head and squinted.

Neves locked the door, sat at a wooden table across from Tiago, and lit a cigar.

A smell of burnt tobacco filled Tiago's nose.

"How long have you been counterfeiting passports?" Neves asked.

Tiago turned his head away from the light.

Neves leaned over the table. He drew on his cigar, flaring the ember, and ground it into the back of Tiago's hand.

Pain seared through his skin. He jerked but the shackles held tight.

Neves removed the cigar and relit the end with a metal lighter. "You'll talk. I might need to go through a box of cigars, but eventually you'll tell me everything."

He's a sadistic lunatic. Tiago's pulse pounded in his temples.

"Let's try this again," Neves said. "When did you begin counterfeiting passports?"

His heart told him to fight, but his brain knew that it would be of no use to remain silent if he wanted to convince Neves that he acted alone. He buried his pain and emotion and said, "At the start of the war."

"That wasn't so hard, was it?" The agent flicked ash. "Are all of the papers for Jews."

"Yes."

For several minutes, Neves interrogated him on the forging of documents for refugees. Tiago answered each question in a manner that, he hoped, would make him appear as if he were the sole counterfeiter.

Neves puffed on his cigar and blew smoke through his nostrils. "What does your clerk know about this?"

"Nothing."

"We have her confession," Neves said. "She's admitted her guilt. I want to hear your side of it."

He's lying. Rosa wouldn't easily crack, even under intense interrogation. "She's a clerk at my bookstore, nothing more. I hired her to run the shop to allow me the freedom to create papers for refugees. I'm out of the store much of the time, which you may already know from your surveillance."

Neves stroked his mustache. He took a drag and said, "Where did you get the gold?"

Tiago felt a smidge of relief with the questioning moving away from Rosa. His mind raced. "A donation from a wealthy asylum seeker."

"Tell me their name."

"Uri Malkin." Tiago hoped the fictitious name would buy time, given that it would take days, perhaps even weeks, to search emigration records.

"Is he a Jew?"

"Yes."

"How did he obtain German gold?"

"I don't know," Tiago said. "I presume he stole it."

"How did you meet him?"

"He heard rumors at the shipyard that I forged papers. He came into my bookstore."

"Did you provide him a passport?"

"I altered his existing passport," Tiago said, "It was expired."

"Why did he pay you in gold?"

"He paid me in escudos," Tiago said. "The gold was a gift."

The agent rubbed his jowl. "What was his reason?"

"Six members of Malkin's extended family were arrested by the Germans in France. He wanted me to use the gold toward helping refugees leave Europe."

"How much gold was given to you?"

"Four small bars," he said, deciding it was best to reveal all of his gold. "Three at my apartment and one at the shop, which I was planning to have melted down and sold."

"I searched your apartment," Neves said. "I didn't find any gold. Perhaps you misplaced it."

The bastard stole it and he wants me to know it. His face turned hot.

"But I did find this." Neves reached into his jacket and placed a pistol on the table.

Tiago squinted.

Neves moved the desk lamp.

Tiago blinked and his eyes slowly focused on his Astra 400 pistol. Dread filled his stomach.

"Where did you get a Spanish service pistol?"

"I bought it."

"When?"

"Soon after I found you in my apartment. I felt that I needed protection."

Neves stood, clenched his fist, and struck Tiago in the jaw.

Pain shot through Tiago's face. He took in breaths, attempting to clear the fog from his brain. He swallowed and tasted blood.

"You lie." Neves adjusted his black necktie. "And you underestimate me. I've been investigating you for months. Earlier this week, I spoke with a woman named Leonor."

Oh, no.

"She claims that she and you had an affair while you were studying at the university in Coimbra, and that she ended the relationship when you went off to fight in the Spanish Civil War."

An acidic burn rose into Tiago's esophagus.

"According to government records, you aren't on the list of

soldiers that Salazar sent to support Franco's nationalist forces. Therefore, you must be a communist."

"I'm not a communist," Tiago said.

"If one opposes Salazar and the Estado Novo regime, that would make one a communist."

Cold sweat dripped down his back.

Neves removed a fresh cigar from his jacket and lit it. He puffed and blew smoke in Tiago's face. "We have much to discuss. By the time I'm through with you, you will have told me all the secrets in your head."

Tiago buried his trepidation. *I'll take his punishment. No matter how much suffering I endure, I will not divulge anything that could harm Rosa and Maria.*

Chapter 33

Lisbon, Portugal—January 11, 1944

Maria, hoping to see Tiago, climbed the stairs of his apartment building. At the landing, she froze at the sight of his broken front door. She crept inside to find the contents of the kitchen drawers and cabinets scattered over the floor.

"Tiago," she called, her voice trembling.

She entered the living room, where the furniture was overturned and the cushions destroyed, as if rabid dogs had ravaged the apartment. The vacuum, where Tiago hid his banned books, was broken in half with its dust bag turned inside out. In the bedroom, Tiago's clothes were strewn over the floor and the mattress was ripped open to expose its guts of wire springs.

Maria, her heart racing, fled the apartment. Minutes later, she arrived at the bookstore to find a padlock on the front door. A note taped to the window read, "Property of the New State."

Portuguese secret police raid, she thought. Her angst grew as she peered through the storefront glass at the books and smashed radio on the floor. She clasped her hand and prayed that Tiago and Rosa were far away when the raid took place. Feeling shaken and helpless, she left for home.

At her apartment, she inserted her key and discovered the door unlocked. Her adrenaline surged.

"Maria?" Pilar's voice called.

Thank God. She darted inside to find Pilar and Rosa in the kitchen.

"What's happened?" Maria asked, her voice quavering.

Pilar wrapped her arms around her. "Tiago was arrested."

"No!" Maria's legs turned weak.

Pilar released her. "I stopped by to visit, and I found Rosa outside the building searching for you. I let her in with my spare key."

Maria turned to Rosa, her left eye red and swollen. Her chest ached. "Did they hurt you?"

"I'm all right." Rosa clasped Maria's hand. "I have much to tell you."

"If you need privacy," Pilar said, "I'd be happy to leave."

"No," Rosa said. "If you're a friend of Maria's, I know that I can trust you."

They sat at the table. For several minutes, Rosa told them about the PVDE raid on the bookstore.

"The secret police knew precisely where to search," she said. "They confiscated forgery supplies, passports, money, and a Nazi gold bar from a hiding place in Tiago's office."

Maria lowered her head. Tears welled up in her eyes.

"In the police vehicle," Rosa said, "an agent gloated about our paperboy being an informant for the PVDE. I should have been more careful."

"I'm so sorry," Pilar said.

"They took me and Tiago to PVDE headquarters to interrogate," Rosa said. "They roughed me up a little, but I convinced them that I knew nothing about the gold or the forgeries. After five hours of questioning, they let me go. They're misogynistic pigs who are incapable of believing that an old woman could have the skills to create counterfeit documents."

"What are they doing with Tiago?" Maria asked.

"He remains detained by the PVDE." A tear dribbled down Rosa's cheek as she looked into Maria's eyes. "It should be me, not

Tiago, behind bars. He's a fledgling counterfeiter. I'm the one who forged most of the documents, including your pink list."

"Oh, Rosa," Maria said. She squeezed her hand.

Pilar stared with wide eyes.

"I gave Tiago the money and gold," Maria said. "It'll be used as evidence against him."

"Your gifts will have little impact on his fate," Rosa said, as if trying to comfort her. "The secret police fabricate charges to suit their agenda of suppressing those whom they deem to be a threat to Salazar's regime."

Pilar clasped her hands and leaned forward in her chair. "Is there anything I can do to help?"

Maria, struggling to set aside her heartache, ran through options in her brain. "We should notify the OSS that our best book supplier is under arrest. I'm not sure what they can do, but it's worth a try."

"I agree," Pilar said. "I'll take care of informing the OSS, and I'll make Roy aware of the situation when I see him."

"Thank you," Maria said.

Rosa wiped her eyes and stood. "I'm going to speak with a lawyer who I used to work for. He owes me a favor for my years of being a pawn in his devious deeds. I'll let you know what I find out."

"Where can I reach you?" Maria asked.

Rosa, using a piece of paper and pencil from her purse, scribbled her address. She hugged Maria, and left.

Pilar drew a deep breath and exhaled. "I don't want you to feel obligated to tell me everything that is going on. I suspect that you're working on a confidential OSS assignment. Otherwise, Roy and I would not have been relocated to another section of town. I want you to know that I'm here for you, if you should need anything—anything at all."

Maria nodded, feeling grateful for her friend's selfless support.

"He's going to be okay," Pilar said. "We'll find a way to get him freed from jail."

"We will," Maria said, despite her angst.

Maria hugged Pilar goodbye, walked her to the door, and watched her disappear down the stairwell. Alone in the apartment, the seriousness of Tiago's predicament weighed heavy on her heart. She sat on a sofa, wrapped her arms around her knees, and cried.

I shouldn't have given him the gold with Nazi markings. It'll only make matters worse for him. In the privacy of her apartment, she revealed her vulnerability. And she knew that once she stepped outside, she'd shed her weak skin. She had no choice, she believed, but to be strong. Resilient. The OSS needed her to plant misinformation on the Allied invasion of France. Thousands of lives were at stake. She wiped away her tears, retrieved her bottle of German invisible ink and codebook, and drafted a message to place in her Abwehr dead drop.

Chapter 34

Estoril, Portugal—February 20, 1944

Maria, dressed in evening attire, left her apartment building and was greeted by Lars's chauffeur. He helped her into the back seat of a black Mercedes-Benz, closed her door, and took his place behind the wheel. As the vehicle pulled from the curb, an uneasiness grew in her stomach. Hours earlier, Lars had telephoned her to say that he was sending a driver to pick her up and bring her to his home. He provided no detail, other than the matter was important and he needed to speak with her as soon as possible. She thought it might have something to do with Admiral Canaris or his Abwehr agents, considering that her dead drop messages had gone unclaimed for the past two days. Rather than dwell on speculation, she leaned back in her seat and tried to relax but her mind drifted to Tiago.

The OSS had refused to get involved with criminal cases of the PVDE and Salazar's regime. Additionally, Rosa's lawyer had no success with creating cause to release Tiago, who was charged with multiple crimes—including forgery of government documents, possession of stolen gold and currency, and being a communist with the intent to overthrow Salazar's regime. Within days of his arrest, Tiago was sent to the Peniche Fortress, a maximum-security political prison.

"There might be a chance of gaining diplomatic efforts to free him after the war," Argus had said, during a recent clandestine meeting with Maria.

Maria was devastated. Driven by her sense of duty, she carried on with her role as a double agent. She delivered misinformation to her Abwehr dead drop, performed her cover role as a representative of the Library of Congress, and gambled with Lars at Casino Estoril—all the while hiding her shattered heart. To complicate matters, she had to secretly fight for Tiago's release. If she openly protested against the PVDE or Salazar's regime, she risked being deported. Operation Fortitude's deception was vital to the success of the Allied invasion of France. Millions had perished in the war, with thousands more being killed each day. She had no choice, she believed, but to help mislead the enemy to give the Allies a chance at a swift victory and an end to the bloodshed. Once Hitler was defeated, she would devote every fiber of her being to free her Tiago.

As days wore on, Maria's desperation to reunite with Tiago grew unbearable. Last week, she'd put on a disguise—consisting of a black wig, headscarf, and raincoat—and traveled two hours by bus to Peniche. Under high winds and a pouring rain, she'd stood for two hours along a steep, jagged coastline, several hundred yards away from the fortress. Violent waves crashed along the rocks below the prison, positioned high on a peninsula that jutted into the Atlantic. She'd relived their time together, reimagining the gentle manner in which he bandaged her wound on the day they met, his countless sacrifices to provide refugees a chance at freedom, his commitment to family, and the joy she felt when he held her in his arms. Tiago was everything she'd dreamed of in a man. *I'll find a way to get you out*, she'd vowed with rain pelting her face. *The light that we have together will continue to shine.* Maria, soaked and shivering, had left Peniche with determination burning in her heart.

The driver stopped the vehicle at Lars's home and helped her from the back seat. She approached the front door and was greeted by Lars.

She kissed him on the cheek. "Where's your staff?"

"I gave them the evening off."

She entered and followed him to his office, a large wood-paneled room with a pedestal desk, leather wing chairs, an upholstered sofa, and a fireplace. Along the far wall was a cocktail bar, and the air contained a faint smell of cigarette smoke.

"Drink?"

"Only if you're having one." She sat on the sofa and placed her purse on the floor.

He made her a gin and tonic and poured himself a glass of schnapps. "Here you are," he said, giving her the drink.

"Thank you."

He sat next to her and sipped his schnapps. "Canaris is out."

She turned to him.

"Hitler dismissed him and abolished the Abwehr."

A jolt shot through her. "When?"

"The day before yesterday. It appears that Germany's führer believes that his intelligence agency is incompetent, given their failures to predict events in North Africa and in Italy."

Maria took a gulp of her drink, spiked heavy with gin. She was glad to see the ineffectiveness of Hitler's intelligence, but her pathway to spread misinformation collapsed with the abolishment of the Abwehr. She'd expected a change with Canaris, but not his entire organization. A wave of uncertainty stirred inside her, yet her exterior remained calm.

"I thought something might be wrong," she said. "The messages in my dead drop have been unclaimed for the past two days."

"Don't use it again. It's no longer secure."

"How should I relay my intelligence?"

"Give it to me." He ran a hand through his hair. "Canaris's role and the functions of the Abwehr are being taken over by SS-Brigadeführer Schellenberg of the Reich Security Main Office. I'll use my banking connections to forward your information, and I'll make sure you are continued to be paid."

Maria nodded.

"Was there anything of high importance that the Abwehr failed to pick up from your dead drop?"

"Yes." She set her drink on a side table and picked up her purse. She removed a blank piece of paper and gave it to him. "I didn't want to leave it inside the dead drop."

He examined both sides and furrowed his brow.

"It's written in invisible ink, and it's in code."

"Do you mind telling me what's on the message?"

She shifted her weight.

"The agents at the Reich Security Main Office in Berlin might not use the same codes as the Abwehr agents in Lisbon. It could cause delays in the decipher. I suggest sending this uncoded until you receive a new cypher book." He took a sip of schnapps and swallowed. "I'm going to read your message, so you might as well tell me."

I have no choice, she thought. *He's my sole link to Berlin*. "Two of my subagents, one in Washington and one in Liverpool, have reported that US troops are being deployed to Britain."

He straightened his back. "Where?"

"South East England."

"Does this army group have a name?"

Maria's mind raced with the deceptive information she'd received from Allied headquarters in London. Pressure grew inside her chest. "First United States Army Group—FUSAG for short. It's comprised of one hundred and fifty thousand men and commanded by General George Patton."

His eyes widened. "Are you sure about this?"

"Yes. My subagents are unaware of each other's existence, and they're reporting similar information."

He swirled his drink. "How many troops have arrived in England?"

"I don't know," she said. "My sources only provided the news that FUSAG is being deployed there."

Lars drained his schnapps and set aside his glass. "Knowing where and when an invasion of France will happen could change the tide of the war for the Germans. At the very least, it would prolong the war, perhaps for years."

She nodded.

He stood and refilled his glass with schnapps. "With a long war, I'll make a fortune from my wolfram banking deals."

Her skin turned warm, and she crossed her legs.

He sat, inches from her side.

"What's in it for me?" she asked.

Lars tilted his head. "What do you mean?"

"If my intelligence contributes to you making enormous sums of money, I'm thinking that I should receive a piece of the action."

"You're already being paid by the Germans."

"I *was* being paid by the Abwehr, which is now dissolved. Until I begin receiving payments from the Reich Security Main Office, I need to look out for myself. And, if I'm assessing the situation correctly, it appears that you need me as much as the Germans." She looked into his eyes and smiled. "If there's one thing you taught me, it's to seize lucrative opportunities."

He laughed and placed his hand on her exposed knee. "If your intelligence leads to increasing my wealth, I will gladly reward you."

"How much?"

"It'll depend on if, and how much, your intelligence impacts the war." His eyes gravitated to her legs. He caressed her kneecap with his thumb. "If things work out well, it could be more money than you ever dreamed of."

Disgust grew in her stomach. She fought the urge to push him away. "I have no doubt that you will treat me well." She patted his hand. "I should probably go. I have much work to do tonight."

"I thought you might like to join me for dinner."

"I would love to," she said, "but duty calls. I need to prepare a readable report on my intelligence. I'll deliver it to you first thing in the morning. Perhaps we could have coffee together."

Lars nodded. He slipped his hand away and took a gulp of schnapps.

She looked at him, his eyes filled with disappointment. It was clear, to Maria, that Lars was sexually attracted to her, despite his original claims that she was too young for him. She worried that her rejection of his advances, if not handled delicately, would sour their relationship and put an end to her ability to infiltrate German intelligence. *It might be better to string him along for a while.*

"I've given some thought about joining you for the wedding in Switzerland," Maria said.

He set aside his drink. "Have you made a decision?"

She nodded. "I think I'll be ready by June to get on a plane. I'd like to join you, assuming your invitation is still good."

His demeanor brightened. "It is."

She smiled and extended her hand.

He clasped her fingers and helped her up from the sofa. They exited his office and walked outside to the Mercedes that was parked in the rotunda.

The chauffeur, who was resting behind the wheel, got out and opened the rear door.

"Good night." Lars kissed her on the cheek.

"See you in the morning," she said.

Maria got into the back seat and Lars closed the door. The chauffeur took his place behind the wheel, started the engine, and pulled away. As Lars and his mansion disappeared from sight, a mixture of relief and apprehension stirred inside her. She felt fortunate to have avoided a catastrophe with the dismissal of Canaris and the Abwehr, and she was confident that Lars's banking connections would enable her to continue sending misinformation to the Germans. But she worried that she was making a mistake by promising Lars that she would travel with him. She had no intentions of going to Switzerland. The promise had bought her time. She hoped that the invasion of France would commence in the coming months, or she'd need to fabricate a good excuse to let him down.

Chapter 35

Peniche, Portugal—March 12, 1944

Tiago, his back bruised and throbbing from a beating by three prison guards, crawled across the concrete floor as the solid steel door of his cell slammed shut. The sound of the departing guards, one of whom was running his wooden baton over the corridor wall, filtered through a crack beneath the door. With pain flaring down his spine, he labored his way onto his bunk and curled into a fetal position. He took in deep breaths, laced with the foul odor of an old, soiled mattress. It was his second clubbing in the past month, both of which were led by a guard who promulgated his view that all political prisoners should be executed, rather than be a burden to Salazar's authoritarian regime. The attacks Tiago suffered were random and brutal, but he wasn't the only prisoner who was suffering abuse. All of the inmates in his wing of the prison endured the same incessant punishment.

Tiago's cell was a ten-foot-by-six-foot space with a barred window that was whitewashed to prevent him from having a view to the outside world. The room contained a metal frame bunk, a wall-mounted sink that dispensed brown water, and a corner cupboard that housed a slop bucket. He was the sole inhabitant of the damp, dark chamber. The Peniche Fortress—known as the harshest of Portugal's political prisons—consisted solely of individual cells, as if its architects were charged with designing a jail to punish prisoners through isolation. Due to the prisoners' seclusion, they rarely spoke to other inmates. Tiago never left his cell, with the exception of one hour per day when prisoners were permitted to walk on a roof terrace for fresh air.

Additionally, books and newspapers were prohibited. With long periods of seclusion and the lack of brain stimulation, some of the prisoners suffered mental breakdowns. Two weeks into his sentence at the prison, Tiago witnessed a man, his eyes dark and absent of spirit, throw himself over a terrace wall. He was killed upon impact with the jagged shoreline, far below the fortress. To torment the prisoners, the guards left the man's body on the rocks for a week, until his remains were swept away by a king tide.

Determined to fight against his mental and physical decline, Tiago recited poems by Luís de Camões. He paced the floor of his cell, all the while counting his steps, and he did push-ups and sit-ups to curtail muscle atrophy. Despite his sparse food rations—consisting primarily of a watery pottage made from moldy potatoes, onion peels, and fish scraps—he forced himself to exercise and think, rather than succumb to sempiternal sleep. In the evenings, his cell became a silent, stygian crypt. To suppress his pain, he relived his brief but joyful time with Maria, over and over in his head. He prayed that she was safe and that she would have a long and beautiful life. Although she would always remain in his heart, a future with her was no longer possible, given that political prisoners never left Peniche Fortress alive.

Of all the charges brought by Agent Neves and the PVDE, the alleged crime of being a communist was, by far, the most severe. The offenses of forgery and the possession of stolen gold and currency might have resulted in a prison sentence of five to ten years. But Salazar strongly opposed communism, which he viewed as a threat to his regime. Therefore, Tiago received no trial or judicial hearing. Instead, he was labeled a communist, given a life sentence of imprisonment, and transported in shackles from the PVDE jail to the Peniche Fortress. In the end, it wasn't his crimes to aid refugees that changed the trajectory of his life. It was his volunteer service in the Spanish Civil War—to fight the spread of fascism—that had sealed his fate.

As weeks and months passed, he often wondered if his grandparents were still alive, and how his parents were managing to work through the heartache of knowing that they would never see or communicate with their son again. In addition to his family, he deeply missed his friend Rosa. Each day, he prayed that she was safe and that she'd convinced the PVDE that she had nothing to do with his crimes. He liked to imagine that Rosa had outwitted Agent Neves, and she'd found a way to continue their mission of helping refugees to flee Europe.

A loud whistle sounded.

Tiago opened his eyes. *If I remain in my bunk, I'll receive another pummeling.* With pain flaring through his back, he rolled out of his bunk and shuffled to the cell door. A key rattled in a lock, and the steel door squeaked open. He shuffled to the corridor, where guards were unlocking a dozen cells. Prisoners migrated into the hallway, where they lined up in single file. Coughs and the clearing of phlegm filled the air.

A whistle sounded.

The prisoners made their way down the corridor, climbed two levels of concrete stairs, and exited through an arched doorway to a stone rooftop terrace.

Sunlight pierced Tiago's eyes. He squinted and inhaled fresh salt air into his lungs. His eyes adjusted and he saw a gray-haired prisoner named Danilo, who was sitting on the ground with his back against the wall. The man had dark, sunken eyes and protruding clavicles, and he'd lost a large amount of weight since Tiago's arrival. He'd told Tiago that he was fifty years old, but after eighteen months of imprisonment he'd aged a decade, if not more.

Danilo, his face haggard, raised a hand and lowered it to his lap.

Tiago shuffled to him.

"How badly did they beat you?" Danilo asked, his voice hoarse.

"Not enough to keep me from missing my hour of fresh air."

The man gave a nod.

"You should try to walk," Tiago said.

"Too weak." The man's eyelids drooped.

"Are you eating?"

"I can't keep anything down."

"You must try," Tiago said. "We need to consume every morsel if we want to live."

"It doesn't matter. We're never getting out of here."

Tiago placed a hand on his shoulder, frail and bony. "If we give up, we let them win."

The man blinked back tears and wiped his eyes.

"Let's try walking." Tiago helped the man to his feet.

They slowly sauntered over the terrace. But after several minutes, Danilo's breathing turned labored, forcing him to rest on the ground. Tiago, refusing to give in to his pain and fatigue, walked along the wall. He pushed his body to carry on, step after step, until the sound of a whistle pierced the air.

Chapter 36

Lisbon, Portugal—June 2, 1944

Shortly after sunset, Maria retrieved her suitcase from a closet and placed it on her bed. As she set out clothing to pack, a knock came from the apartment door. She went to the foyer and peered through the peephole to find Argus standing in the hallway. Her eyes widened. She unlocked the door and Argus entered the apartment.

"I'm glad I caught you," Argus said, bolting the door. He turned to her. "I need to speak with you."

Maria clasped her arms and nodded. She thought it must be something urgent, otherwise Argus would have scheduled to meet at a clandestine location.

They went to the kitchen and sat.

"When are you leaving?" he asked.

"Six in the morning," she said.

"It's not too late to back out."

She shook her head. "Lars is our sole channel to pass information from Lisbon to German intelligence, and we need to do everything possible to keep him believing that my material is real. If I go with him to Bern for a wedding, I'll keep his trust in me."

Argus rubbed his jowl.

"I received a new package from London headquarters. It came

in on a flight this afternoon with my microfilm supplies." A memory of examining the contents of a manila envelope flashed in her brain. "It contains explicit misinformation about the location of an Allied invasion. It's critical that I relay it to Lars."

"Maybe you could deliver the information and make up an excuse to bail out of the trip."

"I've already decided," she said. "I'm going."

He drew a breath and exhaled. "All right."

Maria had initially planned to back out of joining Lars for the wedding, but she gradually changed her mind over the past few months. Her role as a double agent in Operation Fortitude had become more important, she believed, given the frequency and magnitude of disinformation she was supplied with from London headquarters. The Allies were counting on her to help mislead the German military on the location of the invasion of France, and she wasn't about to let them down.

Argus placed his hands on the table. "Tell me what you know about the wedding."

"It's in Bern for a family friend named Margarete—I think Lars said that her last name is Brauen. Her fiancé is named Hermann, whom Lars hasn't met."

"Do you feel safe to be alone on a trip with Lars?"

"I can handle him," Maria said, leaving out that Lars's flirtation had grown. "And as for the trip, the Swissair flight route is secure and avoids combat airspace. Switzerland is every bit as neutral as Portugal. I'll be fine."

"I expected that you wouldn't change your mind. So, I brought you a few things to take with you." Argus reached into his jacket and removed a tube of lipstick, a silver compact, and a metal gadget that looked like a writing pen with a small lever.

She furrowed her brow. "What are these for?"

"Protection."

He unscrewed the bottom of the lipstick and held it to her. "Inside is an L-pill."

Lethal pill, she thought. She stared at the rubber-covered tablet.

"Bite down on it and death will occur in under fifteen seconds."

Maria's skin turned cold.

He screwed on the bottom of the lipstick and retrieved the compact. He opened it and popped out the mirror to expose several tablets. "These are K-pills, otherwise known as liquid knockout drops. The contents of one pill, inserted in a drink or food, will render a person unconscious."

She swallowed.

He put away the compact and picked up the pen-like object. "This is a Stinger pen gun. It contains a twenty-two caliber cartridge. To use it—remove the safety pin, point it at your target in close range, and press the lever."

Good God! She shifted in her seat. "I won't need this."

"It's only a precaution," Argus said. "You might feel better to know that you would have already had these in your possession had you gone through OSS paramilitary training."

She straightened her back. "Actually, it makes me angry that the librarians of the OSS didn't get the same tools and instruction as agents deployed to enemy-occupied countries."

He looked at her. "I see your point."

She set aside her feelings and said, "I appreciate you looking out for me. I'll take them with me as a safeguard."

"I'm leaving for Madrid. Leave word at that embassy if you need to reach me." Argus stood and shook her hand. "Good luck."

"Thank you."

Argus left, and Maria returned to her bedroom and packed her suitcase. Afterward, she went to the kitchen and placed the lipstick and compact inside her purse. She picked up the pen gun and paused, running a finger over the cold steel of the small weapon. Her skin prickled. She'd never held a gun, let alone fired one, and she had no plans of using it, or any of the pills. *Argus is being overly cautious. I'm more likely to have the pen gun accidentally discharge in my purse than use it in self-defense.* But deep down, her instincts prodded her to protect herself. So, she wrapped the weapon in a handkerchief and hid it beneath the lining of her purse.

Chapter 37

Lisbon, Portugal—June 3, 1944

Maria, sitting next to Lars in the back of his Mercedes-Benz limousine, looked through her window as the chauffeur turned the vehicle onto a road leading to the Lisbon Portela Airport. The sun, peeking above the horizon, cast golden fingers of sunlight over a cobalt blue sky. Instead of traveling to the terminal, the chauffeur steered the limousine to a gate, where an airport employee waved them through and onto the tarmac. Maria twisted her sapphire ring on her finger as they stopped near a Swissair twin-engine plane.

Lars, as if sensing her apprehension about flying, placed a hand on her arm. "It's going to be all right."

She nodded.

While the chauffeur gathered their luggage, Maria and Lars got out of the limousine and were greeted by a steward.

"The plane is ready for you to board," the steward said, gesturing to stairs at the tail section of the plane.

Lars tipped his hat.

Maria, her legs feeling weak, followed Lars up the stairs and into the plane. She glanced over the cabin of fourteen window seats, all of which were empty. "It looks like we're early."

"We're on time," Lars said. "It's only us."

"Did you charter the plane?"

"Yes. It's mine on a permanent basis; I hired the entire aircraft and crew."

She forced a smile.

He led her to the middle of the cabin and gestured to a seat.

She sat, holding her purse to her belly.

Lars walked down the aisle, knocked on the cockpit door, and entered. While he spoke with the captain, the copilot went to the tail section of the aircraft. The steward climbed aboard, placed their luggage in an overhead rack, and exited the plane. As the steward rolled away the portable stairs, the copilot closed the aircraft door and made his way to the cockpit.

Lars sat next to Maria with the aisle between them.

"Is there no steward?" she asked.

"I prefer privacy. There are prepared foods and drinks in the back. Once we're airborne, I'll show you where everything is located."

The cockpit door closed. A minute later, the engines coughed, then roared to life. The propellers buzzed, sending a vibration through Maria's seat. Her muscles tensed.

"What kind of plane is this?" she asked, buckling her seat belt.

"The safest kind," Lars said. "It's a DC-2 with two exceptional pilots. I've flown this route countless times." He pointed to a lever. "The seats have been customized to fully recline. You'll be well rested for our arrival this afternoon."

I doubt that I'll sleep a wink.

The plane taxied for a hundred yards and turned onto a runway. The engines roared. The wheels rumbled over the ground as the plane accelerated for takeoff. Maria tucked her purse beside her and gripped the armrests, digging in her nails. An echo of the *Yankee Clipper*'s wing being sheared away flashed in her head. Her heart thudded inside her chest. Seconds later, the nose lifted and the plane was airborne.

Sunlight streamed through the cabin windows. She drew in deep breaths and loosened her grip on the armrests. As the plane gained altitude, she peered through her window to the city of Lisbon and the Tagus River, which flowed to the Atlantic. The sight of the coastline resurrected memories of the crashing waves at Peniche Fortress. She silently prayed that Tiago wasn't suffering, and that she'd find a way for him to be released from prison. The plane banked to the right, and her view of the shore disappeared.

The aircraft reached cruising altitude and Lars lit a cigarette.

Maria, compelled by her sense of duty, set aside her thoughts of Tiago, as well as her apprehension of flying in a plane. She turned to Lars. "I received new intelligence."

He took a drag and exhaled smoke. "Did you bring it with you?"

"I did." Maria retrieved her purse and removed a manila envelope. She slipped out a small photograph and gave it to Lars.

His eyebrows rose. He examined the grainy, black-and-white image of Allied naval landing craft that were anchored in what appeared to be a tidal river. "Where did you get this?"

"It was taken by my subagent, Hazel. She's a twitcher in South East England."

"What's a twitcher?"

"An amateur birdwatcher. She took the photograph at an estuary. She claims there are dozens of landing craft."

"Are all of the vessels in South East England?"

"Yes—outside of Dover to be precise." She crossed her legs and smoothed her skirt. "Also, two of my informants have reported that FUSAG, commanded by General Patton, is stationed nearby."

"How do they know?"

"Barracks have been erected in the vicinity of Dover Castle, and convoys of supply lorries have been seen rolling in and out of the area." She looked at him. "I suppose it takes a monumental effort to house and feed an army group of one hundred and fifty thousand men."

He rubbed his chin. "Dover?"

She nodded.

He looked at the ceiling, as if he were attempting to visualize the geography. "That would make the closest invasion point in France to be Pas-de-Calais."

"It appears so."

He glanced again at the photograph. "Well done."

"Thank you," she said, "but I have more intelligence. Another informant, a wireless telegraph operator for the Women's Royal Naval Service, reported that the Allies are planning a diversionary invasion."

"Where?"

"She doesn't know. She intercepted a communication about a sea to land attack—designed to distract the German military—that will take place a few days before the real, large-scale invasion of France."

"Does she know when this will happen?"

"Likely within the week. Her report indicates that the Allies are waiting for the sea and weather conditions to clear." She looked at him. "The invasion could happen at any moment."

He unbuttoned his collar and loosened his necktie.

She removed a page of handwritten notes from her envelope and gave it to him. "I always draft reports about my subagents' intelligence, but at this point I don't think it matters. By the time you get it to your contacts, the invasion might be underway."

Maria watched him examine the scribbled message, absent details of the sender. She looked for signs in his facial expression and body language that might indicate suspicion, but she found nothing.

"This could change the war for Germany." He held up the paper. "For this, they should award you the Iron Cross."

"I prefer gold over iron."

"So do I." His lips formed an impish smile. "If the German military has been acting on your intelligence, the war will be prolonged, and I'll be rich."

She felt sick to her stomach. "You promised me a piece of the action."

"I always keep my word. If the Allied invasion fails and Germany's war machine continues, I'll make you a wealthy woman."

"Fair enough."

Lars stowed away the intelligence in his monogramed briefcase, leaned back in his seat, and smoked his cigarette.

Maria, desperate for a reprieve from conversation, converted her seat into a cot. She curled on her side, closed her eyes, and pretended to sleep.

Hours passed and Maria's angst about flying gradually faded. There was little, if any, air turbulence, and the landing to refuel in Barcelona had gone smoothly. For lunch, they had a tin of caviar with toast points, crème fraiche, lemon wedges, hard-boiled eggs, and a bottle of champagne. Based on Lars's demeanor, she was confident that he accepted her intelligence as valid. *I've cleared the first hurdle*, she'd thought, sipping champagne. *I'll pretend to enjoy the wedding, avoid his advances, and tomorrow I'll be back in Portugal.*

Six and a half hours after leaving Lisbon, the plane landed at a small airport in Bern, Switzerland. Maria drew a deep breath and exhaled, feeling tension evaporate from her neck and shoulders.

Lars tamped out a cigarette in an ashtray.

She smoothed her skirt. "At some point, I need to change my clothing."

"We won't have time to stop at the hotel before the wedding ceremony," he said. "I suggest changing in the back of the plane."

"Are you sure?"

"Yes," he said. "There's a curtain for privacy."

While the plane taxied along the runway, she gathered her purse and suitcase, and went to the tail of the plane. She pulled a curtain across the fuselage and undressed. As she removed a black dress from her suitcase, the propeller engines turned off and the plane slowed to a stop. She slipped on her dress and put on peep-toe high-heeled shoes. Using the mirror of her compact, given to her by Argus, she freshened her makeup and lipstick. She packed away her travel clothes and put on a black-and-white pillbox hat.

Let's get this over with. Maria slid back the curtain and made her way forward with her luggage. Through a window, she saw a fuel truck near the front of the plane with a man in an oil-stained coverall rolling up a hose. She approached Lars, sitting in his seat and smoking a cigarette.

"I'm ready," she said, putting down her suitcase.

He stood. His eyes traced her body. "You look stunning."

"Thank you," she said. "Do you need to change?"

He lifted his necktie. "Not unless you think it doesn't match with my suit."

"You look swell."

He grinned.

The fuel truck drove away. Propellers turned over and the aircraft's engines rumbled.

Her body stiffened. "What's happening?"

"We have another short flight."

She swallowed.

The buzzing grew and the aircraft rolled forward. Lars stashed her suitcase in the overhead rack, and then helped her into her seat. The plane turned, and it shimmied side to side as it accelerated down the runway.

Her adrenaline surged. She buckled her safety belt and gripped her armrests. "Where's the next airport?"

He took a drag on his cigarette. "Austria."

CHAPTER 38

PENICHE, PORTUGAL—JUNE 3, 1944

A guard whistle sounded, sending a chill through Tiago's body. Weak and hungry, he crawled out of his bunk. A bolt unlocked and the steel cell door squeaked open. He shuffled to the corridor and lined up with the prisoners of his cellblock.

A guard, holding a clipboard and pencil, walked down the line and counted the men. He furrowed his brow and turned to another guard, twirling a chain with an attached whistle around his forefinger. "We're missing one."

The guard stuffed his whistle into his pocket and inspected cells. Halfway down the corridor, he stopped. "Get up!"

Eyes of the prisoners fell on the guard.

That's Danilo's cell. His pulse quickened.

"Don't make me come in there," the guard said. "I'll thump your ass."

Please get up, Tiago called inside his head.

The guard slipped his baton from his belt and entered the cell.

Oh, no. Tiago expected to hear the gruesome thwack of wood pounding flesh. Instead, the guard exited the cell and looked at his comrade. "He's dead."

Tiago's heart sank.

The guard with the whistle pointed his baton and called out to two prisoners, one of whom was Tiago. "Carry him to the morgue."

Tiago left his place in line and entered the cell, where Danilo's lifeless body lay on his bunk. The man's partially open eyes were hazy and gray, like a spoiled fish. Tiago, using his hand, gently closed his friend's eyelids.

"Hurry up!" the guard shouted.

The other prisoner grabbed Danilo's wrists.

"Be careful with him," Tiago whispered.

The prisoner nodded.

Tiago clasped Danilo's ankles, bony and cold. He blinked back tears.

They lifted Danilo, stiff with rigor mortis, from his bunk. The man's clothing slid down his shins and arms, revealing old scars and fresh bruises. *Bastards.* Anger burned inside Tiago. He wanted to retaliate against the guards but he, as well as the other inmates, were too frail and malnourished to fight. They lugged the body out of the cell and down the corridor. At the morgue, a masonry room in a subterranean level of the prison, the guard ordered them to place the man's body on a low, wooden bench. Tiago gently lowered Danilo's legs and silently prayed for him and his family.

"Get moving," the guard said.

Tiago and the prisoner left the morgue. The guard, running his baton along the wall, followed close behind them as they made their way back to the cellblock. A wretched ache grew in Tiago's chest, and he wondered how many days would pass until his remains were carried away by his fellow prisoners.

Chapter 39

Salzburg, Austria—June 3, 1944

Maria, her eyes wide, turned to Lars as the plane shot down the runway. "I'm sorry, I must've misheard you. I thought you said that we're going to Austria."

"You heard correctly," Lars said. "The wedding is in Salzburg."

Fear flooded her veins. The plane lifted into the air, pressing her into the seat. "You told me that the wedding was in Bern."

"I said that we'd be *flying* to Bern."

She struggled to remain calm. "You should have told me that the event was in Austria."

"I apologize." He placed a hand on her arm. "I was worried that you wouldn't join me for the trip."

She fought back the urge to pull away. "You're right," she said. "I wouldn't have come. It's not a good idea for me to be in an Axis country."

"You'll be perfectly safe. You're a spy for Germany."

"True," she said. "But I'm carrying an American passport."

"Leave the passport in the plane. You won't need it while you're with me. You're fluent in German and will fit in. If anyone questions your background, tell them that you're Portuguese."

This is madness! Her mind raced to find a solution to escape this nightmare. But she decided that there was nothing she could do while flying thousands of feet in the air. *Remain cool and confident, and you'll get through this.*

The plane banked to the east and leveled off.

"Some women love surprises," she said. "Me—not so much."

He slipped his hand away.

"On our next trip together," she said, "I expect that you'll be forthright about our itinerary. Will you do that for me?"

Lines on his face softened. "Yes."

"Good," she said. "Is there anything else that you haven't told me about this journey?"

He placed his fingertips together. "The wedding is for Margarete Berta Braun."

"Yes, I know."

"Margarete goes by Gretl."

Maria tilted her head. *Gretl Braun.*

"She's the younger sister of Eva Braun, Adolf Hitler's companion."

She swallowed. "You're joking."

He shook his head. "Her fiancé is Hermann Fegelein, a high-ranking commander in the Waffen-SS."

Oh, God.

"My clients are powerful people. You're well aware of my connection with Portugal's prime minister and his banker. Are you shocked that I have a similar relationship with Germany's führer?"

Her blood turned cold. "No."

"Germany's gold flows through me to acquire wolfram. It's made me a rich man, and it's important for me to pay my respects at weddings and funerals of their elite."

Maria's brain struggled to absorb his words. "When were you going to tell me about all of this?"

"When we landed in Salzburg." He ran a hand through his hair. "If I had told you earlier, you would have made an excuse not to come. Selfishly, I wanted you by my side at the wedding."

"Why?"

He looked into her eyes. "Because I care about you."

Her breath stalled in her chest.

"When Gisela died, I thought that I'd never have affection for another woman. But when I'm with you, I feel alive. I thought that by spending time away with me, you might begin to feel the same way."

"I do care about you. It's just that—everything you told me is a lot to take in."

"I understand. I'm sure you're upset with my lack of transparency."

"I'm not angry with you," she lied. "I simply wish you had told me everything from the start."

He paused, adjusting a gold cuff link. "May I ask you a question?"

"Yes."

"Do you think it's possible that someday you'll view me as more than a friend?"

A knot twisted in her stomach. She wanted to reject him, but doing so could jeopardize her life and Operation Fortitude. *I'm at his mercy. To get out of this mess, I'll need to use his affection for me to my advantage.*

"I do." Maria, hiding her disgust, clasped his hand. "Would it be okay if we take things slow?"

He caressed her fingers. "We can take as much time as you need."

An hour and a half after leaving the Bern airport, the plane landed on a hilltop airfield in Salzburg, an Austrian city on the border of Germany. Maria peered out her window. Miles away, snowcapped alps and evergreens covered the landscape. The plane taxied to a tarmac, where a landing crew and limousine were waiting for them.

Maria, her head reeling with scenarios on how to survive the trip, exited the plane and descended the stairs. She walked with a confident gait, her heels clicking on the pavement, as she followed Lars to the limousine.

"*Hallo*, Herr Steiger," the chauffeur said, opening the rear door of a sleek, black Mercedes-Benz.

"*Guten Tag*," Lars said.

They got into the back seat. Their luggage was loaded into the trunk and the chauffeur took his place behind the wheel. The engine started and the limousine pulled away from the tarmac.

Fifteen minutes later, they arrived at Mirabell Palace, a lavish Baroque-style building in the city of Salzburg. They got out of the limousine and made their way across a stone-paved rotunda. Maria's eyes locked on two broad-shouldered Waffen-SS officers—wearing gray-green uniforms emblazoned with medals—who were approaching the entrance.

Lars placed a hand at the base of her back and lowered his voice. "How are you?"

She buried her fear. "*Mir geht es gut, danke*."

He smiled, placed her hand on his elbow, and escorted her inside the palace.

They traveled down a long hallway and climbed a white marble staircase, decorated with blithe, chubby-cheeked cherubs. The clack of jackboots on the stairs above them sent chills down Maria's spine. On the upper floor, they entered a room called Marble Hall. An arched ceiling towered over a multicolored marble floor with geometric designs. The walls contained large displays of decorative plaster that were covered in gold leaf, with the exception of an outer wall that was comprised of ten-foot glass doors that led to Juliet-style balconies. At the front of the room was a long, marble-top table that resembled an altar. In front of the table was a row of four chairs with red velvet upholstery, which Maria presumed was for the bride, groom, and their witnesses. Four rows of guest seating, angled to provide a view of the ceremony, had been placed behind the bridal chairs.

Maria silently counted the chairs. *It'll be impossible to blend into the crowd with only twenty guests.* Her chest felt tight, as if it were being compressed in a vise.

Lars led her to a back row where they took seats on the end. Soon, guests entered the hall and settled into their places. All of the men were in military uniform, with the exception of Lars and a bespectacled man who walked with a limp. And given the insignias on the uniforms, it appeared, to Maria, that they were likely members of Germany's high command.

A woman in her early thirties—wearing a silver silk gown and holding a small movie camera—entered the hall and stood off to the side of the crowd. She had high cheekbones, skin like alabaster, and shoulder-length wavy brown hair that was parted on the side with a bow.

Lars leaned to Maria and whispered. "That's Gretl's sister, Eva. She's a photographer, like you."

Maria's heart raced. She scanned the crowd but saw no sign of Hitler.

Gretl—who looked remarkably like Eva, except for shorter hair and a black dress with a white lace collar—entered the hall with her fiancé, Hermann, a tall Waffen-SS officer with a V-shaped hairline. They sat in the front row with two military leaders.

Maria recognized none of the guests, until an officer with round-rimmed glasses and a neatly trimmed mustache walked to the front table and faced the audience. Based on her microfilming of Axis newspapers with photographs, she recognized him to be Heinrich Himmler, one of the most powerful men in Nazi Germany. A wave of dread washed over her.

For twenty minutes, Himmler officiated a pagan wedding ceremony. He spoke words of the fatherland, bloodline, and the superiority of the Aryan race. Eva, smiling and looking through the viewfinder of her movie camera, filmed her sister's special day. Himmler directed the couple to drink wine from chalices and ended the ceremony by having Gretl, Hermann, and witnesses sign their names in a ledger.

The guests rose from their seats and followed the newlyweds out of the hall and down the stairs. Maria hoped that she'd make it to the limousine without having to converse with guests, but as she and Lars were exiting the palace, Gretl and Hermann approached them.

"Lars!" Gretl gave him a hug and kissed him on the cheek. "I'm overjoyed to see you."

"Me too." Lars turned to Hermann and shook his hand. "Congratulations."

"*Danke*," Hermann said.

"And who is this lovely flower?" Gretl asked.

"This is Maria," Lars said.

Maria gathered her courage and smiled. "It's an honor to be here for your celebration."

Gretl hugged her. "I'm delighted that Lars brought you with him. How long will you be staying?"

"We leave tomorrow," she said.

"You must stay longer," Gretl said. "Our party will last for days. It'll give us a chance to get acquainted."

Her skin prickled. "I'd love to but—"

Lars placed his arm around Maria's shoulder. "Unfortunately, I have business to tend to."

"You work too much," Gretl said. "If you must leave tomorrow, then we need to catch up tonight."

"I look forward to it," Lars said.

Hermann clasped his wife's arm and led her away. They got into the back of a black convertible limousine and drove off.

Maria walked with Lars across the rotunda. *I can do this. If I can make it through the wedding, I can survive the reception.* They got into their Mercedes and the driver sped away.

"What do you think?" Lars asked.

"Interesting ceremony," Maria said, concealing her outrage at Himmler's words of racial superiority.

"It's the civil marriage service used for SS officers."

She adjusted the bottom of her dress. "Gretl is cordial."

Lars nodded. "She's quite fond of social events." He lit a cigarette and partially lowered his window.

"Where's the reception?"

He took a drag. "Kehlsteinhaus."

Eagle's Nest, Maria thought.

"You'll be impressed. It's a chalet that sits on a ridge, high atop a mountain in the Berchtesgaden Alps.

"Is it far?"

"Forty minutes. But before we get there, I have some business to tend to at the Berghof." He flicked ash out his window. "It's the führer's vacation home."

Her stomach turned nauseous.

"The wedding party will be stopping at the Berghof to pay their respects to the führer and take photographs. Afterward, everyone will go to the reception."

"Will I be joining you?"

"No," he said. "It's best that you go on ahead to the reception. I won't be long."

"All right," she said, feeling both relieved and powerless.

The limousine left the city of Salzburg and winded through the mountains. As they gained altitude, the temperature dropped. Goose bumps cropped up on her arms. Thirty minutes later, the driver stopped at a gate house with two armed guards.

Lars raised his hand.

The guards, who appeared to recognize Lars, waved the vehicle through.

They traveled to the end of a long driveway and stopped. Ahead, the newlyweds were climbing stone steps to the entrance of the home.

Lars placed a hand on her knee. "I'll see you soon."

"Okay."

He slipped away and got out of the vehicle.

The driver opened the trunk and handed Lars his briefcase.

A flicker of hope stirred inside her as she watched Lars approach the Berghof. *He's carrying my misinformation.* She prayed that he would deliver the intelligence, and that it would convince Hitler and his high command that the Allies would soon embark on an amphibious attack at Pas-de-Calais—far from where the real invasion of France would take place.

The driver started the engine and pulled away. The vehicle traveled several miles up a steep alpine road with five tunnels and a sharp, hairpin turn. Eventually, they approached a large car park, where wedding guests were making their way on foot to a tunnel in the side of the mountain. Several hundred feet above the tunnel's entrance was the Eagle's Nest, perched on the summit. Maria, peering through her window at the chalet, recalled Lars's words. *Everyone will go to the reception.* A thought of Hitler, giving a toast to the bride and groom, flashed in her mind. Her breathing quickened. She twisted her mother's sapphire ring, attempting to vanquish her trepidation, and made plans in her head.

Chapter 40

Obersalzberg, Germany—June 3, 1944

The limousine door opened and Maria stepped outside to frigid, high-altitude air. She shivered as she followed the chauffeur to open the trunk of the vehicle. *Now I know why Lars instructed me to pack warm clothing,* she thought, removing a wool coat from her suitcase. She slipped on her coat and retrieved her purse.

The driver closed the trunk. "Enjoy your evening."

"*Danke.*"

Maria followed a group of guests, all of whom were wearing coats, to the entrance of the tunnel. They passed through open steel doors to a subterranean passageway large enough to fit a delivery truck. Chatter of guests echoed over the marble-lined walls of the tunnel, illuminated by suspended electric lamps. Maria, feeling like she was on a passage to hell, willed herself to walk deeper into the tunnel. Four hundred feet into the interior of the mountain, they reached a large elevator. Some of the guests, including Maria, rested on benches in a domed waiting room.

Once the group thinned, Maria boarded a polished brass-paneled elevator with green leather benches. As she sat in the corner, a Waffen-SS officer entered and blocked the doors from closing with his arm to allow two women in fur coats to board the lift. Maria, hoping to avoid conversation, lowered her eyes and listened to one of the women talk about her son, who was assigned to the eastern front.

Doors closed. The elevator jerked and slowly ascended.

"Good evening, *fräulein*," a baritone voice said.

Maria looked up to see a German officer, who was approximately thirty years of age. He was clean-shaven with a lantern jaw, and his cap had a silver skull-and-crossbones emblem. "*Hallo.*"

"May I sit?"

"*Ja.*"

He sat and removed his cap to expose blond hair—long on top but shaved at the back and sides. "What's your name?"

The elevator creaked and groaned.

"Maria." A menthol scent of hair tonic penetrated her nose.

"I'm Wilhelm." He adjusted an iron cross, worn close to his neck, and leaned in. "Are you here with someone?"

"I was supposed to be, but he's been called away on business."

The officer smiled. "Who's the unfortunate fellow?"

"Lars Steiger."

The officer straightened his back and created space between them. "I hope I didn't offend you, *fräulein*. Please pay my respects to Herr Steiger."

"I will," she said. "What is your full name?"

He swallowed. "Sturmbannführer Wilhelm Brandt."

The elevator doors opened. The officer put on his cap and exited ahead of the women.

He knows and fears Lars, Maria thought.

She walked out of the elevator, gave her coat to an attendant, and traveled down a corridor that opened to a large reception room. Timber beams spanned the ceiling, and the walls were made of massive blocks of stone. A large fireplace with burning logs filled the air with a scent of charred birchwood. Electric candle sconces adorned the walls, giving the chalet the appearance of a medieval castle. Guests—a mixture of military and civilians—were mingling around oak tables, one of which contained seating for twenty people. Given the number of place settings, the gathering was bigger than the wedding ceremony but far from a huge assembly. And she assumed that the guest list was reserved for members of Hitler's inner circle.

I can do this, she thought, admiring a bouquet of flowers. *Pretend that I belong here, like when I gate-crashed the Astor mansion to meet Colonel Donovan.*

Maria went to the largest table, which she assumed was reserved for the bride and groom. Name cards written in calligraphy were at each of the place settings. Through the corner of her eye, she scanned the cards as she walked past two gray-haired men, one in a tuxedo and the other in a business suit. At the head of the table, her skin turned cold upon seeing the names Eva Braun and Führer. She glanced at an empty crystal water glass and continued her exploration of the chalet.

After touring the rooms, including the women's washroom to freshen her makeup, she traveled down the corridor and descended a set of stairs to a pine-paneled room that was being used as a tavern. A musical trio—comprised of a violinist, violist, and accordionist—were entertaining guests. Maria made her way to the bar and ordered a glass of Riesling. With her wine in hand, she mingled upstairs, retrieved her coat, and went outside to a large terrace with a view of the Alps. A few of the guests, bundled in coats and hats, were drinking champagne and smoking cigarettes. At the railing, she peered down to the town of Berchtesgaden, thousands of feet below. Cold wind nipped at her face. She sipped her wine and contemplated her fate.

Maria had been raised a pacifist and believed that all life is valuable. But Hitler, an evil dictator who was responsible for the deaths of millions of people, had to be stopped at any cost. If she did nothing, she'd live her life, assuming she would survive this ordeal, regretting that she could have done something to curtail the war and save countless lives. And if she acted on her plan, she likely wouldn't leave the Eagle's Nest alive. She weighed the alternatives and made her decision. *I'm committed to liberating Europe and saving lives. So, I have no choice but to kill the bastard.*

She had three means, she believed, to do it. She could use her Stinger pen gun, which was hidden inside her purse, but it had only one low-intensity .22 caliber cartridge, which was designed more for escaping than killing. Therefore, she would need to be standing next to Hitler when firing the weapon. She could try to place the cyanide from her L-pill into his water glass but there were two obstacles: it would be difficult not to be seen, and the liquid from the L-pill might be absorbed through her skin, when crushing the capsule with her fingers, and she'd be dead before Hitler took his first sip. Her last option was to snatch a pistol from an unsuspecting officer and fire it at the führer, but it would be difficult to pull off, given her strength and lack of firearms training. Her choice of weapon, she decided, would depend on how close she could get to him. She finished her wine and watched what would be, in all likelihood, her last sunset.

Crowd noise grew from inside the chalet and Maria left the terrace. She returned her coat to an attendant and went to the reception hall. The bridal party had arrived and Gretl—who'd changed into a sleek, ivory-colored silk wedding dress—was making rounds to greet guests. She scanned the room but didn't see Lars or Hitler. To avoid standing out by being alone, she located the *sturmbannführer*, whom she had spoken with on the elevator.

"Pardon me," Maria said, approaching him at a bar.

Sturmbannführer Brandt, holding a glass of wine, turned to her. His eyebrows rose.

"Would you mind keeping me company until Herr Steiger arrives? I'm sure he will be most appreciative of you looking after me."

He smiled. "Of course. May I get you a drink?"

"Tonic water."

For thirty minutes, she chatted with Brandt. She initiated most of the questions, which limited the amount of talking she had to do about herself. Throughout their conversation, she stealthily eyed a leather pistol case that was attached to his belt with a polished buckle that read *Meine Ehre heißt Treue* (My honor is called loyalty). Based on the design of the pistol case, she would need to undo a leather strap to remove the weapon. Her only hope of snatching it would be if Brandt's reflexes were slow. Therefore, she ordered him a glass of Jägermeister as a gesture of appreciation for his hospitality.

An attendant wearing white gloves rang a small bell, signaling for guests to sit for dinner. Maria left Brandt and sat at a table, adjacent to the wedding party, with a place card that read "Guest of Herr Steiger." Her nervousness grew as bowls of *hochzeitssuppe*, a chicken-broth-based wedding soup with small meatballs and asparagus tops, were served. For an hour, she forced herself to eat bits of a four-course meal, all the while chatting with an elderly couple who were related to the groom.

As a server was placing plates with slices of cake on the table, she felt a hand touch her shoulder.

"I'm sorry I'm late." Lars sat next to her. "Are you having a good time?"

"Yes," she said, her stomach in knots. "You missed a delightful meal. I asked the server to save you a plate in the kitchen."

"That was considerate of you. But tonight, I'm in the mood for dessert." He flagged the server and ordered a glass of schnapps.

"I take it your meeting went well."

"It did."

She glanced to the empty chair next to Eva Braun, who was talking with her sister. Her anxiousness grew. "Will the führer be coming?"

"No. He's detained with military affairs."

A mix of relief and defeat washed over her.

He picked up a fork and took a bite of cake. "It's good. You should try it."

Before she could reply, he forked cake and held it to her lips. She opened her mouth and accepted the offering, a sweet layered tree cake with nuts and honey.

Soon, plates were cleared and tables were moved to create a small ballroom. The musical trio performed a modern waltz for

Gretl and Hermann's first dance as husband and wife. The music continued and the newlyweds were joined by guest couples.

Lars finished off a second glass of schnapps and extended his hand. "Will you honor me with a dance?"

She clasped his fingers and followed him to the center of the floor. As they waltzed, he pulled her close. His right hand gently caressed her back.

"You're a superb dancer," she said, hoping to distract him.

"Having the right partner makes all the difference."

As they glided to the rhythm of the waltz, her understanding of Lars's persona became clear. In addition to being a Swiss banker who'd sold his soul for riches, he was an intelligence informant with direct ties to Hitler. For quite some time she'd viewed him as a Nazi sympathizer, but seeing him here, surrounded by members of the führer's inner circle, she saw him for who he truly was—an accomplice to Hitler's quest for racial cleansing and world domination. Anger burned inside her. She struggled to remain calm and fought the urge to push him away.

For three hours, they celebrated with guests, most of whom knew Lars quite well. With each encounter, Lars introduced Maria as his Portuguese companion. He did most, if not all, of the talking, and she played the role of a demure lady friend. Two women, one of whom was Gretl, had privately commented to Maria that they were happy to see that Lars was moving on from the death of his wife. Also, Lars consumed much more schnapps than usual and, as the evening progressed, his speech grew louder and his touch became more frequent. To ensure that she maintained her faculties, she drank tonic water and coffee.

"I'm having a lovely time," Maria said to Lars, "but my energy is spent. When do you think we will leave for our hotel?"

"Now, if you like."

"That would be lovely."

They said their goodbyes to Gretl and Hermann, gathered their coats, and took the elevator down to the tunnel. At the car park, Lars pecked on the window of the limousine to wake the chauffeur, and they got into the back seat. Maria leaned against the door and pretended to sleep until they arrived at a hotel in Salzburg.

At the front desk, Lars spoke with a clerk while Maria sat on a sofa in the lobby. A bellhop retrieved their luggage from the limo and disappeared up a staircase.

Lars approached her. "Ready?"

Maria, her body and mind drained, stood and followed him up two flights of stairs. At the end of a hallway, Lars stopped at a door and removed a key from his pocket. He squinted as he attempted to insert the key into the lock.

"May I help you?"

"I got it." He scratched the key's tip over the lock and eventually found the hole. He opened the door.

"Is this my room or yours?"

"It's for both of us," he said. "There are no more rooms available. It was reserved when you were undecided about joining me on the trip."

She held her purse in front of her. "Perhaps I could stay in another hotel."

"The chauffeur has left for the evening," he said. "I've stayed here before. It's a large suite with a sofa. There's room for both of us."

She glanced inside to the well-appointed room with a poster bed and their luggage in front of an armoire. *What choice do I have? I have no money, I'm in enemy territory, and I need him to fly me back to Lisbon.* Reluctantly, she crossed the threshold. As she placed her purse on a dresser, her eyes gravitated to a metal stand that held a bucket of ice with a bottle of champagne.

Lars shut the door and bolted the lock. "Splendid—they remembered." He picked up the champagne, removed the casing, and popped the cork.

Maria clasped her arms.

"We must toast," he said pouring champagne into glasses.

"To what?"

"To your intelligence." He handed her a glass. "Germany's

high command has committed Panzer tank divisions to defending Calais."

Thank God.

They clinked glasses and sipped champagne.

Lars took a gulp and set aside his drink. He moved close—their shoes nearly touching—and he took her glass and placed it on a stand.

Oh, no.

He placed a hand on her shoulder. "We make a good team, don't you think?"

"We do," she said.

He glided a finger over her cheek.

A chill traveled down her spine. "I thought we were going to take things slow."

He leaned in, his breath smelling of alcohol, and kissed her neck. "This is slow."

Her mind raced. *There's no talking my way out of this. He's a man accustomed to having everything he wants—and he intends to have his way with me.*

His hand slid to her breast. He pressed his body to hers, pinning her back to a wall.

Maria hid her disgust and ran her fingers through the back of his hair. "Give me a moment to change into something more comfortable."

Lars, his eyes glossy and bloodshot, eased back and smiled. "Don't be long."

"I won't."

She slipped away and removed a nightgown from her suitcase. She retrieved her purse, entered the washroom, and locked the door. Her heart thudded inside her chest. She leaned her back against the door and drew in deep breaths to gather her composure, and then removed her clothes and put on her nightgown. She turned on the faucet to create noise. As she removed her compact from her purse, Argus's instructions echoed in her head. *The con-*

tents of one K-pill, inserted in a drink or food, will render a person unconscious.

Using her fingernail, she picked at the compact's mirror but it didn't budge. She plucked a hairpin from her purse and pried at the mirror's edge. The glass snapped, sending shards and pills over the floor. *Damn it!* She got on her hands and knees and searched over the tile floor. *How many were there?* she thought, plucking a pill from behind the toilet.

A knock on the door. "Is everything all right?"

"Yes," she said, struggling to remain composed. "I'll be right out."

She picked up the pills, hoping that she found them all, and deposited the shards of mirror into a trash bin. She tossed her compact and all of the pills—except for one—into her purse. She wedged a K-pill under the band of her sapphire ring and left the washroom.

She ran a hand over her silk, form-fitting nightgown. "How do I look?"

His eyes traced her body. "Beautiful."

She approached him and placed a hand on his chest. "It's been a while since I've been intimate. I'm a little nervous and was hoping we could take our time."

"I'll be gentle."

"I know you will." She ran a finger down his tie. "Get comfortable, and I'll pour us more champagne."

He looked into her eyes and nodded.

As Lars was removing his jacket, she retrieved their glasses. With her back to him, she cracked open the K-pill and dripped the liquid knockout drug into his glass. She hid the shell of the pill in the ice as she removed the bottle from the bucket. She poured champagne and turned to find him in trousers and a white undershirt.

"Here," she said, giving him a glass.

He took a gulp.

She sipped her champagne.

He took another swig and put down his half-full glass.

Her adrenaline surged. "Let's finish our drink."

"Later." He took her glass and set it aside.

"I was hoping we—"

He pulled her to his chest and kissed her hard.

She felt him trying to open her lips, but she pressed them tight. Fear flooded her body. *I should have used more pills!*

Using his weight, he forced her onto the bed. He clasped the back of her hair and pulled her head back. His breathing quickened, and he lowered his open mouth to her neck.

Maria struggled to push him off, but he was too strong. She felt his hand, pulling up her nightgown, and she prayed for the knockout drug to take effect.

Chapter 41

Peniche, Portugal—June 3, 1944

Tiago, unable to sleep, rolled out of his bunk and stood on weak legs. His cell was dark and silent, except for the muffled sound of waves crashing against the shore. It was late at night, he believed, given that it had been a long time since he'd been fed and his stomach ached with hunger. He whispered poems, hoping they would dispel the horrid visions of carrying his friend's lifeless body to the morgue, but the words did little to alleviate his turbulent mind. Forgoing his recited verse, he paced back and forth over his cell.

One, two, three, four, five, six, seven, eight, nine, ten.

He turned and shuffled.

One, two, three, four, five, six, seven, eight, nine, ten.

Although his cell was nearly absent of light, he was able to traverse the space with his eyes closed, ending with less than an inch of space between his nose and the cell wall. For an hour, he shuffled over the floor while the other inmates on the cellblock slept. *I need to exercise my mind and body, or I'll end up like Danilo.*

An iron door at the entrance to the cellblock squeaked open. A sliver of light beamed under his cell door.

Tiago froze. He listened to the night guard's boots clack over the floor as he conducted his rounds. Minutes later, the cellblock door clanged against its metal frame. He stared at the ray of light over his floor, and he was grateful that the guard had, for the third time this week, forgotten to turn off the corridor light.

He lifted the end of his metal bunk frame and slid it away from the wall to reveal a faint chessboard, scratched into the surface of the concrete floor. Using his fingers, he carefully plucked game pieces from a hole in the bottom of his mattress. He sat on the floor, the damp cold radiating through his bottom and legs, and arranged the pieces on the chessboard. Games of any type were banned at Peniche Prison. If he were caught, he would be severely punished. But for Tiago, it was worth the risk. It kept his mind sharp and, more importantly, made him feel human.

It had taken him two months to create the chess set. The board, scratched into the surface of the concrete with a tiny stone, had taken less than a day. It was the chess pieces that had required the most time and effort. He'd created them from wool and horsehair—which was the stuffing in his mattress—and bits of old bread. The first step in the process was to separate the white wool from the chestnut-colored horsehair. Using a paste made from bread crumbs and water, he molded the hair to resemble chess pieces. His first attempts were a disaster, with the rooks, bishops, and queens indistinguishable and resembling upright fuzzy caterpillars. Despite his failure, he'd laughed at himself and wondered what Rosa would have said about his lack of artistic talent.

After much trial and error, he'd mastered the process of making the pieces. At first it was difficult to play a game of chess by himself, but eventually he learned to condition his brain to remain unbiased and always strive to make the best move. Playing chess had not only occupied and exercised his mind; it had resurrected fond memories of his parents.

Tiago had learned to play chess at eight years of age. After an arduous day of labor in the vineyard, his father and mother played chess in the evenings for entertainment. Tiago had learned the rules and strategy of the game by observing and asking questions about their moves. Within weeks, he was whispering suggestions into their ears about which moves he thought they should make. And soon after, the three of them were taking turns to play matches.

As a child, he'd thought it was only a fun game to pass time. As he matured, he gradually understood that his parents were teaching him the importance of togetherness, problem-solving, and how to graciously win and lose. He thought that he'd someday teach his own children to play chess, just like his parents had done for him. But the war and Salazar's regime had stolen his future with Maria. Late at night, when the cellblock was still, he often imagined what it might have been like for him and Maria to teach their children how to play chess.

God, I wish things could be different.

Tiago, his heart aching, moved a white pawn forward two squares. He scooched across the cold floor to the other side of the chessboard and compartmentalized his mind. After some thought, he moved a black pawn. He played for two hours, until the night guard conducted another round and remembered to turn off the light.

CHAPTER 42

SALZBURG, AUSTRIA—JUNE 4, 1944

Maria's pulse pounded in her eardrums as Lars slid his hand beneath her nightgown and squeezed her thigh. His body pressed against her, pinning her back to the bed. She turned her head and squinted her eyes.

"I need to stop," she said. "This is too fast—it doesn't feel right."

"It'll—It'll be okay." He pressed his mouth to her cheek.

His sour breath filled her nostrils. Her leg muscles flared as she struggled to press her knees together. As she fought to push him away, her eyes locked on a crystal ashtray. She stretched out her arm but couldn't reach it.

He gripped her waist.

She strained her arm, getting her fingers within an inch of the ashtray.

Lars's respiration slowed and his muscles relaxed. His hands dropped to the bed.

She felt his full weight on her chest, making it difficult to breathe. Using all her strength, she rolled him to the side. She scrambled out of the bed and slumped onto the sofa. Tears flooded her eyes. Her body trembled as she wrapped her arms around her knees.

For several minutes, Maria watched Lars's diaphragm rise and fall. Not knowing how long the drug would last, she left the sofa and prepared for when he woke. She sniffed his glass and detected a faint chemical smell, despite that the drug was colorless. So, she disposed of his champagne, as well as what was left in the bottle, in the sink. She scoured the washroom floor and discovered a K-pill under the claw-foot tub. She hid all of the remaining pills inside the lining of her purse and removed the pen gun, which she placed in the interior pocket of her navy-colored suit jacket that she planned to wear for travel.

Hours passed and Lars remained unconscious. She ran water in the tub to make it appear she'd bathed, and then got dressed and put on makeup. She packed her bag, sat on the sofa, and listened to the cadence of his breathing. *I can't keep him drugged. He's my only ticket out of here.* She ran a hand over the lump in her suit jacket. *But if he tries to force himself on me again, I'll shoot him.*

Long after sunrise, Lars began to stir.

Maria, burying her angst, approached the bed. "Lars."

He groaned.

"Lars." She nudged his shoulder. "It's late. We need to go."

He slowly rolled over on his back and rubbed his head.

Maria opened the curtains, allowing sunlight to stream into the room.

He covered his eyes. "What time is it?"

"Nine thirty. I let you sleep in."

He sat on the edge of the bed with his face in his hands. "My head is throbbing."

"How much schnapps did you drink?"

"Too much," he said, his voice hoarse.

She gathered her courage and approached him. "Do you remember what happened before you fell asleep on me?"

Lars raised his head and wiped his mouth with the back of his hand. "I think we were about to—"

He paused, as if he were trying to clear fog from his brain.

She placed her hands on her hips. "You were aggressive with me."

His eyes narrowed. "I—I don't remember—"

"I do," she said, cutting him off. "You behaved like a brute."

He ran a hand through his hair. "I was drunk."

Anger burned inside her but she remained poised. "That's no excuse."

"I'm sorry."

"I care for you, but I'm not ready to be intimate. I hope you can respect that."

"I do." He raised his palms. "Are you mad?"

"I'm disappointed."

He stood and approached her.

She crossed her arms, preparing to grab her pen gun.

"I don't make a habit of boorish behavior—you must know that about me." His eyes filled with regret. "It won't happen again."

Maria nodded. "We need to leave. There's a London flight coming in to Lisbon, and I need to see if my shipment contains any news on troop movements."

"All right." He shuffled toward his suitcase but stopped at the champagne bucket. He picked up the empty bottle and examined it.

A memory of hiding the K-pill casing surged in her head. Her breath stalled in her lungs.

Lars shook his head, as if he was ashamed of himself, and lowered the bottle into the bucket. He picked up his suitcase, entered the bathroom, and closed the door.

Maria waited for the sound of running water, and she fished the pill casing out of the bucket. She hid the evidence under the mattress and placed her packed suitcase by the door.

Twenty minutes later, they left the hotel and got into the limousine. The chauffeur drove them to the airfield, where the plane was being checked over by the pilots. Maria and Lars boarded and took their seats. Propellers turned over and the engines grew to a roar. The plane rumbled down the runway and lifted into the air.

As the aircraft leveled off, Lars turned to Maria, across the aisle from him. "I'm truly sorry about what happened last night. I don't know what came over me."

"I don't want you to worry about it." She patted his arm. "We'll work it out. Get some rest."

Relief filled his face. He leaned back in his seat and closed his eyes.

Despite not sleeping for nearly thirty hours, Maria was unable to relax. She peered out the window to the snowcapped peaks of the Alps. Her mind reflected on the surprise wedding venue, her foiled plan to put an end to Hitler, and her agonizing night with Lars. *I don't know how much more of this I can take.*

In an attempt to restore her confidence, she recounted the reasons she joined the OSS—to serve her country and fight fascism. But her time in Lisbon had broadened her sense of purpose. She'd witnessed the impact of Nazi anti-Semitism with the masses of Jewish refugees who were escaping persecution through the Port of Lisbon. Tiago had opened her eyes to what was not being reported in newspapers. Not only had he lost his grandparents to Hitler's plan to purge Europe of Jews, he'd sacrificed his own freedom in helping refugees to flee to America.

An Allied victory is within reach, she thought. She envisioned a liberated Europe, and Tiago walking out of Peniche Fortress and holding her in his arms. *I know you won't give up, Tiago. And neither will I.*

CHAPTER 43

D-DAY—LISBON, PORTUGAL— JUNE 6, 1944

Maria poured a cup of morning coffee and carried it to her microfilm table. She took a sip, hot and bitter, and set aside her drink. Her airmail was scheduled to arrive from London in a few hours. To occupy her time, she picked up her camera and microfilmed a German newspaper. The camera felt comforting in her hands, and the repetitive click of the shutter release was relaxing, if not meditative.

Despite having been back in Lisbon for two days, Maria remained mentally and physically exhausted. She'd refused to rest and continued her duties of feeding misinformation to Lars, which painted a picture of the fictitious First United States Army Group—comprised of 150,000 men and commanded by General George Patton—that was preparing to cross the Channel to Pas-de-Calais, France. It was unnerving for her to interact with Lars after his beastly conduct on the trip. Fortunately for Maria, he'd kept his advances in check for the past forty-eight hours. But it was only a matter of time, Maria believed, before he resumed his ploy to seduce her.

A knock came from the door.

Maria put down her camera, went to the foyer, and checked the peephole. Her tension eased at the sight of Roy. She opened the door and let him in.

"Jeez," Roy said. "Are you all right? You look tuckered out."

"I am." She closed the door.

"Pilar and I stopped by to see you a few days ago but you were out. Where have you been?"

"You wouldn't believe me if I told you."

"You want to try me?"

"Another time."

He raised his nose and sniffed. "I smell fresh coffee."

"Come on," she said. "I'll pour you a cup."

Roy followed Maria to the kitchen. His eyes widened at a large arrangement of flowers. "Nice bouquet."

"I thought it would brighten up the apartment," she said, deciding it was best not to reveal that the flowers were a gift from Lars. The arrangement included a handwritten apology note, which was stashed in a drawer. She wanted to toss it out when it was delivered, but she kept it in the event that Lars paid a surprise visit.

She poured a cup of coffee and gave it to him. "Where's Pilar?"

"She'll be along in a minute. She stopped at a newsstand on our way here."

"Oh," Maria said.

"It was supposed to be a surprise," he said. "If we found you here, we were going to steal you away for breakfast. It's been far too long since the three of us have gotten together."

Maria smiled. "That would be lovely. I'm free for an hour. Will that be enough time?"

"Plenty."

Footsteps grew on the stairs outside the apartment. They turned as the door flung open and Pilar dashed inside.

"It's happening!" Pilar shouted.

Maria's eyes widened.

"What are you talking about?" Roy asked.

Pilar sucked in air. "The Allies have landed in France!"

Maria's hope soared. "How do you know?"

"It was on the radio at a newsstand," Pilar said.

Maria darted to the living room and turned on the radio. Several seconds of silence passed as the vacuum tubes warmed, and the male voice of a Portuguese news broadcaster filled the room. They huddled around the radio and listened to the announcer's claim that multiple German news agencies reported early this morning that an Allied invasion of France had begun with Allied paratroopers dropping out of the dawn skies over Normandy and amphibious forces landing near Le Havre. Also, the news broadcaster reported that Allied warships were bombarding the German-occupied French port of Le Havre at the mouth of the Seine River, two hundred kilometers west of Paris. He then repeated the reports for listeners who might be tuning in.

"Hot damn!" Roy said.

Maria clasped her hands. "It's really happening."

"It is," Pilar said, smiling.

Maria's mind flashed to the Eagle's Nest, where the several-day wedding celebration for Gretl Braun and her husband, Hermann, was likely still taking place. She imagined military guests—upon hearing news of the invasion—fleeing the mountaintop retreat and bringing the party to a halt. She prayed that the German high command was surprised by the attack and, more importantly, had fully committed the majority of their defenses to Calais, far from the Allied invasion point.

The phone rang.

Hairs rose on the back on Maria's neck.

The phone rang again.

"Are you going to get that?" Roy asked.

"Yeah," Maria said.

Pilar reached for the radio's volume knob.

"Leave it on," Maria said. "But remain silent while I'm on the phone."

Roy raised his brows.

The phone rang for a third time.

"I'll explain later." Maria drew a breath and picked up the receiver. "Hello."

"Have you heard the news?" Lars's voice asked.

Her heart rate quickened. "Yes. I just turned on the radio."

"The Allies have landed between Le Havre and Cherbourg, along the Normandy coast."

Maria swallowed.

"The reports indicate a large-scale attack," he said, his voice agitated. "Are you certain your intelligence is correct."

"Yes," she said. "It's a deception."

Pilar and Roy looked at each other.

"What if your subagents are wrong?"

"They're not wrong," she said. "They are independent sources. Everything they've reported indicates that the real invasion will take place at Calais."

Roy's jaw dropped open. Pilar's eyes widened.

Maria looked at them and placed a finger to her lips, signaling to remain silent.

Pilar nodded and clasped Roy's arm.

"The Allies have been planning this for months," Maria said firmly. "They want the Germans to believe that the attack is in Normandy, so Panzer divisions are diverted away from Calais, where the real invasion will take place in a few days."

"If you're wrong about this," Lars said, "we'll be killed."

"My intelligence is correct, and you know that I'm right. You must do everything possible to convince the Germans to keep their forces in Calais. Otherwise, all will be lost when General Patton's troops cross the Channel." She gripped the receiver as she waited for his response.

"When will I see you?"

"There's a flight coming in from London today. After I check to see if I've received new intelligence, I'll come to your house."

"Very well," he said. "I'll be here."

"See you soon." Maria hung up the phone.

"What the heck is going on?" Roy asked.

"I'm not at liberty to reveal details," Maria said. "But I will tell you that I'm working for the OSS to supply misinformation to German intelligence. You'll need to trust me."

He rubbed the side of his neck. "Okay."

Pilar looked at Maria. "What can we do to help?"

Maria thought of Argus, who'd gone to Madrid and hadn't been debriefed about her trip with Lars. "Go to the embassy and leave word for Argus that I'll be in Estoril. He'll understand why I'm there."

"Okay," Pilar said.

"Are you sure it's safe for you to leave?" Roy asked.

"No," Maria said. "It also isn't safe for the thousands of Allied soldiers battling their way ashore in Normandy. And if I don't go to Estoril, there's a chance that many more lives could be lost."

Maria, fearing that it could be the last time she saw her friends, hugged them tight. She slipped away, grabbed her purse, and left the apartment. Outside she got into a taxi and traveled to the airport. *I can't fool Lars much longer, but if I can keep up the masquerade for forty-eight more hours, it might be too late for the Germans to defend against the invasion.*

Chapter 44

D-Day—Peniche, Portugal—June 6, 1944

A whistle blew in the cellblock and Tiago labored to stand from his bunk. A key jostled in the steel door and it opened, revealing a guard and the prison superintendent—a barrel-chested man with sweat stains under the armpits of his khaki uniform. The presence of the superintendent, based on Tiago's time on the cellblock, usually meant a surprise inspection, random punishment, or both.

"Stand aside," the guard shouted.

Tiago placed his back to the wall.

The guard rummaged through the cell. He pulled away the mattress, toppled the metal frame of the bunk, and inspected under the wall-mounted sink and inside the cabinet that contained Tiago's slop bucket.

The superintendent, standing in the doorway, folded his arms.

"It's clean," the guard said, pushing a tattered blanket with his boot.

Tiago's shoulders relaxed.

"What's that?" the superintendent said, pointing to the floor.

Tiago's pulse rate quickened.

The guard examined scratches in the concrete. "It looks like a checkerboard."

The superintendent looked at Tiago. "Where are the pieces?"

"I don't know what you're talking about," Tiago said.

"Help him remember," the superintendent said to the guard.

The guard removed a wooden baton from his belt and struck Tiago in the stomach.

Pain shot through his abdomen and he fell to his knees.

"Tell me where the pieces are hidden," the superintendent said.

Tiago gasped, struggling to bring air into his lungs.

A guard examined the mattress and located a hole, the size of a small coin. "I think I found it, sir." He tore at the opening and fished out the pieces.

"Restrain him," the superintendent said.

The guard shoved Tiago against the wall. He pressed his baton over his throat, cutting off his air.

Tiago's head throbbed as he strained to breathe. He pushed the baton with his hands, but he was too weak to fight.

"Enough," the superintendent said.

The guard released his stranglehold and Tiago slumped to the ground.

"Did you make the checkers?" the superintendent asked.

Tiago sucked in air.

"I'll ask you one last time," the superintendent said. "Where did you get the checkers?"

Resistance burned within him. He raised his head and looked at him. "They're chess pieces, not checkers."

A scowl formed on the superintendent's face. "Give him half rations and no outside privileges for three months."

"Yes, sir," the guard said.

The men left the cell and locked the steel door.

Tiago sat in the corner of his cell and stared at the etched chessboard. Dread chewed at his gut. At Peniche Prison, most prisoners died when placed on half rations for more than sixty days.

Chapter 45

Estoril, Portugal—June 8, 1944

Maria, holding a manila envelope that arrived with her daily airmail from London, sat next to Lars on the sofa in his home office. She removed four photographs, one of amphibious landing craft and three of American Sherman tanks, and gave them to him.

"From my subagent, Hazel," Maria said.

"The birdwatcher."

"Yes."

"Where were they taken?"

"Dover, England—same as the other photograph that we received." Maria turned to him. "General Patton's army is still in South East England. The invasion at Calais, France, is imminent."

Lars rubbed his chin and examined the images.

For the past two days, Maria implored Lars to convince German High Command that the attack in Normandy was a deception. Fortunately for Maria, the OSS had armed her with daily airmail from London that contained fake evidence for her to keep up the sham. "Hitler's Panzer tank divisions need to remain in position to defend against the real invasion that will take place in Calais," she'd said, showing him an intercepted wireless radio transmission from her subagent in Liverpool. But as hours and days passed, and as radio and newspapers reported on Allied military successes in Normandy, Lars's consternation grew. He spent much of his time talking privately on the phone and checking news reports. To maintain his confidence in her, she remained at his residence, with the exception of her trips to the airport and sleeping at her apartment.

Lars set aside the photographs. He took a drag on a cigarette and snubbed it out in a crystal tray overfilled with ash and butts. "I thought they would have invaded Calais by now."

"Me too," she said. "It shouldn't be much longer."

Lars crossed his legs and ran a hand over his necktie. "Newspapers are reporting that the Allied attack in Normandy is doing better than expected. There are claims that Bayeux has been captured and a fierce fight is taking place for Caen."

"We need to be patient and stay the course," she said, looking into his eyes. "In a few days, you'll look like a genius to the führer. With a long war, you'll make a fortune from your banking arrangement with Germany to acquire Portugal's wolfram."

He adjusted a cuff link and nodded. "It'll also make you a rich woman."

She smiled. "Indeed, it will."

The phone on his desk rang.

"I'll let you get that," Maria said, standing. "Do want anything from the kitchen?"

"No, thank you."

She left his office and closed the door. She attempted to eavesdrop by pressing an ear to the door, but the wood was thick and Lars spoke in a soft tone. Rather than risk being detected, she went to the kitchen and prepared a bowl of seasoned black olives. The house was silent, given that Lars granted his staff, including the chauffeur, time off work to provide him with complete privacy. Although Maria and Lars were alone together, she felt less threatened by him than she had all week. With the Allies in Normandy, he was consumed with Germany maintaining the upper hand in France.

Maria placed a bowl of olives and a dish for the pits on a silver serving tray. She carried it to his office and tapped on the door.

"Come in," he said.

She entered and approached him, standing at a small bar and pouring a glass of schnapps. "Everything all right?"

"Yes."

She held out the tray. "You haven't eaten, so I prepared some olives."

He selected one, placed it in his mouth, and chewed.

"How is it?"

"Good." He deposited the pit into the dish and took a sip of schnapps.

"I'll put the tray on—"

He cocked back his arm and slammed his glass to the side of her head.

Pain shot through her temple. She crumpled to the floor and everything went black.

Chapter 46

Covilhã, Portugal—June 8, 1944

Dazed, Maria struggled to lift her head. She felt her hands pulled tightly behind her back and her wrists tied together with cord. Gradually regaining her strength, she cracked open her eyes to see Lars slip a handkerchief from his pocket, shove it into her mouth, and cover it with tape. *It's over.*

She attempted to get away but her body felt broken. Blood dripped from a gash on her scalp, turning her hair wet. Helplessly, she watched Lars bind her ankles together with rope and slip a pillowcase over her head.

He grabbed her legs and grunted as he lifted her onto his shoulder.

She squirmed, sending a sharp, shooting pain through her head. Unable to fight, she allowed her body to go limp in an effort to conserve her energy.

Lars carried her from the house and lowered her into the open trunk of his Mercedes-Benz.

The trunk lid slammed shut, turning her space into a dark crypt. Her heart pounded as she breathed recycled air. The automobile started and pulled away. She tugged at her bindings, but it was of no use. Her wrists and ankles were securely bound, cutting off the circulation to her hands and feet. For several minutes, while the vehicle drove through winding roads, she slowly arched her neck back forth until she was able to work the pillowcase above her nose.

Her ability to think gradually improved, and with it came the understanding of her plight and fate. *Lars knows what I've done, and he's taking me someplace to kill me.* Eventually, her absence would alert Pilar, Roy, or Argus, and the OSS would come to her aid. But by the time help would arrive, it would all be over. Fear flooded her veins.

She expected Lars to pull over at a remote area outside of Estoril. Instead, he drove without stopping for hours. The interior of the trunk grew intolerably hot, and the air turned stagnant. Sweat dripped from her forehead and burned her eyes. Her mind and heart ached for a future that would never be. She prayed for her father, her friends, refugees fleeing persecution, and for an Allied victory to bring an end to Hitler's tyranny. And she wished for a miracle that would free Tiago from prison.

The vehicle turned onto a rough road and traveled up a steep incline. Maria curled into a fetal position as she bounced around the trunk compartment. Several hours after leaving Estoril, the car stopped and the engine turned off. Her adrenaline surged at the sound of Lars opening his door and walking to the trunk. A key was inserted into a lock and the lid opened. The pillowcase was removed from her head, and she squinted at the sunlight.

Lars grabbed her left arm and leg, and he lugged her out of the trunk.

She fell to the ground, knocking the wind out of her lungs. She struggled to take in air through her nose, and she gagged on the wadded handkerchief in her mouth.

Lars undid the binding on her ankles, but left her hands tied behind her back. He placed his hands under her armpits, lifted her to her feet, and led her to the rear door of the vehicle, where he removed a miner's lamp from the back-seat floor.

Using the corners of her eyes, she scanned the area. The remote, mountainside terrain was covered in rock and evergreens, and there were no paved roads or houses in sight. She assumed they were somewhere near Covilhã, the wolfram mining town where Lars spent much of his time.

He slipped a pistol from his jacket and pressed it to her back. "Walk."

With her feet numb from the bindings, she limped along a narrow earthen path. A few minutes into the trek, her circulation improved enough that she could feel her toes and the ground beneath her feet, but she continued to hobble and groan, pretending to be in pain. They traveled forty yards up a steep trail until they reached a padlocked, wooden door in the hillside.

He pushed hard on her shoulder, forcing her to kneel.

Oh, God! She winced, preparing for him to place the pistol to her head and pull the trigger.

Lars picked up a rock and struck it against the rusted padlock, breaking its shackle. He opened the door and retrieved his cigarette lighter. He rolled the flint wheel several times with no success.

If it doesn't light, he's going to kill me here.

On the eighth attempt, the lighter produced a miniscule flame. He quickly lit the lamp, and then got her to her feet.

She felt the nose of the pistol press against the back of her neck. "Move!"

Powerless, she entered the mine.

Lamplight illuminated the low ceiling of the passage, which was supported by vertical timber beams. A mine railway—its steel covered in rust—ran through the center of the tunnel. Sections of the ceiling had partially collapsed, and the mine appeared to have run out of wolfram ore and was abandoned. The temperature dropped as they traveled deep underground. She limped onward, all the while searching for a means of escape.

"Stop!" he shouted, his voice echoing through the tunnel.

She froze.

He put down the lamp and approached her.

She felt the tip of the weapon pressed to the base of her skull, and the tape pulled away from her mouth.

He stepped back. "Turn around."

Maria spit out the handkerchief and faced him. "Why are you doing this?" she cried.

"I found a pen gun and pills hidden under the lining of your purse."

He searched it when I was in the kitchen. "It isn't what you think. It's for protection." She wriggled her hands behind her back, attempting to loosen the cord.

"You betrayed me."

"No—I don't understand," she pleaded. "You hurt me, Lars. I need a doctor."

"Stop the lies! I know your allegiance is to the Allies. The attack at Normandy isn't a deception—it's the real invasion. You've been using me for months to mislead the Germans."

She swallowed, her throat dry and raw. "You don't have to do this, Lars."

He aimed his pistol.

"We can find a way for both of us to get out of this," she said soothingly.

"It's too late for that. We had the world at our feet, and you threw it all away for goddamn patriotism."

She looked into his eyes and slowly shuffled toward him. "Please, Lars. I know that you don't want to kill me."

He hesitated, stepping back. His arm trembled.

She shot to the side and kicked the miner's lamp, smashing its glass and extinguishing the flame. The gun exploded, a bullet ricocheting over the wall, and she darted into the black abyss.

Maria ran blindly into the tunnel. She tripped over a steel rail and fell on her chest, sending a twinge through her ribs. A flash of gunfire and a bullet whizzed above her head. Her heart pounded. She rolled to her side. Using her legs, she pushed her back against the wall and worked her way into a standing position. She heard Lars trying to light the lamp, and then smashing it to the ground.

"I'll find you!" Lars's voice echoed through the tunnel.

She scuttled away, leaning her shoulder to the wall to avoid tripping over the rails. Seconds later, her shoulder struck a timber pillar of a roof support. As she carefully inched her way around the pillar, her foot kicked a rock. She froze at the sound of the stone clattering down a mine shaft. *It's the end of the line.*

Lars's footsteps grew close. He flicked his lighter, again and again, producing nothing but a spark.

Maria crept back a few feet from the shaft. She pressed her shoulder blades and restrained arms to the wall. Using a heel, she slipped a shoe from her opposite foot but left her toes inside.

A few feet away from Maria, a flint wheel scratched, producing a spark. She gently raised her foot, balancing her shoe on her toes. *Please, God.*

"Maria!"

Dread surged through her. She held her breath.

He flicked his lighter, and it produced a miniscule flame.

She flipped her shoe toward the shaft, striking its wall.

Lars shot forward and fired his pistol.

Air brushed Maria's face.

Lars screamed as he tumbled down the mine shaft. A thud, and then silence.

Maria's legs trembled. She leaned against the wall to gather her composure, and she slogged her way back through the tunnel.

She emerged from the mine to a warm afternoon sun. She drew in deep breaths of fresh air, and then rubbed the rope on her bound wrists over a splintery wood post at the entrance to the mine. Slivers of wood gouged into her skin. Her arm and shoulder muscles burned. Ignoring her pain, she pushed on for thirty minutes and the rope snapped.

She rummaged through Lars's Mercedes-Benz but found no spare key. She did, however, find a handkerchief in the glovebox, which she used to wipe her bloodied wrists. With one shoe and her mind and body ravaged, she trudged down from the mountain.

PART 4

LIBERATION

Chapter 47

Lisbon, Portugal—August, 25, 1944

While on her walk to meet Pilar and Roy, Maria stopped at a newsstand and purchased a special edition newspaper. She'd heard the report on a radio broadcast, but there was something real and meaningful about seeing the news in print. A feeling of triumph swelled within her as she read the headline.

PARIS LIBERATED!

She folded the paper and navigated her way through cobblestone streets. At the Rossio, she entered a café, sat at a table, and read the newspaper while she waited for her friends to arrive.

The past two months had been a time of healing, both physically and emotionally, for Maria. After escaping the mine, she'd plodded her way to the nearby town of Covilhã. Fearing that some of the town's inhabitants might have a connection with Lars and his wolfram smuggling operation, she sought refuge at a Catholic church. A nun named Cristina had cleaned and bandaged the wounds to her head and wrists. Maria had told the woman that she was abducted by an unknown assailant in Lisbon, and that she escaped her captor by jumping out of a moving vehicle. Although Cristina appeared skeptical of her story, she respected Maria's wishes not to notify the police. Maria had insisted on having her own physician, rather than the local village doctor, examine her scalp, which likely needed a few stitches. So, Cristina arranged for a parishioner to drive Maria to Lisbon.

Maria had delayed seeking medical treatment. At her apartment, she'd washed, changed clothes, and put on a headscarf to cover her bandage. She arrived by taxi at Casino Estoril shortly before midnight. Instead of entering, she walked to Lars's home to retrieve her purse, which she feared could be used as evidence to lead either the PVDE or a German agent to her. With his staff away, she'd entered the home by breaking a glass pane on a French door. Within minutes, she'd scoured the house, recovered her purse and its contents, and left.

The following morning, after having three stitches placed in her scalp, she'd met with Argus and debriefed him on everything—Lars's relationship with Hitler and his High Command, Gretl Braun's wedding, the reception at the Eagle's Nest, using a knockout drug to thwart Lars's sexual advances, her two days of trying to persuade Lars that the Normandy invasion was a deceptive attack, and her abduction.

"You've been through hell," Argus had said. "Your courageous service has been instrumental to the success of Operation Fortitude. I think you've done enough, and it's time for you to go home."

She'd declined his offer, even when Argus warned her that she might be at risk of assassination if she remained in Portugal. After much insistence, he agreed for her to remain in Lisbon to perform microfilm duties. Also, Argus had promised to arrange—through his OSS and MI6 connections—to dispose of Lars's Mercedes-Benz in Covilhã. She was confident that Allied intelligence services would do everything possible to erase any evidence that would lead a German agent back to her, but there were no guarantees. Also, she'd expected that the PVDE would eventually pay her a visit about Lars's disappearance, considering that they were often seen together at his home and Casino Estoril.

But days turned to weeks, and weeks turned to months, and the police had yet to contact her. And she'd often wondered if Lars, a Nazi-collaborating banker without living family members, was presumed to have cashed in his chips and fled Europe for South America.

Maria was relieved to end her role of a spy acting as a double agent. She no longer feared for her life, and she was glad that her web of lies was over. Most importantly, she could now dedicate more time and effort to free Tiago. She'd asked Argus and Kilgour to initiate efforts to help Tiago, whom she described as a bookseller who aided the efforts of the OSS. They agreed to escalate the issue through their chain of command, but told her that there was likely little the OSS could do to free an imprisoned Portuguese citizen. Also, she'd written Colonel Donovan but hadn't received a reply. And for the past several weeks, she'd visited the American embassy to lobby Raymond Henry Norweb, the United States Ambassador to Portugal. Eventually, she convinced Norweb to initiate a discussion about Tiago with the Portuguese government. She was optimistic that Norweb might be able to help, until she was summoned—two days ago—to the embassy.

"I'm sorry," Norweb had said. "Salazar's regime refuses to consider the release of any political prisoner. There's nothing further we can do."

Maria had left the embassy feeling shattered, but she refused to give up. *To hell with diplomatic channels. I'll take matters into my own hands.*

Pilar and Roy entered the café and paused, scanning the room.

Maria set aside her paper and waved.

"We did it!" Pilar said, running to Maria and giving her a hug.

Roy removed his pipe from his mouth and grinned.

"Yes, we did," Maria said, feeling a strange mix of joy and sadness.

They sat at the table. To celebrate the liberation of Paris, they ordered coffee and pastries.

Pilar nudged Roy. "Tell her the good news."

"I've been selected for T-Force," Roy said. "It's a special group attached to the military. I'll be on a document team to recover books and publications left in the wake of the retreating German army. I leave for Paris this afternoon."

Maria smiled. "Congratulations."

"Thanks," he said. "Maybe Kilgour will send the both of you to join me in a few months, like he did when deploying us to Lisbon."

"I hope so," Pilar said.

Maria took a sip of coffee. "I won't be joining you."

"Why?" Pilar asked.

"I've resigned from the OSS."

Roy's eyes widened. "When?"

"Yesterday. It won't matter much anyway. With the liberation of Italy and France, the Lisbon outpost will likely be closed by the end of the year. Eventually, the librarians of the OSS will become members of T-Force, like Roy."

Pilar placed a hand on Maria's arm. "You've done more than any agent could hope to do in this damn war."

"I agree," Roy said. "You're the bravest person I know."

Maria blinked, fighting back tears. She hadn't told them everything about her role as a double agent, nor did they probe her for details.

"When are you going home?" Pilar asked.

"I'm not," Maria said. "I'm staying in Lisbon to see what more can be done for Tiago."

Pilar looked at her. "Someday, he'll be free."

"Yes, he will." Maria drew a breath and raised her cup. "Enough about me. Here's to us, and the librarians of the OSS. It's been an honor serving with you."

"The honor is mine," Pilar said.

"I'll drink to that," Roy said, clinking their cups.

They ate their pastries and celebrated the liberation of Paris. It was only a matter of time, they believed, before the rest of Europe would be liberated and Nazi Germany defeated. For the first time in many months, they were joyful. Knowing it was the last time that the three of them would be together, they hugged goodbye and promised to keep in touch. As Maria left her friends, a deep determination burned inside her. She crossed the street en route to speak with the only person whom she believed was capable of helping her free Tiago.

Chapter 48

Lisbon, Portugal—August 25, 1944

A block away from Graça Convent, perched on Lisbon's highest hill, Maria stopped at the address written on her piece of paper. She entered a building, its frontage covered in blue tiles, and traveled down a dimly lit hallway to a first-floor apartment. She knocked on the door.

A dog barked in a neighboring apartment.

Maria fiddled with the clasp on her purse. Footsteps approached and the door opened.

"Maria!" Rosa wrapped her arms around her. "It's so good to see you."

"You too," she said, squeezing her tight. "I've missed you."

"Please come in." Rosa ushered her inside and closed the door. "If I would have known you were coming, I would have fixed my hair and prepared you something to eat."

"You look lovely, Rosa. My apologies for the unannounced visit. Am I catching you at a good time?"

"Of course," she said.

Rosa led Maria to a small living room, where they sat on a gray Victorian-style sofa. The room was covered with framed family photographs, and a scent of burnt beeswax and cleaning solution filled the air. Along a wall was a home altar, consisting of a crucifix, a Bible, prayer beads, and lit votive candles.

"You just missed my husband, Jorge," Rosa said. "He's having a good day with his arthritis, so he decided to go for a walk."

"I'd like to meet him."

"Hopefully he'll be back before you leave." Rosa adjusted her glasses. "Did you hear the news about Paris?"

"I did. Things are looking up for an Allied victory."

"Hitler will lose his war and all of Europe will be liberated." Rosa frowned. "But the Portuguese people will be stuck with their dictator until the day he dies."

"I'm hopeful that democracy will eventually prevail." Maria's eyes gravitated to the home altar.

"I have prayer candles for Tiago and his grandparents," Rosa said.

"That's thoughtful of you. I'm sure he'd be grateful for your wishes for him and his family."

Rosa nodded. "Last month, I went to see Tiago's parents in Porto."

"How are they?"

"Heartbroken."

"I wish I could have gone with you," Maria said, feeling guilty for not having met Tiago's parents.

"You've been committed to winning the war," Rosa said. "Soon, you'll be able to meet them. And I'll go with you."

"I would like that very much," Maria said.

"Have you heard any news on Tiago?"

An ache grew in Maria's chest. She told her about the failed diplomatic efforts of the US ambassador to Portugal. "He said that Salazar's regime refuses to consider the release of political prisoners."

Tears welled up in Rosa's eyes. "I wish there was something I could have done to protect him from the secret police. And I'm sorry that my former lawyer boss could do nothing to fight for his release."

Maria removed a handkerchief from her purse and gave it to her.

"*Obrigada*." Rosa wiped her eyes and wrinkled cheeks.

"There might be something that can be done."

Rosa lowered the handkerchief. "What do you mean?"

"I've come up with a plan to get him out of prison, and I'd like your help."

She arched her eyebrows. "Count me in."

"I don't want you to accept until you hear what it's about," Maria said. "It's a long shot that it'll work, and it comes with great risk."

"How much danger are we talking about?"

"Enough to keep one in jail for the rest of their life."

Rosa raised her chin. "A life sentence doesn't scare me. They won't get many years of imprisonment out of an old woman like me."

"You might change your mind when you hear my idea."

"I won't," Rosa said. "Tell me your plan so we can get to work."

Chapter 49

Peniche, Portugal—August 25, 1944

Tiago cracked open his eyelids and peered up at the grooves running along the concrete ceiling of his cell. He shivered and pulled his blanket to his chest, but it did little to warm him. He'd lost an extreme amount of weight and, no matter how tightly he bundled himself, he remained in a constant state of cold.

His eyes were dark and sunken, and his muscles were atrophied to the point where he was no longer capable of shuffling over his cell for exercise. He felt lethargic and spent most of his existence in a deep, dreamless sleep. Despite his reduced rations, he'd lost his desire for food and water. His brain struggled to think, and he was unable to recite verses to his favorite poems by Luís de Camões. Worst of all, he struggled to remember the faces of the people he loved.

Tiago pressed his eyes shut, searched through his memories, and strived to piece together a picture of Maria in his head. The curvature of her nose. The shape of her chin. The softness of her hair. The timbre of her voice. The smell of her skin. But all he could visualize was a faded image, like a watercolor portrait left out in the rain.

A whistle blew, signaling roll call. One by one, cell doors were unlocked.

Tiago, his limbs feeling like lead, pushed the blanket from his chest. He rolled from his bunk and fell to the floor, striking his hip.

"Soares!" a guard shouted from the corridor.

He tried to stand, but could only manage to get to his hands and knees. His head turned dizzy.

"Show yourself!"

He drew in breaths, hoping his vertigo would subside and he could gather his strength.

A clack of footsteps grew in the corridor. The guard entered, swung back his leg, and kicked Tiago in the ribs.

Pain shot through his diaphragm. He crumpled onto his side. Depleted of energy, he made no effort to protect himself.

As the guard removed his baton from his belt, the prison superintendent appeared in the doorway.

"Leave him," the superintendent said. "He's dying."

The guard put away his baton and left, locking the cell door behind him.

Tiago, too weak to move, remained on the floor. He listened to water drip from a faucet until his pain deadened and sleep took him away.

Chapter 50

Cascais, Portugal—September 5, 1944

The taxi driver turned into the entrance of a palatial, Mediterranean-style home and stopped in a rotunda. Maria paid the driver to wait and exited the vehicle with a briefcase. Her heart rate accelerated as she approached the entrance of the home of Ricardo Espírito Santo, a close friend and banker to Portuguese dictator António de Oliveira Salazar. She rang the doorbell and waited. Chatter and laughter echoed from behind the home.

A middle-aged woman wearing a gray-and-white maid's uniform opened the door. "May I help you?"

"My name is Maria Alves. I'm here to speak with Ricardo."

"I'm sorry. Senhor Santo is with guests."

"It's important," she said. "You'll need to interrupt him."

"I'm afraid I can't do that. I'd be happy to let him know that you—"

Maria turned and walked across a manicured lawn toward the side of the home.

"Excuse me, *senhorita*," the woman called. "You can't go back there."

Maria lengthened her stride. She turned the corner and soon reached a rear garden, where Ricardo and his wife, Mary, were hosting two couples for drinks on a patio. The group, all of whom were dressed in country club attire, turned their heads to Maria. Their chatter faded.

"I'm sorry, *senhor*," the maid said, scurrying into the garden. "This woman insisted on speaking with you."

"Hello, Ricardo," Maria said calmly. She looked at his wife. "How are you, Mary?"

Mary put down her cocktail. Tension filled the air.

"I'm Maria. We met at Prime Minister Salazar's home."

"Now is not a good time," Ricardo said.

"Oh, but it is," Maria said, raising her briefcase.

Ricardo's eyes locked on the monogrammed case. He rose from his seat and looked at his wife. "I won't be long. Would you entertain our guests?"

"Of course, darling," Mary said.

Maria glanced over the grounds. "You were right about your garden, Mary. Your plants and flowers are every bit as spectacular as the ones in Salazar's garden."

The woman lowered her eyes, as if she'd committed blasphemy.

"Follow me," Ricardo said, crossing the patio.

Maria followed him into the house and down a long travertine tile hallway. They entered an office, filled with golf trophies and several photographs of him and Salazar.

Ricardo shut the door and turned to her. "What are you doing with Lars's briefcase?"

A memory of breaking into Lars's home flashed in her head. She'd intended to reclaim her purse, but she'd also rummaged through his office for intelligence and had taken his briefcase.

"He left it at my apartment." She sat in an upholstered wing chair in front of his desk and placed the briefcase on her lap. "Do you know where he is?"

"No. Do you?"

"I'm afraid not. But if I had to guess, I'd say he's likely enjoying an early retirement in Argentina."

"Give me the briefcase and leave."

"I came to deliver it to you." She placed the case on his desk with the latches facing a leather chair.

He folded his arms.

"I'm going to stick around for a few minutes. You might have some questions for me after you open it."

Ricardo walked around the desk and sat. He paused, placing his hands on the latches.

"Go on. It's not going to explode."

He clicked the latches and lifted the lid. He raised his brows. "What's this?"

"Microfilm."

He removed a spool of developed film with tiny images.

"It contains Swiss bank documents."

He undid the spool and held the images up to the light. His face went pale.

"Those are small to read," she said, "so I took the liberty to include a larger photograph of one of the documents. It's tucked behind a divider in the briefcase."

He examined the photograph and placed it facedown on his desk. "Where are the originals?"

"In a safe place," she said. "I also have many copies in microfilm."

"Give them to me, or I'll have you arrested."

"No." She crossed her legs and smoothed her skirt. "If you are foolish enough to have me incarcerated, my friends will deliver copies of the documents to the British, American, Canadian, and Australian governments. Also, there are copies slated for newspapers in London, New York, Washington, Toronto, and Sydney. And a special copy for General Charles de Gaulle, Chairman of the Provisional Government of the French Republic."

Ricardo scowled. "You have no clue about what you are doing."

"You're wrong about that," she said. "I know everything about your gold laundering operation."

His jaw muscles twitched.

"According to Lars's records, Germany purchased wolfram from Portugal using gold, but there was no direct transfer of gold from Germany to Portugal. Instead, gold was deposited in a complex scheme into Lars's Swiss bank in Bern, and then transferred to the Bank of Portugal. The documents show that the bank is transferring Portuguese escudos in exchange for gold, in which Lars's bank acts as a trustee. It's a clever plan."

"You're a fool," he said.

"I don't think so. Based on my math, there was over one hundred tons of Nazi gold transferred from Germany's Reichsbank."

Ricardo clenched his hands.

She leaned forward. "Allied leaders will be eager to learn about the world's largest gold laundering operation involving German, Swiss, and Portuguese banks."

He swallowed.

"The gold in your bank was stolen. Nazi Germany looted it from occupied countries and their citizens—including jewelry taken from Jews who were sent away to prison camps."

Ricardo, appearing agitated, looked down and away.

"Hitler's demise is imminent. Within months, the remaining occupied countries will be liberated. If their governments find out that their gold is sitting in the vaults of your bank, they're going to want it back. And I have little doubt that American and British governments will seek personal action against you and Salazar."

He wiped his forehead with the back of his hand. "What do you want? Money? Gold?"

She looked into his eyes. "I want a political prisoner released from Peniche Prison."

Ricardo's forehead wrinkled.

"His name is Tiago Soares. He was unjustly imprisoned."

"I don't understand."

"You don't have to," she said. "The thing is—we both get what we want from this deal. You and Salazar get to keep the gold in your bank a secret, and I get Soares released."

He glanced to a framed photograph of him and the dictator,

dressed in business suits at a banquet. "It'll take time to consider your demand."

"You have thirty-six hours to free Soares and deliver him to me. Otherwise, the records will be released."

"The prime minister will require more time."

"Thirty-six hours—nothing more."

He shifted in his seat. "If we should reach an agreement, I assume you'll turn over all copies of the bank records."

"Only the originals," she said. "The microfilm copies will be stowed away in a safe deposit box for insurance. If any retribution should be taken against me, Soares, or Soares's family and friends, the copies will be released."

"If he is let out of prison, what will prevent you from later releasing the copies?"

"I care about the welfare of Soares and his family, otherwise I wouldn't be here. If I did publicize the documents, Salazar would have them punished, and I don't want that to happen."

"I do not think he'll agree to your demands."

"My terms are nonnegotiable." Maria removed a slip of paper and placed it on the briefcase. "You can reach me at that telephone number. I'll see myself out."

She left the office, exited the home through the front door, and got into the back seat of the taxi. As the vehicle left Cascais, Maria lowered her guard. She slumped in her seat and stared out the window, shocked by the enormity of what she'd done. Her hands trembled. She recalled working with Rosa to alter Lars's documents. The papers provided details on the gold transactions, but omitted the names of banks and individuals for secrecy. It was Rosa who added the identities, and she'd helped her piece together how the gold laundering scheme operated. *In thirty-six hours, either Tiago will be free or we'll both be in prison.* She closed her eyes and prayed that the microfilm images of the forged bank documents were convincing enough for her plan to work.

Chapter 51

Lisbon, Portugal—September 7, 1944

Maria, standing at the entrance to the harbor and docks at Alcântara, watched a line of passengers—many of whom were Jewish refugees—make their way onto the *Serpa Pinto* bound for New York. The crowd gradually diminished as passengers cleared through customs agents, climbed a gangway, and boarded the ship. She glanced at her watch and her anxiety grew. *We're running out of time.*

Yesterday afternoon, she'd received a telephone call from a man who didn't identify himself. He'd told her to be at the docks at 8:00 a.m. to exchange documents for Soares, and that she and Soares would board a ship to America.

"The demands are agreeable with one stipulation," the man had said in a guttural voice. "You and Soares are banished from Portugal."

With nothing left to negotiate with, Maria accepted. She'd hung up the receiver and wept with joy. As she gathered her composure, her brain prodded her to be cautious. *It could be a trap*, she'd told herself, placing clothes into her suitcase. *But there isn't a thing I can do about it—Salazar has made his decision and our fate is sealed.*

Maria, expecting that she was under surveillance, had waited until nightfall and sneaked her way to Rosa's apartment. While her husband was asleep in the bedroom, they sat in the living room and Maria told her the news. Rosa was elated, but when Maria informed her about his exile, the woman's eyes filled with tears.

"He'll be free," Rosa had said, holding her prayer beads. "That's all that matters."

Maria had requested Rosa not to come to the dock out of fear that it could be a ruse to arrest her. She'd given her a bag of escudos—equivalent to $90,000—that the Germans had paid her but she hadn't yet turned over to the OSS. She'd asked Rosa to use the money to help Jewish refugees find freedom, and then hugged her goodbye.

A black automobile with flared fenders pulled to the entrance and stopped. Maria's breath stalled in her lungs as the driver's door opened and a man, wearing a black suit and hat, approached her. Based on his appearance and demeanor, she assumed he was a member of the PVDE. She strained to see if Tiago was one of the men in the back seat.

"Maria Alves," the man said.

"Yes," she said. "Where's Soares?"

"Documents first."

Maria opened her suitcase and gave him a package.

The man peeked inside. "I have a message for you."

Her mouth went dry.

"If you should break your pledge of secrecy, Soares's parents, Renato and Lina, will serve life sentences in prison for aiding a communist."

"I understand."

The man gave her boarding tickets and a set of travel papers with Tiago's name on them. He approached the automobile and signaled with his hand.

The rear doors of the car opened and two agents removed Tiago, his head drooped, from the back seat and pushed him to the ground.

Maria sprinted toward him. "Tiago!"

The agents got into the vehicle and sped away.

She kneeled to his side and wrapped her arms around him. Tears flooded her eyes. "Tiago!"

"Maria," he breathed.

"I'm here," she cried, squeezing his frail body. "You're coming home with me."

He placed a hand to her cheek.

She leaned back and looked into his eyes, dark and sunken. He wore civilian clothes, several sizes too big, and his hair was long and brittle. His once clean-shaven face was covered in an unkempt beard. "You're free. Everything is going to be all right. I'm going to make you well."

A smile formed on his lips.

A ship horn sounded.

"We need to go." Tears streamed down her cheeks. "Are you able to walk?"

"Yes, but I'll need some help."

Maria labored to get him to his feet. She wrapped his arm around her shoulder and she held him tight, feeling his protruding ribs against her hand. *Oh, God, what have they done to you!* As they shuffled forward, two dockworkers came to their aid and helped them to board the ship with her luggage. Minutes later, they were on the deck of the *Serpa Pinto* when its horn gave a long blast.

They leaned against the rail, overlooking the harbor and the city of Lisbon.

"You saved me," Tiago said, gently touching her arm.

"I had help." She clasped his hand and pressed it to her lips.

Tears filled Tiago's eyes. "I hoped and prayed that I would see you again."

"Me too." Waves of emotion flooded her body. "I never stopped thinking about you."

"Nor I. It was my thoughts of you that gave me the strength to live. To never give up." He wrapped his arms around her.

Together, they wept. The dam holding back the time and space between them collapsed.

Tiago kissed her tears.

The ship pulled away from the dock. They held each other tight and peered over the railing for one last look at Lisbon. And their eyes were drawn to a familiar old woman—standing on the shore and waving a white handkerchief—with her chin raised to the sky.

AUTHOR'S NOTE

While conducting research for *The Book Spy*, I became captivated by the real-life librarians who were recruited by the Office of Strategic Services (OSS) to serve as intelligence agents. On December 22, 1941—two weeks after the Japanese attack on Pearl Harbor—President Roosevelt signed an executive order to create the Interdepartmental Committee for the Acquisition of Foreign Publications (IDC), a force of librarians and microfilm specialists. The IDC was proposed to Roosevelt by Colonel William "Wild Bill" Donovan, the head of the Office of Coordinator of Information (COI), which would soon become the OSS. The objective of the librarian agents was to acquire enemy newspapers, books, and periodicals for American war agencies. They were deployed to neutral European cities, such as Lisbon and Stockholm, to pose as American officials collecting materials for the Library of Congress, which was attempting to preserve books during the world crisis. The agents used local currency and bartered with American magazines, like *Time* and *Life*, to order Axis publications through bookstores and secret channels. Once the publications were acquired, the agents microfilmed them—reducing size and weight—and then transported the film to intelligence staff in either the United States or Britain for analysis.

Maria's character in the book was inspired by a real agent named Adele Kibre, who was stationed in Stockholm. Kibre was an expert in microphotography, fluent in seven languages, and was—according to research records—the most accomplished of the IDC agents. During her overseas service, she was able to obtain a copy of a secret directory of German manufacturers called *Industrie-Compass 1943*. Kibre was intelligent, confident, brave, and intrigued by espionage. Also, she wasn't afraid to break rules and act independently, which sometimes annoyed her boss, Frederick Kilgour. In the book, I strived to use many of Kibre's attributes to create Maria's character.

During my research, I was moved by stories of Jewish refugees fleeing Nazi persecution. During the war, Lisbon, Portugal, was considered the last gate out of Europe. An estimated one million refugees fled there to acquire ship passage to either the United States, Canada, or Latin America. I discovered varying accounts as to how many of the refugees were Jewish, which ranged from sixty thousand to hundreds of thousands. Also, there were many refugees who secretly fled to Portugal without proper passports and visas. Some of the refugees, fearing they'd be sent back to where they came from by the Portuguese secret police, sought the aid of underground networks to obtain travel papers. In the book, I imagined Tiago and Rosa to be the masterminds of a secret channel to forge documents for freedom seekers. It is my hope that this story will commemorate the refugees who fled German-occupied Europe.

During World War II, neutral Lisbon was a city of espionage. The hotels, most notably Hotel Palácio and Hotel Atlântico near Casino Estoril, were crawling with Allied and Axis spies. Informants were everywhere, and the city was swirling with rumors and counter-rumors. Maria's role as a spy was inspired by a real double agent named Juan Pujol Garcia, code-named Garbo by the British and Alaric by the Germans. He was a Spanish spy who moved to Lisbon and acted as a double agent loyal to Great Britain against Germany. He was a persuasive actor and invented a team of twenty-seven fictitious subagents, all of whom were funded by the Germans. Also, Pujol played a critical role in Operation Fortitude, the plan to mislead Hitler and conceal the real location of the Allied invasion of France. The Germans paid him over $300,000 for his fake intelligence and he was awarded the Iron Cross. After the war, Pujol—fearing retribution from surviving Nazis—faked his death with the help of British intelligence services and moved to Venezuela where he ran a bookstore.

Wolfram (tungsten ore) was a critical element to supply Hitler's war machine. This rare metal was needed for the manufacture of hard steel in tanks and armor-piercing shells. By 1942, Germany was almost entirely dependent on Portuguese and Spanish wolfram, and Portugal's dictator, António de Oliveira Salazar, used the sale of wolfram to essentially buy his country's neutrality. Nazi gold, which was looted from the vaults of conquered central banks of Europe and victims of the Holocaust, was used by Germany to purchase Portugal's wolfram. Salazar, who was also selling wolfram to Britain, wanted to keep his financial dealings with the Germans a secret. Therefore, a complex gold-laundering operation was created between German, Swiss, and Portuguese banks to avoid direct transfer of gold from Germany to Portugal. Allied intelligence estimated that Portugal received four hundred tons of Nazi gold, which is likely underestimated. After the war and years of negotiations, Salazar and the Allies eventually agreed that Portugal would return a mere four tons of gold.

During my research, I discovered many intriguing historical events, which I labored to accurately weave into the timeline of the book. For example, the summer of 1942 was when Colonel Donovan gave a speech at Vincent Astor's mansion, and I used the event to create a way for Maria to be recruited to the OSS. The arrest of Tiago's grandparents is set during the German roundup of Jews in Bordeaux, France. Between July 1942 and May 1944, ten trains departed Bordeaux with over 1,600 French Jews, including children, en route to Auschwitz concentration camp. Also, Pan Am's *Yankee Clipper* crashed in Lisbon's Tagus River on February

22, 1943, and twenty-four of the thirty-nine people on board perished in the accident. The probable cause of the crash was inadvertent contact of the left wing tip of the aircraft with the water while making a landing. In addition to using the *Yankee Clipper* to transport Maria to Lisbon, I wanted readers to experience this little-known event and commemorate the passengers and crew. Additionally, Operation Fortitude took place between December 1943 and March 1944, and I used key events of the Allied deception plan as part of Maria's role as a double agent. The wedding reception for Eva Braun's sister, Gretl, took place at the Eagle's Nest on June 3, 1944, three days before the D-Day invasion. I attempted to accurately reflect the timeline of war events. Any historical inaccuracies in this book are mine and mine alone.

Numerous historical figures make appearances in this book, including Franklin Delano Roosevelt, Colonel William "Wild Bill" Donovan, Frederick G. Kilgour, Vincent Astor, Mary Benedict "Minnie" Cushing, Eugene Power, Jane Froman, Tamara Drasin, Ben Robertson, H. Gregory Thomas (Argus), António de Oliveira Salazar, Ricardo Espírito Santo and his wife, Mary, Eva Braun, Gretl Braun, and Hermann Fegelein. It is important to emphasize that *The Book Spy* is a fictional story, and that I took creative liberties in writing this tale. Maria, Tiago, Lars, Rosa, Roy, Pilar, and Agent Neves of the PVDE are fictional characters. In the story, Maria changes seats with Ben Robertson on the *Yankee Clipper*. In real life, Jane Froman had given her seat to Tamara Drasin, who was killed in the crash, and this action was reported to have plagued Froman with guilt throughout her life.

Numerous books, documentaries, and historical archives were crucial for my research. *Information Hunters: When Librarians, Soldiers, and Spies Banded Together in World War II* by Kathy Peiss was extremely helpful with learning about the librarians of the IDC. *Lisbon: War in the Shadows of the City of Light, 1939–45* by Neill Lochery was an exceptional resource for gaining insight into the events taking place in Lisbon, especially the refugee crisis, wolfram wars, spy activity, Salazar and his personal banker, and the Nazi-gold laundering operation. Additional research books included *OSS: The Secret History of America's First Central Intelligence Agency* by Richard Harris Smith; *Operatives, Spies, and Saboteurs: The Unknown Story of the Men and Women of World War II's OSS* by Patrick K. O'Donnell; *Sisterhood of Spies: The Women of the OSS* by Elizabeth P. McIntosh; and *Shadow Warriors of World War II: The Daring Women of the OSS and SOE* by Gordon Thomas and Greg Lewis. Also, a video by Mark Felton Productions titled *The Fegelein Wedding: Nazi Fairytale or Nazi Nightmare?* provided actual film footage of the event and was a tremendous resource for writing the scenes of Gretl Braun's wedding.

It was a privilege to write this book. I will forever be inspired by the valiant service of the OSS's librarians, and I will never forget the one million refugees who escaped through the port of Lisbon in search of freedom. It is my hope that this book will pay tribute to the men, women, and children who perished in the war.

The Book Spy would not have been possible without the support of many people. I'm eternally thankful to the following gifted individuals:

I am deeply grateful to my brilliant editor, John Scognamiglio. John's guidance, encouragement, and enthusiasm was immensely helpful with the writing of this book.

Many thanks to my fabulous agent, Mark Gottlieb, for his support and counsel with my journey as an author. I feel extremely fortunate to have Mark as my agent.

My deepest appreciation to my publicist, Vida Engstrand. I am profoundly grateful for Vida's tireless efforts to promote my stories to readers.

It takes a team effort to publish a book, and I am forever grateful to everyone at Kensington Publishing for bringing this story to life.

I'm thankful to have Kim Taylor Blakemore, Tonya Mitchell, and Jacqueline Vick as my accountability partners. Our weekly video conferences helped us to finish our manuscripts on time.

My sincere thanks to Akron Writers' Group: Betty Woodlee,

Dave Rais, Ken Waters, John Stein, Kat McMullen, Rachel Freggiaro, Cheri Passell, and Corry Novosel. And a special heartfelt thanks to Betty Woodlee, who critiqued an early draft of the manuscript.

This story would not have been possible without the love and support of my wife, Laurie, and our children, Catherine, Philip, Lizzy, Lauren, and Rachel. Laurie, you are—and always will be—*meu céu*.

A READING GROUP GUIDE

THE BOOK SPY

ABOUT THIS GUIDE

The suggested questions are included to enhance your group's reading of Alan Hlad's *The Book Spy*.

Discussion Questions

1. Before reading *The Book Spy*, what did you know about the librarians who served in a special unit of the Office of Strategic Services (OSS) in World War II? What did you know about the Jewish refugees who escaped German-occupied Europe through the neutral port of Lisbon?

2. What are Maria's aspirations while working as a microfilm specialist at the New York Public Library? How does the death of Maria's mother influence her to join the OSS?

3. What are Tiago's motivations to forge passports and visas for Jewish refugees? Describe his relationship with Rosa.

4. Describe Maria. What kind of woman is she? How does conning her way into an elite social event at Vincent Astor's mansion persuade Colonel Donovan to recruit her for the OSS?

5. While working in Lisbon, Maria and Tiago fall in love. What brings them together? Why does their relationship develop so quickly? At what point do you think Maria realized she loved Tiago? How is the war a catalyst for their affection? What are Maria's and Tiago's hopes and dreams?

6. Prior to reading the book, what did you know about Hitler's need to acquire wolfram (tungsten ore) from Portugal, and the Nazi-gold smuggling operation between German, Swiss, and Portuguese banks? What did you know about Operation Fortitude, the plan to mislead Hitler and conceal the real location of the Allied invasion of France?

7. What are the major themes of *The Book Spy*?

8. Prior to reading this story, what did you know about the fate of Pan Am's *Yankee Clipper*?

9. Why do many readers enjoy historical fiction, in particular novels set in World War II? To what degree do you think Hlad took creative liberties with this story?

10. How do you envision what happens after the end of the book? What do you think Maria's and Tiago's lives will be like?